NEVER SPEAK

A DEEP PSYCHOLOGICAL THRILLER

JOHN MANCHESTER

1

Ray woke to the tinkle of breaking glass. *Susan, crashing into the concrete.* He shook his head blearily. It must be an accident out on Warren Street. He rose from where he was lying on the couch and stumbled a couple of steps to the round window. He peered out, but the street wasn't visible from this high up in his house.

It was still night. But he was awake, more or less, and had to see what was going on. He shuffled down the hall in gloom barely penetrated by streetlights, then clanked down the spiral stairs from the third floor, listening for sirens. He passed the kitchen on the second floor and continued down the metal steps into his art gallery on the ground floor. Cold air struck his legs, coming from the street side of the room. He stopped and came fully alert. It must have been some accident to blow the door open. And where were the sirens?

He gazed at the back of the window display. The sculptures still sat there, but something was missing. It took a moment to get it. The name of his business, Ray of Darkness, painted on the glass, was gone. Because the *glass* was gone, except for jagged shards sticking from the frame.

Kids throwing rocks? He'd never heard of anything like that in Hudson before. There was always a first time. His eyes scanned the floor. Just glass shards, sparkling in the streetlights. Maybe they used a baseball bat.

Should he call the police? *We'll send a squad car.* He'd stand around while they eyed the weird contents of his gallery and made a report. All that time—with idiot Rockefeller drugs laws still on the books—he'd be worrying about his stash of dope in that cigar box up in the rafters.

It was getting light, almost six. Ray called Bodine.

"Did I wake you?"

"It's okay. About time to get up, anyway."

"Someone just busted my front window."

Bodine said, "Bummer. Especially with it being so chilly. I'll come over with some plywood."

Ray got his coat and stood huddled in it as he waited. The wind gusted through the jagged hole in the glass. He was cold and felt exposed. Goddamn it. He'd have to get new glass, paint Ray of Darkness on it…but at least the sculptures in the window were okay.

What broke it? He got down on hands and knees, careful not to cut himself, and looked under his desk.

Ah. A brick. He fished it out and stood and held it to the first rays of sun streaming in the window.

An *old* brick. The shivers he'd been holding at bay broke through.

A billion old bricks in the world. It couldn't be….

He turned it in his trembling hand. Stamped in big plain letters was the word "LENT."

***

Two weeks earlier…

They say never Google your ex.

> A New Jersey woman died Saturday in a fiery crash on I-89. Susan Brandon was traveling in the southbound lane north of Saugerties around midnight when she apparently lost control. Her car crashed into a bridge abutment and burst into flames.

The words punched Ray in the gut. His eyes flicked away from the computer screen and for a long moment his mind was blank aside from the vague shapes of sculptures in the gallery. He read on.

By the time rescue vehicles arrived, her body had been burned beyond recognition…

Ray sipped tiny breaths high in his chest. Some wickedness in his mind had him at the scene of the accident, rubbernecking, staring at twisted flaming wreckage, at a black lump that used to be Susan. And now, the thought came: *I killed her.* The rage that had consumed him thirty years ago at the end of their relationship had finally spread to her, burned her to a crisp.

He shoved the thoughts away. Tried to picture her alive. Standing there the last time he saw her as he drove from their house, her face twisted in sorrow, but also full of that terrible resolve. His only solace at that moment had been, *This is as bad as it gets.* Only this was worse. A hole opened in him, filling with raw anguish. Back then, he'd never wanted to see her again. Now, he truly never would.

It was time to stop, close the computer, with its windows on things no one should ever see. But he searched for her obituary. Paused for a moment, then clicked.

> Susan Branford is survived by her loving husband, Phillip Roberts
> of Monson and daughters Megan, 13, and Beth, 10. Susan excelled
> at everything she took on in life, in her position as claims adjuster
> at Mutual Insurance of Central Jersey, on numerous local boards,
> as a wife and devoted soccer mom…

The hole in him expanded. *Married.* That was no surprise, but still unwelcome news. *Two kids* was harder. *Those kids could have been ours.*

What path could have taken her from fervent spiritual seeker to insurance claims? Her faith had never been in the things of this earth, but in the promise of that un-seeable, unknowable *something*.

Saugerties was just ten miles south of here. *She'd been coming to see him.*

Southbound—so she came north to Hudson, changed her mind, headed home…no, she couldn't have been coming to see him. They hadn't spoken in thirty years. She must have been at some business meeting in Albany, a late dinner. Was she drunk? Impossible. Susan rarely drank, would never think of driving less than sober.

When did it happen? Just a year ago last November. That somehow made it worse. Like maybe he could have done something about it.

He found a photo. A group shot in a hotel lobby, plastic name tags, some kind of conference. She had aged well. Even after all this time and that bitterest of ends, she still sparked something in him. She was pretty as ever. And under the obligatory grin, she was still dead serious, even noble. The bozos smiling to either side of her probably thought they took their jobs seriously. Nobody took any job as seriously as Susan, whether it was assessing damage for an insurance claim, or chasing down God.

He stared at the picture, at the trace of something in her eyes. A shadow.

Sadness? Defeat? He was probably projecting his sorrow onto her. She was just showing her age. When was this photo taken? Barely a month before the…accident.

He finally tore himself away from Google. Closed the computer and looked up, blinking at the bright street outside.

At least she'd kept her maiden name. *That* was the old Susan. It's how he'd found her. The obituary didn't mention anything about a long-ago *ex-*husband, but of course it wouldn't.

***

Actually, it was Bodine who'd said, "Never Google your ex," capping off a lecture about the perils lurking behind that friendly search box. Bodine was well aware of Ray's curiosity, should have known that telling him not to type something into Google was like telling a kid not to look in that box up on the shelf in the closet. That it was the first thing he'd want to do. The only surprise was how long he'd resisted.

Except curiosity didn't really explain it. Ray could see any of a number of other exes online. Google them up, find out where they were, even who they were hanging with now, no harm. But why did he Google Susan? It made no sense. He'd been in a gruesome funk for months now, deep in the shadows. No news of her could possibly brighten his mood.

But this was pure blackness. It launched him from his chair and toward the door. He grabbed his coat. On his way out he flipped the sign to Closed. The icy air slapped him in the face. He hesitated on the sidewalk. Should he go tell Bodine? No. Ray didn't need another lecture right now. He headed across Warren Street to Jo's Joe, his friend's coffee shop. She might have a few minutes before the lunch rush.

The warm air in the little foyer embraced him with its promise of the essentials of caffeine and sugar. The prospect of unloading to Jo kept the terrible news at bay. He eyed the armchairs in front enviously before parking himself at his usual table in back. Jo reserved it for him in the slow hours between breakfast and lunch. Jo was strict about no eating in those comfy chairs. Besides, Ray needed to reciprocate her reserving his place by taking it.

He looked around for Jo, and a minute later she appeared from the kitchen bearing four late breakfasts without benefit of a tray. She delivered them along with her great smile to some day-trippers up from the city. They caught the smile, her straight, flaxen hair framing that wholesome face, heard the hint of Scandinavia on her tongue, and assumed she was a simple soul from the Midwest. A farm girl, maybe. Which she was. They didn't know of her fierce intelligence, the tangled nightmare of a family she'd escaped back in Minnesota. They couldn't guess that she cursed like a sailor and loved her longtime partner Louise like no one Ray had ever known.

Jo got the food on the table and came over to Ray. Jo's great smile, to those who knew her, actually had at least a hundred variations, expressing everything from joy to sorrow and even anger.

This smile remained in place—nothing short of the death of a close one could erase it—but her forehead knotted, and she laid a hand on his shoulder. "What's wrong?"

"I just found out my ex-wife died."

"Oh, Ray, I'm so sorry. I didn't know you were ever married."

"It was a long time ago." He looked away. He'd come here to tell Jo about Susan, but now, he couldn't talk about it.

She got that. Reached down and gave him a quick hug. "The usual?"

"No, just a cup of coffee."

As he drank it, then another, the news of Susan faded, like a summer squall retreating over the horizon. And it was just another morning at Jo's, the same as everyone for months. He stared from the window at the drops melting from icicles on the roof, the hum of chitchat rising and falling like waves, punctuated by the tinging of silverware.

Ray had been a fixture at this table since the day his art career ended. That ending came with a literal bang when he slammed his latest sketchpad down on the pile, yanked the curtain closed on his studio, and stalked over here.

The essential lever, the mysterious piece that hooked his eyes up to his hands, that performed the alchemy of art, had broken. His eyes still saw, but the only result was junk thoughts. His hands—which once made art, art that sold!—had turned useless, jittering and fussing, tapping polyrhythms on the table's edge and worrying his napkin into fine shreds.

Not today. Susan had retreated over his mind's horizon—chased by caffeine and habit. But something was different about his hands.

They were itching.

Ray waited until Jo was in the kitchen, tiptoed up, and grabbed a pen from behind the counter. He sat down with his placemat and drew. He sketched a couple of women across the room. He could tell that they were old friends, knew they were dishing about somebody or something, but all he'd gotten down was lifeless hair and a couple of empty smiles.

He gave up and doodled in the margins the arabesque pattern from the tin ceiling.

He'd filled the placemat, but his fingers still itched. Why? Because what had them itching was the poison fruit of his Google snooping. It had set off a storm in him, and he needed to vent it. Sketching those women didn't do it. And he wasn't drawing a fiery wreck.

He turned the paper over and started…writing. He filled the page in no time. While Jo was in the kitchen, he snagged more placemats from where she kept them next to the silverware.

"You're drawing again!"

Startled, Ray looked up at Jo beaming down at him and his left hand shot across his work, covering it while the other whisked her pen under the table.

Jo reached down and gently pried his fingers off the placemat. Her smile slipped a hair and her eyebrows rose. "Oh. You're writing. What the fuck? I knew something was up with you." A bell chimed in the kitchen, and she rushed off to deliver someone's lunch.

What the fuck about covered it. Was he really writing? He peeked down at the placemat. Words. So he guessed he *was* writing. He folded the placemats and stuffed them in the pocket of his leather coat, placed a twenty on the table, and left.

The cold air smacked his cheeks. He huddled down Warren Street toward the river to Bodine's. The snowbanks were mostly melted, revealing dark lumps of greasy trash from last fall and road sand that blew in his face.

The only evidence of the abandoned Palace Theater on Warren Street was the faint scar where the marquee had been. The windows were covered with weathered plywood and the doors sealed with a rusted chain. The sole entrance now was the old emergency exit on the alley in back. As Ray turned right on Fourth Street and headed for it, he heard the faintest trace of pumping bass. He smiled. He was one of the only people in town that knew Bodine lived there.

Ray's knock on the door was answered by howling and the thunder of approaching paws. A minute later, Bodine cracked the door and Mingus barged out, gave a yip, and abruptly changed gears, sucking up to Ray for a pet. His tail beat on the dirt of the alley.

Bodine leaned out of the door. "Hey." He nodded for Ray to come in. Ray's friend was tall and thin, with straight blond hair in a ponytail. He looked a decade, or even two, younger than his fifty odd years, depending on the light.

Ray nodded at the dog. "Good doorbell. How can you work with that…shit?" Some kind of mindless techno. Ray and Bodine had been in a band for years, and as musicians agreed that for them there was no such thing as background music. If it was on, they couldn't help but listen, for better or worse. Worse in this case.

Bodine laughed. "This is just a little experiment. You'll notice it has absolutely no content. And no, I'm not losing my good taste. It's terrible. But it might actually help me concentrate."

"Is it working?"

Bodine just gave a little smile.

Mingus trotted across the theater and back upstairs to Bodine's office in the old projection booth. The theater was unheated and dark, the museum cases and neat piles of Bodine's odd private collection hulking in the dim light leaking from above.

Ray followed Bodine up into the office, and Bodine shut off the music. Ray asked, "This a bad time?"

"It's fine. Just let me finish this." Ray leaned against the ancient theater organ. Bodine sat at one of the towers of computers. Doing what, exactly? His work. But what was that? Ray didn't ask. He wasn't sure he wanted to know. He stole a glance at the screen. Columns of numbers racing by. Windows opening and closing. E-trading? He doubted it. That was too capitalistic for the old commie. Hacking was more like it. Whatever it was, it had to be very hard to do. Probably dangerous, too, or Bodine would have long since gotten bored and quit.

Bodine slammed a few keys with the finality of the ending chords of a song. Only five minutes, but Mingus was already crashed out in his bed. Ray sat in a swivel chair and spun around to Bodine, who looked at him. "What's wrong?"

Jo's question. "Is it that obvious?"

Bodine laughed. "Your face is what I believe they call an open book."

"Let me show you." Ray walked to Bodine's computer, bent over, and winced at the strings of code. "This thing have Google?"

Bodine clicked a few keys. Ray reached around him and brought up Susan's obituary and sat back in his chair as Bodine read.

"I'm really sorry, man. Even if you guys happened a thousand years ago."

Ray pulled the placemats from his pocket, unfolded them, and showed them to Bodine. Bodine glanced at them, then looked at Ray. "What is this?"

"What I just did over at Jo's."

"Writing." Bodine's eyes bugged. "There are strange things in this world—two headed zebras and smart rednecks and… You want to be a writer?"

"No, no. This terrible thing happened, and I couldn't draw it."

"And being the tortured artist, you had to get it out of yourself somehow, or you'd…explode, or whatever it is you creative types do."

"Something like that."

"So you wrote about it."

"Well not the accident, but…" he choked the name out. "Susan."

Bodine sighed. "The little writing I've done falls somewhere between doing taxes and getting a root canal. Maybe several."

"You pay taxes?"

"When there's a 1099… But maybe writing will be good for you. Horrible as that thing with Susan is, it might be the kick in the butt you need to do…something."

Mingus snorted in his sleep, as though agreeing.

Bodine said, "Well, if you're going to do it, I hope you don't use a pen and paper." He made the writing tools sound like horse and buggy. "This is the twenty-first century, Ray."

"I've got a computer."

Bodine groaned. "What, that old piece-of-shit PC?"

"What's wrong with it?"

Bodine held up a finger—one minute—and disappeared into the closet. They might be best friends, but vast reaches of Bodine's psyche were off limits. And so was his closet. Given all the stuff Ray had seen come out of it, it must be huge.

Ray went over, leaned down and scratched the dog's head, the way Mingus liked. Bleary eyes looked up at Ray. Would he rather be still sleeping or being petted? Ray didn't care. He was a dog. His job was getting petted.

Ray heard Bodine returning and stood. The object in his friend's hand gleamed in the overhead halogens. It was a different color, but the same shape as the placemat. And the same shape as something else. They formed a *series*. One, two…Ray frowned as he lined them up in his mind.

Bodine looked at him. "Ray?"

He raised a hand—nothing. Bodine handed him the laptop. It was cold. It was completely different than the placemats. Just a computer. There was no series.

Ray said, "You don't need it?"

Bodine pointed to his array of hardware. "Does it look like I do? Got one exactly like it in the living room."

"Where'd you get it?"

Bodine lifted a finger to his lips. "Must have fallen off a truck."

A perk of Bodine's mysterious computer business.

Bodine scowled. "This is going to be like trading in an old shitbox for a Ferrari. You don't watch out, it might run away from you. But hook it up to Wi-Fi and you'll be able to go online anywhere you want in that house of yours. But please promise me you'll get some security."

"Security?"

"Nobody would have the patience to hack into that old clunker of yours. But this new one... You never know when someone in some *white van* is gonna sneak up outside your place with a satellite dish and break into your computer."

"Come on. What do I have that anybody wants?"

"You never know. There's some good freeware out there. You can Google it. Hacksafe, Botgard." Bodine's eyes flicked to the closet. "You need anything else? Crack cocaine? A rocket launcher?"

They both laughed. Bodine was a confirmed pacifist and didn't have any rocket launcher in there. Or crack.

Other illegal substances were another matter.

Ray headed home. He turned onto Warren, the main street of Hudson, the funky-chic little city on the river that gave it its name. Only a few thousand folks lived in town, but it boasted 165 antique stores. That naturally encouraged specialization. An icy wind raced toward the water, blasting him in the face.

Ray's eyes may have become useless for making art, but they hadn't lost their habitual hunger. Nor their capacity for judgment. The next block was like stepping back through time in the period rooms of a museum, each shop covering a different era. He frowned into a big display window packed with mid-century modernist crap. He smiled at the store with its svelte Art Deco lamps and chaise lounges. Gave an appraising eye to a smaller shop with

Victorian chairs and couches, and finally yawned at a stuffy Second Empire living room.

A fast rattle of Spanish from some guys entering a bodega reminded him that Hudson wasn't just a weekend playground for upscale New Yorkers. A block north of Bodine's, seedy Columbia Street crawled its way down to housing projects by the river. A couple of blocks to the south, a state prison hunched under a bluff.

But this section of Warren east of Sixth Street was headed upmarket. And here was a brand-new women's clothing store with silk dresses in dazzling colors, flowering a little early for spring. Shit.

Liz. This was the kind of stuff she just loved. He started sliding down a familiar muddy slope. His home was across the street in the next block. He peered up at its brooding face. Bodine called it the House of Usher, and it definitely had a gothic vibe. It stood tall and unnaturally thin, like a severe old man, its ornate cornice a brow, and tucked beneath it a single, round, cyclopean window. What that architecture course back in art school had taught him was an oculus. Right now, it was glowering down at him.

This was night and day from seeing it the first time, ten years ago. He and Liz had driven up from the city house hunting. Laughing and chattering away the whole length of the Taconic Parkway, his hand in her hair, her popping chocolate truffles into his mouth.

They'd been right where he was now when a flash of light caught Ray's eye. The sun gleaming off the round window. He pointed and said, "Look," but the gleam was already gone, just a trick of the sun's angle. Later, Ray would joke with her: "It was winking at me."

"You made that up. You and your famous imagination." She liked it, then.

He eased the key in the door and pushed it open, his other hand muting the string of bells he'd chosen for the creepy mismatch of their tones. Their purpose was fair warning to all who entered, though the window display ought to ring a few bells as well. It contained the last of the reliquary parodies he'd made his stock in trade in recent years, somewhere in the uncanny valley between fine art and horror movie props. If you still didn't get it, there was Ray of Darkness painted in shiny black Gothic script on the display window.

11

Weenies and kids not admitted! The sign in the door said Closed, but there was no need to flip it: The gallery only opened mornings, and even then, at his whim.

While he was fond of his sculptures, he did not like the twin phantoms that haunted his house. The ghosts of Liz and his muse were the cause of his extended funk. He slipped his shoes off and stepped softly so as not to wake them. He tiptoed up the rusted spiral staircase, making only a faint metallic hum. He glanced across the kitchen at the closed door of the bedroom, which he hadn't dared enter in months.

Though it made no sense, he gripped the laptop like it was a shield or talisman that might protect him. He headed up the continuation of the spiral steps to the third floor. Tiptoed down the narrow hall past his studio. Nothing stood between him and that mausoleum of hopes and ambition but the red curtain he hadn't pulled open since that last day. He couldn't see the chisels, brushes, half-finished pieces, and stacks of musty materials entombed there, but he could smell their charnel breath of linseed and old glue. And he could feel them, accusing.

He retorted: It wasn't *me* who left. Two more steps, and he entered the turret room behind the oculus, with the comforts of the purple velvet wingback couch, the window, and his bottle of absinthe. The one place in his house where he was safe from the ghosts.

He sat, pulled a placemat from his pocket, and read, shaking his head. He eyed the silver laptop. Maybe Bodine was right. Use the tool of the times.

He opened it, fired up a Word doc, and started typing.

2.

The fall I met Susan, Bodine had moved to the City with his current girlfriend and I was sharing a house in the country with our rhythm section. It was a big step up from our previous place on Alton Road—no roaches, a working furnace, and a downstairs bathroom that didn't have the one upstairs leaking down on you while you sat on the toilet.

Our band, The Nightcrawlers, was scrabbling its way up into the big time. We weren't rock stars yet. Not just another bar band, either, but the money was still short. When our drummer Frank moved out, we needed a new roommate. Finding one might have well precipitated a psychotic break in Bassman, so I had to do it.

Susan was a grad student. I showed her the room and made her instant coffee. We sat downstairs, she on the shabby couch and me in a sprung armchair. My plan was to interview her, find out if she could pay the rent, and make sure she wasn't too crazy.

Somehow the questions and answers stopped, because I found myself looking at her, and her at me, silently for the longest time. We stared directly into each other's eyes. Soon there were just those eyes and a clock ticking more and more faintly from the kitchen. Her face began shifting, almost melting, like I was seeing different people in her. Or maybe past lives, though I've never believed in such things. My limbs felt heavy, my head dreamy, as she hypnotized me with her incandescent gaze.

Finally, I moved. I crawled to the couch and embraced her. We didn't make love, didn't even kiss. If there was a sexual element to whatever brought us together, it was only in the sense that there's a sexual element in everything.

She moved into the house and, some months later, my room. Within the year we were married.

Susan was studying for a religion degree, but that was just the cover for her burning desire to find it, find The Answer, Enlightenment, God. I was surprised that she hadn't done psychedelics, had never even smoked pot. She said, "I need to get to this on my own, without artificial tools." Like some people won't touch food that isn't pulled right from the ground, grown without chemicals, she needed her God served up straight.

So where did I figure in the equation? Did she really care about me, or was I just a spiritual project?

She said, "Ray, I believe in you. Not who you are, but who you can become. You're a seeker, like me." Was I? I didn't know much about religion, but drugs had shown me without a doubt that there was something out there, beyond this mundane world, something even greater than rock 'n' roll.

***

A car horn from below rocketed Ray back to the present—his butt on the couch, the cold wafting from the window, the late afternoon sun burnishing rooftops across the street. He'd returned from far away, because he hadn't just been writing about the past. He'd *been* there. Conjured his younger self and brought Susan back to life, and them together. Happy.

And so it was a shock to be back here in a haunted house. With a third ghost now, lurking in the laptop. And unlike Liz or his muse, Susan was really dead. Knowledge that still ached in him. Yet there was also a new spark: The inkling that this writing might be magic. And this silver tool might be part of it.

The stuff on the placemats had just been words. This had…juice.

***

The sex was good for me. It seemed just okay for her. I asked, and she said, "Oh, no, Ray, it's fine." I always felt that she wanted more than I or lovemaking could give her. What was an orgasm next to the promise of reuniting with the Godhead?

Whatever her motivations, she got me setting my sights higher. Which was why

I married her. I'd hitched my spiritual wagon to her star. Marriage was the guarantee that she'd forever carry me up and up.

Which makes the next part ironic. Without me, she would have never met...

***

Karl. Like that, Ray was violently coughing, tears running down his cheeks. Must have gotten something caught in his throat while he was consumed with writing. It took minutes to get the cough under control. Better now, but his throat still felt wrong. Was he coming down with a cold? He gazed out the round window and drank in the late afternoon light. A whirring of rush hour out there. His eyes flicked to the floor next to the couch and he smiled. It was almost time for his medicine. It should soothe his throat.

Every day it worked its charm, chasing away his twin ghosts. It ought to work against this third phantom, Susan. But Karl? There was one way to find out. He looked at the clock on the computer. It read 4:55. He slapped the laptop closed, stuffed it under the couch, and waited. Rituals must be honored. He sat still, his mind a blank.

Five bells sounded from the Episcopal Church down the street. As the last faded, he reached over the armrest and lifted the bottle.

It was half filled with green liquid, the word Absinthe rendered in Art Deco script above a picture of a voluptuous specter seeping like green vapor from the top of her own bottle. Her arms transformed into vines as they reached down to embrace the man sprawled in his chair, eyes closed, and lips open in anticipation of the kiss of the Green Faerie. That's what they called this drink back when it became fashionable in Victorian times. Ray's patron saint, Edgar Allan Poe, had loved the Faerie. Ray was getting there himself.

It was potent medicine. Not only 180-proof but infused with the psychoactive ingredient in wormwood.

He fished around next to the couch for his tumbler and flask of water. He popped the cork and splashed a generous portion into the glass. Chased it with water and the green paled, remained clear for a second, then turned opaque. It was like some magician's trick, as if the Faerie had slipped from her abode in the ether and into his glass.

Back when he was making sculptures and just drinking beer, his five o'clock ritual had been more than an excuse to drink. His theory was that after putting out all day creating things for people to look at, you needed to take in. The first act of visual art was looking, just as the first act of music was listening. Daily practice honed your inner eye so that you came to see in more detail, depth and nuance. As Ray peered out of his oculus, and as the booze took hold, he'd imagined it as an eye, his house itself sentient, an art machine that drank in the visuals of the street and popped sculptures out the door below into the hands of his customers.

Nothing fashioned by his hand left this building anymore. But he still needed to look from his window. The root of this impulse was his terrible, insatiable desire to see the invisible. The setting sun painting the ice dams on the eaves across the street was a fine sight, but he wanted more.

He wanted to see inside the houses, see how the people lived. He yearned to peer inside their heads and hearts. To know what it was like to be another person, to live another life.

He'd long ago admitted this was a hopeless quest. But a proper dose of green medicine and he didn't care. The first sip lit a dot of fire in his belly. With each additional sip, it grew and grew, into a pulsing, molten golden coin whose heat radiated to the tips of his fingers and toes. As the Faerie wrapped him in her velvet embrace, the round glass of the window hummed in sympathy with the coin inside and began to glow itself with faint phosphorescence.

The Faerie rose to full strength. This was the sweet spot where body and heart were fully satisfied. No more longing for Liz, for his lost muse or billions of lives unseen. Perfect bliss.

A streetlight glinted on the glass in his hand. It had passed its midpoint, from half full to half empty, warning him that the Faerie's embrace, like all embraces, would not last. Outside, fine snow had begun sifting past his window. The desire burst in his chest to see every snowflake before it fell. And a twinge pinched his belly, as he knew it couldn't be.

And now, the ghosts stirred in the empty house.

Before they got him, he'd be asleep. He lay down and pulled Liz's afghan over him.

***

Ray woke to the sun peeking through the top of the window and stabbing his eyelids. He was sweated up under the cover. Even with the register up here turned off, the heat from downstairs came up the stairs and pooled in this little room at the end of the hall. He stood. His head was fuzzy. While absinthe chased the ghosts away, with its hangover they returned with a vengeance, taunting him.

He limped past the red curtain, the stink of his muse's breath causing his stomach to do a half flip. He shuffled downstairs, careful of that missing step.

Liz hissed at him from her fancy coffee machine, shooting a needle between his eyes. Caffeine would fix that, at least. He brought the steaming cup down to the gallery. The sculptures glared at him. *What's the matter, big boy, can't get it up anymore?* With the exception of the pieces in the window, his gallery was filled with the work of other artists.

He sat at his old clunker PC and remembered the laptop upstairs. And Susan, and the writing…

The discordant bells announced customers. A couple with teenaged daughters shuffled in, sleepwalked around the gallery past all the bizarre works with the bemused looks of Walmart shoppers, then marched out into the street without a word.

As they were leaving, an impeccably dressed Asian man arrived and stared for a long minute at Ray's friend Maurice's "Untitled #13," which Ray privately called "Psycho Ax-Murder Baby." A doll's torso and head, eyes staring blankly, the right leg a weathered ax with a rusty blade for a foot, the left a small chainsaw. Ray suppressed laughter as the guy asked about the provenance of the materials: "What brand of chainsaw is this?" "How old is this doll?" as if any of it mattered. The man stood back, gave it a last look, thanked Ray for his time, and left.

The third customer made Ray's morning. The dusty little guy looked around for a few minutes, then came up and got right in Ray's face, saying, "You are one sick man." He stalked out and Ray laughed out loud. A moment later, his spirits drooped. What horrified the guy was not Ray's art, but only his curations. Ray's identity was bound up in his creations, not his questionable skills as a gallery owner.

Now that he was idle, he felt it in his hands again. The itching.

He climbed upstairs, got more coffee and the laptop from under the couch on the third floor, and brought them downstairs. He opened the computer to the last words he'd written.

Without me, she would have never met...

He closed the document and launched a blank one, as if it would make a difference. But there was just a cursor blinking, wagging at him like a scolding finger.

His fingers needed to write. But he wasn't getting any further with this piece of Susan.

Flipping the sign in the door to Closed, he headed to Jo's. He sat in his usual spot. She was busy with customers. His fingers tapped rhythms on the table—or was that frustrated writing?

She finally came over. "Isn't your gallery open today?" She was a nicer scold than that cursor.

"I had a flurry of customers this morning. I'm hungry."

"You sell anything?"

"No."

At a chilly gust from the front of the restaurant, Jo turned her head and stiffened. Ray looked. The woman's back was to him as she looked at a menu. But he'd know her if he spied her from across the river. A hundred and fifty bucks worth of gloss on her already fine auburn hair and a sleek black coat.

Liz.

He rose from his chair. Jo grabbed his arm. "You sure you want to talk to her?"

"I can handle it." Of course he could.

He came up beside her. When she saw him, she jumped. "Oh. I was going ask Jo where you were. Why's the gallery closed?"

Another scold, and this one had teeth. "So I can eat?" He pasted on a smile. "You're looking good."

She gazed at him, and her eyes danced away. "You, too." She said it without conviction. She broke the awkward silence by delivering one of those white people hugs, leaning the top of her body toward him, lightly touching the back of his shirt with her fists, for an instant brushing hair against hair, then springing away to her rigid upright stance. He bit his lip.

She said, "Um, I was over at the house. I didn't want to just let myself in. I came to get the rest of my stuff."

Uh oh. She'd cleared out most of her things last September. What remained in the closet off the bedroom he'd invested with hope.

She said, "And we need to talk."

She was laying it on thick, no mercy, like he imagined her delivering a closing statement at trial, not that her corporate cases ever made it to a courtroom.

She left Jo's all business. He followed her across the street. Inside she stared at the sculptures, frowning. "Any luck?"

"Luck?"

"With the art. None of this new stuff looks like yours."

As if luck had anything to do with it. He said, "Actually, I've been doing a little writing." *An hour's worth.* Where did that come from? Desperation.

"Writing?" She blinked rapidly and gave a small shake of her head: What the hell does writing have to do with anything?

He followed her upstairs, averting his eyes from her skirt sliding over her ass. She opened the door of the bedroom and entered. He hesitated. It was here in the nights after she'd left that he first became aware of her ghost. Her voice murmuring in the radiator's indigestion. No matter how many times he washed the sheets, her scent was still in the bed. He finally stepped into the room. Just a musty odor in here now.

She turned toward him, her lip trembling. He could see that she sensed some of what he was feeling, and hope raised its foolish head. He took slow steps up to her and for the first time she actually looked at him.

She said, "Oh, Ray. I'm being such a miserable hard ass. It's just..." She started to cry. He reached her, and now she gave him a real hug.

He pushed her up against the dresser, reached down to undo her pants. She said, "You've been watching too many movies. Real people do it in a bed."

Their bed, which was conveniently a couple of feet away.

Only it wasn't quite theirs anymore. Her body was the same, and his response to it. And afterwards they lay just the same way as always, her head on his shoulder, his hand stroking her hair, breath settling back to normal as the happy chemicals gave him that best of mini vacations.

But something was off. What? For one thing, they weren't talking. He was never a roll over and go to sleep guy. Not with Liz. Afterward they talked up a storm. Today there wasn't a word.

And they remained silent as he helped her carry her things down to her BMW. Clothes. Books: Doris Lessing, Dorothy Sayers, *Our Bodies, Ourselves*. Law tomes. The last items included a spring coat. And spring was coming one of these days. But that didn't explain the rest of the stuff.

He finally spoke. "Liz, why are you getting all this now? You said we had to talk."

She didn't answer, just gave him a terrible, sorrowful look. And suddenly he knew what she was going to say, because he'd been here before, with Susan. The bad sex, and *I'm sorry,* only that time with Susan *he'd* been the one to drive away, and never see her again.

Liz said, "There's a real shitstorm brewing down at the office. Some of our best people are getting axed, and I worry that I'm next. They're already cutting back my hours."

That's all? He tried to suppress his grin. "Oh. Sorry."

"I haven't gotten a cent from you in months."

"I know, I know, I'm…"

"Listen to me. I'm having trouble carrying this house along with my place in the city. The condo fees just went up again. And that's with me still having a job. If you can't keep up your part of our deal, I'll have to…sell."

His grin slipped. No house meant no shop. No way to make a living. And no home.

"So, I need a check. I need all of what you owe me, and soon."

She climbed in her car, pulled out onto Warren Street. She didn't wave.

3.

Ray made a beeline for Bodine's. Just because it wasn't what she came to talk to him about didn't mean she wasn't doing it: banging another guy. That sex had been off. Its pleasant residue still lit up his cells, but an ache in his chest was emerging, like pain breaking through an analgesic.

And it was a familiar, very specific ache. He flashed on Susan's face, the last time he saw her in the flesh and the pain deepened to a dark throb.

No music leaked from the theater this time. Mingus howled, and Bodine let Ray in without looking at him. Bodine had replaced the old chandeliers downstairs in the theater proper with modern overhead fixtures, which cast even light on his museum. The original sconces still glowed on the walls. Ray followed Bodine over to one of the brass Victorian-era display cases. A space heater next to it put a small dent in the chill. The glass lid of the case was raised. It bore the sign: *Lost Love.*

Ray couldn't help himself. He laughed.

Bodine asked, "What?" But he was ensconced in his work, removing invisible dust with a tiny feather duster. Ray looked over his shoulder, though he knew the contents well. They were meticulously arranged: the mildewed wedding dress of a bride jilted at the altar in its shroud of desiccated cellophane; a stack of "Dear John" letters, senders and sendees long dead; a wheel of Enovid birth control pills from the first year they were issued, 1960, never used, turned to powder in their plastic coffin. Flanking these items on either side down the length of the cabinet was Ray's contribution to this part of the collection: a pair of nun's gravestones.

Bodine finished and looked up with a sigh of satisfaction. He raised an eyebrow a millimeter, his way of shouting. "Speaking of love, if I'm not mistaken you just got laid." Now, a tiny frown. "By a hyena? Because though you have the vibe, you do not look happy. Put upon, even. Who was this creature?"

"Liz."

Bodine didn't mince words. "If I've said it once, I've said it a thousand times: No sex with your ex. That's worse than Googling her. Lost love, indeed."

Ray winced at that terrible word "ex." Liz wasn't an ex. They were just *separated.* Bodine was only enjoying one of his many adages about exes. You needed a bunch if you had as many former lovers as he did.

Bodine twisted the knife. "So, was it a pity fuck, or does she want something?"

Pity fuck. He winced. "She wants something. My part of the mortgage on the house."

"Uh-oh. How far behind are you?"

"Five months. Far enough that I don't have a prayer of getting it. She's demanding all of it, or she's going to sell."

"Well, you are fucked. If you pardon the expression."

Ray glared at him, and they both laughed.

Bodine said, "Before we get to your mess, how about a little curatorial advice?"

"Sure." Ray smiled. Advice almost always flowed from Bodine to Ray, and he relished the rare exceptions.

He followed Bodine to the newest case at the end of the third row. The sign on the glass said, *Outmoded Media.* A box of old type, Teletype, and mimeograph machines, carbon paper, Wite-Out, floppy discs, eight-track, cassette, and VHS tapes. A turntable and a parlor radio. An answering machine. An abacus.

Ray said, "Cool. What's the problem?"

"The case is crammed, and I'm just getting started."

"The way things are going with technology—no thanks to guys like you, need I remind you—you'll have to turn this category into its own museum."

Bodine said, "That's what I thought. Damn. It's hard work putting order to a chaotic universe."

"But you are the man to do it." Ray scratched his chin. "You could always edit. The eight-track and cassette are redundant, so you could lose one."

Bodine frowned.

"The abacus is a little precious."

Bodine scowled.

"You're in love with your creation. Which—trust me—beats hating it."

Bodine rolled his eyes.

"You'll figure it out."

His friend took a breath. "So...*your* problem. Does it require coffee...or beer?"

"It's almost five, but...coffee."

"I don't have a fancy machine."

"Which is a good thing." They'd come up in the pre-latte times, when coffee was simple.

Bodine headed up. Ray said, "I'll meet you upstairs. I need a little museum time."

Ray loved museums—the Metropolitan in New York, and all the great ones he'd seen with Liz when she took him to Europe. There were no Rembrandts here, but that didn't stop him from enjoying the sweet whiff of decay, the sight of yellowing papers in a still room.

He peered into the case titled *Lost Dreams*. It had just seemed like trash until Bodine explained the contexts of the items: cereal box coupons, cut out and ready to redeem, for products long discontinued by companies out of business; unused airline tickets on BOAC and Pan Am. A bag of losing lottery stubs, tickets to Woodstock, never redeemed when the fences came down. Now, as Ray looked, he felt a bittersweet tide rise in him from the great ocean at the bottom of his heart.

He heard his friend upstairs. He clicked the downstairs lights off as he climbed to the office.

Bodine handed him a steaming cup, and they sat. "How's that writing going?"

Ray snorted. "As well as everything else. What's that got to do with anything?

"Hear me out. As long as we've been hanging out you've been making art, and before that, music. I've known plenty of starving painters and deadbeat musicians. But you always make a living at it."

"Except this year."

"Because you stopped doing it! You can't expect anyone to pay you to sit around and mope."

"Where are you going with this?"

"Hold on. I'm almost there. You made money playing guitar and making those spookola sculptures of yours. You can make money...writing."

Ray stood and went over to one of the old projector slots and stared down on the cases hunched in the gloom. "Aw, come on. I don't know shit about the writing business. And I've barely started."

"Unh-uh. You wrote song lyrics back in the day. And I'll bet you your art skills translate."

"A literary career takes time. As in forever, if the writers I know are any indication."

"True." Bodine was silent. "Unless you find a shortcut. A leg up."

Ray turned and looked at Bodine. "Knowing somebody in the business? Well, I don't."

"Neither do I...but hold on."

Bodine moved from his swivel chair over to the old pump action theater organ. Before they were born, it had accompanied silent films downstairs. He pumped his feet on the treadles. A faint squeaking and rush of air as the instrument built up a head of steam.

Ray stared into the dark theater. Bodine's idea was a ridiculous long shot. More like a pipe dream, and Bodine hadn't smoked weed in years.

Ray was startled by the sudden sound of the organ. Bodine stabbed out the three most famous chords in rock 'n' roll. He sang, "Uh Louie Lou-eye, oh baby yeah, me gotta go...yeah, yeah, yeah, yeah..." He stopped playing.

Ray grinned. "Haven't heard that in forever! What a great, shitty song. You know it's the five minor that makes it rock."

"That it does."

"So?"

"I'll give you a hint. Alton Road."

"That shithole!"

"You say it so fondly."

"Lou. Of course. What was his last name?"

"Goldman."

"The writer." He'd been one of the assorted hangers-on who lived or crashed in the first band house, along with an army of cockroaches. Before the record deal. Before Susan. "With the glasses."

Bodine laughed. "Those terrible tortoise-shell jobs nobody in their right-hip mind would get caught dead in. Only one of the twenty-seven reasons that no matter how long he grew that fur on his head, he was never going to be remotely *with it*."

"You think he's still writing?"

"He's doing something. Because another of those twenty-seven reasons was that he was always hitting it."

"Hitting that fucking typewriter in the room off the kitchen."

"No matter how early you dragged your ass out of bed, he was already working. Guys like that who have a dream generally end up living it."

"How'd he earn the moniker Louie Lou-eye?"

"How'd I get from Bob to Bodine? Ask the fucking hippies."

They laughed.

Bodine said, "He was a hardcore fan. Remember him in that basement?"

Ray had been happily riding a wave of nostalgia. He blanched. *Freezing cold, an endless expanse of bricks to lay, and more to go...* "Lou was never there. And we didn't practice after..."

Bodine said, "No, not *that* basement! The one at Alton Road."

Ray recovered. "The smell down there. What was that?"

"Mold, plus sewer gas? Fuck if I know. Incense didn't knock it down much, either."

"It took dedication to practice down there. But we hung in there."

"Until it flooded."

Ray said, "And poor Bassman..."

"Lost his amp. His Fender Bassman."

"Which is how he got his name."

"He never did have much luck with basements."

Ray glared at him. "This isn't like you, tripping down nostalgia lane."

"I'm not. I'm trying to help you out."

"How?"

"For all we know, Lou is a famous writer." Bodine was still punching out the chords to the song.

Ray said, "Will you stop that?"

Bodine stopped.

"Even if he is, so what?"

"So he has an agent."

"It's been too long. I barely remember him."

"But I'm sure he hasn't forgotten you. Your guitar."

"Oh. Right." It had been the time of the Guitar gods, and in their scene, Ray was the reigning deity. Writers were the heroes of their parents' generation, which was one of those twenty-seven reasons Lou was so unhip.

Bodine said, "Lou worshipped the ground you strutted on. Wished he'd been born with the gift for music, but he was tone-deaf. I'm going to Google him."

Ray flinched, but Bodine was walking to the computer and didn't notice. Google again. What if Lou was dead too? Strangled with a typewriter ribbon or lung cancer? He had been a terrible smoker.

Bodine muttered, "L-o-u, or L-e-w-i-s? Real estate. Trust law. Ah. Check this out."

Ray came over and leaned down and peered at the screen as Bodine read. "Lou Goldman Associates, New York literary agency." He clicked on the link and laughed. "Look at the logo."

The header of the home page was a big pair of tortoise-shell glasses.

Bodine said, "This is him. And he's turned those nerd specs into the signature of his brand. Which proves my rule—anything stays around long enough, it becomes hip. Look at Tony Bennett."

"Tony's never going to be hip in my book."

Bodine rattled off some writer names from the agency's roster. He said,

"You know this isn't my scene, but even I have heard of some of these cats." He clicked on a tab, "Lou Goldman – Author."

Novel published in 1978. Articles in *The Atlantic, Time Magazine, New Yorker*.

A sheet-music icon: "Song Lyrics."

Lyricist for several notable bands.

Ray looked at Bodine. "The Resentments? The Conniptions? You ever hear of them?"

"Can't say that I have. Which is good. He's still a wannabe musician, and his attempts to get into music didn't go anywhere. You can use that. Come on, you must have some of the old hustle in you."

"So, what? I just call him up?"

"You just call him up."

Ray got up to leave. Mingus hopped up from his bed. Bodine nodded at the dog. "He needs to go out. I'll come with you." He leashed Mingus up and followed Ray out into the alley.

Bodine said, "Still cold as a bastard. But at least it's sunny." Following some mysterious canine logic, Mingus tugged Bodine around the yard, sniffing. A truck rumbled past the theater. Mingus eyed it but didn't bark. Went back to sniffing. Bodine addressed the dog, "If you're just going to fart around, we're going back inside. My ass is starting to freeze off. Five more minutes."

Ray admired the last light of the sun. His artist's eye had strong opinions, and they didn't apply only to shop displays on Warren Street. Sights evoked in him a wide spectrum of emotion, all the way from awe down through a narrow band of indifference to visceral disgust.

What was before his eyes now, most would consider shabby. Crumbling bricks on the back wall of the buildings over on Columbia Street, the porch on the house across Fourth Street fallen half off, dirty insulation leaking from its tar-shingled walls.

For Ray, this scene ranked toward the upper part of the spectrum. The natural process of decay was central to his art. And painted in the last golden rays of the dying sun, what was before his eyes shone with a poignant beauty.

Except for the little flagstone path that led from the theater door to the street. He'd never liked it. He cast a baleful eye on it. Why did it displease him? The stones glistened with snowmelt. Maybe he didn't like that kind of stone. He was particular about rocks, too. He hated volcanic ones.

Bodine came up beside him. "I got played. Mingus just wanted to come out because it's spring."

"Doesn't feel like it…" But he was distracted, watching the sun inch down, the stones one by one catching fire. His jaw clenched.

Though Ray was stock still, Bodine must have sensed the current pulsing through him. "What?"

"Nothing." But Ray wasn't listening, his entire consciousness distilled into the light on the stones before him. He hadn't liked them before, but he'd never counted. One. Two. As the last rays of the sun hit magic number three, a door, long closed, sprung open.

Three stones gleaming in the sun. But not here. And not at sunset. A finger pointing at them, and that inimitable voice clear as if it spooled from some old reel-to-reel tape machine, murmuring, *One stone is just a rock. Two are just two. But three is a…a path.*

Bodine said, "Ray?"

Ray jerked a hand up. Bye! And he rushed home, sentences already forming in his head. He ran up Warren, weaving through strolling tourists by instinct. He was blind to the street as the visual memory came to life. He crossed Warren, and a car swerved and honked, almost hitting him.

Key fumbled at the lock, bells jangled, then he plucked the laptop from under the desk where he'd hidden it. He bounded upstairs to the third floor with the clamor of troops on a battleship. Rushed into his sanctuary and onto the couch.

***

It was chilly that morning, working in the shadow of The House. The sun crept across the lawn—it seemed to take a month—but finally reached my face. I squinted. In minutes I was sweating. I'd been raking since dawn without a break. My tongue was leathery with thirst. I kept snagging the metal tines of the rake on tangles of weeds in the overgrown garden. As I overheated, my hands squeezed the rake until they hurt. But I forced my facial muscles to go slack. You must never betray frustration, let alone anger in this place.

The tines clattered on something hard. The shock of the impact shot up my arms. It had to be a stone. I raked on. A moment later, I struck another.

Fuck. I was going to have to dig them out. It wouldn't be the first time, and it was a pain. I got a shovel from the neat row of tools around the side of The House and went to work.

The top of the stone was…flat. And the edge was straight. Another edge at ninety degrees. I reached down and brushed the dirt off. A flat, blue stone. I uncovered a second, then the beginnings of a third. All flat and square.

An old flagstone path buried under decades of autumn leaves. These stones led to a door to the basement of The House.

In the opposite direction, if the path continued the two hundred feet or so across the gardens, it should run into the pile of junk at the bottom of the hundred-foot cliff.

I studied the first stone I'd uncovered. My face flushed, and I gave a fearful glance at The House looming tall above me. Shit on shit. I'd dinged it with my rake, made a silver mark. Wounded it. I kneeled, spit on the stone and frantically rubbed dirt into the scratch, but it was no use. The scar was permanent.

My eyes darted around. No one was watching. I casually raked soil over the stones. Bury them and who will know?

"Ray." The voice was behind me. I started, then stood rigid as a statue. Sun, breeze, the smell of earth all vanished as I became my ears. Became the listening. The voice was soft, just at audible volume, but it penetrated to my core. "What have you found?"

***

Ray's hands stopped on the keyboard. He returned to his body, which, aside from shallow breaths, was frozen. The velvet arm of the couch touching his forearm, and the soft cushion against a stiff back. Where had he just been? It was like the words had written themselves, springing from some deep vault, pure, unsullied by recollection in the intervening decades.

He was coughing again. He tried to clear his throat. He stopped breathing, felt his face heat up. The coughing subsided. But now, there was something *in* there. A lump. A fast-growing tumor... He shouldn't go there. He massaged his Adam's apple, but it only made the lump seem to grow. Like a small animal burrowing inside.

Even as he focused on his throat, his hands idle, the story continued in his head.

Karl.

One stone is just a rock...

He heard the exact words, as from a tape recording, and the exact voice, with its lustrous overtones and British accent.

Karl must have been looking at Ray as he spoke. He always did. But his face was missing from the memory. All he saw was a dark form, taller than Ray, wider, looming over him, casting a shadow. Like The House.

He always just appeared, sneaking up without a sound, as from thin air.

Ray was suddenly a kid again who'd done a very bad thing and was about to be punished. No question, this writing was magic. Black magic. It had got him running over here from Bodine's, telling tales out of school.

No more. Ray closed the file and dragged it into the trash. He trashed the Susan piece, too. He picked up the placemats from where he'd dropped them on the floor, balled them up and clanked downstairs and out to the cans in the alley. Pickup was tomorrow morning.

He came back upstairs and hit the absinthe hard. He'd passed that crucial midpoint of the glass—definitely on the half-empty side tonight—when he remembered. He'd thrown away the physical writing but forgotten to empty the trash on the computer. He leaned down and fished the laptop out from under the couch. When he sat up again, he was a little dizzy.

"Are you sure you want to permanently delete the two items in the trash?"

A click of the mouse pad and they were gone.

The rest of the glass, and he was too.

***

The sun woke Ray the next morning. Something was hanging over his head.

Absinthe? No, that happened every morning. He battled Liz's coffee machine, had almost conceded defeat and headed to Jo's when it spit out a cup of something. He carried it downstairs and sat. The coffee fixed his head.

The thing was still hanging over it.

He looked out the window at the sidewalk. *Three stones, that blank face.* Had he actually written about Karl? That must be what was hanging. But then he remembered: he'd deleted it.

So what…

The mortgage. Fuck.

What time was it? A little after nine. When did book agents get to work? If it was like the music business, ten at the earliest. He puttered around the gallery until quarter after ten, then sat in his chair and called Lou.

As the phone rang, he flashed on Lou at one of their gigs, standing awkwardly behind those monster glasses, looking right at Ray, no, at his *guitar,* like it was a magical scepter. He smiled. Maybe this would work.

The receptionist, who sounded about twelve—though a well-educated twelve—said, "Will he know what you're calling in regard to?"

"Just tell him it's Ray Watts."

And here was Lou. "Raaaay! The Nightcrawlers. Fastest Telecaster in the East. Tell me you're still playing."

Twice maybe in the last year. "Absolutely."

They reminisced about the early days of the band. Lou sounded like they were recounting the rise of the Beatles in Liverpool. Good.

Ray said, "I caught your website. Very impressive."

"Ahhhh. Yeah, I'm a big shit these days. It still ain't rock 'n' roll. I've written a few song lyrics myself."

"I saw. Great. Actually…I've been barking up your tree lately. Doing a little writing."

"Hey, those songs of yours were far out!"

"These aren't song lyrics."

"It doesn't matter. Send me whatever you've got. I promise, no jive-ass bullshit. I'll tell you if I can sell it."

"Thanks, man. This address here on the website?"

"Oh, don't bother with snail mail. Attach them to an email. I look forward to it."

Ray did a little dance around the gallery. He caught himself. It wouldn't do for prospective customers to see that. But it sure had been easy. He'd have to thank Bodine, lay a case of Magic Hat on him, maybe three.

Ray's exuberance lasted about thirty seconds. Attach what? He'd trashed the writing. That piece about Karl was definitely out, but the thing about Susan? Some of that was on the placemats, though it hadn't been as good as the stuff in the computer. But he could reconstruct it. Had they taken his garbage yet?

He raced into the alley behind the house. The cans were empty. Back inside the gallery he called Bodine. "Fiddlefarts!"

"What now?"

Ray told him about Lou and trashing the writing.

"Upside, Ray. He wants to look at your stuff."

"I know. Thanks for thinking of him."

"You brought up the guitar and that sold him."

"Didn't have to. *He* brought it up."

"Why d'you trash what you wrote?"

"I guess I'm a temperamental artist."

Bodine paused. He wasn't buying the lie. But he let it pass. "What have you done on the computer since?"

"Nothing."

"Then you're in luck. Bring that sucker over here, and I'll show you a little trick."

Ray hit the street with the laptop.

They sat in the office. Bodine said, "Fiddlefarts your latest word of the month? I'd expect with you becoming a writer and all, you'd be going a little more upmarket. Using a thesaurus."

"No. It's the mot juste."

"French—that's more like it."

Ray handed him the laptop. Ray leaned over the organ and noodled silently as Bodine worked on his computer. He didn't know any jazz like Bodine, but he could play three chords. In C, anyway.

A couple of minutes later Bodine said, "Here's your stuff."

"You're fast."

"That's what they say."

Ray came over and looked over his shoulder as Bodine clicked on the folder of retrieved items. "Hey, don't…"

"'Susan.' Why d'you trash that? And 'Stones?' You getting into a little music criticism while you're at it? Geology?"

Ray shuddered and frowned.

Bodine shook his head, misunderstanding Ray's look. "What a shame. Not my style, but Susan was a fine woman."

***

Back home he was in the gallery, about to send the Susan file to Lou when he stopped. She was dead, but he really ought to change her name at least. He called Bodine.

Bodine said, "Use 'Bulk Replace.' But be careful. It's a powerful tool."

"Thanks again."

Sally? Sue? It didn't make any difference. *Ann.* He used bulk replace to swap out the Susans for Anns. He was about to send it to Lou when he thought to proofread it.

The replace seemed to have worked. But as he read, he felt himself falling back into the past, back into the good times. He winced and dragged himself back to the present. She was still dead.

As he hit Send, he felt a little shiver. It wasn't just Bulk Replace that was powerful. All this tech stuff was, especially the internet. Just like the President could push a button and blow up the world, you could poke a little plastic key and make big things happen in your life.

Though this would probably be just a little, painful thing. *I don't know how to break it to you, buddy, but you ought to stick with music.* Okay, so maybe not so little.

4.

The poke of a key had started this. He'd clicked on Susan's obituary, and the next thing he knew he was diving headlong into the past, writing.

It was too late for Susan's funeral to send flowers. Not too late to know how she'd lived, to find out what she'd become. He could call the husband.

Her widower. The prospect made him a little queasy, but he Googled Phillip Roberts and found his profile on LinkedIn.

He poked more keys, and there he was.

Ray was stunned. Not that Roberts was a middle manager at a pest control company or that he coached Pop Warner football. But by the fact that this bullet-headed, crewcut guy with the dead eyes and blank face could have gotten the time of day out of Susan, let alone married her and fathered her children.

Ray found a number and tapped it into his phone with a sick feeling.

"Ray Watts. I'm not sure if Susan ever mentioned me…"

"I know who you are."

Do you?

Barely into the conversation and Ray had to restrain the urge to end it. He forced the next words. "I'm very sorry for your loss, for your children's loss…is this a good time?" He sounded like an idiot. A callous idiot.

Ray gripped the phone through a long silence. He flipped the sign in the door to Closed. This wasn't the kind of conversation he wanted to share with the public. Or anyone. He walked to the back of the gallery by the bathroom.

Finally the guy said, "What do you want?"

"I want to know…was she happy?"

"Happy? Of course she was happy. *We* were happy."

A happy family? Happy couple? Ray would have understood if the guy sounded uptight, hearing from the old ex-husband of his dead wife. But he seemed shut down, like his tongue was made of wood, like he was reading his lines from a manual at the pest control company. It must be grief.

"I know this has got to be hard, but when she had the…accident, she was close to my house."

"Sheer coincidence, I'm sure."

"Do you have any idea where she was going?"

"No. She had nothing scheduled with the company, nothing in her appointment book." For the first time Ray heard some feeling.

"So what do you think happened?"

A pause, and when he spoke his voice was raised. "I have no idea. She was completely sober, going the speed limit. And then she just slammed into a bridge abutment."

"So you don't think…"

Roberts lost his cool, raising his voice. "Susan would never harm herself. She believed in life." So he understood one thing about Susan. And whatever she'd felt for her husband, she would have loved her kids. She couldn't do that to them. The guy said, "I have to go."

Ray said, "Well, thank you, and again, I'm sorry." But Roberts had hung up.

***

Ray paced, weaving his way between the sculptures. A whole lot of sorry going around.

He was sorry he Googled Susan, sorry she was dead. And sorry Susan ended up with that putz. It just didn't make sense. Ray had heard no evidence of imagination in the guy's voice. He was boring, with no spark. Ray liked to think she'd had better taste in men.

And what was with *I have no idea*? Maybe he was one of those guys who goes for angry because he can't do sad. But it sounded like maybe he did have an idea. Whatever it was, Ray wasn't going to find out from him. He couldn't imagine any circumstance in which they'd speak again.

The conversation left him with weird energy in his body. It was concentrated in his hands. But he wasn't writing until he heard back from Lou.

Ray's guitar playing had been the thing that got Lou interested in seeing his writing. Bodine had been hassling him for some time to come play a gig with him at some local dive. Ray wasn't ready for that, but it did rouse an old guilt. He'd devoted a good part of his young life to learning guitar. He'd never let a day go by without at least practicing scales. Now, whole months went by with his guitars sleeping in their cases in the closet.

He left the sign in the window closed and brought his Martin acoustic up to the couch.

Playing guitar was like riding a bike. He fell right into a blues in E, with all those nice open strings, and his hands felt good. For ten minutes, at which point his un-calloused fingers started complaining. More tomorrow, maybe.

How long did it take to read some pages? Ray gave it three days before he called Lou back. He tried in the morning. "In a meeting." Left a message, but Lou didn't return the call. He tried again at two-thirty. The twelve-year-old receptionist said, "He has your number. He's still at lunch."

Weren't three martini lunches confined to the Mad Men set? So what did they do all that time, now—guzzle fizzy water?

He was up on his couch, five bells approaching when he gave it a last shot. The receptionist didn't seem the least bit annoyed to hear from him again. Maybe that's what writers did all day long—called their agents.

"Are you sure Lou got my message?"

"Hold on, that's him in the hall."

Lou said, "Sorry, buddy. Business must be attended to."

"It's alright. I'm just curious…"

"I read your stuff." Ray's pulse started beating in his temples.

"The good news? The writing's decent. No surprise there. I knew you had it in you."

Ray waited for the blow to fall.

"But an ex-wife? No offense, but if I were looking for a kiss-and-tell, I'd be talking to Bodine."

Ouch.

"But stay in touch. I gotta fly."

Stay in touch. Agent speak for go fuck yourself.

Ray called Bodine and told him about Lou. Ray said, "I was going to get you a case of Magic Hat. Two, maybe."

"Yeah. Next time you're by, you can bring me a bottle of Miller Lite."

"It's not your fault. It was a good idea."

"You need money? Come to my gig."

Ray scoffed. Bodine was always looking for an excuse to get Ray to play with his band.

"Twenty-five bucks is going to really put a dent in that mortgage."

"Well, I can pay you fifty, but yeah. I could…" Lend you the money.

"No."

"This latest software gig has got me kind of rolling in it."

"No, and don't ask again. 'Never lend friends money.' I'm surprised it isn't one of your sayings."

Bodine sighed. "I dig it. But you're in a pickle. A jar full of them."

***

Over the next three days, Ray sank back into his gloom. He shuffled around his haunted house, dusted sculptures, surfed the net, and gave customers half-assed sales pitches. Counted the church bells until five. But he did hit the guitar every day. He could do fifteen minutes before his fingers warned him of impending blisters.

Ray had just opened the gallery a little after ten and was slouched in his chair when Lou called.

"Ray, I'm glad I caught you." Agentry had turned Lou breezy, a dry gust from the southeast. Now, something had him blowing faster, almost tripping on his sentences.

"You won't believe who I had lunch with yesterday. A senior editor from Random House. A guy our age. A music fan. And guess who his favorite band of all time is?"

"I don't know. Pink Floyd? Velvet Underground?"

"Blues Revolution."

Oh. The bells on the door jangled, and it began to open. "Uh, hold on, Lou, somebody's here."

Three guys in their twenties sauntered into the gallery. A pork-pie hat on one, ratty beard on another, plaid all around. They had to be hipsters from Brooklyn. Ray moved to the back of the room and kept an eye on them. He said to Lou, "Sorry. Go on."

"This editor still idolizes Karl Maxwell. I told him I'd just spoken to you. He remembers seeing your band open for them on that tour. Now, I may have stepped out of line—I was smelling a sale—but you knew Karl pretty well. Weren't you guys up at his house, doing séances or something?"

Not séances. "Yeah." The hipsters were twenty feet away, peering at sculptures, cackling, but Ray could smell the reek of marijuana from here. Stoned hipsters. No wonder they thought his stuff was hilarious. "Sorry, Lou. Just one second."

Ray approached the guys, lifted a price tag and showed it to Pork-Pie. "You break it, you buy it."

"Whatever, man."

Ray returned to the back of the gallery. He said to Lou, "I'm back."

Lou said, "Anyway, this editor says a week doesn't go by without him wondering—Whatever happened to Karl Maxwell?"

"Uh, where are you going with this, Lou?"

Pork-Pie draped an arm around the back of "Psycho Ax-Murder Baby" and tongued its cheek as his friend snapped a photo. Ray shook his head and gestured the guy away with his hand, but the jerk ignored him. Fucker.

Lou said, "If you answer the question of what happened to Karl Maxwell, I think I can get you a book deal. Karl Maxwell is this guy's pet project. He'll buy your manuscript just so he can read it. What I need you to do is write a sample. I'll help you polish it. Then land you a fat advance."

Ray blinked rapidly. Karl…a book…an advance… It was too much. He finally got himself together, got his voice working. "Great. I don't know what to say."

"You don't need to say anything. Just get to work. You got to strike while the iron's hot." Lou hung up.

Had he just agreed to this? He hadn't said no. What had he said? *Great.*

And it was great. The solution to his problems. It would get Liz off his back. Buy his way back into her house. And…maybe her heart.

Lou's idea was also terrible. The worst.

Ray focused on the guys in his gallery. Pork-Pie approached Ray, shaking his head sadly, like the joke had worn thin. "This shit is dark, man. Why so dark?"

"Did you notice the name of this place?"

"Nope."

"Ray of Darkness. That would be me."

The guy practically crossed his eyes trying to figure that one out.

Ray said, "You know what? My good friend has a restaurant right across the street with all kinds of goodies."

"Goodies?"

"A triple choc-o-late torte. With whipped cream."

Pork-Pie beamed and crooked a finger at his buddies. He waved as they hightailed it to Jo's.

Ray had been young and hip and stoned once. Rude, too.

He sat still in his chair for a long time and gazed out on the street. It had been raining on and off all morning. The kind of end of winter rain that sneaks dank fingers beneath doors and the edges of windowpanes. He was on the verge of shivering. It didn't matter. He had to get out.

Business was always slow with weather like this. He flipped the sign to Closed and stalked down rain-slick Warren Street toward the River. While most of the fine buildings he passed were from Ray's preferred Victorian period, in its last blocks the street stepped back in time to its origins when it was a thriving port. The houses shrank, and their fancy trappings dropped away to the clean, boring lines of Federalism. The whole scene fell apart in the final block, the south side of which was consumed by a butt-ugly sixties-era community center. The sixties had been great for sex, drugs, and rock 'n' roll, but had been the worst time in the long history of architecture. Warren ended at Promenade Park on a cliff overlooking the Hudson. It was Ray's go-to place for pondering.

It was in the low forties. By the time he reached the park, his pant bottoms were soaked, slapping icily at his calves. He stood at the railing before a cliff with railroad tracks below and the river just beyond. The far bank was shrouded in fog, sheets of rain angling down, lashing at whitecaps.

The news from Lou was great and…terrible.

The page appeared from memory, as if it sat right before his eyes. The paper was handcrafted, a rich cream, with finely woven fibers. The kind you didn't get at the local stationery store. The words were handwritten in an odd, elegant script, unlike any he'd seen since:

NEVER SPEAK

NEVER SPEAK ABOUT WHAT WE DO

And if that hadn't been warning enough, there'd been that voice: *Ray.* A sound that caressed the ear and lulled the mind. *Remember.* Still lulling, until the next moment—and there always was that next moment with Karl—*You don't remember?* Without raising a decibel in volume, without changing timbre, the voice turned cold and sharp:

Never speak about what we do. Never repeat a word of what I say, not even to each other. Never mention my name.

You could mess around with semantics, get all legalistic and argue that speaking and writing weren't the same thing. And Karl would give you a look that would burn you to the ground. He'd have a point. Writing was just another way of speaking.

Why? Because rules were rules. Especially when Karl laid them down. Ray hadn't seen his old teacher in decades. But unless Karl showed up—God forbid—and spelled out a change, the rule was still in place.

What to do? Ray just stood, staring into the mist across the river as if it might hold the answer. He was suddenly overtaken by violent shivering.

He rushed home and took a long hot shower. Opened the gallery again and sat.

Ray had never spoken to anyone about his time in the group, not Liz or Jo, not even Bodine, who was there for part of it. Speaking and writing were out.

Karl didn't say anything about looking at him.

Ray stared out at the street. He wasn't going to see Karl out there. He climbed upstairs to the couch. He cracked the lid on the silver laptop, poked a key and the machine grumbled its little complaint and came awake. His new window, with views across the country and back in time. The Great Google.

He typed, "K, a, r, l, M, a…" and his fingers froze. He was that guilty kid again, hanging from a sill, pulling himself up to peer in at some kind of adult business.

Come on. This was public knowledge. He shook off his reluctance and finished typing.

Karl Maxwell. Wikipedia was the first hit, with the history of Karl's band, Blues Revolution, his abrupt departure from life under the lights and a discography. Nothing Ray didn't know. He navigated to images: publicity shots, old stage pictures. He flinched at the childish magical thought—*If I can see him, he can see me.*

The photos of Karl were all from before. Ray stared at the eyes. Did Karl have it yet—the power, the supernatural charisma? No. Not fully. There was a gleam here, but either it hadn't reached maximum wattage, or Karl was deliberately hiding it from the public. He was certainly capable of that.

Ray found a link to an old article from the *Times*: "Rock star leaves the stage, but where is he now?" It must have been a frustrating assignment for the reporter, for the best answer he'd come up with was: "Rumored to be secluded in a house upstate." The writer didn't mention what town. Upstate New York was a big place.

Another link to an old *Rolling Stone* article, which Ray remembered reading at the time. He skimmed it.

This was the public part of Karl's life. Before. If some cat from the *New York Times* could write about it, why not Ray? He opened a new Word document. Closed his eyes for a minute, then typed.

***

Karl Maxwell was the front man for Blues Revolution. They were part of the second wave of British invasion bands after the Beatles and Stones. They stormed the US in sold-out tours in '66 and '67.

By 1972, they were on their way down, on the long slide that lands you in Vegas, if you're lucky. Our band, the Nightcrawlers, had just recorded our first album. We were on the way up and intersected the declining trajectory of Blues Revolution, opening for them on a tour of medium-sized venues: old movie theaters, college hockey rinks, and the bigger nightclubs. Onstage, Karl was still a formidable presence. Prancing around, playing tricks with the mic stand, howling his lines, and wailing on his harmonica. Some called him the greatest white blues-harp man alive. Paul Butterfield might have argued, but I wouldn't.

Karl's band was tired. At the smaller venues, they were phoning it in. But that just made Karl work harder. At the end of every show, girls lined up by the stage. The road manager, a wizened guy with a ponytail, would point at the foxiest and hand her Karl's hotel key.

We did our job well. Bodine himself was a fine front man but had been in the game long enough to know to dial it down a couple of notches, not to risk upstaging the main act. Warm them up, but not too hot.

We glimpsed the members of Karl's band backstage, but as the A-team players, they kept their distance from us. Their guitarist—Joe "Winker" Doogal—and I exchanged the competitive glares lead guitarists did in those days. I ragged on Winker's playing to our guys: too damned stiff. I heard he thought my blues were too American, which gave me a good laugh, given that the Brits had stolen the blues from us in the first place.

A week into the tour we had our first night off. Winker passed me backstage, sticking his tongue out. I gave him the finger. He laughed and said, "So."

I said, "Hey, how about a drink back at the hotel?" The best offer of entertainment I could come up with in Akron, Ohio. I figured Brit rockers had a long-standing reputation to uphold as fearless partiers, so I was confused by the worried look that passed over Winker's face. He looked around to see if anyone was listening, then whispered. "Okay, but in your room?"

Back in the room I shared with Bodine, I introduced Winker to Hilton's recent innovation—the mini-bar. He said, "You Yanks are clever!" I soon came to understand his nickname—though you couldn't see it onstage, up close his left eyelid fluttered. As the nips of Jack Daniels sank him deeper into his chair he blinked uncontrollably. This evidence of frailty in a big Rock Star made me start to like him. He had a strange way of talking, and it wasn't just the accent. He referred to his band mates as "cunts," which obviously had a different meaning over in England. It had me laughing, because Karl's guys were all beefy pirates.

Suddenly Winker said, "Oh, bloody hell. How many of these have we had? Spare me some mouthwash? I mustn't have the other blokes knowing about this." A minute later he came out of the bathroom, wiping his mouth, and left. The only thing I could figure was he'd been on the wagon and wanted to hide his falling-off from the other band members.

Bodine arrived back at the room a little later. I said, "I figured you found a new friend." Bodine picked up groupies more nights than not. Which was fine by me—it meant I had the place to myself.

He scowled. "Akron's a cold town." He opened the mini bar. "Started without me, did you?"

"No, believe or not, I had a few with that Winker. Is he supposed to be on the wagon?"

"Not that I know of."

"So why was he sneaking around, coming here to have a drink with me?"

He shook his head. "There's something weird about those guys."

A week further into the tour, after the show in an old opera house, the Blues Revolution road manager came up to me. "Mr. Maxwell wants to meet your band."

As I approached Karl's dressing room, I spotted Bodine. He glanced at me, shrugged and stepped in before me. The light was dim inside. Our drummer Frank, Bassman, and Karl's band and roadies were all there.

I looked around for Karl. "Sit," rang out in the room with the force of a command, though it was barely above a whisper. It sounded like Karl, but could it be? I'd only ever heard him shout and scream. And how did you command with a whisper?

We scrambled in the gloom for chairs. Musical chairs, I remember thinking, hiding my grin at the bad pun. Bassman ended up sitting on the floor. Though he did it faster than I'd ever seen that slowpoke move. Now that we were all seated, I could see Karl, sitting at the front of the room facing us. It was the first time up close. I had known how big he was from watching him onstage, but not how solid. Solid as stone. And as still.

Ten minutes before that he'd been rocketing around on stage, turning it up full for an encore that brought the crowd roaring to their feet. I flashed on a Buddha I'd once seen in a museum, in dim lighting like this...

I was startled when he finally moved. He turned his head with a fluid grace and whispered something to a guy who scurried over and closed the door.

I studied his face. Oddly, his eyes were a dull shade of gray. The stage sweat was gone from his cheeks. They glowed in the dim light, like they were polished. Even for that big body, his head was too wide, his forehead too tall below a raven widow's peak. His face was oversized, but unquestionably handsome. Perfect for a rock star. And perfect for his new role.

He began speaking, his lips barely moving, in a voice soft as silk, rich in mellow overtones as an old Martin guitar. The accent was British—no surprise—and upper class.

It was a little frightening that one person could instantly transform like that, as if some switch had been thrown, reversing his polarity.

Karl was famous for his knockdown cover of Screamin' Jay Hawkins "I Put a Spell on You." And it was a killer. I suppressed another giggle. Talk about putting a spell on. I don't recall a word he said that night, only that murmuring voice, and the warm stillness that like a palpable stream flowed from him out into the twilit room and into my body, calming me, one by one switching off the circuits of my mind.

His mouth had, of course, always been the source of his power on stage as he howled and blew on his harp. But by some law of inverse proportion, the softer that voice grew, the more force it exerted.

It was making me stone like, still and chill except for this fluttering in my chest. The feeling was finally too much, and I looked away from him and around the room. It was the same as our funky dressing room, just a little bigger—flaking plaster above wainscoting scuffed by a thousand jostled guitar cases.

Only the space had transformed. It was like the stillness pouring from Karl had suffused this humble place with a soft glow, touching up the shabby plaster and wainscoting so it now seemed elegant. Like the grand foyer of some fine house.

And then it was over. Karl knitted his hands together, bowed in a blessing. He rose and glided across the floor. The same guy who'd closed the door before opened it, and Karl was gone. I felt an acute pang of loss. But then I was up, gliding out, too, in my own way on some kind of cloud—already imitating him? And the pang left. Because though the meeting was over, it was also the beginning.

***

Ray looked up from the laptop and frowned. The beginning of what? He was missing something here. Something had to have happened in that room aside from a guy mumbling in a strange voice. That meeting had changed his life. He stared sightlessly from the window and it came.

***

I do remember one thing Karl said. How could I forget? "You've all been searching. Some of you for a long time. Searching for this." He raised a hand and held thumb and forefinger an inch apart. "Searching for this jewel of consciousness." And the way he said it I could see it sparkling, feel it cool in my palm. And I wanted it, desperately.

Afterwards our tour bus rumbled toward the next night's venue. No one spoke for a long time. Finally, our drummer Frank did. He was the most practical of us. Dabbling in the spiritual was common among everyone we knew, musicians and non alike. Astrology, every kind of Eastern religion. We lost more than a few friends to Scientology and Jesus Freaks. But Frank just kept his foot on the downbeat, and his eyes on the next gig.

He looked around at the rest of us—Bodine, Bassman, and me—and what he saw in our faces made his sad. "Charles fucking Manson, if you ask me." He retreated to the little room at the back of the bus. I glanced at Bodine—his face was unreadable as always. But shy Bassman actually held my gaze for a moment, in which something real passed between us. Solidarity in this thing, whatever it was.

A few days later, he asked me about that dressing room scene. "Is this really it? Is Karl a true teacher?"

I didn't hesitate. "I guarantee you; this is the real deal."

"Thanks."

Those words would haunt me. They still do. I'd given Karl my blessing, and Bassman had believed me.

5.

Ray was so lost in the writing that the jangle of the bells downstairs made him spring from the couch—*Christ, it's Karl!* He rushed downstairs.

It wasn't Karl. It was business. A tall woman appeared in the door, smiling as the warmth hit her flushed face, followed by a man who didn't smile. Rare customers for such a frigid day in March. From the looks of them they were New Yorkers—handsome, early fifties, elegant with a slight bohemian edge. Wedding rings. The wife worked her way into the room, looked around, and her smile brightened a notch.

She passed Ray, weaving through the grove of standing sculptures and display cases. Her husband hesitated then followed. She stopped short before "Untitled #13." Psycho Ax-Murder Baby. She said, "Oh, this is priceless!"

Ray hung back. He knew not to hover. Let the couple do his work for him. And he knew to hold his silly tongue—*it's not priceless, lady, only forty-five hundred bucks.*

The husband joined her. "Where would we put it?" It was a reasonable question. It would be the rare living apartment edgy enough for that thing to just fit in.

She raised her eyebrows, shot the guy a fierce look, and he flinched. He asked Ray, "Can I use your restroom? Long ride up from the city, had a double espresso across the street." He nodded toward Jo's.

Ray pointed to the back of the narrow gallery. "To your left."

The woman said to Ray, "He likes it—he just needs a little time to think about it."

Ray waited for him to return. When people got back from the bathroom, they either made a quick exit from the store to the safety of Warren Street, or...

The man zigzagged his way through the sculptures and display cases, fast, his eyes bright. He gave Ray a penetrating, appraising look. Hooked a thumb toward the bathroom, "You do that?"

Ray nodded.

The man finally smiled. "That's something." He turned to the menacing figure and glanced at his wife. "We'll take it."

Her husband sold, it was her turn to have doubts. "Where *will* we put it?"

He said, "Good question. *Our* bathroom! It can't make it any weirder than what he's got back there."

She looked at him questioningly.

He said, "Weird. But wonderful. You look at it."

She said, "No thanks. I'm good." The man took out his checkbook, and Ray finally relaxed.

What kept Ray in business was not art, but edge. Dark accessories that let Tribeca loft folks indulge in the conceit that they were more than moneymen and lawyers. They looked at Ray and pictured themselves back in college, hip again. For a couple of grand they could bring some of that edge to their lofts, to show off to their friends.

Ray lifted one end of the sculpture, the man the other, and they shuffled it out to a Range Rover. As they drove away, she turned to the guy, and Ray knew what she was asking: "What was with that bathroom?"

Ray bounded upstairs and dove back into the writing.

***

We were home at the end of the long tour, nursing road wounds, sleeping half the day, getting reacquainted with wives and girlfriends, when I got the call. It was Ethan, who worked in the office of Karl's management company. He, too, had a British accent and spoke just above a whisper. It annoyed me, and I soon realized why. He was imitating Karl's voice, but with none of its effect. He just sounded like an upper-class Brit prig. "You are invited to Mr. Maxwell's house in upstate

New York, next Monday. If you do not come, this invitation will not be repeated."

We were on break with nothing better to do. But I think we would have shown up—at least Bassman and I—even if we were still on tour, halfway across the country. Karl had set the hook in us.

Ethan didn't call Frank. Our drummer headed to LA, where he remains, playing on everything from hit records and jingles to live at the Academy Awards. And the Nightcrawlers were never seen or heard from again.

Neither was Karl, at least in public. He'd simply dropped off the map. There was precedence for his trajectory—a rock star going spiritual, quitting the business, and disappearing into relative obscurity. Cat Stevens had done it, and Peter Green of the original Fleetwood Mac. And Mel Lyman of the Jim Kweskin Jug Band. Lyman played harp, too, and became a guru around the same time as Karl. And from what I've read, he had other things in common with Karl.

***

Ray stopped. He massaged his throat. That lump was back.

He was also aware that the sale he'd just made—the first in weeks—would net him all of fifteen hundred after Maurice's cut. Buying him less than two months with Liz.

He saved one last time. Before he could change his mind, he needed to email it to Lou. Another momentous punch of the key. As his hand reached forward to hit Send, he had an almost out-of-body experience, the sense that this was not his hand, that he was not him. Yet soon as he heard the whoosh of the message leaving, he felt a huge rush of relief. That hot potato was Lou's problem now.

***

Ray woke the next morning breathing fast and shallow, his body cold but his palms slippery with sweat. The sun streamed in the round window, too bright.

Fuck. He'd emailed the writing. Lou's problem now. What bullshit. What time was it? It was before nine, but Bodine should be up by now. Ray sat up and called him. "I sent an email. I don't think the person's gotten it yet. Any way I can un-send it?"

"If your account's set up right, you have five seconds."

"Shit. It's been over twelve hours. Can't you, you know, go into somebody's computer and…?"

"Maybe I could, but I won't. Let's back up. What's this email you're so intent on not sending? Oh. You drunk-emailed Liz, didn't you? That's what you get."

For sex with your ex. "No, I…" Ray was embarrassed to tell Bodine about this Karl book idea. And, frankly, this morning it seemed terrible again. He'd only tell him in the unlikely event that the thing came through. Which, right now, he was hoping wouldn't happen.

"You what?"

"Nothing."

"What are you doing, Ray?"

"I've gotta go."

He went downstairs. Lingered over coffee and toast. He wasn't writing today. Wasn't writing until Lou got back to him. And it was going to be a no. Then he'd be off the hook.

Except for the mortgage. At the thought of Liz, the desire to call her arose like an early flu symptom. He shook it off. He had nothing to say to her. And all she had to say to him was, "Where's my money?" As he puttered in the gallery, rearranging the pieces to fill the hole Ax-Murder Baby had left, a feeling tugged at him.

He wanted to write. And it wasn't just the money. He *needed* to write.

Why?

Of the multitude of subjects for his curiosity, few in his life had held the power of Karl. Karl was the most secretive, opaque person he'd ever known. Who was Karl? In those years Ray had never had a clue. But just a few pages had revealed things he'd been oblivious to at the time.

Like that thing Karl did with his voice. Ray had been so enthralled by it, so immersed in his reactions that he hadn't noticed that it was a whisper. Until now.

What if he could see inside of Karl? Maybe he could. Because writing *was* magic. He clanked upstairs to the laptop.

***

The first time we visited The House, Bodine drove from where he was living in the City and picked Bassman and me up. It was several hours to the Helderberg Mountains southwest of Albany. Bassman slouched in back, being his morose self, while up front Bodine and I jived as usual. But I felt an edge.

I fished a joint from my pocket and was about to light up when Bodine said, "No, I don't think we should." Bassman in the back looked relieved. Just the smell of the stuff gave him the willies. I stashed the joint back, oddly guilty.

Later, I'd see that as a pivotal point. Our last moment of innocence, the last time we were still happy-go-lucky hippie musicians. Nothing had stopped us from getting high—we'd smoked once in some kid's backyard not twenty feet from a cop station, watched officers coming and going, laughing our asses off. Until now.

We rode silently past dreary overgrown farmland, falling down barns and trailers. Bodine said, "This is the northern tip of Appalachia."

I said, "When are we going to see these famous mountains?"

Bodine said, "We're already there. Sneaking up their rear end. I did a little research. This is a limestone plateau. The slope is so gentle from this direction that you barely notice. The other side is sheer cliffs." Bodine had always been interested in geology.

We descended sharply into a deep valley. It was a long way down. We came around a curve, and the cliffs loomed above. My breath sucked in.

Bodine said, "Not quite the Alps, but they beat the hell out of those wimpy Catskills."

A steep, wooded slope rose a thousand feet to a hundred-foot cliff. Bodine handed me directions scribbled on the back of an envelope.

I read, "Left at a dirt road, a mile and a half past the white church."

A few minutes later Bodine said, "That must be it." White was being charitable. The church was more gray, most of the paint chipped off. It looked long abandoned. In fact, this valley showed even fewer signs of life than the plateau.

I said, "Not quite the neighborhood I expected Karl to be living in."

Bodine said, "Yeah, it's beat. But we haven't seen his place yet. He must be going for secluded."

We lurched onto the dirt road. It was rough, potholed, and quickly climbed into a series of switchbacks. Bassman looked out the window and squealed. "I can't do this. I hate heights."

Bodine said, "A little late. I don't see any place to turn around."

Like that, I became aware of the absence of a guardrail. I peeked down at the chasm beside the car and felt a little sick myself. Though it might have been anticipation of where we were headed.

I closed my eyes. We finally leveled off. I opened my eyes as the road plunged into darkness—a narrow slot sliced into the sheer limestone, the walls less than a foot from the car. Bodine turned on the headlights.

The cliff continued on our right, and appeared to on the left, until I noticed windows. A stone building. I craned up to see more, but we were driving so close that all I caught was a glimpse of a porch. I said, "Is that the house?" but we were already past it, climbing again steeply around a bend.

Bodine said, "That must be it. But there was nowhere to park." We approached a line of cars parked on the left, half in the road. Not a great spot if one of the locals screamed down in a pickup truck. If there were any locals. Bodine pulled in behind the last car.

We climbed out, stretching after the long drive from the City. We walked back the way we came. Rounded the corner and there it was. I stopped and stared as the others continued. I gazed up from the bottom, counting three rows of tall windows, capped by the wide cornice of the roof, black against a sliver of gray sky darkening with dusk. Odd lumps punctuated the cornice. It took a moment to identify them: the remains of concrete gargoyles, missing arms and, in one case, the side of a head.

With Edgar Allan Poe as my mentor, I should have loved the place. But I knew something of architecture. How proportions based on the "golden ratios" discovered in the Renaissance evoked a feeling of harmony in the viewer. The builder of this pile must have used tin ratios. He'd assembled the elements of a great house—massive walls, ornate window frames, that looming cornice—but he'd measured all wrong. The effect was not only less than the sum of its parts, but downright unsettling.

After we'd been there a few times, Bodine did more research. He explained how Karl's place was set in an abandoned quarry that once had provided limestone for houses and bridges in the City. It made the owner rich. He opened a new excavation behind the old one farther up on the plateau and built this house.

What was weird was that its facade—which if nothing else had cost a fortune—faced a cliff across a narrow dirt road. Even when some mansion hides behind hedges and gated walls, there has to be some place, some great lawn from which to gape at the thing. Otherwise, why bother? There was no vantage point from which to admire it.

I had a moment's real doubt: What was Karl doing in this place? I forgot about it when a figure appeared in the gloom, approached and hissed, "Don't ever park there again." Where, then? It was the first inkling of the conundrums that I would soon find were the meat and potatoes of Karl's scene.

By the time I reached the porch, the figure was gone. I was alone. The others had gone in. I hesitated. Maybe some wisdom was telling me that this door might be a lot easier to enter than to leave. Or maybe it was just that monstrosity of a house.

Finally I reached for the doorknob.

The first time I went in The House...

***

Ray's hands curled into fists, and his forearms collapsed on the computer keys, like someone had snuck up behind him and was holding them down. He glanced over his shoulder but of course no one was there. His breath came in short gasps.

His damned throat. The burrowing creature in there had died, hardened into something sharp, like a ragged chunk of glass. He squeezed with his hand, but it only got more painful. He swallowed several times and gagged. Leaned forward and puked on the carpet.

This deal Lou was talking about would be predicated on distributing what Ray wrote about Karl to the whole world. Where anyone could read it. Ray could dance around about whether what he'd written up to now violated Karl's rule. But there was no question, the rule applied to everything that had ever happened, that had ever been said within that house. He felt like Karl had sealed the door of The House shut by some spell, and if Ray even dared to open it a crack...

See inside of Karl? He couldn't even peek in the windows of his place. It

53

wasn't just that he couldn't write about it. He couldn't even think about it.

He tried. Tried to remember what had gone on in there. They had meetings, meals… those were just words. When he attempted to recall actual moments, his mind slammed shut. All he could see inside that house was the black of a moonless midnight.

At the same time, his fingers gripped the computer, so hard that its edges cut into his palms. This is *mine*. Not the laptop—that was Bodine's. The story.

Before he could second-guess, he emailed the latest to Lou. "Another stab at it. Want to make sure I'm on the right track."

He checked his email, and came on a new one, with the subject line: "LAZY **SUSANS**…" His heart fumbled a beat. "VOTIVE **CANDLES**…" The words flashed from the screen like they were in Day-Glo 3D. He flashed on a vision of Susan's ashes in an urn in some chapel, surrounded by flickering votives, him creeping up and slotting coins in a box, lighting a candle. She'd been cremated, but first she burned alive…twice burned.

It was only imagination. For all he knew, she'd been buried in the ground. Which was just as bad.

He opened the email.

"Decorative trays… Home items on sale, 20% off!!!"

Fucking spam! *Lazy Susan.* She was the last person in the world he'd call lazy. It was more like busy bee Susan. He slammed the delete key.

***

The next day, Ray did some actual work. He went online and researched gallery trends. Called Maurice and told him the good news about Psycho Ax-Murder Baby and asked if he had anything new. "No, but I will." Artists were easy that way. He didn't fool himself into thinking this was going to pay the mortgage. But he had to do something. And he wasn't writing. Not if he couldn't get in that door.

He set the sign in the gallery to Closed and climbed upstairs and played the acoustic, but it didn't feel right. What he really wanted to do was wail on his electric. He hauled his '67 Telecaster up to the couch, tuned it up, and started bending the crap out of the strings. Now, that was more like it. The only thing missing was a stack of Marshalls.

He played a solid forty minutes before his fingers got too sore. He was headed downstairs for a late lunch when his phone buzzed.

"Lou here. Are you sitting down?"

Ray plopped himself down at the kitchen table. "I am."

"That editor I told you about—he bought it!"

Ray hopped up and paced the length of the room. "Uh, that's super!"

"You bet it is. And the next part's better. I promised I'd get you an advance."

"Right. How much?"

"A hundred grand—fifty now, and the other half on completion, minus my fifteen percent."

Ray leaned his forehead against the fridge and closed his eyes. A hundred grand was more money than Ray had ever seen, ever dreamed of making. Crazy energy coursed through his body. It streamed up into his brain and made pictures. A stack of bills piled on the sidewalk outside, higher than the roof. Him reaching out his round window—never mind that it didn't open— and grabbing a handful.

Lou said, "You there?"

Ray opened his eyes. "Yes. What do I have to do?"

"Well, you could sit there and wait for the contract to arrive in the mail, then sign it. Or I can send it to you in an email that you can take care of right away electronically."

Ray sat at the table. "Uh, email's fine."

Ray was speed-dialing Liz before he could think. He took the phone up to the couch.

"Elizabeth Fairchild." He'd forgotten that corporate voice of hers.

"It's Ray."

"Why are you calling me?"

"I've got a book contract, with an advance!"

"What book?"

"I told you I was doing some writing. It's a lot of money. I'll be able to pay you every cent I owe you."

"That's good." *Good?* "Listen, I have a meeting."

She was gone. Unbelievable. She was getting her fucking money. She could at least pretend to be a little bit happy for him. More important, he had his new life, new career! Wasn't that what she wanted too?

But he was too pumped up to get dragged down by Liz.

A book. His ever-eager imagination went wild. He saw his name on the *New York Times* bestseller list. He was signing at Barnes & Noble, women in line waiting to meet him. Smart women who read. There he was on TV, on *Oprah*.

Was Oprah even on TV anymore? He shuddered with embarrassment. This was not him, at least not since he was kid in a band, dreaming of being the next Beatles.

But this *was* him, getting Lou's email with the contract, climbing downstairs, and figuring out how to hook the new computer up to the old printer. It was him, finding a pen—not so easy these days—and signing. Futzing with the printer to get it to scan. He worked fast, aware that he was doing it before he could change his mind. And then he was at the last thing—hitting send.

It was done. He sat in the chair and stared out past the sculptures at the street.

This was not the same as looking from the oculus. He was too exposed here. And this window was too square. Still, it was a window and, like the one upstairs, could serve as a device to see things that weren't there.

He gazed out at cars, a couple walking by. The scene dissolved, like some movie trick, and The House appeared. Like a scene from Hieronymus Bosch, it morphed in his mind into sentience, into Karl's big head. Ray stood in front of The House, staring up at the facade, the door a mouth taunting, *You'll never dare!* The windows turned to eyes, black pools. And inside was the void.

A hundred grand…a hundred million. He still couldn't write about Karl. He called Bodine.

"You busy?"

"No."

"I'm coming over. I've got some news."

6.

Bodine and Mingus met him at the door. Bodine looked at Ray. "You said you had news. Not that you just got raptured. I'm taking you out to lunch."

"How do you know it's good news?"

"It isn't bad."

"Actually, it's a little of both."

"Of course. You're Ray. You hungry?"

"Starved. With all the excitement, I forgot to eat."

Mingus gave Bodine an imploring look. He said, "Sorry, bud. You want to come to a restaurant, we need to move to France." He led the dog upstairs and closed him in the office. He returned with his laptop.

Ray eyed it.

Bodine said, "Never know when the coding muse will call."

"You sure Mingus won't tear something up?"

"He's not that kind of dog."

He didn't sound sure.

Warren Street was rapidly on its way upscale but still had Sal's, a bar where they knew a lot about pouring drinks and enough to more or less cook a burger.

They sat in a booth. A tattooed waitress in her early thirties came by, and they ordered burgers and beer.

Ray said, "Lou called. He got me a book deal. With an advance."

"What, five grand?"

"Nope."

"Three?"

"Wrong direction."

"Ten? You're buying lunch."

"A hundred."

"Fuck me. Now you owe me lunch and a truckload of beer. I'm assuming that's the good news. Though you have a way of seeing the downside to anything."

"No, it's good."

"The bad?"

"The book has to be about...Karl." He leaned forward and whispered, almost choking on the name.

Bodine barked an ugly laugh. "I can come up with a lot more pleasant subjects. Pictorial history of the Khmer Rouge. Principles of Proctology. And..." He shrugged. "What the hell. You need the money. So you're going to whore yourself out. There's no shame in that. What do you think we used to do playing for drunks in all those dives?"

"It's more complicated than just money."

"Isn't everything with you? So, what else?"

"I feel like it's...calling me."

Bodine rolled his eyes. Ray explained how writing was magic, how he wanted to *see* inside of Karl.

Bodine shook his head. "I haven't done enough writing to speak on this magic business, though I have my doubts. But one of the things in my life I'm truly grateful for is that I never have to *see* that motherfucker again." He sighed. "I get the money. But calling you? It doesn't mean you have to answer. Can't you just scribble some glossy thing?"

"Hey."

"Yeah, yeah, Ray the artist. So you're really going to get into it."

Ray was silent.

Bodine said, "You sure you're ready to dig that shit up?"

Ray was still silent.

The waitress brought the beers and Ray took a long swallow.

Bodine asked, "Are you after revenge?"

"No."

"This calling business—you might want to figure out what, or who, it is you've got on the line. Is something wrong with your throat?"

"Huh?" Ray became aware of his hand massaging his Adam's apple. He hadn't known it was still hurting until Bodine spoke.

"You sound hoarse. Is it sore?"

Ray said, "No. More like something's stuck in there and won't come out. It's been that way for a while."

"Since you started this writing business."

"Yeah."

"You don't get why?"

"No."

"That's your third chakra. Karl had some rap about it."

"What'd he say?"

"Fuck if I remember. The usual crap—you better line all seven of them up, tout de suite, or you'll be cursed unto the twelfth generation. But good luck doing it, because nobody, not even the Dalai Lama, can pull off that trick. That said, it doesn't mean there isn't something to chakras."

"Like what?"

Bodine set the laptop on the table and went online. "Good beer and working Wi-Fi. What else does a man need?" He laughed, "Oh, this is sweet. The third chakra has to do with creativity and self-expression. Which would be your bag. When it's closed, we decay. Open that sucker up, and we experience wisdom."

"So my creativity's stuck. That's been the case for months. How am I supposed to open it?"

Bodine surfed. "Let's see. Aromatherapy. Frankincense, jasmine, ylang-ylang."

"Right. If you can't pronounce it, I ain't trying it."

"You can rub crystals on it. Lapis lazuli, tanzanite…"

"You know I don't do crystals."

"What about chanting 'HAM' in the key of B?" He made a ridiculous humming sound, in what Ray assumed was the key of B, since Bodine had perfect pitch.

"Bodine…"

But his friend was on a roll. He was a scientist at heart and couldn't pass up an opportunity to poke fun at all the wackadoodle new age therapies out there. "Wouldn't you know—it has its very own color."

"Or course. All that horseshit does."

"Sky blue. Go outside, look up, and you'll be on your way."

"That I could do. If it ever stopped raining. Are you done?"

"Sure."

Ray held up his beer. "This helps."

"That helps everything. Until it doesn't."

"So what does?"

Bodine looked at the computer. He got serious. "How about this? It says, 'Speak the truth.'"

"That's exactly what I've been trying to do, with the writing, but something's stopping me."

"Writer's block already? I'd think it was a little early for that."

"No, writing's easy. It's…" Ray got it. He forced himself to speak, though his voice was practically a croak. "How could I miss it? It's obvious. This thing in my throat is… that old taboo. You remember." Ray was half whispering. He looked around the restaurant. It was almost empty this late. Still, he was glad they had the privacy of a booth.

"Who could forget? But you can't still believe it?" Bodine put on a decent imitation of Karl's portentous whisper. "Never speak."

Ray winced, then stared into space. "I believe…" Believe what? Ray suddenly remembered Karl explaining the reason for their silence: *This energy we accumulate here in one day of our practice is more precious than all the treasures in the world. To speak of what we do, to speak of me, is to waste it. If I gave you a hundred-dollar bill, would you toss it out the window?* He supposed he'd believed it back then. What about now? "Why do you think Karl insisted on our silence?"

"Oh, come on! If you were doing all that nasty shit, wouldn't you need a way to keep people's lips sealed?" He gave Ray a wondering look. "You're still afraid, aren't you? And not just to speak. You're still afraid of Karl."

Ray looked at him, and the blood rushed to his face. He *was* afraid.

Until he'd started writing about Susan, he'd barely thought of Karl in years. But hidden away from the light of consciousness, Karl had grown. He'd become fantastic, larger than life, some mythological creature. Which had blinded Ray to a very real possibility: that Karl was alive, out there somewhere. And if he was, he would surely find out that Ray was writing.

Bodine caught his look. "What?"

Ray looked away. Their waitress was coming with lunch. He leaned over to Bodine and whispered, "Do you think Karl's alive?"

Bodine said, "The question never occurred to me." He looked at Ray. "I doubt it."

"Why?"

"I don't know…what goes around comes around, I suppose. Did you Google him?"

"Yeah. There was nothing more recent than thirty years ago."

The waitress set the plates on the table. "Ketchup?"

Ray said, "And hot sauce, if you have it."

She nodded to his glass, which was almost empty. "Another beer?"

"Sure."

She looked at Bodine. He said, "I'm good."

She left, and they ate. Bodine said, "This burger's fine, but these fries are a little…soggy for my taste."

"They say grease calms the nerves."

"Who says? When taken with enough beer, I suppose." Bodine frowned. "You know Karl was a junkie back in the sixties."

A junkie? "That's impossible."

"I knew musicians who shot up with him."

Ray shook his head. He pictured Karl, an oldish man. Raising his arms to a sunset in a canyon of Big Sur. Or laughing with some fellow Lamas in Tibet. Back in England, in a country manor, presiding over a new group. "If he's alive, where is he?"

"Sucking on a jug in some alley. Sing Sing? Most likely rotting in the ground." Bodine laughed. "Hey, maybe he's still sitting up there in The House."

Ray didn't think that was funny at all. "Oh, shit." He pictured The House, not as some nightmare face, but very real, in daylight. With its ancient stones looking exactly the same, and…Karl in it. Less than two hours away. He shuddered.

The waitress brought his beer.

Bodine said, "Hey, I was kidding. He's not in The House."

"Why not?"

"How could he keep that big place up? Blues Revolution records didn't sell *that* well."

Ray had a worse thought. "But what if he still has the group?" He downed a slug of beer.

Bodine snorted. "We were all fools, I'll admit, but I doubt any of us were that foolish. And my gut tells me that group is long defunct. It was in a death spiral when I left, and that wasn't even the end."

"I don't know. If you're wrong, how could we find out if a member were still involved?"

Bodine nodded. "It would be hard if they were still signed into Karl's secrecy shit."

Ray said, "What if I call someone, they play dumb with me, then get off and ring Karl?"

"If he has a phone. Remember? He didn't believe in electricity."

"So, they could go see him, 'Hey, guess who called me the other day, asking about you?'"

"Why are you so uptight about him finding out?"

Never speak… Ray paused and thought. "I don't know." And he really didn't. "If they still have the group, you think they have a website?"

Bodine scratched his chin. "It's been a long time. People change. He changed once—from rock star to guru. He could have changed again."

"Karl might have changed his tune on technology. But he'd never stop being cagey."

Bodine said, "Let me see if they have a website."

Bodine searched, and Ray drank.

Bodine said, "What did we call whatever nonsense it was we were doing?"

"The Way."

"Right. But that was just from some stuff Karl said. As far as I recall—which isn't too far—he never actually called it anything."

Bodine typed. "The Way is so generic; I'm not pulling much up."

Bodine thought. "You really want to know, you need someone who left after us, who could tell something of what happened after that. But who we're sure isn't involved now."

"Lorraine."

Bodine said, "Of course." Lorraine was one of the few members of the group Ray had stayed friends with. She maintained a wider network of relationships than Ray or Bodine. "She's always got an ear or two tuned to the grapevine. I never knew how she survived during all those years of enforced silence. If anybody knows anything, it's her."

"But can I trust her to keep her mouth shut?"

"Good point. That old grapevine cuts both ways. You have to be careful what you say. Because you know whatever you tell her is going to be all over Greene County ten minutes after you get off the phone."

"So?"

"Just keep it casual. You ask the right questions; she'll open up and tell you everything you need to know." Bodine looked at him hard. "So, you going to write this thing or not?"

"I already wrote some. That first meeting backstage. Our first trip to The House. But I got stopped at the door."

"Portals, man. Karl didn't call them doors."

"Right. It's like he cast a spell on that place, no shit, and I can't see a thing inside."

"You have it bad, and I don't think gargling or lapis lazuli or all the good healing vibes in the world are going to fix it. You know if this book with Lou is one of those 'big deals' like we were always getting promised in the music business, it'll never happen anyway."

"True."

"Then you'll be off the hook."

Ray didn't know how he felt about that.

The waitress brought the check. Ray had the beer in his right hand, so he grabbed it with his left.

Bodine was watching and said, "Hey, let me see those fingers." Ray reluctantly splayed them on the table.

"No, the tips." Ray showed him. "What I suspected. You've been playing."

"A little."

"From the looks of these a couple more weeks, and you'll be ready for our gig."

Ray rolled his eyes. "A couple more lifetimes."

Bodine got up and went in the kitchen. He returned a minute later with a large bone. "Mingus's reward for being so good while I was gone."

"How do you know he's been good?"

"Because he wants this bone, that's why." Ray paid the check and they left. They went their separate ways at Bodine's street.

***

When he got home, Ray climbed upstairs to the couch and called Lorraine.

"Ray Watts! How nice to hear your voice."

"And yours." It was.

"How's Liz?"

"Gone."

"I'm sorry. Is she…"

"Coming back? I don't know."

"How about the art?"

"That's kind of over too."

"It sounds like you've been going through a rough time."

"You could say that. And the shrink business?"

"Okay. People aren't getting any less crazy."

They shot the shit, and then as off-hand as he could he said, "Hey, you ever wonder what happened to Karl?"

A dead silence. The roof across the street gleamed in the last sun.

Finally, she laughed weakly. "Remember the end of the group? Karl was all I wanted to talk about. You listened, but even then, you were still obeying him. Not talking about it. And here you are bringing it up. Why?"

You couldn't put anything over on Lorraine. She was smart about people. Which probably made her a fine shrink. "Uh, Lorraine, I have a situation here. When your patients come to you…"

"Clients."

"Okay. When your clients come to you, you're sworn to secrecy."

"Absolutely. Unless they confess to murder."

"Can you keep what I'm about to say quiet?"

"Hm. You're a friend, not a client. But I suppose so."

"Okay. I've been doing some writing."

"Instead of art."

"Yes. A book."

"Wow. I want to read it! What's it about?"

He opened his mouth, but nothing came out.

She finally asked, "You still there?"

"Yeah. I'm writing about…Karl."

"Oh." A pause. "I haven't thought about all that in a long time. You know what I remember?"

"What?"

"Those silent meals. Have you ever known such an uptight scene? Thinking about them still gives me a stomachache."

No, he hadn't remembered. Lunch grumbled in his gut. "I know what you mean."

"The Dining Hall."

Ray's breath caught, and he stood and leaned his forehead against the cold window. She'd nailed Karl's peculiar enunciation, better than Bodine even. Now, all the names came back. The Kitchen. The Meeting Hall. The House. Ordinary words transformed by Karl's skilled tongue so that they hummed with esoteric meaning.

She said, "Sorry. I didn't mean to freak you out."

He sat back down. "It's just that you do his voice so well. Have you heard anything about him?"

"Nothing."

"And if you haven't heard…"

"Nobody's heard."

"Do you think there's still a group?"

"It's hard to imagine there is."

"Is he even alive?"

She paused. "If he died…someone would have told me."

It was true. Ray's gut clenched—*he's alive.*

She said, "Why are you writing this book?"

"Money."

"Which means it's going to get published."

"It looks like it."

"I can see why you want to know if Karl's still around. As you remember, any of a number of things made him unhappy." She laughed. "If someone folded his napkin wrong… But revealing his darkest secrets? After him commanding us not to speak? Whew. And I'm speaking as the one who started talking back then."

"I know. And I'm glad you did. I never would have been able to leave if you didn't."

"But that was only to you and a few other friends. Not to the public. Are you sure you're just doing this for the money?"

Smart Lorraine. "No. I'm…trying to deal with some of what happened too."

"I'm sure. Which could be a good thing, but also dangerous. And I don't just mean if Karl finds out."

"How do you mean?" Her words made him nervous. He stood and rocked from leg to leg in the small room.

"Ray, in my business, in order to get to a better place, sometimes you have to go through a worse place. And it can get…rocky. You never told me what happened, but judging from what I know about others, plus of course Susan…"

He cut her off. "I can handle it. What I'm worried about is Karl. Are you still in touch with anyone from the group?"

Silence. He sat and leaned back on the couch. She said, "Harold's around."

"I don't think I want to talk to him." There was bad blood, something to do with a gig Harold got the band, and they never got paid... He didn't like the guy. Or, more importantly, trust him.

She laughed. "You know who I ran into just a couple of years ago? Fred."

"Jeez. I almost forgot there was a Fred. Almost."

"He's as weird as ever. He gave me one of those looks—you remember."

"Oh, yeah." The disciple deadeye, staring right through you.

"And I wondered for a moment if he might not be still involved with Karl. Then I figured—he's just being Fred. I see clients like him. I think he's somewhere on the spectrum."

"Makes sense." Talking to the guy was a chore. Fred didn't get the give and take of human interaction. He'd express deeply personal things with all the affect of a robot. He'd blurt out insults to your face like he thought he was only giving you the time of day.

Ray suddenly understood something. He said, "You know when Fred whispered, wagged his finger, bored his eyes into you..."

She laughed.

"He was trying to *imitate* Karl, probably unconsciously. He was so bad at it that I never got it. Until now."

"I think you're right."

"Can you imagine Karl putting up with him all this time?"

"No. I saw Fred down in Rhinebeck. Maybe he's living around there. I have to get to a dinner. But great to talk, as always. And good luck with the writing. Tough, isn't it?"

Ray remembered Lorraine had done a bit of writing herself. Was it tough? Ray hadn't been doing it long enough to know. "I suppose."

"And listen, any of that stuff starts getting to you, you can call me. Not on a professional basis, but as a friend."

"Thanks."

He hung up. Could he trust her to keep her mouth shut? It was too late now. He had to. He looked out the window. Night had stolen in while he was on the phone. He didn't want to talk to Fred now any more than he ever had. Didn't have any other ideas. He found a number down in Hyde Park. He paused. This was a bad idea. His fingers went ahead and dialed.

"Yeah." No hi.

"It's Ray. Ray Watts." He stood and leaned against the wall.

"Yeah." Flat.

"Am I interrupting your dinner or something?"

"No."

"How have you been? It's been a long time."

"I'm fine."

Fred didn't inquire about Ray. He said, "I'm curious. Have you been in touch with Karl?"

"No."

"Heard anything about him?"

"No."

Fred hung up.

Ray remained standing. He shook his head violently, shrugged his shoulders and wrung his hands, trying to rid himself of the conversation. He felt the usual awkwardness from talking to Fred, but also the fear that Fred might tell. But tell what? Ray hadn't said a word about writing. Still, he pictured Fred slinking up to Karl, tattling, trawling for points as they all did.

Karl whispering, *What is it, Fred?*

Ray was asking about you.

Was he? Where is Ray?

***

Ray woke the next morning. He'd been dreaming, the same recurrent one, plus or minus a detail, that he'd been having since he left the group. He switched on lights as he fumbled downstairs. As he made coffee, the dream replayed:

He stands at the edge of a clearing in a wood. Winker, Ethan, Susan and others mill around. He's steeped in dread. But the other people seem uncharacteristically relaxed. They lazily trim bushes, shoot the shit, something they never did back then. Ray steps from the trees, and one by one they turn toward him and smile. Warm and friendly. Even Bassman's morose face is smiling.

It's wrong. None of them ever smiled.

The talking stops. Everyone looks to their right, to a dark opening in a rock, a cave entrance. Karl emerges from it into the sun, like the hermit Saint Anthony in a painting. He approaches Ray, beaming with compassion, his arms outstretched—welcome home! His eyes shine with forgiveness. Ray opens inside, letting the warmth in.

Karl reaches Ray and places a soft palm on his shoulder. He explains in his most eloquent whisper, as only Karl can, how it was all a misunderstanding, how Ray's leaving is just a small thing that will float away, like a leaf on a stream.

All's forgiven. But Ray is inching backwards from Karl, across the clearing. Turning and running into the woods, consumed by terrible guilt.

The dream was dissolving, but Ray clung to its remnants, trying to understand. It always ended with the same feeling: his guilt for leaving the group. For years now, he'd believed himself free of Karl. But that was when he was awake. By night the old guy had been regularly visiting, radiating an affection he'd never shown in reality. And the terrible thing was that in these dreams Ray returned it.

Some part of him *loved* Karl. How could that possibly be, after everything that had happened?

The dream left a smudge on the morning. Lunch made him sleepy. He trudged up to the couch, idly surfed around on the net. He seamlessly transitioned from sitting to lying down, now to just get the afghan over his legs…

***

He woke to the tinkling of glass. *Susan.* He found the broken window downstairs. He called Bodine, and he found the brick.

7.

Ray was still staring at the brick when Bodine knocked on the back door. Ray laid it on his desk and let him in. Bodine's Mustang convertible was in the alley, the top down, a piece of plywood perched in the back seat.

In the front of the gallery, they stood before the window. Bodine said, "Kids? The little fuckers ought to be in school."

Ray didn't say anything.

Bodine looked at him. "What?"

Ray handed him the brick with the "Lent" side up.

Bodine stared at it. He gazed at Ray, and it took a moment to get the expression, because it was so rare on his friend. Bewildered.

Ray asked, "You recognize it too?"

"That depends. Where's that laptop?"

"Upstairs. It's warmer up there. And there's coffee." They climbed up to the kitchen, and Ray got the computer. Bodine sat with it as Ray fired up Liz's espresso machine and stood waiting for it to heat. He was embarrassed by the dirty dishes and sticky counters, but his friend was too busy to notice.

Bodine typed. "This thing was made around 1910 by the Lent Brick Company, a half hour upriver from here."

"So?"

Bodine read, then said, "Brickmaking was big business back then around here. 'Lent' was one of 130 companies, each stamping their bricks with their name. Which makes the odds slim that a brick from this particular company would randomly smash your window."

Ray said, "Why would you remember 'Lent' after all this time?"

"I can't speak for you, but it was spring, if you recall. And I had the heretical thought—with Karl, it's Lent all year round."

Ray laughed. "True."

Bodine said, "Which is why it stuck with me. How'd you remember?"

"Repetition. Ten thousand is a shit ton of bricks."

"The question is—what the hell was this brick doing coming through your window?"

The computer pinged. They ignored it.

Ray said, "It's got to have something to do with…the writing."

"Which is about Karl. What have you done so far?"

"That's the thing. Precious little. I'm still stuck trying to get in that house."

Ray ground the beans and was tamping coffee into the filter basket when the computer pinged again. Annoyed, Ray stalked over, grabbed the laptop, and opened his email. He leaned over and read. The subject of the first message was "Maxwell House." Ray looked at Bodine. "What the hell? You think it's okay to open it?" Ray pulled his chair around next to Bodine's, sat and they looked.

Bodine said, "I don't see any attachments."

Ray clicked.

Good to the last drop.

Bodine asked, "Some joke. Only the joker is Karl, or somebody that knows what you're doing."

The second email had the same subject line as the first. Ray said, "They sent it twice." He opened the new one. This message was different:

DON'T

THINK

Bodine said, "Fuck me."

They looked at each other. "Don't think" was one of Karl's favorite whispered commands. Despite his growing panic, Ray's mind still churned on, wondering how he'd never noticed before just how much of Karl's language was couched in the negative. *Don't. Stop. Never.*

A third ping.

This email seemed to be blank. Ray scrolled down, impatient as the scroll bar slowly crawled down the screen. He was about to give up when the words appeared:

NEVER SPEAK ABOUT WHAT WE DO

STOP WRITING

Ray said, "The brick came from The House. From…Karl."

Bodine hit the scroll bar. "Hold on. There's more."

~~Karl Maxwell was the front man for Blues Revolution. They were part of…~~

Ray said, "I *wrote* that. They crossed it out. How did they get it?"

"A lot of questions here. First, how'd they get your email address? And a physical address, to deliver that brick?"

"And how do they know I'm writing?"

Bodine shook his head. "Did you call Lorraine?"

"Yeah."

"You told her you were writing?"

"Uh-huh. But she swore she'd keep it confidential, like I was one of her clients."

"You trust her?"

"I think so."

"You need to call her back and ask if she told anyone."

"Okay." That was going to be fun. Ray's voice took on a chill. "Susan. She has something to do with this."

"You just showed me her obituary. What—her ghost flew up from Jersey and tossed a brick through your window?"

"I know. It's crazy, but it was seeing that news about her that triggered the writing."

Ray got up, finished making the coffee, brought it to the table, and sat.

Bodine said, "You didn't install that software I told you to, did you?"

Ray gave Bodine a guilty look.

"I warned you about mysterious white vans out on the street. They can suck the bits right off your hard drive," Bodine pointed to the computer, "as easy as an anteater at an ant fest."

"I haven't seen anything like that." But Ray was picturing a blizzard of ghostly atoms of information, the air swirling with teeny scraps of notepaper and Post-its and random letters, phantom figures chasing after them with nets, grinning. "I'm not getting it. Karl sending someone out with a bunch of high-tech equipment? Karl hated technology. He didn't even believe in electricity."

"Well, somebody does. What if Karl's got some minion doing this for him? He certainly had no trouble getting us to do loads of shit for him." Bodine clicked around. "Here's where these emails came from: Bud269@comcast.com."

He typed some, then said, "As I suspected. It's a nonsense address. They're using anonymous remailers. Even if they were sending it from right up the street, they could have routed it to Bangkok, then Brazil, then up to Kazakhstan—twice around the world. It would be hard to trace."

"Really. *You* couldn't trace it?"

Bodine shook his head, "It would take weeks. Well, at least we can plug the leak. I'm installing some serious security software."

"Don't you need to go home to do that?"

"I'll download it."

Ray brought their cups to the sink and rinsed them. When he returned to the table Bodine handed him the computer.

"Here you are. Locked tighter than the Muscle Shoals rhythm section. Still, you tell me if you notice any vans lurking."

"How serious do you think they are about stopping me?"

"Assuming it's Karl, I can see him showing up and browbeating the fuck out of you. But something… violent would be beneath him."

"That brick was violent."

"Somewhere on the spectrum of violence. They didn't burn your house down."

"And if it's not Karl, but someone he's handed it off to?"

"That's scarier. Somebody else might get a little overzealous."

"Jeez."

"At least with that new software they won't know you're writing." Bodine stood. "I must get back to it. Let's patch up that window. You wouldn't want to scare off all those customers."

Ray snorted.

They got the plywood up.

Ray said, "Thanks."

"Any time. Though hopefully there won't be a next."

Bodine left. Ray sat in his chair, stared at the plywood. Somebody knew where he was, had demanded he stop writing. This time the brick had broken his window. Next time…he could just picture them, sneaking up behind him on the street. Or breaking in here at night when he was in an absinthe stupor, creeping up to the couch and bashing his brains in.

***

The next morning, Ray sat in the kitchen drinking coffee and tried to face his mess. Everybody was demanding something from him. For Liz, it was the mortgage. For Lou, a book. The brick-thrower insisted that he stop writing.

Or else.

It was impossible, and all the caffeine did was get his fingers back to their bad habits—drumming on the table and shredding napkins. If he could only write, he'd stop worrying about all this stuff. Because when he was working, in the flow, everything else disappeared.

Even before yesterday's email had explicitly commanded him to stop writing, the old taboo about speaking had him stuck outside Karl's door. No way he was trying to get in there. Not today. But his hands needed to write.

When he'd written about Susan, she'd come back to life, back when it was good between them. It had been good with Liz once too. He brought the laptop up to the couch.

***

I was an hour into my first real gallery show in Soho, my cheeks aching from too much smiling, my nerves jangling up a storm despite the Pinot Grigio I kept sucking down. I saw her first. She stood in profile, facing one of my pieces on its pedestal. It was the best thing I had on display. She had taste.

She was tall, with wavy reddish-brown hair, pretty in a severe way. She wore a long black dress and string of shiny pearls that said money. As she stared at my piece, a private smile stole onto her face. I felt immensely flattered. The expression didn't match those clothes. It moved up into her eyes, which moistened with a look of wonder. The contradiction between those clothes and that look put a hitch in my breath, propelling me across the room, past my usual shyness.

I said, "You like it?"

She turned toward me, but I could tell she didn't even really see me at first, that she was still seeing my piece.

"Like it?"

She paused. "It's alive, it…" She clutched at her heart with both hands, a gesture that I felt in my own chest. "Speaks to me? No, that's a cliché. It sings to me."

The last of the fake smile I'd been hauling around all evening melted into a real one as a shameless bubbling feeling overcame me. I gobbled up her praise like a kid handed a three-scoop ice cream cone with sprinkles.

"I'm Ray Watts."

Her eyes finally focused on me. My nerves jangled again, for I somehow just knew our future would be written in the next moment.

Her face was transparent. Dismay—oh, an artist. An actual Bohemian. Reconsideration—but he made that thing. He's…not bad looking.

Resolution. What the hell.

"I'm buying this piece for my apartment. Can I buy you dinner too?"

Well, she wasn't shy.

She took me to the fanciest restaurant I'd ever been to—not that the greasy spoons I was used to set the bar very high.

Her West Village place was elegantly furnished, with a stunning view of lights on the Hudson.

More wine, then she showed me her king-sized bed. The way I was living, I was still camped out on an old mattress on the floor. The black dress came off, along with the last traces of law school diction and table manners. I started getting acquainted with the secret person her initial smile had hinted at.

***

Ray looked up from the computer and out the window. And for a moment, it was still then, still before her leaving, and she was just in the city at work, and she'd come home, and they'd cook a nice dinner together, because that's something they were really good at, aside from that other thing, of course.

The spell dissolved, and he closed his eyes and clenched his teeth. He dove back into the magic.

***

We were fulfilling some cliché, the bohemian artist kept by a society girl. The old commie hippie in me grumbled about her cleaning lady coming twice a week, and Liz just gave me a look. She'd been to my sty down on the Lower East Side. Once. It was amazing how quickly my scruples fell away once I discovered steak-au-poivre, crème caramel, and a red that didn't come out of a jug.

Our opposite natures made for good chemistry. And made moving in together a bad idea. Fortunately, we both understood that. Practical Liz, as always, had the solution. She had some bonus money she needed to park. She'd buy a place in Hudson and keep her apartment in the City.

While it was the round window that sold me on the house, for Liz it was that spiral staircase. The house was for sale by the owner, a crusty old painter. When he gave us a tour of the house, those steps were the first thing he pointed to. "That goes all the way to the attic on the third floor. I just repainted it. It's a one-of-a-kind piece."

I wasn't going to argue with him. It was an Art Nouveau wonder—cast-iron vines in emerald, jade leaves sprouting from them, the whole thing gleaming, winding up to the roof like...Liz smiled at me. "Jack and the Beanstalk."

I said, "I hope there's no giant waiting up on top."

The owner said, "Nah. Just my studio."

Liz looked at me. "Your studio."

In just a month, the paint started flaking off that staircase. But life was good. During the week, I holed up in the house while Liz did her lawyer thing in a glass tower in Manhattan. Friday, she'd clean out the nearest Gristedes and drive up in her Beemer and cook me a meal that was every bit as delicious as what was in those restaurants.

Skinny Bodine eyed my belly and said, with fake disapproval, "You aren't quite looking the starving artist anymore."

The gallery was her idea. I'd had a few smaller shows since the one where I met her but wasn't close to making ends meet. One day, we were sitting downstairs, and I was moaning to her about fuckhead dealers. The sculpture that she'd been staring at when we first met was sitting in the corner. She pointed at it. "You sold me. Now, sell them," she said, sweeping her arm out at the world.

"What am I supposed to do? I've taken my portfolio around to every dealer. I call all the galleries. I go to—"

"Shh." She stood and paced. And that woman could pace. Her voice lost a bit of its edge. I'd say it got dreamy, except Liz doesn't do dreamy. She said, "I was in Umbria a few years ago, in a town called Deruta. It's famous for its pottery."

"Of course." I was lying. Another hoity-toity thing I didn't know about.

"The artisans' studios are right on the street with a sales counter up front. As they worked on their pots, they explained to me, in that lovely accent, what they were doing. I felt like I was witnessing magic. And if I bought something, I could participate.

"Keep the studio upstairs. Open a gallery here, and you can sit and do your finish work, sanding and polishing."

It worked like a charm. It was a rare golden time, making hay with the sun high in the sky. I leapt from bed every morning. I couldn't wait to yank back the curtain on my studio and get my hands on my latest baby.

I'd long known that consorting with the muse was the sacred thing, not whatever progeny resulted. But Liz taught another indispensable thing. If you want to have real self- respect as an artist, you need proof that you're a valuable, functioning part of society. And the proof is, bluntly put, sales.

The first day I was open I sold two pieces. I called her at her office, and she said, "Oh Ray, that's great! Which ones? I'll miss them."

I got off the phone and ran all the way upstairs to get back to work.

8.

Ray looked up from the writing again. This time the illusion shattered. And the real Liz, the current one, stormed into his head. Distracted when he called to tell her about the advance. She just couldn't be bothered. And then there was that terrible sex.

Never Google your ex. What did Bodine know about exes? He might have a ton—a shit ton. But once they were out the door, it was like they hadn't existed. He'd never mentioned any of their names, not once.

Ray was about to set his hand back on the flaming burner. He hit the bookmark for Google, and in less than a minute, he was seeing Liz. Seeing and burning.

Here she was at some conference. He couldn't help but flash on the last picture of *Susan*. She had been at a conference too. Only there was no shadow smudging Liz's fine face. She was grinning. And so was the guy standing next to her. The bottom dropped out of his stomach. It was time to stop, but he was scrolling down the page. Here they were again, arm in arm. These smiles weren't look-good-in-the-quarterly-bar-review smiles. They were can't-wait-to-get-back-to-the-hotel-room-and-fuck smiles.

She was fucking a *lawyer*. He stared. No. Something told him, this guy was worse than a lawyer. Banker? He was about to scroll some more—maybe he could catch them in bed, really beat himself up—when the phone rang.

Liz. She said, "Is this a bad time?" She always did have a sixth sense with him.

He leapt from the couch, and his feet did a nervous dance. He wanted to howl with demonic laughter. His tongue twisted with sarcasm. He suppressed it by speaking slowly, with a flat affect. "No, this is good. It's excellent. What's up?"

"Have you been drinking?"

His eyes flitted to the absinthe bottle at the side of the couch. If only. "No. I never drink before five."

"Except when you do. I need the money. Now."

The check's in the mail? No, the truth. "It hasn't come yet. When it does, you'll know."

"Don't you get pissy with me. You *are* drunk."

He carefully closed the phone. He wanted to smash it into the wall, but once he started down that road, he might not stop until he'd burned the house down. No, he wasn't drunk. But he would be soon as five o'clock rolled around. Now, it was barely two.

He stalked over to Jo's. The sun was bright, thinking about putting out some warmth. He glared up at the sky—*it ain't the thought that counts.* The north wind was stuck back in February.

Jo was busy. The room hummed with the lunch crowd, with just a few tables empty. But it didn't roar like it would if she served alcohol. Which meant he could think. And that he wouldn't be tempted.

He sat at his table and got right up to his old habit, finger drumming. Jo caught his eye, mouthed, "The usual?" and he nodded, even though he wasn't hungry.

She brought his sandwich, and he picked at it. Jo finally came and sat. She said, "I haven't seen you in a while. What's up with your window?"

"Kids."

"They better not try that here. I'll sic Louise on them." They laughed. Jo's partner was five feet tall, gentle, and taught second grade. A man, one of the last lunch customers, waved a check at her. "I'll be right back."

She returned and sat. "Last time I saw you, you were headed out with Liz. How'd that go?"

"It was weird. I had the sense that she's been…seeing someone else."

"Oh, shit." But she said it like she wasn't too surprised. She looked at his plate. "You're off your feed."

"Yes, Mom." He groaned. "I Googled her, and I saw them together."

"Aw, Ray. Computers! You should stay away from those fucking things. Nobody had to see that shit before they came along. Nobody needed to know." She lowered her voice. "What did this asshole look like?"

"Like a fucking banker."

"I'm not surprised. Liz is reacting. This new guy is the anti-Ray. She's trying out rich and straight just to see what it feels like."

"Reacting to what? What did I do?"

She closed her eyes for a moment and got a faraway, sad look, like she was revisiting some old heartbreak. She opened her eyes and put on her best sympathy smile. "Try to see it from her perspective. She falls for this artist, for his art. Helps set him up in a nice gallery. Suddenly he doesn't feel like doing the art anymore. And soon he isn't selling anything, because he isn't producing. And—no offense—but while this is happening, he's not the cheeriest guy on the block."

"But you don't understand—the art left me. I couldn't help it."

"I understand. Liz doesn't. She can't. You guys are different. Different can be good. But too different…"

"Then why the hell did we just end up in bed?"

"Oh, no." Her face curdled in horror. "That was a very bad idea."

"I didn't figure out she was with this guy until after."

She shook her head. "Naughty Liz. But naughty you too. You should know better."

Despite himself, he started laughing.

"I'm not joking!"

"No, it's just the thought of you and Bodine agreeing on something."

"On what?"

"He told me, 'No sex with your ex.'"

She made a rude sound. "A stopped clock's right twice a day." She and Bodine did not get along. He was a techie, she a Luddite. She wasn't thrilled by all the girlfriends he'd been through, and he knew it. She bit her lip.

He said, "What?"

"Uh, I shouldn't say this. But if Liz has this guy but bothered to come all the way up here just to sleep with you, maybe she's having doubts."

Crazy hope welled in his chest and must have shown on his face.

"Oh, Christ. My fat mouth."

The hope collapsed. "No, she didn't come here for that. She came here for money. I owe her for the mortgage."

"What are you going to do?"

Should he tell her? If it happened it would be public soon enough anyway. "I'm writing a book."

She brightened. "A book. I saw you writing. You seemed more…energized."

Her nice way of saying less depressed. He smiled.

"What's this book about?"

"I'd love to tell you all about it, but I can't. Writer's superstition. You'll be the first to get a signed copy when and if it comes out."

"I can't wait. If it's half as brilliant as your art…."

Ray gave her a hug, then went home. It was still freezing out. Jo was right. The writing *was* good for him. Tangled up as it was in the mortgage, Karl's taboo, and God knows what publishing hassles awaited him, the actual craft of it gave him a purpose, made him feel more alive.

He headed upstairs and glanced at the closed bedroom door. A vivid picture of Liz and her new fuck buddy flashed in his head—here, in their bed. His nails cut into his palms, and he clamped his teeth together. When Liz was with him in there that last time, he'd sensed she was with this asshole because of her vibe. She was holding a part of herself separate from him in a way she'd never done before.

He'd recognized that vibe because Susan had been exactly the same when she started cheating. Putting some vital part of herself high on a shelf, and he kept reaching. Was still reaching after all these years.

For Susan? Liz? Did it matter?

He wanted to Google Liz again, just like you worry a sore tooth with your tongue. Instead he climbed up to the couch and searched again for Susan. He studied the picture of her at the convention. No question, something was missing from when he'd known her. Her spark. But time could extinguish the brightest sparks.

Susan Brandon must be common name, because each Susan on the page was different, from eight months to eighty, blond, brunette. He scrolled down. And there was an earlier photo of his Susan. In front of an office building with five others, squinting in the sun. Her expression was impossible to read.

He scrolled. Two pictures of her next to a shorter woman with dark hair. In one, she was really smiling. In the other, they grinned at each other, conspiratorially. A friend.

He navigated back to her last picture, that group shot. Compared to what he'd just seen she looked positively haunted. He checked the dates on the earlier shots. They were from two and three years ago. What had happened to her in the time between? It looked like she'd *lost* something.

One of the photos with the friend was captioned. *Joan Telford.* What was that company Susan worked for? Mutual of Central New Jersey. He closed the computer. Called and asked for her.

Joan had a nice voice, younger than her picture.

"This is Ray Watts. I was a good friend of Susan Branford's."

"Oh, Susan. I haven't heard her name in months, but I think of her all the time."

"I just found out about what happened."

"Really?"

He could feel her distancing herself. What kind of good friend is so out of touch that they don't hear for over a year? Open up to her, and maybe she'd respond. "I hadn't spoken to her in a long time. We were married once."

"Oh. She never said anything about you." But she was warming up. "I'm sorry. No matter how it ended between you, it must be hard."

"Thank you. So, you were friends?"

"I'd like to think so. Yes, yes, we were friends."

"I called because I can't stop thinking about how she died. It doesn't make sense."

"I can't think about it at all. It's so awful. I just try to remember her alive, always with a kind word for me, and so…*there.* You must know what I mean."

So present. "I do. This is a strange question, but was there anything going on with her in the last months, before…"

"How did you know?"

Know what? "I don't. Just guessing. I found some photos of her online. In the most recent one she looked different than in the earlier ones."

"You're perceptive. What do you do?"

"I, uh, am an artist."

She laughed. "I just had a terrible thought. About her husband. Artist fits her a lot better than pest control. I just met you on the phone, and I'm already liking you better than—what's his name?"

"Phil."

"He came to an office party. Don't get me wrong. He was nice enough. But he didn't seem her caliber."

"I spoke to him. He seemed a little dull."

She laughed. "As dishwater. *She* certainly wasn't." Joan sighed. "Losing her was going to be hard no matter how you sliced it. What's harder is the depths I sensed in Susan that she never revealed to me. And now, I'll never get to know that Susan. We had lunch fairly often. She spoke about her kids, hassles at work, the usual. She was always big on eye contact. And I returned her looks, hoping for a glimpse of that hidden part of her."

"I know exactly what you mean." Ray had been trying to open to Joan to get her to talk, but now it was coming automatically. He was starting to like her.

She said, "Tell me. What was she hiding in there?"

The House, looming above him, Susan rushing in the door, more than any of them making sure she wouldn't be late.

He shook his head, wrenching himself back to the present. He said, "I can't…"

"What?"

"Just our history."

"I understand." She paused. "Even when she wasn't doing the eye contact thing, she always looked right at me when I spoke."

She did. Joan had known Susan. "She was a good listener."

"The best. But in those last months, she'd sometimes look away. Often enough that I knew something was going on. I asked if her kids were okay, and she said fine. And Phil…Susan laughed and said, 'Phil's Phil.'"

"How was her marriage?"

"She never brought it up. I had the feeling that she was making the best of it, like with everything in her life."

"Did she ever talk about her past?"

"What, before her husband and kids? Never a word, now that you mention it. Why, was she hiding some dark secret?" She laughed nervously.

"No, no." *The House again, towering over him, now the shabby farmhouse he and Susan shared those last months of hell.*

She must have caught something. "What are *you* hiding? Sorry. I have no right to pry."

"Neither do I, but…" He was a curious bastard. "Do you remember when this change happened in her? Anything around that time?"

"She was that way the fall before the accident, not in the spring before, so it must have been…Oh."

He didn't push. A long silence.

She finally said, "I need to think about this."

About what? But he held his tongue.

She said, "I don't mean to be mysterious, it's just that I don't know what's right. Anyway, I'm glad we talked."

"Likewise."

"It's good to know someone else cared about her. Give me your phone number. But don't call me again, please."

I need to think about this. Phil, when Ray asked what he thought happened to Susan, protesting too much, said *I have no idea.* Was something going on here? He had to know. But with nothing else to work with, the two cryptic statements just chased each other around his brain until five o'clock.

When the bells rang, he poured himself an extra measure of absinthe. The knowledge of Liz's lover had ripped the wound of her absence wide open. It throbbed in his chest. But with each sip, the pain receded, and he gained perspective.

Right now, Liz was some rough surf, no doubt. But she was just the edge of a sad, sweet ocean. Susan's betrayal had, at the time, practically drowned him. Now, she was merely a gentle swell out past the shore.

Karl's jewel of consciousness? He scoffed aloud. Ray's memories were his gemstones, the pearls he harvested from this sea. He'd spent much of his life plucking them from the waters, curating them, dusting them off, polishing them to hold gleaming to the light.

The writing had upped the game. The simple process of making words netted treasures he'd never known existed.

Ray was deep into the waters, deep into the absinthe when something became clear. Liz, Susan and the rest had all come and gone. And terrible as it was to think, the joy and sorrow they'd brought hadn't really had all that much to do with who they were. The sting of Liz's betrayal wasn't that different than with Susan.

All along he'd had one steady, one true love. An unrequited love. She never left him, but he could never have her, either. She stood just out of reach, just past the next wave, eternally enticing, eternally breaking his heart. She was the reason he fashioned reliquaries from dead things. The reason the first thing that came to his fingers when he picked up a guitar was dusty forlorn blues.

His one true love, the past.

9.

Ray woke. He cracked his eyes and immediately closed them. Way too bright. He opened his eyes again, hand over his brow. Where the fuck was he? He grasped at something wooly. Liz's afghan. He turned his head and saw the back of the couch.

He stood. The room spun. He staggered to the wall and leaned against it. His head cleared. He hobbled down the hall, gripped the railing of the stair as he inched his way downstairs.

Jo's? Too much trouble. The scream of Liz's coffee machine triggered a spike of pain above his right eye. The light was still too bright. Liz's stainless-steel refrigerator gleamed with a jittery penumbra. Everything looked a little blurred.

He carried coffee and a piece of toast downstairs without dropping them. Progress! He choked the coffee down but couldn't even look at the toast.

The diagnosis for these symptoms was no mystery—he had a wicked hangover. But it didn't make sense. He never, ever had more than one glass of absinthe. Okay, maybe he'd poured a little heavily, but that did not explain this devastation.

Where was the laptop? Upstairs in the side table drawer. He always stashed it in case of burglars. He humped up the two flights of stairs, panting. Somebody was driving that spike into his forehead now. Red mist pulsed at the edge of his vision.

The drawer was empty. He frowned. Could it be downstairs, in the desk drawer? No. He hadn't had it down there. He looked around. Got down on hands and knees, which just pissed off that asshole driving the spike.

The laptop was on the floor, hiding behind the arm of the couch. The lid was open.

He picked up the computer and sat, his heart pounding even harder than a minute before. He punched a key and the screen lit up. Word was open. He knew he'd closed the program. His eyes focused on the words.

***

Bodine and I were outside clearing brush. It was cold, late winter. Karl appeared, holding something by his side. He lifted it, with the grace of performing a ritual. An old brick. He said, "You need to get me more."

Bodine said, "How many?"

"Ten thousand. And not from some dealer. They would be"—he looked like he had a bad taste in his mouth—"spoiled. Dig them from old barns, abandoned houses. Make sure no one sees you. Then clean them."

I said, "Clean them how?"

Karl gave me a look of contempt. Shall I tie your shoes for you too? He added, "I need them here, neatly stacked outside the basement, in one week."

My mouth fell open—impossible! Karl ignored me but nodded his head once as he caught the look of skepticism on practical Bodine's face.

"All right. Ten days. That's only a thousand a day."

Bodine and I drove out that afternoon, found a barn, and managed to collect about a hundred. We obviously had to work harder. Starting the next morning, we rose before dawn and worked until after dark, crawling through the bowels of tumbled down barns, pulling bricks from the crumbling foundations. I alternated between the fear that the police might come and fear that we'd bring the walls down on us. We got filthy and soaked.

When we finally returned to Karl's, we huddled out back—no making a mess inside—and scrubbed each brick with a wire brush until every speck of mortar and dirt was gone. It was tough with numb fingers.

Karl came out once around halfway through the ordeal. He eyed the stack then walked away. We got his point. We'd counted. We were never going to meet the deadline.

***

Ray stared at the screen. He didn't for the life of himself remember writing this. But he had. The only person who knew this story was Bodine, and he hadn't snuck in here in the night while Ray was sleeping and done it.

He'd blacked out. Something he'd never done before. Where was that absinthe bottle? He found it tucked behind the couch, like someone had hid it in shame.

No wonder. It was three or four inches lower than he remembered. He sat on the couch with the laptop again and scrolled down—there were pages more of this stuff. It was obvious why he was so tired—he wasn't just hung over, but had been up half the night, writing.

Automatic writing. He cringed. That was old school hokum, spiritualist crap that went with crystal balls and spirits tapping behind curtains.

His hangover had him on the wrong side of everything, but a stronger feeling was emerging. It screwed his mouth up and had him cold inside, even though he'd turned up the heat.

Fear. Not just of whoever was out there that didn't want him to write, but of the part of himself that had written last night. He had no control over it.

He could stop drinking if he wanted to. It wouldn't be much fun, but he'd done it before. He wasn't sure if he could stop writing.

Filled with the rectitude of the mortally hung over and three cups of strong coffee, Ray resolved to make something of his day. He went down to the gallery, murky with the plywood in the window. He measured the frame, called a glazier, left a message.

He sat at his desk and checked his email. Lou: "We still on track? Waiting for pages." Ray didn't answer. He wasn't sending him last night's efforts.

Snail mail clanked into the slot in the door and tumbled to the floor. Bills, bills. Credit card offerings. Something from Lou. He began to tear the envelope open. Stopped and gingerly pulled out the contents. A check for $42,500.

He headed to Bodine's. Mingus howled, and Bodine came to the door. Bodine said, "I've got something for you."

Ray followed him and Mingus up to the office and sat. Bodine disappeared into the closet. He appeared holding a green bottle. He said, "As they say, absinthe makes the heart grow fonder."

"Ouch. That's for me?"

Bodine handed it to Ray and sat. "Don't drink it all in one sitting."

Ray said, "My lucky day. Look what else I have." He held up the check.

Bodine scooted his chair over and looked. Mingus caught their energy and sprung from bed and trotted over and looked too. *Doggie treat?* He sniffed at the check, then lay on the floor, disappointed.

Bodine said, "Huh. Not that I didn't believe you, but this sort of makes it real."

"That it does." Ray's fingers were squeezing the check like it might run off. "I need this money. And that's not all I need."

"What else?"

What indeed? It came in a rush. "I need to *know*. Know if he's alive. Where, with whom. How he is."

Bodine sighed. "That's what I was afraid of. What's been calling you is your goddamn curiosity. How far are you willing to go to find out?"

Ray started to reply, but Bodine interrupted him. "Don't tell me. I know how far. To the fucking moon. I know you, Ray Watts. Once you get determined, nothing can stop you. I'm certainly not trying."

"And I don't just need to find out. I need to write."

"And not just for the money."

"No."

Bodine nodded. "It's like how you had to play that guitar. Which was a good thing." He sighed. "So, you're still spooked by that brick."

"Yeah, but you fixed the problem with my computer."

"I believe so."

Ray sighed. "More than that is that old taboo. I can hear Karl: *Never Speak.*"

"And you're still listening." He slitted his eyes and did his Zen Master imitation. A minute later he opened them and gave Ray a crafty look. "Wait here."

Bodine disappeared into the closet again, returned and handed Ray a tiny vial. Ray raised his eyebrows.

"Take a peek inside."

A couple of wisps of paper in the bottom. "That's not…"

"Blotter acid."

"You must be kidding." But Ray knew he wasn't. A few years ago Bodine had confided in Ray, "I still trip once a year, around the summer solstice. Every year, religiously." His eyes twinkled at the pun. Up to now, Bodine's ongoing psychedelic adventures had been just a part of his myth. But that was real LSD in his hand.

Ray stared at the vial and tiny teeth of fear gnawed at his gut. He was well acquainted with that drug. Too well acquainted. "Where'd you get it?"

"My buddy Spider, out in Sausalito. Used to be a roadie for The Grateful Dead. He says it's Owsley."

"Owsley? Come on."

"It was made back then, anyway."

"And it still works?"

Bodine nodded sagely. "Mm."

"How's it going to work for me?"

"There's a direct line between that substance and Karl. Acid was the thing that opened our eyes to the notion of a spiritual path."

"True."

"Never mind that Karl turned out to be a major detour."

"I think I'll stick with my poison." Ray pointed to the fresh bottle of absinthe on the floor.

"You want to channel Baudelaire? Your buddy Poe? Fine. But those guys were way before our time."

"Where are you going with this?"

"Acid got us to Karl in the first place. Maybe it can take you there again. Think of it as supernatural intercession."

Ray was reminded that while Bodine was essentially scientific in nature, his yearly acid trips suggested a less rational aspect to him. With it came flashes of intuition.

Maybe he'd just had one.

Ray stared at the vial, so hard that it seemed to vibrate in the air. Could it be the key to The House?

He was sitting in pitch darkness, black filled with a million horrific colors. Freezing. Monks chanting, over and over. He started half up out of the chair, his eyes wild.

Bodine said, "Whoa! Where did you just go?"

"Nowhere. But now, I'm going home."

"Suit yourself."

Ray placed the vial on Bodine's desk carefully, like it might explode. He carried the absinthe bottle to the door, stopped, and held it up. "Thanks for this. I was almost out."

Bodine came over and pressed the vial into Ray's hand. "I'm trying to help you out here. I really think it might do the trick."

Ray stood for a long moment casting a stink eye onto the vial. Finally, he took a deep breath.

"Oh, fuck it." He pocketed the vial and left.

Up on Warren Street, he searched for the nearest trash can. It was after eleven, and the town had come to life. Too many people. LSD was still illegal in New York, a lot more so than the little bit of weed up in his rafters. He was aware of his paranoia—folks threw stuff in trash cans all the time, that's what they were for—but he kept the vial and headed to the bank to deposit Lou's check.

He saw the guard by the door and blanched. He sweated out ten minutes in a long line, waiting for the guy to come over and arrest him. Fortunately, the young woman at the window was off someplace that didn't include old guys like him. Ray pocketed the receipt and made it outside and took a deep breath. He'd send Liz her money tomorrow. Or maybe the next day.

He headed down to the park on the river. It was in the fifties, but the park was dreary as ever. So was the Hudson, in this final gasp of winter. A desolate scene in black and gray. The last ice was gone from the water. Its sullen surface mirrored the leaden sky. There was no snow either, just bare trees on the island in the middle and on the far banks. Hard to believe they would ever show color again.

Ray yanked the vial from his pocket and stood to pitch it in the river. But the railroad tracks were between here and the water. He'd never been much of a ball player, doubted he could throw it far enough. It wouldn't do for some kid to pick it up, suck on those papers, and lose their mind. He stuffed the vial back in his pocket and kept his hand there as he headed home. By the time he got there, the vial was greasy with sweat.

He needed to give it back to Bodine. If he wouldn't take it, Ray would sneak the thing into the museum. But not right now. For all his hemming and hawing about trying to write about Karl's house, he hadn't actually tried in days.

He made coffee and brought it up to the couch. He opened the laptop and the K document.

***

I reached for the doorknob...

***

He willed his fingers to type, but his mind was blank. No words, no thoughts. That door might as well be a massive stone wall, extending up and to the sides beyond sight. He rubbed his thumbs on his forefingers, tapped on the front of the laptop.

He remembered Lorraine invoking The Kitchen and Dining Hall. They appeared as little flashes of light in the darkness but immediately winked out. Because when he tried to recall, there were no faces, no words, no traces of sensation in his body. Just a vague feeling of gloom.

He forced himself to picture the porch as if he were actually there. Creeping up the stone steps to the door. Standing with his nose an inch from it. Peering in one the narrow windows that flanked it. But inside was just blackness.

But his vision was adjusting to the dark. A dim figure, *Karl,* stalked back and forth in the hall like he had on stage, like an animal in a cage. Age had sunk his eyes in his head. But they still burned.

Ray glanced away, but too late. Karl caught his eye for an instant. Ray's heart lurched in his chest. He turned and fled the porch and ran down the road.

Though there were no new words on the screen, here on the couch he shrank back.

He sat paralyzed, pulse racing, barely breathing.

But he still had to write. He relaxed.

He could write about something else.

10.

I was what, ten? My buddy Joey would just not stop lording it over me about this mummy he'd seen in a museum. "It was a real one, and it was all rotted." When Mom brought me to the Metropolitan in New York, I saw my chance. She dragged me through endless corridors, the walls plastered with a million boring paintings. I kept asking, "When are we going to see the mummies?" After about a hundred hours, she finally gave up on my art education and took me to the Egyptian collection.

More boring stuff in cases. Joey was a dirty liar.

A sarcophagus. I ran for it. Mom grabbed my hand and stopped me. "You're going to have nightmares."

I broke from her grasp and flew to the case and lifted myself by the edge and looked in.

My mother yelled, "Ray!" An alarm rang, and a guard barreled over, shouting, "Son, don't touch that!"

In the seconds before they reached me and dragged me away, I'd seen enough. Enough to last a lifetime.

Mom was right about the nightmares. In the dream that night I was looking in the casket. Here there were no linens. Just the face, brown skin flaking off like autumn leaves, showing bone beneath. The eyes popped open. They were desiccated and black as walnuts, but they looked right at me. The mummy lurched up and chased me through endless museum corridors as I screamed.

It was the worst nightmare of my young life. Except next thing I knew, I was reading everything Edgar Allan Poe wrote.

***

The day Liz and I moved into the house in Hudson, I went to use the downstairs bathroom. Something was holding the door closed. I shoved it open and found some curious boards on sticks, like signs, hand painted, a name and dates on either side. Next to them sat...a pelvis.

Liz clanked down the spiral stairs. "Ray?"

"In here. Check this out."

She gave a quick look at the booty, then frowned at me. "I want this junk gone before dark."

I called the previous owner. He laughed nervously. "Uh, those are 'nun's gravestones.' I guess they painted two names on a sign to save wood. And don't worry, that's just a cow pelvis. I can come get them if you want."

"I'll take care of it." I drove the stuff over to Bodine's. He had a lot of space in the old theater.

"Nun's gravestones, huh?" He grinned. He lined the items up carefully with the rolled-up theater curtain and a few remaining seats. Neither of us knew, but it was the beginning of his museum.

That night I woke around four a.m. and peed in the upstairs bathroom. I pictured the toilet bowl set into that pelvis and laughed.

***

Liz got a Christmas bonus and took me for her version of the Grand Tour of Europe. On the plane home, the highlights played in my head. Reliquaries in Rome: intricate gold coffers housing the tibia or skull of a saint. The Capuchin Chapel: decorated with the skeletons of thousands of monks. What were they doing there? A placard explained the wisdom of the Memento Mori, "What you are now we used to be, what we are now you will be."

By the time we landed, my path stood before me: I would fashion modern reliquaries. Parodies, with punning names. I made my first piece, "I'm Cross." A rat skeleton, shrouded in its own gray skin, mounted on a cross, the bar of a rattrap pinching the neck, tiny arms to the sides and tail curling down. I stuck a scalpel in the side from a dissection kit I'd had as a kid and crowned it with thorns fashioned of barbed wire. More followed.

It was good fun for a while. Most of them sold. But after the better part of a year at it, I was getting bored.

It was time to dig deeper. I saw an exhibit at the Met with this baroque masterpiece made of amber. They called it a casket. On the train home, I was on the edge of sleep and images played in my head. That pelvis bone…mahogany paneling in a tearoom in London…that amber casket.

I started awake. A casket was a reliquary. I yanked my sketchbook from a pocket and drew. Back home, I stayed up all night sketching at the desk downstairs, periodically running to the bathroom with a tape measure.

The next morning, I slathered casting resin on the walls and thick in the corners until the space was like a giant bubble in dark amber. I buried bone fragments in the still-tacky substance, like fossils in limestone. When it dried, they were vaguely visible through the translucent surface. I stained the walls and sink housing mahogany and lacquered and polished everything to a silky patina.

I set dim halogen lights like Bodine had in the ceiling. The effect was a room whose lustrous walls cried out to be touched. But when you moved closer, you saw those bones and recoiled.

The centerpiece was the medicine cabinet. I framed it with historical shaving implements, stacked in ascending chronological order like an archeologist's section through shaving trash, from straight razors up to Bics. I gilded them with spray paint and capped them with Gothic spires.

The hardest part was setting the toilet in that cow pelvis. I was about to call a plumber—which would have been fun!—when I realized I could saw the bones in half, assemble them around the bowl, then glue it together.

I'd been surfing the artistic flow, pumped on adrenaline. I stopped and frowned into the mirror. It needed one last touch.

I touched my face. Bones beneath the skin. I ran up to the closet and found my Visible Man, a toy from childhood that had followed me through countless moves. It was a foot-high plastic skeleton standing inside plastic skin. I'd apparently saved it for this moment. I replaced the mirror with clear glass and set the mannequin behind it.

A philatory is a transparent reliquary. Here was a full-body one. A Memento Mori.

When it was done, I showed it to Liz. She looked for a long time, a series of expressions playing out on her face. Finally, she turned to me, smiled, and gave me a huge hug. "Ray, this is truly great."

Great? That was a big word. But I knew it was the best thing I'd ever done.

My bathroom installation—that was the official art world term for it—became locally famous. People came to the gallery just to see it. It was featured in an art magazine. And then the New York Times.

The critic wrote: "Mr. Watts has tapped into that vast collective memory that has had the living enshrining their dead since the beginning of history. Everyone from shamans with their fetishes of bone and feather, to Christians with their shards of saints, have done the same thing—groped toward immortality.

"The most obvious example of this, of course, is the Egyptians, who elevated funerary art to perhaps its highest point."

***

Ray closed out the document. He patted the computer and laughed. It was a reliquary too. A glittering thing that housed the relics of his life—those precious memories.

He frowned. He was just treading water, writing about Liz, about his muse. Ray of Darkness, spawn of Edgar Allan Poe, had a dark tale to tell. It awaited him right inside the door to Karl's house.

But he was not getting in without a key. The vial was still in his pocket. The shriveled papers sleeping in it woke. As if the drug were already acting on him, he imagined them mewing like kittens. They were already making him crazy, and he hadn't touched them. But he didn't flush them down the toilet.

***

The glazier came the next morning and fixed the window. He said, "Kids, huh?"

Did he look hopeful, that maybe he'd see an uptick in business?

"Yeah."

The sky was cloudy, but the temperature was in the upper forties. Not too cold for painting. And it would be nice to be out in the spring air.

The new Ray of Darkness sign was just as good as the old. It was fun simply pushing a brush without the burden of having to make art. And by the time he was done, his dilemma didn't seem so dire. He'd figure something out. He went back in the gallery and checked his email.

Lou: "You get the advance? And I don't want to be a noodge, but do you have some stuff for me? That editor wants to see more."

He answered, "Check received. I'll have more writing for you very soon."

And he was back in the soup.

The potion in the vial stopped mewing. It started humming—a quiet but utterly demented tune. Taking this acid was a ridiculous idea. As far as Ray knew, it was fine for Bodine. But Bodine had never stopped dropping it, was used to its effects. For Ray to take that shit after all these years? And with the state he'd been in? He might as well just stick an icepick in his forehead.

The drug burst into song, nonsense syllables, on the pitches of some unearthly scale. He did his best to ignore it. He finally climbed upstairs to the couch with the acoustic guitar. Strummed up a storm and the vial finally shut up. His fingers got sore.

He went down to the gallery, flipped the sign to Open and dusted the art works, starting at the front.

Liz called. "It's what I feared. I'm not exactly downsized, but they've shrunk my hours to nothing. If I don't get your check today—all of it—I'm driving up to a realtor tomorrow at nine a.m. and putting the house on the market."

He threw the dust rag on the floor. "I've got your goddamn money. A bank check work for you?" Your banker fuck buddy can cash it. He leaned against the wall, tapped a fist on it.

"You really have it? I need it on my desk by five today."

"I'll drive it down."

"No. You don't have to do that. FedEx it, I'll get it tomorrow morning."

Was she easing up on him, or did she just not want to see him? In either case it was his cue to explode. "I saw your new boyfriend."

"You what? Where?"

"So, you don't deny it. I Googled you, and…"

Somebody on the street was looking in the display window. Ray turned and stomped to the back of the gallery.

She said, "I can't believe it. You're *stalking* me. Do I need to remind you that I'm an attorney?"

"I'm not stalking you. Anybody can search for pictures on the internet. I imagine it's quite legal."

"Ray, I'm going now. Don't look me up online anymore. And send me that check."

"I'm doing it this fucking minute."

He hung up on her. He stomped down to the bank, then the FedEx office and sent her the money.

He flew out onto the street. Slowed down. Where was he going? Not home, back to the couch and cold laptop.

He stopped on the sidewalk, closed his eyes, and pictured the blackness inside The House. He changed channels to Liz and her lover on some king-size hotel bed, then slammed the dial away to the Nutso Channel, the vial in his pocket.

He opened his eyes. Fuck. He had just committed to the book. Ten minutes ago he could have still returned the advance. Now, he'd spent a good chunk of it.

The tempest in Ray's head stopped. He sensed the early March sun on his face, radiating actual warmth for the first time since the fall. He drank it in.

Orange Sunshine. The "brand" of the first acid he'd dropped. Back then, a bunch of loony acidhead chicks liked to sing that old song: "Please don't take my sunshine away," with a spooky quaver in their voices that suggested somebody ought to take it away, right now. The same genre of music the vial was into.

He strolled down to the river. At the park he stood at the railing atop the cliff. Sun glinted off the swollen river. He'd been here just yesterday, but something was different: the lightest dusting of red on the narrow island midstream.

Spring. He sat on a bench, slid a hand in his pocket, and rolled the vial between thumb and forefinger. He flashed on Aladdin with his lamp. What was inside might as well be a genie. He imagined it waking and whispering to him. Telling of how back in May of '68—in the springtime of his life—LSD had transformed Ray of Darkness for a few hours into Ray of Sunshine. He'd stepped out into the May sun, grass and flowers so bright, so alive that it was like that moment in *The Wizard of Oz* when Dorothy steps from black and white into color. He felt as though he'd suddenly woken from a dreary lifelong sleep to a miraculous day.

But those ecstatic hours had never returned, any more than his youth would now.

The genie whispered. *What have you got?* No Liz, no art. Only a ghost house. *And you need that money.*

But never say never. It's never too late.

He imagined the vial growing warm in his pocket, starting to glow, the color of the sun, and suddenly the song it sang was sweet and rich.

He returned home, slowly, with a final pretense that he was still deciding. By the time he arrived at the couch upstairs, the vial had gone silent. He pulled it from his pocket and looked at it. Just a couple of wisps of paper curled in an old glass bottle. He popped the cork and used his pinky to tease out a single paper. Before he could change his mind, he tossed it onto his tongue and chewed it up.

He'd asked Bodine, "Why two?"

"I'm not sure of the strength anymore. If one doesn't do you, two will."

When you're taking a trip, you want to make sure you've pumped enough gas to get there. He swallowed the second one. Flutters kicked up in his stomach. It must be like this skydiving, when you're about to jump. I'm gonna fly! Better hope the chute opens. He waited. If he remembered, it took about twenty minutes. He was already thinking trippy thoughts.

This round window, this eye, was about to become magic.

The genie was about to overpower Karl's spell, and Ray would see into The House, into that lost time. And then he would write.

The first sign that the acid was coming on was the sensation of that glass chunk in his throat. It had never gone away, just become so constant that he was no longer aware of it. He was aware of it now. Suddenly he *was* that chunk, every ounce of consciousness concentrated in that centimeter of aching gristle.

But things were moving right along. A tingle of electricity raced up into his head then down into his body, growing in intensity by the second. The chunk of glass throbbed with his pulse, glowed and hummed like the vial in his pocket had, as if he hadn't swallowed the magic paper, but it had stuck to his vocal cords.

Was this pain or pleasure? With sensations this strong, who could say?

A knot arose in his belly, an angry fist, competing with the throat for attention. Another chakra, what was its name? Never mind. This was definitely pain.

Which was somehow connected to the terrible disappointment that his oculus had not transformed into a magic window. Instead, it had become a fritzy old TV. He'd never seen a round one before, but there was an awful familiarity about it. Unbelievably, it was tuned to the same idiot channel as when he'd last tripped long ago. It was still playing the same fucked-up program!

Somebody needed to tell the assholes running this station that this wasn't the seventies anymore. The colored patterns on the set rearranged themselves over and over in the same order. How could something be both terrifying and colossally boring at the same time?

His throat and stomach roared at the peak of every pulse in an explosion of noise, radioactive light, icy fire, and physical agony.

An agony which acidhead wisdom told him was the somatic analog for a feeling. Dread, the knowledge that the very worst was about to happen any second. When the next second came and it didn't happen, the feeling just grew. All his muscles twisted like rubber bands, tightening and tightening, bracing themselves for some executioner's blow.

The thought: *This was a bad idea.* The homunculus occupying his couch laughed.

Bad? He was supposed to be a writer now. Where was his thesaurus? Let's see, it was a moronic, hideous, nincompoopish idea. If memory served, there was no unplugging this idiot box for at least another twelve hours.

As dusk crept up outside the oculus, the channel finally switched to endless cascades of diamonds the color of blood and sewage. A sizzling sound—was his brain catching fire? No, just rain against the window. The wind had picked up and turned the drops to the burst of a thousand machine guns.

It was full dark outside. He fumbled around on the floor, found a candle, and lit it. The TV was off. His window was now a mirror. A real mirror. He gazed in, and a long, weary face with salt-and-pepper stubble and messy hair stared back. Like Escher's "Hand with Reflecting Sphere," a man who also looked at himself, aghast, in a round glass, as though seeing a ghost. Except its coloring was a lot more Van Gogh than Escher.

Ray's body had the sudden impulse to move. He rose and crept silently past the studio curtain. It wouldn't do to wake whatever was in there tonight, not with a rack of cold chisels at its disposal. He hit the steps, a hand tightly gripping either railing. He bridged the missing step like it was a bottomless chasm. Why had he moved? A deep, deep question. Ah. Because that chakra between his legs—the sixth, or was it seventh?—was screaming.

He needed to pee in the worst way.

The upstairs toilet was closer but through the bedroom. Demon Liz was in there, hiding behind the door. He reached the downstairs bathroom. The splashing in the bowl was deafening. He was about to leave when he glanced at the medicine cabinet. With all the other psycho-crap going on in his head, he hadn't noticed that the Imp of Bad Jokes was lurking. It pounced. *I don't need any more medicine, Doc, I took a double dose!*

Be gone, asshole.

When Ray had erected this trick mirror, it had been no more than an artistic conceit. Now, he looked at the Visible Man, at this bag of bones, and for the first time in his life really got the truth: that all his flesh and hopes and suffering were soon enough going to be gone, leaving that skeleton. No, not that plastic one, but *this* one, every bone of which presently ached within its temporary coating.

This was the reason for his dread. It was the fear behind all the other fears, cold and black, growing with each breath and tick of the pulse in his neck, as he moved ever closer to the end.

That wise-ass devil returned, picking up one of those giant Mexican guitars and strumming some awful mariachi tune. The skeleton in the mirror—*his* skeleton—started shimmying, doing a little dance. A cut-scene of a blackened corpse in a wrecked car, barbequed flesh melting away, then Susan's skeleton stood beside his. She wasn't in the mood for dancing, and who could blame her? But the devil picked up the tempo, her bones trembled, and now the two of them were shaking it side by side, like south-of-the-border puppets.

They turned to each other. Embraced. And they made chattering, clacking love.

Ray was a glutton for this kind of punishment. But enough was enough.

He climbed back up to his couch. Though it seemed an eternity, only three hours had passed since taking the drug. He tried to play the Telecaster, but it sounded like insects chittering. The next moment, he felt them nibbling on his fingers. His hands flew up, and he stashed the guitar under the couch where he couldn't see it or them.

The trip finally wound down. Bargain-basement hallucinations still cobwebbed the window, but their colors were fading. The dread crawled down the dial to nine, and his body began to loosen.

He assisted. Poured the last of the absinthe into a glass. As he finished it, he felt the first tendrils of weariness pull him down into a slouch.

***

He'd been dozing when, with a shock that practically stopped his heart, he sprung straight up from where he sat.

He was *inside The House.* Not hallucinating, exactly, but vividly imagining. Not in the front hall behind the door, but all the way inside, in a narrow corridor in back, standing before another door. The door to The Backroom.

His hand worried the knob. It was locked, thank God. But he still wanted in. With a colossal effort he turned around, inched his way from the door as though held by a great magnet. Finally, he hightailed it down a long, long corridor, out The Front Door and into the night.

Here on the couch he sat up straight, gripped the velvet skin of the arm, and did everything in his power to stay here, in this house, in his room with its window on Warren Street.

Sometime later, a strange light appeared in the oculus, and he panicked. And then laughed. Just a bedraggled sun crawling to the job. The window had reverted. It was no longer magic. Just a window, a dreary window looking out on an empty street.

He lay down and tumbled into the mercy of oblivion.

11.

Ray woke around eleven. He headed to Jo's. She came over to take his order, looked at him then quickly away.

He said, "I know."

"You look like…"

"A ghost."

"I wasn't going to say it, but yeah. You look like somebody took a big hose and sucked the juice right out of you. What have you been doing?"

"You do not want to know."

"I don't think I do. If you need anything, though, I'm here."

"Thanks. What I need now is coffee. A pot of coffee."

"That I have."

He reached up to his throat. What?

The glass chunk was gone.

He headed home. The LSD had left behind a residue of magical thinking. This throat had been guzzling the nectar of the Green Faerie. The acid genie had freed it of its pain. In turn, he must pay the price: go on the wagon. The beer wagon, anyway. He was laughing at himself, at these crazy thoughts, even as he took the full bottle of absinthe to Bodine's.

His friend and Mingus met him at the door. Bodine glanced at him with a little nod. "So you did the acid."

Ray fished the empty vial out of his pocket and handed it to Bodine.

Mingus sniffed at Ray. Bodine laughed. "Even Mingus can tell." He looked at the vial. "You took both."

"Unfortunately. I can't believe you do that every year."

"Practice makes perfect. Bet you didn't wait before taking the second one, like I told you."

"No. Hindsight."

Ray handed him the absinthe bottle. Bodine said, "What, this brand isn't up to snuff?"

"I haven't opened it."

Bodine frowned, then laughed. "You're giving it up! You know, back before it got all illegal, LSD was quite effective in curing alcoholics."

"I'm downgrading to beer, anyway."

Ray followed Bodine and Mingus up to the office, and they sat.

Bodine said, "Kicking absinthe is a nice side benefit. But did it do the main trick?"

"What trick?"

"You know. Get you into Karl's old haunted house."

"Fuck. I forgot that's why I took it. It *did*. At the tail end after…you don't want to know what nonsense."

They sat, the silence only broken by the dog's gentle snores. It was amazing that you could suck on a couple of wisps of paper and overcome a psychological barrier like that. Ray's eyes got wide. There was something even more amazing.

Bodine asked, "You having an acid flashback?

"No. That trip didn't just get me into Karl's. That thing calling me?"

"Your curiosity."

"Yes, but beneath that."

"The creative urge. To write."

"Even beneath that."

"Whoa. Going deep on me."

"It all comes down to this. I want to be free. Free of Karl. And in order to do that I have to know that his way was bogus, that he was bogus. And that's where I'm getting with this writing. It's the reason I Googled Susan in the first place. As long as any part of me still sees something divine in Karl, I will never be free."

Ray had to credit Bodine. His friend didn't snark on him for being so dramatic. He just stood and put a hand on Ray's shoulder.

"So, go write your book."

Ray headed home. Spring was hiding again. A bitter wind spit rags of rain at him. He didn't care. He knew now what he was doing, and why. And paradoxically he'd come out of the other side of a semi-psychotic experience feeling newly sane. As he climbed the stairs, his house felt like just a house. No ghosts here. That had been just a conceit, like that ridiculous genie in the bottle, carrying on, singing to him. It was only a potent chemical.

It was a plain old house, but he wanted to keep it. Which required not only writing about that other house but publishing it. His new sanity informed him that though he'd breached that threshold—Karl's portal— whoever had tossed a brick through his window was still out there. It was going to be hard enough creating this book without worrying that they might return at any moment with a brick or worse.

They wouldn't get him in public. He could bring the laptop to Jo's. That would mean closing the gallery. Missing out on the slim chance of a sale. Never mind. Writing was really his new job.

He crossed the street. Luddite Jo had never seen this computer and wasn't likely to approve of its entry to her realm. He clutched it to his side nervously as he made his way to his table. But it was getting onto lunch, and she just waved on the way into the kitchen.

***

As I pulled open the heavy door that first time and crossed the threshold, The House exhaled a sour, diseased breath. It was the opposite of the sweet incense of that first meeting backstage. Inside, the plaster was half-gone from the walls, revealing the bare lath skeleton.

But the floor was swept clean. Shoes were lined up along one wall. I'd been in hippie houses where they asked that shoes be left at the door. They were—in a pile. These were arranged with each pair perfectly squared, and every pair the exact same distance from the others. I removed mine and placed them at the end. I looked twice to make certain I had them right. I still wasn't sure.

I entered a great two-story chamber with a grand staircase. It was early evening and last shafts of sunlight from windows high up pierced the gloom, revealing that the place was a ruin.

I wandered into a smaller room. Half the ceiling had come down. A once-grand couch, set of easy chairs, and walls splotched with green, black, and white mold. It must be the source of the bad smell. I began coughing.

I flashed on Xanadu at the end of Citizen Kane, Dracula in his ruined abbey. An old Grateful Dead song, "Brokedown Palace," started playing in my head. Except I had just arrived. What good could come in a place like this?

My thoughts were interrupted when Karl's lieutenant, Ethan, stalked in the room with a scowl. In a clipped British accent, he hissed, "What are you doing in here? You're late! Don't let it happen again."

We musicians always made fun of ourselves, wondering how it was that people whose living depended on expert timing could be late all the time. Late to practice and gigs. For a musician, I was fairly punctual, so I had never worried about it. Until now. I had just discovered that you were never late for anything with Karl.

I followed Ethan to another room. It was in somewhat better shape, the walls recently painted white. People were sitting on cushions, lined up in rows as meticulous as the shoes in the front hall. Everyone's back was ramrod straight. I took a cushion in the last row.

In front sat a larger, empty cushion. Karl's! To my disappointment, instead of him, one of his elder students came in and took it. He settled into it with an exaggerated care I'd soon be exhibiting myself. He rattled on for an hour, in a vague and pedantic manner, about what we were doing there. He had none of Karl's charisma. By the end of his spiel, I was wondering why we'd driven all that way.

It was the same the next few times. Drive three hours, and no Karl. I finally asked Winker where Karl was.

He gave me a knowing look. "Patience."

We'd been going up there a couple of months when we were invited up for a full day. We had to get up before five in order to arrive by eight sharp. One minute late and they locked the door, and you had to drive all the way home.

We were still on musicians' schedules, crashing well after midnight. So, I was glad Bodine drove. I dozed in the car. Dawn was breaking as we approached the switchbacks leading up to The House. I asked Bodine, "Why is the place such a wreck?"

He explained, "One of Karl's 'blokes' told me the house was abandoned back in the twenties. Water breached the slate roof in the fifties. It worked its way down through the floors. The damage is apparently worse on the upper floors. Whole walls have collapsed. The beds have lagoons of stuff living in them. But don't worry—we won't be going up there any time soon."

"Why not?"

"Upstairs is reserved for the inner circle. Karl's band, that guy Ethan? I'm not sure exactly how it works."

An inner circle. I wanted to be up there. To belong.

***

Ray looked up and blinked like he was coming awake. The room was filled with the lunchtime roar of conversations. Sun gleamed on a couple of empty tables. It seemed a vast distance, returning from Karl's dark house to this cozy, familiar place.

He had a disconcerting sensation, like his innards no longer quite fit in his skin.

He'd crossed the Rubicon. He'd pried open Karl's door using the acid. Now, just under the influence of a little caffeine, he'd willfully written about that house. Which explicitly broke Karl's taboo.

Never speak about what we do. His fingers, lying idle on top of the keys, started trembling. Random letters appeared on the screen.

He froze at the distinct sense that someone was standing next to him. *Karl.* He'd slipped silently into Jo's in that way of his, was right now looking over Ray's shoulder, and if he turned, he'd see that face, and hear that voice. *Ray...*

"Ray?" He jerked his head to the side. It was Jo. "I didn't want to interrupt. You seemed miles away."

"Mm." About a hundred, actually.

"Writing again?"

"Yeah." He eased the laptop lid down so she couldn't see.

"Need anything?"

"More coffee."

"I know that. Food?"

"No thanks."

Customers arrived, and she went to their table. Jo hated cellphones even more than computers. Ray was always careful to silence his whenever he was over there. He checked it and found a message from Susan's coworker, Joan Telford. He walked outside into the alley by the restaurant and called her.

He said, "I wasn't sure I'd hear back from you."

"You almost didn't. I've been wrestling with this thing. And I've...decided."

"Oh."

"I wasn't going to tell you, because even though Susan is gone, the notion of anyone thinking badly of her... Then I realized I actually had no idea what this thing meant. And that I wanted to know what it was. Maybe you have some idea." She sucked in a loud breath.

A truck rumbled by, and Ray cupped the phone to his ear as she continued. "So one day in the July before the accident, Susan was late to work. A young guy came by with the company mail. I was shuffling through mine when I found an eight-and-a-half-by-eleven manila envelope with Susan's name and our address handwritten on it. I looked for the guy, but he'd gone. I was going to put it on her desk but decided to give it to her in person. In case...in case it was important."

"Why'd you think it would be?"

"I don't know. It wasn't the kind of thing we get here."

"Where was it from?"

"I don't remember. When Susan showed up, she apologized for being late—not that I was her boss. She was just that way. I gave her the envelope, and she looked at it and froze. It was like she released an electrical charge into the room. She recovered, smiled, and headed for her cubicle. But then...she didn't go in. She walked down the hall. Came back a few minutes later, and the envelope was gone."

"What did she do with it?"

"There was a trash can in her office, like mine. She would have thrown it there. There's…a shredder down the end of that hall."

Some people came by on the sidewalk and Ray turned away.

"What would she want to shred?"

"Nothing. You know Susan. She would never have been involved in anything that wasn't above board."

"I'm sure she just threw it out."

"I have to go."

He wasn't sure. But he couldn't think about it now. He had to write.

He went back to Jo's.

***

As I approached the door that morning, the last of my sleepiness vanished in a torrent of anticipation. I whipsawed between promise and threat. The promise that great secrets were about to be revealed. And the threat of…what? Nothing concrete, but it was there from my first moments inside The House.

I sat on my cushion and closed my eyes as we did at the beginning of meetings. That voice shattered the silence, though it was barely a whisper. I slitted my eyes. Karl sat up front. In the same room as me. Why did it feel so extraordinary? He hadn't done anything yet. In fact, it was the first time I'd seen him since that meeting back when we were on tour.

We were still allowed to talk then, so maybe people told me things. Or maybe I'd been waiting a lifetime for my Answer Man, and when Karl showed up with all the trappings, I projected all my desire onto him.

Karl said, "Those meetings were preparation for the real practice." Which was what? I didn't care. As he spoke, his voice began to fill me with a delicious warm calm. I was just getting comfortable when he abruptly stood and left. So soon? I felt abandoned.

But everyone was standing and walking out toward the Front Hall. I followed them.

They were milling around something. I worked my way to the front of the crowd. An ordinary corkboard, but tacked to it was a page of elegant paper with Karl's odd calligraphy on it.

A list of names with words next to them: our jobs.

Ray—Drawing Room.

I asked Ethan where it was. He frowned as if it was a stupid question and led me to the room I'd stumbled on the first day. He picked up a sledgehammer and handed it to me, pointing to the collapsing wall. "Tear down this plaster. But do not touch the wainscoting." I looked at the stained paneling. What was the big deal? It was all a wreck.

But I was careful. My arms were shaking with fatigue after a half hour. All I could think about was that inner circle upstairs. Never mind the occasional crash that told me they were up there doing the same thing as me. They must be with Karl, experiencing unimaginable wonders.

It seemed impossible not to let the hammer slip and touch the wood. And then two hours of sleep caught up with me, and it did. I'd only left a tiny bruise near the floor, but I felt horrible. Could I pull one of the rotting chairs in front of it, hide it? No. They'd know. I kept working, berating myself for my mistake.

"Preparation for the real practice." That practice turned out to be fixing up Karl's house. Up until then, trips to his place had seemed like a lark. No more. We came up nearly every weekend. It made for a horrendously long day—over sixteen hours by the time we were home. With the exception of the morning meeting and lunch, it was all backbreaking physical work.

When I was done taking the plaster down from that room, I started removing the old finish from the wainscoting. I innocently asked one of the "elders," as we referred to people in the inner circle, why I couldn't use an electric sander. He explained how Karl called electricity "artificial energy," and using it might compromise our delicate nervous systems. I nodded my head and went back to work, but then it hit me: less than a year ago I'd seen Karl on tour happily screaming through a monster PA system, and it certainly wasn't powered by steam. Shrinks call it cognitive dissonance, and for a bad moment I was sweating. Yet before I could start asking myself about other things that didn't quite make sense— like that butt-ugly house, for starters—my mind just flicked the whole business away like a speck of dust. And I didn't think of it again.

As winter set in and the days grew shorter, we worked in the late afternoon by candlelight. The only warmth came from the big marble fireplaces. No matter how we stoked the fires most of the heat flew up the chimney.

The hardest thing was having no running water. There was an outhouse in back. We hauled cooking and washing water into The Kitchen from a well in five-gallon plastic jugs. Their narrow handles cut into our fingers until they were numb.

It would have been a real problem if I was still playing guitar. But I'd stopped. That is, Karl had stopped me. He said, "Writing, painting, poetry and, yes, music are 'Ego Arts.' Unbecoming for a man."

Unbecoming. It was one of his favorite words and spoken such that it was radioactive with judgment. "Ego Arts" evoked more cognitive dissonance. Karl had been a rock star! He'd left the big stage with its blinding lights and lasers for his humble perch on a cushion, lit only by a few candles. Somehow, while we recalled our previous lives with shame, his life before the group was just a natural part of his miraculous evolution.

How could I give up playing with my band, playing guitar? My guitar was central to my identity, the one thing I excelled at in the world. I suffered its loss viscerally in my hands. They alternately ached and felt numb. I looked at them, and they seemed to belong to a stranger. I wasn't alone. Talented poets laid down their pens and vowed to never write another word. An up-and-coming painter from New York just gave it up.

I justified the loss of my guitar by believing it was a sacrifice for my teacher. It leant me hope that I might have the resolve to go all the way down what he warned us was a path of formidable difficulty.

Later, I'd know that this was just the beginning of Karl tightening the screws. Soon he was telling us what to eat. How to sleep. How to breathe.

Karl quoted the Bible. "Many are called, but few are chosen." It would take me awhile to get just how very few he meant. Though Karl was no more a Christian than a Buddhist or Zoroastrian. He lifted quotes from every faith.

***

One morning, an hour before lunch, Ethan came to me where I was working and announced in his usual snotty tone that Karl would like to see me. He led me to a little hall at the back of The House off The Kitchen and left me before a solid oak door. It was closed. I stood there, paralyzed by the quandary: Was I supposed to knock, or just walk in? Finally, I rapped lightly on the wood, immediately cursing myself for not knocking harder.

A rumbling from inside—a voice? Or the settling of the old house? I opened the door and took a tentative step in.

Three of the walls were paneled in dark lustrous wood. The fourth, opposite where I'd entered and at the back of The House, was bare limestone, the inside of the blue-gray blocks that formed the outer walls. Centered in that wall was a rococo marble fireplace, the mantle suspended on the backs of a pair of groaning slaves who faced the blazing fire. It was the only warm room I'd seen in The House.

The windows to either side of the fireplace were bricked in, the mortar fresh. Karl sat in a leather chair and gestured for me to sit across from him.

He pointed at the mantle with its groaning men. "Previous owner."

Was that a joke? About us being his slaves? But he never joked. Or did he?

He asked, "What do you want?"

It was not a question I was expecting. I racked my brains—what's the right answer? What does he want to hear?

"Don't think. Quick, what do you want?"

"I took drugs one time, LSD, and for a few hours..."

"Cosmic consciousness."

"I guess. It was amazing."

"Stay with me, and you'll experience things a thousand times as wonderful."

I believed him. I would have believed him if he told me that the sun revolved around the earth, or that he could sprout wings and fly. Why? Because of his presence. It was invisible but had undeniable substance. It was as potent as one of those drugs they shoot you up with before an operation, that makes you forget that they're about to cut you open. Forget you're a suffering human.

He folded his hands and bowed in a blessing, indicating that my audience was over. On impulse I moved to approach him—to shake his hand, silly as that would be, or embrace him.

He didn't flinch, but something in his manner made me stop cold.

He said, "No man touches me," and I shrunk from him. I forgot about it moments after floating from that room.

Sometime later I found out its name. Hard to know how I learned it, because by then we weren't allowed to speak about anything that happened in that house.

I'd been to The Backroom.

I was high leaving my first audience with Karl, but still needed something to seal the deal. Proof.

That came a few weeks later. I'd finished preparing the walls of the Drawing Room and was up on a ladder, scraping old paint from the ceiling. I'd been there for hours, neck bent back and aching. Would I ever get it straight again once I climbed down?

Karl appeared. My insides jumped, yet my hand kept working. You didn't do anything, or stop doing anything, without being told.

He gave a little smile and tiny gesture of his hand, telling me I could stop. My face flushed. After that it would always happen when he came around.

This time I had good reason to be embarrassed. I'd just been thinking the same thing I had for weeks: What the fuck did all this drudgery—knocking down walls, sanding, painting—have to do with the spiritual practice we had followed Karl here to do?

He moved in close, got right in my face. He didn't speak, only widened that smile slightly, but that was enough to make my heart leap in expectation—he was about to give me something priceless. How rare an audience this was, for him to concentrate all of his presence on one person rather than the whole group.

When he finally spoke, he answered my question. "I know what you're thinking." And I was certain he'd just read my mind.

He showed me his hands, palms up. "With these, we repair this ruin." He gestured with his arms, indicating The House.

"And as we do so, we repair this." He pointed toward his body, then mine. "You once were a baby and possessed the wisdom of the universe. You were wiser than I am now. From that time, you've been descending."

He turned on a dime and gave me a withering look that made me go cold inside. "You are a ruin, like this house. Like everyone out there." He gestured outside The House. "But we are no ordinary carpenters, woodworkers. They only fix a house. We must learn to work with these." He held out his hands. "And, at the same time, in here." He pointed to his chest. "Doing the exercises."

I cringed with guilt. I'd been working for hours and had forgotten to do them. What were they? I knew Karl's words: "See with your third eye. Feel with your head, think with your heart. Expand your aura to fill the room." I tried so hard, but his instructions were always as inscrutable as Zen koans.

Karl fixed his eyes on mine such that I couldn't have looked away if my life depended on it. His face, the sensation of breath going in and out became the universe. A sweet lightness poured down from the top of my head, washing every cell clean, repairing, transforming me into a new person.

Karl murmured, "You see? You're already better. It isn't so hard."

I was high for the rest of the day. He'd made me high, fixed me, but what really amazed me was that I believed he'd read my mind.

I had my proof. I was convinced of his divinity. And certain that I would follow him wherever he went, do whatever he told me to do.

Susan, with her religion studies, had the term for it: conversion. I see, now, that I was ripe for the picking. In the five years since my peak experience on acid, I'd never come close to anything like it. There was a hole in me that nothing could fill. Sex or good dope might sweep me up in their charms for a moment, but I soon was hungry again.

Karl had promised to make me whole. Then he read my mind, proving he had the power to do it. That's why I waited so long for him to make good on his promise.

12.

Ray looked up from the computer. Lunch had come and gone without him being aware. He'd been far away, upstate and decades in the past, but that wasn't what had him disconcerted. It was something about what he'd just written. He was hungry but went home and phoned Lorraine from the gallery.

She said, "How's the writing?"

"That's why I called." He told her about Karl reading his mind on the ladder, about Karl's promise.

"That sounds like Karl. What's the problem?"

"I wrote what I've long believed. And I think I captured how it was. But even as I got it down, there was this weird doubt in the back of my mind. Like I was arguing with myself. By the time I was done..."

"You didn't quite buy it anymore. Ray. Anybody slaving away for a day on that ladder with no explanation for why would be thinking the same as you: What the hell am I doing up here? Karl didn't read your mind. But he did read you. Which was easy. He saw how badly you wanted to believe in magic. And so, he did a magic trick. Like the con man he was."

Karl, a conman? "But what about my acid trip and his promise?"

"He asked you what you wanted. You told him. He said he'd give it to you. Anyone could do that. You want a pony? I swear I'll deliver, stack of Bibles. But did he?"

Ray clanked up to the kitchen, rummaged in the fridge as he talked. "No. In all my time with Karl, I never experienced a fraction of that original experience of enlightenment on LSD. I've always thought it was my fault, that if I'd just hung in there…"

"You still believe that?"

He sighed. "I don't know anymore."

"That's why you're freaked out. Some part of you hasn't let him go. The part of you that still believes. And that belief is finally crumbling."

All that was in the fridge was a hunk of moldy cheese and stale bread. He cut the mold off. "You mind if I eat while we talk?"

"Not at all, as long as it's not in silence. That would give me a stomachache."

"And wouldn't be much of a conversation." They laughed. "You think Karl was like Tom Sawyer, going to all that trouble just to scam us into fixing up his house?"

"No. He was after bigger game. Power."

"That makes sense. But I still…"

"Everybody wants to believe, Ray."

"This is tough."

"I told you it might be. Hang in there. You're coming closer to the truth. You know what they say. The truth will set you free."

"I suppose."

"When are you getting to the good stuff?"

"What good stuff?"

"You know. Because I want to read it."

"Lorraine."

She laughed. "Sorry, old habits."

He got a pint of ice cream from the freezer. There was nothing wrong with it, aside from the fact that it was frozen too hard. He popped it in the microwave for fifteen seconds. He changed the subject. "Listen, I feel terrible bringing it up, but did you…tell anyone I was writing, or that I was asking about Karl?"

"Ray. This isn't like you, not trusting me. You know how seriously I take my job. I said I'd treat our conversation as privileged, and I did. What aren't you telling me?"

He took the ice cream from the microwave and ate it from the carton with a tablespoon. "I'm sorry to doubt you. But I'm in some kind of mess here. It's frankly a little scary."

"What kind of scary?"

"I'm not getting crazy, if that's what you mean. No, somebody...oh, fuck it. Somebody found out I'm writing about the group. About Karl. And they want me to stop."

"How do you know?"

"They threw a brick through my window, followed by threatening emails."

"Whoa."

"One of *those* bricks, that Bodine and I collected."

"Oh. That can't be good. Have you been to the police?"

"No. They aren't going to help. You knew Karl as well as anyone. And you know people. You think Karl could have thrown that brick?"

Half a pint was enough. He took another giant spoonful and reluctantly put the ice cream back in the freezer.

"No. And yes. Throwing a brick is too mundane for him. Plus, he might get those precious hands dirty. But the symbolism is absolutely him."

"Symbolism?"

"You know, a piece of his house assaulting yours. Returning something you got for him along with a nasty twist of irony. Back in the day, he would have put one of us up to doing it."

"So someone's still with him?"

"I can't see that. But it's been a long time."

And, as Bodine said, people change.

***

At five o'clock, Ray grabbed a Magic Hat beer and headed upstairs. He remembered Lou and emailed him the latest.

Ray's hour of grace was almost up, along with his second beer, when Liz called.

She said, "I wanted to thank you for the check."

"Okay."

"I'm sorry I was a little...harsh asking for it. But I really need the money."

"You don't have to explain. Listen, I'm kind of busy."

"I know what you do at five o'clock. It's why I called now, to get you in a better mood."

"Last time we spoke, you accused me of being drunk. Make up your mind." Ray finished the beer and tossed it in the trashcan.

"Ray, Ray. I don't want to end things on this bad note. I'm sorry about when I saw you."

"Why?"

"It was a mistake. Sleeping with you."

He hung up on her.

Fucking Liz. He stomped downstairs for a third beer. The post-acid jag of virtue that had him kicking the hard stuff stopped him on the stairs. And he made another post-trip resolution: to exorcise the remains of Liz's ghost from his house. She had her money, which meant it was as much his as hers.

He marched over and kicked the bedroom door open. There was no scent of Liz's ghost, let alone their last sex, thank God. Just a little must.

Spring cleaning. He tore off the sheets and put on new ones. Opened a window and let in the breeze along with street sounds. He vacuumed and dusted, then lay on the bed and forced a smile. *This is my bed now.*

He climbed upstairs and played some guitar. He wasn't getting a stack of Marshalls—not if he wanted to keep living in Hudson—but the feeble plink-plink of unamplified guitar wasn't doing it for him. They had headphones, now, with all kinds of awesome guitar sounds. He went online and ordered a pair.

Ray went out and treated himself to takeout sushi. He ate it up on the couch—the kitchen seemed empty at night. He was wishing he'd asked for extra ginger when he remembered the conversation with Joan Telford.

He called Bodine.

"How's the writing going?"

"It's going. Finally."

"So what's up?"

Ray explained about the manila envelope. As he did, Susan's widower's voice came to him: *I have no idea.* He told Bodine.

"You're thinking these two things might be connected."

"What, that the husband knew about the envelope? That he sent it?"

"No. That there was something going on. Her coworker caught one part of the elephant, and the husband another. Neither knew what they had, but they both suspected they had something."

"What?"

"I need to think on it." He hung up.

Ray slumped back on the couch and stared out at the night. He tried to picture Susan opening the envelope, then shredding what? Ray couldn't even imagine the Susan he knew in a cubicle in some office, let alone using a shredder. And her husband saying *I have no idea.* Ray didn't quite remember the conversation. Maybe the guy really just had no idea. Like Ray.

Bodine called. "I have an idea."

Ray laughed. "Good thing someone does."

"Huh?"

"Never mind." He picked up the Telecaster, squeezed the phone between shoulder and ear, and started doing scales.

Bodine asked, "Susan died around Saugerties?"

"Yeah. I thought for a moment she might have come up to see me, then changed her mind. She must have had business in Albany."

"What if she was coming back from…Karl's? It's the same direction."

"So's Montreal. And Buffalo. The fucking North Pole. You said you were sure he isn't there anymore."

"Not in The House. There's no electricity there. But maybe he's living in the area."

"What are you saying? Why would she suddenly go see him after all those years?"

"Who said it was suddenly? How do you know she ever left?"

"Come on, man, she was married. With two kids. Karl's deal was no correspondence course. She was going up all those years, and her husband never knew? He's a lunk, maybe, but jeez."

"So it was suddenly. She decides to join up again. The manila envelope was an invitation. She sees who it's from and gets rid of it, because nobody in her current scene knows about that part of her life."

"That makes sense. What about that thing with the husband, him saying he had no idea?"

"Maybe he suspected something was up. This is all speculation. I need more data points." He hung up.

Susan. Now that Ray was into The House, he could write about her there. He was tired but got the laptop out.

***

When I arrived home from the last Nightcrawlers tour, I told Susan about the meeting with Karl. She immediately wanted to meet him. I asked Ethan, and he put me off. "There will be a time for that." Susan kept pushing, and a few weeks later I asked Ethan again. He pursed his lips. "I suppose you didn't hear me before. There will be a time for that. Don't ask again."

But a few days later, he came to me. "The person you mentioned who is interested? She can come. Once."

The week after she did, Karl came up to me. As usual, he got right to the point. "I like your wife. She has something you will never have."

What? I obsessed about it. It must have to do with her passion. If anyone was ever a True Believer, it was Susan.

After that, she came to every meeting and always sat in the front row of cushions. When Karl let us ask questions, hers was always the first. Teacher's pet. But I was also pleased. I'd looked up to Susan in spiritual matters and felt proud to have brought her to The House. Her true home.

***

It had been a bad idea writing about Susan now. He'd turned over this new leaf, banished Liz's ghost from his house, moved back into the bedroom. *His* bedroom, in his house. He wasn't ready for the rest of the Susan story. He might never be. He closed the laptop and went to bed downstairs for the first time in months.

***

Ray's hands woke him the next morning. They were twitching, ready to write. But as he danced impatiently waiting for the toaster to *bing*, he remembered the conversation with Lorraine. He'd told her about the brick. Its violent arrival had somehow gotten buried by the writing and speculation about Susan.

That stuff was ephemeral.

The brick was real.

And so was the person whose hand had tossed it. They'd walked right up Warren Street. Perhaps they'd been in Jo's. She didn't know Karl, or anything about that scene. She wouldn't recognize him.

Ray looked up and down the street as he crossed—looking for Karl—and had a bad moment as he entered the restaurant, thinking he might really be there, at Ray's table, waiting. *What have you got there, Ray? A computer? What did I tell you about electricity? Just what are you writing?*

Yet the moment he opened the laptop the words poured out.

***

Karl's notion of physical work being the door to the spiritual he soon extended to everything we did. According to him, provided you followed his Way, ordinary actions, from speaking, walking, and eating to going to the bathroom and making love had the potential to become imbued with the miraculous.

He called it the Secret Path; a way hidden right below the surface of ordinary life. It had an elaborate philosophy and cosmology, most of which escapes me. That's because he delegated its explication to his subordinates, none of whom held my attention when they spoke at meetings. One part of the philosophy Karl loved to talk about was the magic of the number three. He had his own odd interpretation of the Holy Trinity. He went on about three stages of man, three this and three that. I'm surprised he didn't mention the three members of the band Cream.

Aside from that, he was clear that intellectual theory wasn't the meat of this Secret Path. That could only be accessed by the keys he gave us—the esoteric exercises. No one had written them down. Even if they had they'd have no power, for, as Karl explained, they were only effective when imparted by oral transmission.

Where had he gotten them? From his teacher, back in England. Who in turn had gotten them from his teacher in a lineage that stretched back through all the great prophets of the major religions: Jesus, the Buddha, Mohammed, all members of this secret society. An idea that should have made Susan the religion scholar skeptical, but she bought it. We all did.

I bought the part about oral transmission, because of his voice. No matter where he was—in The Meeting Hall, Dining Hall, even out back, the wind howling—Karl knew how to modulate his speech so that it was always just at the edge of audibility. I was always craning forward to get the words. Eventually, it gave me a chronic stiff neck. And it wasn't just my neck craning forward toward that soft sound. It was all of my being, wanting to get it, get what he had.

According to Karl, his exercises would not only transform us, but over time transform the space we practiced in—The House. As we practiced in it, it was supposedly becoming saturated with some ineffable substance. Karl said, "If a stranger—say, some local farmer—came in here, he wouldn't know what it was, but he'd feel it, wonder why it felt different." And so, this dilapidated mansion was becoming The House, a temple teeming with power. It didn't look so ugly to me anymore, and it wasn't just because of our renovation. Sometimes I thought I could sense the very stones vibrating with energy.

It was an easy sell for the old acidheads among us. We'd tripped and witnessed some skuzzy apartment turn into a miraculous palace, its filthy windows turned to eyes on the cosmos, a dirty sink a sacred fountain.

Karl spoke the names of the parts of his house with an odd cadence, and we imitated him. The Kitchen became the place where we prepared the holy substances that nurtured life, The Dining Hall where we took in those substances. He commanded us to perform Cooking and Eating as sacred acts in which we availed ourselves of the secrets of a universe in which, as he explained, "Everything eats or is eaten. And which are you?"

Karl christened the whole building The House, with an intonation that implied that every other dwelling on the planet was mean as a mud hut. That only within these walls could life be really lived.

Karl said, "Your body is your temple." While the inner exercises were the meat of our practice, they occurred in a physical body. By the same token, all of our work happened in The House. Essential to sanctifying our bodies and The House was a compulsive attention to detail. This extended to our grooming and dress, and to how we moved and spoke—always controlled and measured, just like Karl.

Like shoes and cushions, place settings at meals were laid out in meticulous order. We lifted forks slowly, just so, and replaced them each time at the exact spot on the table. Chewing was even and rhythmic. As if that didn't make eating uncomfortable enough, every meal was taken in strict silence. Pity the poor fool who dinged a utensil against a glass. A flick of Karl's eyes and they were mortified for hours.

Through the long mornings of drudgery, I'd count the hours, then minutes until lunch. Yet soon as I was there, I lost my appetite. I wasn't alone. Everyone picked at their food, because that's what Karl did. The little I could choke down sat unhappily in my stomach throughout interminable afternoons.

Karl said, "Careless gestures, sloppy work betray chaos in here." He tapped his forehead. "That is unbecoming. But what is worse—" he clutched his chest, "—is a black heart. A heart poisoned by negativity. Stop all negative emotions. Cut them off." He sliced his hand down with such violence that the room collectively gasped. "Like you would the dead limb of a tree. And don't let them grow again."

It seemed like simple advice at the time. But what was a negative emotion? Anger? Sorrow? Certainly boredom. Which was what I mostly felt as I slaved away, yearning for those brief moments with Karl, consumed with envy for that inner circle. Envy was surely negative. So was my overwhelming guilt at being unable to "cut off" these feelings. But then Karl never said it would be easy.

I wonder if Karl's command to stop negative emotions had something to do with the peculiar thing that happened to our faces. We learned to keep them utterly impassive, as if by erasing all expression of feelings we could stop feelings themselves.

Karl never expressly told us to do that with our faces. We just learned by imitating him. What he did say was to relax the muscles of the face, which is, I suppose, the same thing. Except, as so often, it became a conundrum. He frequently ridiculed members for their slack faces. What was it? Relax or not? A reasonable question, but no one would dare ask Karl.

Susan and I and the other members of my band did not get to live in The House. That was reserved for the inner circle, who lived upstairs. Susan and I rented a ramshackle farmhouse a few miles away. We worked menial jobs during the day—I was a gas station attendant. But most nights and all weekend we spent at The House.

***

Jo came to his table. "I was going to ask you if you wanted more coffee, but you don't look like you need it."

It was incredible, but he didn't.

"I think you're having fun."

Fun? Not exactly. But he knew this moment from the long practice of music and art. Projects often began bone-dry. Then came a hint of dampness, followed by this trickle. Which would soon turn into a flood. He felt like a kid at the top of the roller coaster just as it tips to head down. Filled with excitement and terror. As he rode, the story was getting steeper. And darker.

Was he ready for the Bassman part? He could try the beginning. As with Susan and Liz, there'd been a before. A better time for his friend.

***

Bass players were the bane of the Nightcrawlers in our early days. We'd just lost our last one to accounting school when Bassman came to audition. He was still Tommy Coogan then. He trudged into our practice room with his axe slung over his shoulder, mumbled something, and gave me a feeble handshake. He wouldn't look me in the eye. There was no way this guy was going to rock. Bodine rolled his eyes at me. Another waste of time.

But soon as Tommy plugged into an amp, he instantly transformed our sound. He proceeded to lay down a bottom that was as fat and solid as the foundation of Notre Dame Cathedral. After a couple of songs, Frank got up and wrapped his arm around Tommy. "Now we have a band."

We didn't care that Bassman was a little weird as long as he played like that. When he came to live in the band house, he rarely left his room. I'd visit him from time to time. There was no rug, nothing hanging on the walls. Just a single bed and stacks of books. He favored stuff from darker branches of the spiritual tree: Alistair Crowley, Arnold Ehret, and Carlos Castaneda. In the safety of his room, he finally spoke. He didn't do small talk but dove right into the big questions—the meaning of life, death, the universe. He might be weird, but I recognized another searcher.

I made some offhand comment about acid and he gave me a terrified look. Had he done it and freaked out? Or was he afraid to because he might? I wasn't asking.

***

Ray winced. He wasn't ready to relive the next part about Bassman. He closed the computer, stood, and got his coat on, preparing for a walk down Warren Street. It was raining, and he didn't have a case for the laptop. He brought it up to the counter and asked Jo if she'd stash it.

She scowled at it. "Sure, unless I put it out with the trash. At least you aren't using it to snoop on Liz anymore. Are you?"

"No."

Ray walked to the river and turned around. There was enough rain pouring down that he didn't need to see more water. Most people were sensible and inside. On the way back, he reached Bodine's cross street. He could pay him a visit, but Bodine had work to do. His friend suggested Susan might still be with Karl. It made no sense. But Ray had also never known what happened to her after the group, and before Phil the roach man.

His jeans were soaked by the time he approached Jo's. He went home, put on dry pants, and called Lorraine from the gallery.

He said, "Hey, sorry about yesterday, questioning your silence."

"Not a problem. You're doing a tough thing."

"When was the last time you saw Susan?"

"Oh. I was going to suggest you call *her* but didn't want to stir up old trouble."

"I understand." He paused. The wind tossed a handful of rain at the window. "She's dead."

"No! When?"

"Just last year. Car crash. It…burned up."

She groaned. "How are you taking it?"

"It doesn't make me feel great."

"You ever want to talk about that…"

"You'll be the first I call."

She sighed. "Susan came to see me a couple of years after we left the group."

"Oh."

"She'd just left herself."

Relief flooded him.

"She said she was done with all that spiritual stuff. She seemed sad about it, and it made me sad, because it was such a large part of who she was. And she seemed kind of washed out, diminished. A lot of us had some rough years after the group. I'm sure she recovered."

"You don't think she might have gone back?"

"No. She was done."

"Well, thanks."

"Sorry, again."

"We'll talk soon." He hung up.

Susan giving up her quest made him sad too. Like a part of him was missing. Because her quest had been so tied to his. What about his? Whatever happened to Ray of Orange Sunshine?

Susan hadn't ever recovered from the group. Why else had she settled for Phil?

He headed back to Jo's. He snaked the laptop from behind the counter and sat at his table. He stared at the screen. It was important that he get this next part right. He needed to honor the memory of his friend. He still had doubts—that if he'd just done this, said that it would have turned out differently. Which was reasonable. But he was so wrapped up in the past that he had the crazy feeling that if he didn't write it, it hadn't happened.

Finally, his fingers moved, and the words tumbled out.

***

After a couple of years with Karl, I was so numbed by the constant overwork and lack of sleep that I wasn't feeling much of anything. But I was still essentially sane.

But Bassman... What I know now is that, without the grounding of his music, he'd been steadily coming unraveled. Bodine and I had chafed when Karl forbade us to play. But playing his bass was essential to Bassman's existence. It was all he had.

It was a bitter morning in early March. Bassman and I were scraping paint off the columns on the front porch when Karl snuck up.

He gestured wordlessly: come. We followed him into The House and down two flights of steps into the basement. The ceiling was almost twenty feet high. We entered the modest semicircular foyer. Karl led us into a great chamber that stretched the length and breadth of The House, aside from the foyer and its twin room on the opposite side.

Karl said, "You are going to lay the floor of the Meeting Hall." He swept his hand across the expanse of fresh concrete. He led us out back and pointed to the ten thousand bricks Bodine and I had gathered and cleaned.

"Neither of you eats or sleeps until it is done."

My first thought was, impossible. I felt the weight of those tons of bricks in my arms and felt myself sinking right into the earth. But then I got it. This was one of Karl's tests. Which could be an opportunity to prove myself to my teacher. If I passed, it might be my ticket to the upstairs, to the Inner Circle. A flicker of excitement. It only lasted a moment.

What if I failed?

I'd laid a few bricks repairing the front porch. Whatever knowledge I had would have to do.

Bassman and I got to work. As usual, I soon forgot about the inner exercises. Instead I obsessively figured and counted: how many bricks, how long it would take. It was going to be a long day and night and part of another day before we were finished.

I remembered the story of Milarepa, whose teacher, Marpa, had commanded him to move a mountain of stones. When he was finally done and went for his reward, Marpa told him to move them back. I'd always laughed at that part of the story. Not now. When we were done, was Karl going to demand that we tear the floor up and lay it again?

Within a half hour of commencing the ordeal, I was shivering. My fingers stiffened and fumbled with the mortar. Bassman started coughing. With no talking allowed, he gestured like his throat was sore.

There were no fireplaces down there. The basement was far enough below ground that it had assumed the temperature of the earth and was above freezing. But the air was still cold and damp and peculiarly musty. It had me breathing shallowly. But at least I wasn't getting sick, like Bassman.

The light from the only window—a casement high in the foyer—did nothing to penetrate the great room. So, we worked by candlelight. After half a day without rest, I entered a state of punch-drunk exhaustion. The candles were a constant danger. One drop of wax on that virgin floor and Karl would be sure to find it. He'd nail me with that dead eye: You ruined it. It was just like Karl to consider a simple floor to be the Foundation of the Group or some such.

Once the mortar started setting you couldn't just tear out a single brick. You'd have to re-lay a whole section of floor.

Bassman's cough degenerated into an ominous liquid bark, and the bouts became longer. He'd sit on the cold concrete, rocking, holding his chest. I wanted desperately to help him. All I could think was to crouch down and put an arm around him, but he feebly shoved me away.

We finally finished, with about a hundred bricks left. My fingers were frozen, belly cramped from hunger, lips cracked and bleeding from thirst. We'd had a single bottle of water and drained it hours ago. I'd been leaning over so long I doubted I'd ever stand straight again.

But we'd done it! I smiled to myself, thinking of that prize. I was headed for the stairs when Karl arrived. How could he know we'd finished? He didn't look at either of us, just gave the floor a cursory glance.

"You can eat now." He left. There'd been no invitation to the inner circle. No nothing. I felt like he'd slapped me in the face with a two-by-four. The next moment, I was seized with a terrible hunger. Bassman had suppressed his cough while Karl was there. Now, he was bent over in an epic fit. But I couldn't wait to eat. I caught his eye and nodded upstairs—I'll see you in the Dining Hall.

He gave me a look that didn't register until later. My body had suffered in that basement, and I was sorely disappointed. But I was still me. Over that day and night and day, Bassman had lost part of himself, and I'd seen it in his face. He *was missing the glue that held his fragile parts together.*

I returned to The House a few days later, still feeling like I'd had the crap beat out of me, filled with resentment. My friend Crystal came up, smiling, carrying a sitting cushion she'd lovingly embroidered with silk thread. "Karl says you can place it up front for him." She looked at me like this was some rare honor.

I carried it downstairs. My hands curled into fists—our beautiful brick floor was practically invisible under an impeccable row of cushions. And the reward for the ordeal of laying it was holding Karl's cushion for a minute.

***

At the end of the day, Ray was up on the couch, feeling that special buzz that only comes from a couple of beers on top of a righteous day's work, when Lou called. Ray frowned. Why did he have to ring now, disturb this time?

Lou said, "You're my last call of the day." Agent's hours, ten to six. "I've been going over the new stuff you sent me. It's coming along. Some nice atmospheric touches—creepy house. But I'm hoping that's what we in the business call foreshadowing."

"Foreshadowing what?"

"Something juicy. Because what you've got so far is a little…quiet."

"Quiet?"

"We're looking for *eyeballs* here. To get eyeballs, we need *dirt*. Sex. Drugs. Come on, this happened in the seventies, right? Would it be too much to hope for a murder or two?"

Eyeballs. "Murder?"

"Just joking. But you have some good stuff, right?"

"Uh, well, that depends on what you call 'good.'"

"Don't weasel on me. You'd better have something good. Because this is not going to fly without it. I don't know how carefully you looked at that contract, but if they don't like the goods, they can demand their money back. And you would not want to tangle with their lawyers."

Ray gave an enormous sigh. "Okay. I've got dirt."

Lou hung up and Ray shuddered.

He had dirt, all right.

13.

Ray woke early the next morning in a foul mood. It was pouring down icy rain. He scurried across the street, the laptop buried under his coat like an infant. He was stepping onto the curb in front of Jo's when a car raced through a puddle and soaked a pant leg. At least the computer was safe.

Jo brought him coffee and a flaky sweet thing. "This is on the house. You look like you could use a little sweetening. What are you pissed about?"

"I'm not." His jaw was set, his hands balled on the table.

"It's raw business when your honey's banging somebody else. Some asshole."

He winced. "Yeah." But that wasn't it. It was the next part of the story.

***

The evening of the first gathering in the new Meeting Hall marked the emergence of a new phase of The Way and a new Karl. He no longer delivered abstract pontifications in a honeyed baritone. He got personal, addressing questions to each of us in turn.

"Bodine, what did you eat this morning?"

"Two eggs and toast with—"

Karl interrupted. "Harold, recite the three rules."

"Uh, let's see. Never Speak. Never—"

He interrupted again. "Ray, what color are Lorraine's eyes?"

I flinched. I had no idea. I glanced over at her, but she was blocked by the person next to me. Which was cheating anyway. "Uh, I…"

"Lorraine, why is Ray blushing?"

I was blushing because Karl had caught me being unaware. Awareness was what we were supposedly after: being there, in the present moment. And if you didn't know the color of Lorraine's damned eyes, it meant you weren't there. Which meant you were no better than all those hopeless people out in the world, what Karl called slugs. Blind, mewling, crawling, stinking slugs.

***

Did anyone ever dare ask Karl what the first thing he ate that morning was? Did he really remember? You'd no more dare that than you would stick your head in the mouth of a dragon.

Ray's face was hot, and he was practically panting.

***

There was no hiding, even sitting at the back of the hall as I did. Karl might, at any moment, turn to me and bore his steely eyes into mine. Though everyone's gaze was riveted up front, I felt seen by all of them, exposed.

It had been cold in that basement laying the bricks. But at least we were moving. Sitting there now with no heat, it wasn't five minutes before the chill started seeping up into my legs through the cushion, then into my belly. I tried to fight it off because I knew when it reached my chest I'd start shivering. Finally, I found the solution: a thick wool cap.

I was sitting still with everyone else, waiting for Karl. He glided in, surveying the room, and made a beeline for me. He plucked my hat off and flung it in a corner with a sneer. I guess I hadn't seen the rule: NO HATS. Was his fashion sense offended?

He leaned down into my face. "That isn't going to keep you warm." Then he addressed the group. "If you were properly here, in this room, properly aware, you'd be filled with energy. So full that you'd be hot to the touch." He laid a hand to my cheek. I flinched. "He's ice." He pretended to shiver, mocking me, and murmured, "Poor Ray." He raised his voice, just a half a decibel, but I practically jumped at the excoriating tone: "Be a man!"

Eventually, Karl would let up on us and go off into his philosophy. Soon as

133

that happened, I had to struggle to keep my eyes open. When I wasn't overcome by torpor, I was consumed by resentment. It had been months since I'd laid this floor, and I hadn't once had a private audience with Karl. He often skipped meetings, leaving that asshole Ethan in charge. I was relieved, because then I could doze. My eyelids would drift down, and I'd jerk awake. I somehow never actually crashed into the people sitting around me. I was on the constant verge of sleep because my body, all of me, was reaching the point of total exhaustion.

The obvious question is, why did I stay? Why suffer and live in constant fear? Because Karl had instilled a greater fear: the fear of being cast from the circle, into the Outer Darkness.

"This Way is the only way. There is no life outside of here. You see the world out there, people in their cars, on the street, bearing their burdens, bearing children. They might as well be dead. Without me, without this—" he gestured around at The House, "—you, too, would be walking corpses. It would be better that you slit your own throat than continue shambling about through days empty of meaning."

He stared at each of us, into each of us in turn, transmitting what he never had to say: Don't think of leaving.

I wasn't about to leave. What was terrifying was the prospect of being "sent away."

Because that's what was happening to people. What were their crimes? Or was Karl just making examples of them?

Let me be clear: Though there were specific days when we were not to speak at all, with the exception of meals, we never took a complete vow of silence. Aside from occasional days of silence, it was acceptable to communicate about practical matters. "Go to the store and buy twelve gallons of milk." "Take those trees out, roots and all." What Karl meant when he commanded, "Never speak about what we do" was that we shouldn't indulge in frivolous speech. Which meant no talking about Karl or the exercises, and nothing remotely approaching gossip. And no revealing our involvement in the group to the outside world: not to mothers, fathers, siblings, or friends.

That didn't stop people from whispering, "What happened to Joe?" or from the anguished reply, "He was sent away," spoken as if poor Joe had been deported to dark Siberia.

My fear of being exiled seems crazy, unless you consider what Susan told me she'd learned in an Anthropology class about the ancestral origins of the terror of being cast out of a group. There was once safety in that circle around the campfire. Safety in numbers and in the fire that kept cave bears and sabertooths at bay. To be sent away into the darkness meant more than the hurt of being an outcast. It meant being literally eaten alive.

Now I can't believe our arrogance in swallowing the idea that out of billions of people, the fifty of us had been chosen to be in this group. The only group that had a prayer of attaining anything of value in this life.

But I did. Because I still felt Karl was working magic on me. I extrapolated from that the belief that this, our circle of disciples, was enchanted. The only thing that could get me to leave was if that circle was broken. I couldn't conceive of anything breaking it.

Taking a page out of Luke, Karl told us that we couldn't follow him unless we put him before our wives and children, even before our own lives.

The wife part was increasingly easy with Susan: Our marriage was crumbling. What else had I had? My music. And as long as the circle remained unbroken, I continued to sacrifice it.

The pitiful thing is that even once we knew we were in the select fifty on the planet, Karl said, "This way is very hard. Only one, maybe two of you will make it."

Karl's questions got very personal. Now, when he spoke someone's name they were to stand.

"When did you last masturbate? Tell us about it."

"Crystal. You're having your period now. I can smell it on your breath. Tell the men what it feels like." I don't remember what she said in response. I was so horrified that I shut down, went away someplace.

It was the seventies. I'd heard of EST and Synanon, with their harsh methods for breaking down the ego, for overcoming hang-ups. In Eastern traditions it was called "crazy wisdom," unconventional, bizarre, even violent acts by a teacher whose purpose was to awaken you to a higher state, to your true self. I figured that's what Karl was doing.

Except those harsh methods never brought me to the light. They only resulted in humiliation and a visceral sense of awfulness.

Leaving the group was out of the question: I wasn't going into the Outer Darkness. But staying was approaching impossible. I felt myself in a vise, and Karl was squeezing, squeezing...

***

A squawk and Ray looked up. Three women sat at the next table, yakking it up, and one had laughed. He hadn't even noticed their arrival.

Jo stopped by. "Heavy lifting today, huh? Glad *I'm* not writing."

That last bit had been rough. Yet his instinct had been correct: The little trickle had become a flood. Before, he'd had trouble starting. Now, he couldn't stop. It was like the old Teletype machine in Bodine's museum had hooked itself up to his fingers. A dispatch would arrive, and he'd start furiously typing away, then, as abruptly, stop cold. The pressure would build, then with no warning, another posting would blast through him. It was as if the automatic writing was happening in bright daylight, without the benefit of absinthe. Just coffee.

As he worked his way deeper into The House, revealing more secrets, his apprehension grew.

Only one thing conferred instant immunity from that fear: the writing. It was like an addiction loop. The writing created a hangover of terror for which the cure was more writing—which fostered worse terror.

He needed to nail this next piece before he chickened out.

***

Karl was more and more absent. Weeks would pass without him appearing. We would meet and just meditate, Karl's cushion before us empty. Hugh was Karl's drummer, and up in the hierarchy right below Ethan. He sat up in the front row near Karl. One night, his cushion, too, was empty.

The atmosphere in the group had become foul and heavy, so oppressive that my discipline about not talking slipped. I caught Winker out at the back of the property alone and whispered, "Where's Hugh?"

He averted his eyes. "Away."

"Not sent away?"

"No, just away."

Was "away" more code, like so many seemingly ordinary words that came from Karl's tongue? I told myself Hugh was probably just in Albany, doing some business for Karl. Except that when he returned a few days later, he looked different.

Then Ethan disappeared. This time it was obvious—when he returned from wherever he'd been, he was no longer his prickly self. His pace was languid, and his eyes had a vacant look. I purposely asked a dumb question, and he just answered, didn't snap at me.

One day in late November, I was raking the last of fall leaves from the garden when Ethan came up without a word and crooked his finger, come! At least he seemed back to his asshole self. He led me to The Backroom and unlocked it. I'd been there for private audiences with Karl. It had never been locked.

Ethan pointed in. I entered, and he closed the door. The fine leather chairs, in fact all the furniture was gone. A single candle sat flickering on the floor. I could feel the cold oozing from the stone wall. I instinctively moved closer to the fireplace, though there was no fire in the hearth. I waited, resisting the impulse to clutch myself for warmth. It wouldn't do to have Karl catch me doing that.

The door eased open, and Karl silently crept in. He sat cross-legged on the floor, gesturing for me to join him. He carried two cups of tea and offered one to me. "It's cold in here. Drink."

Steam was pouring off his mug, but mine was lukewarm. How odd. How unlike Karl. He was the model for our compulsive neatness, attention to the tiniest detail. Though he dressed simply, his jeans fit him like they were tailored. He never spoke a word that wasn't perfectly considered.

I sipped the tea, pretending it was hot, stealing glances up at that impassive face. When I'd drained it, he stood and without a word left, closing the door. At the snick of a key in the lock I shuddered, wincing to suppress any sign of fear from my face, though no one was there to see.

The candle had a few inches remaining, but it was going fast. If Karl was clear about anything, it was that the way into the spirit was through the senses. So, he commanded: listen, look, smell. I tried to attend to the sensations of that moment: the dull ache of cold seeping into my legs from the floor, the guttering candle casting jittery shadows on the wall, puffs of icy air from the flue. What was the point of having a fireplace with no fire on a bitter day like today? I tamped the angry thought down.

As the flame sputtered, then snuffed out, and the room pitched into blackness, I felt a new sensation. Or rather, an old one. My last coherent thought was that I'd been wrong. Karl had been quite precise with the tea. He'd known that LSD destabilizes in hot water.

Moments later, I knew I was in the clutches of a bigger dose than I'd ever taken. There was some ugly tinge to the experience that told me it had been mixed with something else—I kept thinking strychnine.

I couldn't see my hand before my face, but the room wasn't black for long. Soon it was drowning in colors. Terrible colors.

Strains of nasal Tibetan chanting seeped into the room, and I was a hermit in a cave in the Himalayas, my beard down to my knees, shivering in the icy blasts from a glacier above. Now, it was monotonal Gregorian chants, and I cowered in my cell in a Cistercian Monastery in the south of France, the mistral howling through chinks in the stones. Where was this music coming from? From the chimney of course, like that imaginary wind.

***

Ray stopped. He couldn't go any further into this memory. He'd never believed horror stories of acid flashbacks, but that trip had been so intense, so insane, that to write it, even to remember it, would be to risk going back. And maybe never returning. He cut to the end.

***

Eons later, a sound shattered the silence. My head jerked toward it, and a spear of light pierced the darkness. What? Only the door creeping open. I knew I'd been there a long time because my thirst had reached an existential urgency. My mouth was dry, rough, and furred like the lath in the plaster walls. I was certain that if I parted my lips my tongue would clatter to the floor.

I must have been starting to come down, though with such an immense distance to go it was hard to say. To eyes accustomed to pitch black, the light was blinding. A massive figure approached, carrying a candle, a blanket, a warm smile. That expression was so rare on his face that I wasn't sure it was him. Though who else could it be?

My first impulse was to grab that drink and down it. My second was to embrace him. Then I remembered him saying, "No man touches me." So, I just sat there.

He set the candle on the floor. I realized I'd been shivering for hours, and tried to hide it, but it was beyond my control. He draped the blanket over my shoulders, dropped to cross-legged before me, and handed me the water.

"Careful, sip."

The cool wetness touched my tongue, and I felt immense gratitude. As he spoke, I ignored his words, just let that voice wash over me, soothing, healing.

A moment later, something very different rose up in me. A great reservoir of those "negative emotions" had been steadily filling in the years since coming to The House. Not a drop of it had ever been released. It had just been topped off by a waking nightmare.

As if on their own accord, my cracked lips parted, and the feeling spilled out. "But why? Why this?" I immediately wished I could take the words back. I'd instinctively looked away from him as I spoke, but now I felt something and glanced at his face.

I shrunk back, almost falling over. His mouth was filled with sharp teeth, and his eyes were dark pits with hungry fires at the bottom. I remembered his silent, silken step. Behind his elegant mask, Karl Maxwell was a craven predator, pitiless and remorseless. Deadly. A big, black cat.

All this time he'd been wearing a mask. It had slipped for an instant and I'd seen the true face behind it. Even as I thought those thoughts, he dropped the mask on again, smiling. And he was talking again, droning on.

I witnessed myself split into two. One part continued to lap up his voice. I could feel it reaching into my head, rearranging my thoughts, telling me he was good and kind. That this man was goodness and kindness itself. I ignored the fact that he was responsible for my being in that black nightmare room—he'd saved me! I owed him my life.

The second part stood aside from those thoughts, as though a stranger thought them. This part had seen that ravenous feline. And it would never forget.

***

It was a couple of days before I was fully free of the effects of the drug. The part of me that had seen the real Karl retreated into the shadows. I resumed my outer posture of worshipping Karl. And the inner posture, too, except that now I looked at him with a new wariness.

I felt like I wasn't alone. As we disappeared one by one into The Backroom, returning with that vacant look, the group as a whole seemed to grow paler. It was like The Backroom was sucking the life from us. But maybe I was just projecting.

***

Ray came back to the present. His face was hot, his lips pressed tight. Before he could change his mind, he emailed Lou what he'd written. He headed home. The rain had stopped. Ragged clouds flew above, chased by a bitter wind that smelled of snow.

He sprawled in his chair in the gallery and called Lorraine. "Are you busy?"

"Just got out of a session. You sound upset."

"Yeah, well, you remember the Backroom?"

"Oh."

Her voice had gotten small, and he suspected he already had the answer to his next question. "Did he ever take you in there and…"

"Slip a mega-dose of acid on me? That motherfucker. Some things are unforgivable. I still kind of have flashbacks when I'm stressed or get really tired."

"And you're one of the sanest people I know."

"Thank you."

"I just wrote about my experience." He'd been exhausted a moment ago, but telling her about it had him pacing the gallery. He told her about hallucinating Karl as a big cat.

"No wonder you're upset. I hallucinated other stuff. Except, in a sense, that wasn't a hallucination. You saw the real Karl."

"I just figured out that he sent me on that nightmare trip so he could show up the next day and I'd see him as my savior. And, aside from that lapse, it worked."

"He did the same thing to me. It's a classic torture technique. Pull someone's fingernails out and they're wanting Mommy so badly that they fall into the arms of the very monster who did it to them."

Ray shuddered. "What I don't get is, why did he bother to do it? We were already willing to go to the ends of the earth for him."

"Good question."

Ray was headed in the direction of the front door when the letter slot squeaked, and a Chinese menu flopped onto the floor. He scowled. It was the third one this week. "Hold on a sec." He ran out into the street to catch the guy, but he was gone. Fast sucker. He came back inside. "Sorry."

"Here's my take. Near the end, we still considered him all-powerful. But he didn't see himself that way. In order to be our proper guru, he buried his own insecurities deep. But they inevitably started coming out."

He was shaking his head. "What insecurities?"

"Ray. I saw behind his mask too. Not what you saw, not a wild animal. It was different for us women."

He wanted to know where she was going with this, but her voice was tightening up. He didn't push. She said, "So his methods got more extreme as he tried to hold onto us, even though there was no need to do it."

"Like that encounter group stuff."

"Oh, God, I'd forgotten that. 'Describe your last orgasm.' Karl had one real talent, aside from music of course. He had a brilliant eye for other people's flaws. He saw them and exploited them. He could smell fear, like an animal. And he instinctively knew everyone's worst one."

Worst fear. He'd called Lorraine hoping to discharge the crummy feeling writing about The Backroom had evoked. But the conversation was getting him more worked up. He stomped upstairs to make coffee. No. That would just wind him up further. He leaned against the kitchen counter and closed his eyes. "I don't know about worst fear, but here's one: the fear that I don't belong. That I'm on the outside, looking in on the human race."

"Now that you say it, I can see it. And I'm sure Karl could too."

"But how would he…" The memory came, and his face got just as hot as it had then. "Near the end, after I'd been faithfully with him for years, he said, 'You're still a stranger.' He pointed to someone who'd come a few years after me, a 'younger person.' He said, 'She's no stranger.' And I felt so small."

"Bingo."

"How about you?"

"Oh, I know my worst fear. That I'm just a piece of shit."

"And how did Karl use that?"

A pause. She didn't sound like her confident self. "That I can't tell you. I'm sorry. I'm never telling anyone. I have to go."

14.

Ray ate lunch. It was early afternoon, but he was done writing for the day. He bundled up and went out for a long walk. The wind sliced through his coat. It started to snow.

Back home, he sat up on the couch. The guitar headphones had come. He tried them out. They were better than nothing, but no stack of Marshalls. Not even a Fender Pro Reverb. The truth was, he wasn't in the mood for music.

He surfed the internet but wasn't in the mood for that, either. He set the laptop on the floor, watched it snow. He wasn't interested in seeing every flake today. They all looked quite the same. And gravity was pulling him into a slouch, then horizontal.

He thought of Lou and his eyeballs and smiled, gazing over to the cylindrical jar in the corner. It was almost half-full of a marble collection he had started when he was a kid. Alleys and aggies and cat's eyes spanning the colors of the rainbow, made of clay and glass and marble itself.

They'd been slated as the raw materials for his next art project when his muse took a hike. Aside from the marbles, all he had had was a bad idea: painting them with eyes and putting them back in the jar and titling it with some silly pun. *Here's lookin' at you. The eyes have it. Lost your marbles, have you?*

He cringed. Maybe that's why his muse split—she was sick of his cornball humor. He'd been meaning to give the jar to Bodine. The marbles could go in the museum category Outmoded Playthings. It would fit right in with that hoop and stick and the old playing cards.

His eyes drifted closed, and he dreamed.

He's naked at the bottom of an enormous glass cylinder. Marbles the size of basketballs rain down on him. He runs, dodging the marbles, slipping on the glass. They should crash as they hit the floor, but instead make an odd clattering sound.

He somehow avoids being hit but can't escape the merciless gaze of these marbles. Each has an eye painted on it, glaring at him. Looking inside him, seeing his darkest secrets. His envy of Susan and love of Karl. His guilt for Bassman and obsession with Liz.

He stops running. It's hopeless. There's no hiding. Something huge is out there, looking in through the torrent of marbles. Ray stares out, but it's pitch black.

He looks down to the great round floor. It's pulsing, bulging in the middle. A pinprick appears, widening into a black circle. He's standing on the Eye of God—and it can see right through him.

He woke. Hail spit against the round window. He gazed up at it and flinched. The Eye of God, my ass. Lou and his fucking eyeballs.

The computer pinged. Maybe that was Lou now. If so, he was a fast reader.

Ray sat up, picked up the computer. He'd slept over two hours. It was almost four. This writing was tiring work.

The latest email wasn't from Lou.

Subject: "Black cat crossing yr path." He saw no attachment, so he opened it.

A blurry picture of a black cat filled the screen, so black that it looked for a disturbing instant like a hole burned in the screen. The animal lay draped over a computer keyboard, asleep.

Just this morning he'd written about Karl as a great cat. His face got hot. His legs twitched.

The picture was captioned: IZ in yr computer, stealin yr writing.

What was with the weird spelling? He called Bodine. "I just got this email. It refers to something I wrote just four hours ago. Someone is still getting in my computer."

"Forward me the email."

A few seconds later Bodine roared with laughter. He said, "Christ on a croissant. They've sicced LOLcats on you."

"Huh?"

"Laughing Out Loud cats. It's an old internet time waster: silly cat pictures with captions of what they're supposedly thinking. Google cheeseburger and cats."

Ray did, coming up with a website: I Can Has Cheezburger. He scrolled down. "I've got it."

"Those kitties can't spell for shit. Their grammar sucks too."

"Well, I'm not laughing out loud now."

"Sorry. You're right. This is some bad shit."

The laptop pinged. Ray said, "Hold on. Another one just came."

"Send it over. Better yet, I'm coming over there. You didn't get another brick through your window, did you?"

"I don't think so. I was sleeping. What the hell? I was taking a nap when the brick came too."

"A nasty coincidence. But I'll be right there in case they're up to something else."

Ray met Bodine at the front door. They went up and sat at the kitchen table with the laptop.

The subject of the second email was: "Nine minus nine equals…"

Bodine punched it open, to a photo of the same cat lying on the keyboard. But now, there was a gash in its side, and it had bled profusely over the keys. The photo was captioned: OOPSEEZ, curiosity kilt me! Careful it don't get U 2.

Bodine said, "Whoever did this is going to need a new keyboard."

The computer pinged again. Ray said, "One more." He looked at Bodine.

"Karl and his threes."

"You got that too."

This one contained a video, which began playing by itself.

It showed the same cat, apparently resurrected. It played on the floor of a room that was strewn with cat toys—a catnip mouse, a ball of string. But the toy the cat was batting around was a doll's head with black hair.

"This video…" A little knot appeared on Bodine's forehead, a sign of serious concern.

"What?" Ray looked at Bodine, but his friend was looking away. What was going on?

Bodine played the video again. His forehead relaxed, and he looked at Ray. "Never mind. I thought, It's just a cell phone video." He stopped it on the section with the doll head and laughed. "Your hair is still black, more or less."

The joke was forced at best. "I think that's supposed to be me. Bodine, what…"

But his friend was scrolling down and what Ray saw made him forget the strange moment.

The video was captioned:

Don't Forget! I haz 9 LIVES!

PS.

Gotta Pussy sleepin in yr Vulva.

Ray asked, "What the hell? That last line there is an anatomical impossibility, but what do I know?"

"This guy—and it has to be a guy—can't spell any better than those cats. I think he's talking about your car, your Volvo. But hold on."

Bodine Googled around, then brought up a website, Uncyclopedia, and typed *vulva* in the search box.

A satirical article conflated the Swedish car with the female body part. "While it's more common for women to own one, most men would give their right arm to get their hands on a vulva." It went on in that vein.

Bodine laughed. Ray said, "Bodine! You're not fifteen anymore."

"Sorry. I guess part of me will always be. You have to admit this is pretty funny."

"I don't have to admit any such thing." But now, Ray let out a chuckle. He scrolled up to the video of a cat batting around his head and sobered right up. "You and I might be cracked up by that, but can you see Karl coming up with it?"

"Impossible."

Ray said, "This is the work of a teenager or a geek."

"How about both?"

"What would Karl be doing hanging with some teenager? Or geek?"

"I can't see it. He was definitely not into kids."

"Or technology. He has someone young working for him."

Bodine said, "Maybe he has a whole new crop of followers."

Ray flashed on a horrifying image of Gen-Xers, Gen-Yers, pierced, tattooed, shaved bald, or with that spiked hair, sitting in that basement, texting... No, Karl would never allow texting.

Bodine said, "What?"

"Some things are too horrible for words."

"Speaking of horrible, I just had a thought. We need to take a look in that Volvo of yours."

"You think he threw a brick through the windshield?"

But Bodine was already clanking down the metal stairs. Ray followed him down and out the back door to the alley where he parked his car. He was relieved that the windshield was intact. "It's fine."

Bodine stepped closer and pointed inside to the dashboard.

Ray looked. "Fuck. That's a black cat."

"A dead one, I'm afraid."

Ray tried the door. It opened.

Bodine said, "You lock your car?"

"Always. How'd they get in?"

"Oh, easy with a Slim Jim—you know, those strips of metal cops use when you lock your keys in the car."

"Crooks have them too."

They studied the cat.

Bodine said, "That looks like the one in the emails."

"Yep." It had the same gash in its side, only now there was a knife sticking from it. And a length of barbed wire was wrapped around the head.

Ray said, "This is a parody of my piece, 'I'm Cross.' The crucified rat with the scalpel in its side." He was whispering. "You remember it?"

"Vaguely. That's really creepy." Bodine lowered his voice too. It was unlike him.

"And weird. Because my piece is a parody of a reliquary."

"A parody of a parody. Sounds kind of, what do you call it?"

"Postmodern."

"So, now we have a postmodern teenaged geek with a Slim Jim?"

"Add clairvoyant. I sold that piece last year. How the hell would they know about it?"

"Is it on your website?"

"Oh. Maybe." Bodine had designed it for Ray, but Ray never thought about it. It was just something needed for the business. He shuddered and felt exposed, and flashed on the dream, the great eyeball. "My stuff has been sitting out there where any nut could find it."

"Not any old nut. Mystery man. The un-Karl."

"You said people change."

Bodine shook his head and reluctantly fingered the cat. "It's getting stiff. There's a note under it."

It read: Ma kitteh died fr yr sins. Yr car's a kitteh reliquary.

The snow had stopped. It was cold in the car. Bodine said, "Let's go back upstairs."

They sat in the kitchen with the laptop. Bodine navigated to Ray's website and found the cross piece and a section explaining the reliquaries. "I'm going to dig down a little further with these emails. I couldn't get much from those last ones. But those photos…"

Bodine clicked to the first picture and pointed. "That's a Mac laptop."

"Like this one. Which narrows it down to what—only a couple of hundred million people?"

"Certain kinds of people have Mac laptops."

"Me, now."

Bodine opened the email with the video. He hit play. "That's a big room."

"They all were in The House."

"Pause it."

Bodine froze the frame.

"Go back a few seconds. What's that red thing in the corner of the frame?"

"The edge of something. A bed, chair? Probably shot with the same phone as the stills." Bodine clicked back to the picture from the first email. "See this reflection in the monitor?"

Ray saw part of a window. It was tall with a lot of panes.

Bodine said, "Hold on...there's another, fainter reflection here. Another window, at another angle. This is a corner room."

"You remember what kind of windows there were at The House?"

Bodine shook his head. "I remember French doors downstairs. Don't remember windows. And, the way that house is set in the cliffs around it, I don't think any sun got to the first floor."

"What about upstairs?"

"There might have been sun. I wasn't up there...much."

"Me neither." Ray looked at his friend. "What aren't you telling me?"

Bodine looked away and sighed. "Maybe you're not the only one getting a little spooked by the past here. By Karl's scene."

Did something happen to Bodine upstairs? But this was a rare admission from Bodine, and Ray didn't push it.

"I should be able to get the time from this screen shot." He selected the top right corner and enlarged it. The corner of the shot was stamped *Tues 11:17 AM*. "So wherever it was taken has eastern exposure."

"It was taken this morning."

"Or last week."

"No. I wrote about a black cat this morning."

"It's a little after four now. So, whoever did this is within a four-hour drive of here. Unless they flew."

"With a dead cat? The House is less than two hours from here."

"That doesn't mean..."

"I know. But it's certainly possible."

Bodine studied the picture from the second email. "This one's from a slightly different angle. There's only one window reflection. What's this?"

"Fuck, that's a face."

"With a camera blocking it." Bodine enlarged it, enhanced it, but couldn't get it any clearer. Just fingers, the camera, and part of an ear.

"Sorry, this is above my paygrade. You need a Photoshop jock to get better than this. I installed that security package. So, we can assume they didn't get your writing off your computer. Who's seen it?"

"Just Lou. I emailed that section with the cat this morning."

Bodine groaned. "That's it. They hacked into either his email or yours. Probably yours. What do you use?"

"Gmail."

"What's your username and password?"

"Ray247. Password is our band plus a number. Nightcrawlers01."

Bodine snorted. "They just had to keep trying Rays. *You* could figure out the password. They haven't been sucking files off your hard drive. They just guessed your password and hacked your email. I'm sorry. I had this picture of publishing as an old-school business, with you snail mailing what you wrote to your agent, who sent a reply back Pony Express." Bodine typed. "I'm getting you a new password."

"Should I change my email address?"

"Not unless you want to change it on your website and inform everyone you know. Let me take care of that dead cat for you—you have enough trouble right now."

"Thanks. What about the police?" He could throw the dope in the rafters away. He hadn't smoked it in months. Or he could give it to Bodine to keep.

"I think you'd be wasting your time. They're not good with stalking. They like to wait until there's a serious crime."

"Like when I'm dead? No thanks."

Bodine looked seriously at Ray. "Do me one thing. Promise me you'll stop writing. Whoever this is, they mean business."

"Promise."

***

At five, Ray drank and peered out at the evening street, but it was no good. He was no longer gazing on strangers, imagining their lives. Instead he was looking for Karl—or whoever it was. Bodine had said it was his email that was hacked, but Ray wasn't sure. What did Bodine know about stalkers? Maybe they hacked his email *and* had a white van. What had Bodine said, a range of seventy-five feet? It could be in the alley right now, behind his car. But he wasn't going to look. What would he do if it was there?

The laptop sat idle next to him. The window from which he'd spied on Susan, starting this whole thing. Now, someone was watching him.

***

Ray sat in the gallery the next morning. He gazed outside. A kid slouched down the street, head down, with messy hair. Ray leapt up from his chair. Tom! Tom was a kid who'd joined Karl right near the end. He'd sucked up to Karl even worse than the rest of them.

As if somehow aware of Ray's intense gaze, the kid turned for a second.

It wasn't Tom. It didn't look anything like him. And Tom had to be at least forty by now. This kid was about seventeen.

Ray went to Bodine's. After yesterday's snow, it was mild, in the mid-fifties. The sun crinkled his eyes, and a gentle breeze off the river kissed his cheeks.

Bodine was out back with Mingus. "This is the first time I haven't had to force myself to take him out in months." The dog sniffed furiously at a soot-encrusted snowbank, then started frantically clawing.

Ray said, "What's he after?"

"Some rotting hunk of shit. Or maybe he knows I had that dead cat. Though I made sure he didn't see it."

"What'd you do with it? Never mind. I don't want to know."

"You look freaked out. That *was* ugly yesterday."

Ray told him about seeing the kid on the street.

"You're getting paranoid."

"Duh."

"I can't say I blame you."

Mingus got what he was digging for and lay down and started gnawing at it. Bodine leaned down and said, "What do you have there?" Mingus growled at him. Bodine stood and looked away, studiously ignoring him.

Ray laughed, then got serious. "How'd they get onto me in the first place, figure out I was writing?"

"Who knows you're doing it?"

"Lou. That editor. And Lorraine."

"You told her you were writing."

"Yes."

"If gossip had calories, she'd be the size of the moon."

"I don't think she told. She's a shrink now and swore on her shrink bible she wouldn't."

"You believe her?"

"I do."

"What about Lou and that editor?"

Ray sighed. "I haven't given Lou any reason to keep it secret."

"And it's his job to do exactly the opposite if he wants to sell books. So, he blabbed at a cocktail party."

"Or the editor did. He wants to sell books too."

"But who'd they blab to?" Mingus had given up on his new toy—it looked like an old shoe—and started rolling in something.

Bodine said, "Mingus!" He turned to Ray. "We need to get him inside before he does some real damage."

As they headed through the theater to the office, Ray noticed a pile of new items against the wall. He picked up a prosthetic leg. "Cute."

"I've made a new category: Lost Limbs and Lost Lives. It has old X-rays of fatal conditions, death warrants."

"That's dark."

"Right up your alley. And I've added something to your favorite category."

Ray headed over to look.

Bodine said, "I'm feeling bad that I missed the fact that they hacked your email. You take a look while I go up and give this business the old college try."

"You dropped out after a year, but sure."

"You get chilly, plug in the space heater."

Wasted Creations was Ray's favorite category because it was closest to his life as a musician and artist. He walked over and looked.

There were reel-to-reel demos for composers that never got a single job, scores and parts for jingles that never aired; master tapes from never-released albums; scores, complete with parts, from never-performed operas. Ray knew better than most that he was looking at thousands of wasted man-hours. Nothing less than murdered dreams.

The stuff evoked a combination of sorrow for the poor suckers represented here, and relief that at least he'd sold a good deal of what he'd created over his various careers.

The newest addition was at the end: remnants of literary slush piles. He saw rejected articles for magazines defunct since the seventies and stacks of yellowed manuscripts, "No" scrawled on them in red pen. He laughed and climbed upstairs.

Bodine looked up from the computer. "You saw the new stuff. Your book isn't going to end up there, of course."

"Of course."

Bodine gestured at the computer screen, and Ray came over and leaned over it and looked at a Wikipedia article titled "Blackmail."

Ray said, "I don't get it. The agent's blackmailing the editor? Where's Karl come in?"

"No, the other thing: Susan and the manila envelope. I thought Karl was inviting her back to the group, but is that how he'd do it?"

Ray sat. "No. He was the king of oral transmission. Aside from those rules, he never wrote anything down."

"Exactly. Somebody was blackmailing Susan."

"Oh." Ray lit up. "She was having an affair. Once a cheater, always a cheater."

Bodine's eyebrows flew up. "Susan? You never told me."

Ray looked away. "Yeah."

"Sorry. 'Once a cheater, always a cheater.'" He shook his head. "I'm not sure that's true. But even so, why would the guy..."

"She tried to break it off."

"Maybe. Why are you so worked up about it? Whatever happened with Susan, it was a long, long time ago."

Ray groaned. "That wound's been kind of ripped open again. Liz is banging some asshole. A banker or something."

"Ouch. That is gruesome."

"Tell me about it."

Bodine thought. "How would the blackmail work?"

"She tries to end it; he doesn't want her to. Then he gets ugly, shakes her down for money."

"How romantic. If she doesn't pay, he tells the husband, blows up her family."

Ray said, "Exactly. The husband was testy because he suspected something."

"That explains the envelope she shredded. It was evidence of the affair. Compromising photos."

"The question is, where did Susan get the money to pay him off?"

Bodine sat at the pump organ and played silently. Ray walked over to pet Mingus in his bed. He backed off when he caught a whiff of whatever he'd been rolling in. Mingus looked at him, yawned, then closed his eyes.

Bodine finally said, "It's an okay scenario. But it could also be seventeen other things we haven't thought of."

"And I don't know that it's relevant. What I need to know is how Karl found out I'm writing."

Bodine nodded. He teased the organ keys for a minute, then kept playing as he spoke. "So Lou or the editor told someone about the project. And it somehow got to Karl." He stopped playing, looked at Ray. "Who did they talk to?"

"Somebody who was in the group, and who's now in publishing?"

Bodine kept playing, and a tiny wrinkle appeared above one eye. "I can't think of anyone who fits that bill offhand." He stopped playing. "We have to work the other end. Find out who's talking to Karl."

"I've already been down that road, with Lorraine."

"But it's the only road we've got. And it's a wide one. She knows so many people I bet she can't even remember who they all are. Call her back."

Ray left. A nasty wind moaned up from the river trying to slip icy fingers in the seams of his coat.

Back home, he flipped the sign to Open in the gallery and sat and called

Lorraine. He left a message, then checked his email.

One from Lou: "That acid trip is more like it! More, please." Ray moused over to the Word icon but didn't click. He would like nothing more than to finish the story and send it to his agent. But he'd promised Bodine.

He was about to go get his guitar when Lorraine called back.

"I was with a client. I've been enjoying our conversations."

"Me too." Ray told her about the dead cat.

"Yikes! Either somebody has a weird imagination, or they're a candidate for my practice."

"Crazy."

"Cray-cray, as we shrinks call it. Speaking of which—you ever talk to Fred?"

He chuckled. "I see where you're going. I did, but I didn't tell him I was writing. Just asked if he knew anything about Karl."

"Hm. If I remember, he hated animals."

"No more than he hates people. I don't think it's Fred. Anybody else you can think of that we didn't discuss before?"

"There's Beaky."

Ray leaned forward. "Freaky Beaky?" He was named for his humongous nose, which perhaps explained the tons of cocaine and God knows what else he'd sucked up there over the years. That didn't explain all the additional shit he'd smoked, dropped, and shot up. "He's still alive?"

"In Attica prison. Major trafficking."

"I'm not going to see him there. And I can't exactly trust him."

They laughed. Her voice was quiet when she spoke again. "Okay, there is someone else. Crystal."

Ray smiled.

"She left after we did. I didn't bring her up because…I think she got really hurt."

Oh. "Hurt? How?"

"It's icky. There are rumors, which I don't feel comfortable repeating. But maybe she'll talk to you. And she might be in touch with some of the others. You take care with her."

"I will." She gave him Crystal's number. He called.

"Ray Watts. Where are you?" Her voice was a little huskier than back then, but still *the voice,* triggering the same tingle at the back of his neck.

"I'm living in Hudson."

"We're right across the river, in Athens."

The little town was not a mile away as the crow flew. We. A lover? Or a roommate?

She said, "I'd love to see you sometime."

"Great. What's a good time?"

"Any time. I work at home."

"Me too. How about this afternoon, around one?"

"Great."

It was a little precipitous after decades of no-see, but he felt like they'd picked up right where they left off, wherever that was. And Crystal was never much for conventional social calendars.

15.

Ray headed south toward the Rip Van Winkle Bridge, passing the prison on his left and the lowlands by the river on his right.

He'd met Crystal a few years before Karl. She practiced New Age healing, prescribing exotic substances as alternatives to what she considered harsh Western remedies. She'd had Bassman eating clay for his chronic bad stomach. When Frank had back trouble, she had him boiling herbs that stank up the house.

Ray stayed away from that stuff, but he'd had one massage from her. Reiki? Shiatsu? An hour on her table and he reassessed her. She might be into some flaky shit, but whatever she did gave new meaning to the words "healing power."

When she was done, she had asked, "How was that?" in that magical, lulling voice of hers, which was its own kind of balm.

He smiled. "You have real talent."

She showed up at one of their gigs and came up to him after the set. Without a word she clasped his hands in hers, with the same super-light touch as during that massage. She turned his hands over and stared at them, then looked up at him solemnly. She gave him a big warm hug and was gone.

Was she just innocently acknowledging the coincidence of talented hands, or was that the beginning of something?

He didn't see her for a while, and then she showed up in the group. During long days at The House, he found himself catching her eye. She always smiled back. One day Susan—no dummy—caught him looking at Crystal and stopped him cold with a look. After that, Ray stayed clear of Crystal. He eventually put her out of mind.

Now ten feet onto the Rip Van Winkle Bridge, Ray's heart lurched. He slowed to a crawl and stared. A figure with long brown hair stood on the pedestrian walk at about the midpoint, past the opposite lane, their back turned. It was cold for a walk. He stopped the car.

The person didn't notice, just stood there.

Bassman.

He grabbed the door handle. What do you do with people who are about to jump? In the movies you approached them, except that triggered them to leap, and then you stretched out a hand and they were hanging there, threatening to pull you over....

This wasn't a movie. He didn't have any idea what to do. The man in the tollbooth would know. It was on the other side. Ray took off for it, an eye to the rearview mirror.

The figure turned and started walking toward him. A girl in her twenties. Ray shuddered and headed to Athens.

He was surprised to find Crystal living in a modest tract house in an ordinary middle-class neighborhood. He'd expected an enchanted bungalow deep in some forest. But once he was out of the car, the tinkling of wind chimes and a composite of sweet, pungent, and plain weird aromas told him he was in the right place.

She came out from the kitchen and gave him one of her big hugs, then stood, holding both his hands, beaming. Her face was round, with long, curly, honey-colored hair. She wore a spring dress. Which was a bit optimistic, given that it was in the forties, but then she always did look on the bright side.

He said, "You're looking good." She was.

"You too."

In person, her voice had overtones that didn't carry over the phone. And he'd been too young and naïve back then to get its essential quality: seductive. He followed her into the kitchen, and they sat at a table.

The walls were covered with shelves of apothecary jars bearing seeds, stalks, and powders, the source of the odors.

He said, "You're still in business."

"Uh-huh. Tea?"

His eyes flitted nervously to the jars. She laughed. "Don't worry. I've got plain black."

"Sure." She hadn't offered coffee. It was probably not on her list of healing substances. He'd live.

She put on water. He started at a loud whining sound. Circular saw.

"That's my husband, Ted. He's an amazing woodworker. You married?"

Ah, well. He gave her the short version of the scene with Liz.

"Sorry. You've had some bad luck with women." She looked at him, *into* him—checking out his aura? "How's your music?"

"I'm not doing music anymore. I'm an artist."

"That's far out. Well, how's your art?"

"Uh, I'm not really doing art anymore either. I'm…"

She laughed. "What *are* you doing, Ray?"

"I'm…writing."

She took his hand in that gentle way, and he felt the old vibe. She looked at him. "You have a gift. In another lifetime…" She let go of his hands. "You're writing a book."

"How do you know?"

Her eyes twinkled. The teakettle whistled. She put bags in two cups, poured, and brought Ray his. She nodded at the other one. "Let me bring this to Ted." She left the room.

Bad luck with the husband. But Ray was glad the vibe was still there. And accidents happened with power tools. He smacked himself in the cheek but was smiling.

She returned and sat. "What?"

"Nothing."

"What's this book about?"

"The past."

"Your band days. I can't wait to read it!"

"Uh, no. After that."

"Oh." She closed her eyes for a second. "The group."

The chill that came into her voice as she spoke the words assured him she wasn't involved anymore. He was relieved. "Coming here over the Rip Van Winkle Bridge, I saw a woman with long hair on the walkway. Just standing there. And it's a cold day for a walk. For a moment..."

"You thought it was Bassman. That's why I avoid going that way."

She paused and when she continued, her voice was quieter, with a tinge of something—sadness? "Why are you writing this, Ray?"

She wouldn't be fooled if he just said it was for the money. He told her the truth. "Because I have to." The saw started up again. She liked guys with talented hands. "I'm hoping to get free. Maybe heal, even."

She slowly shook her head. A tear ripened at the edge of an eye. It burst and streamed down her cheek. "You know, before the group I believed in the light. And I still do. But Karl taught me about darkness. I've cured all kinds of sickness and suffering, when I could."

Her voice got that chill again, and Ray understood what it contained. Something he didn't know Crystal was capable of: anger. "But there are also...stains. Most fade, with time. Some just won't come out."

She closed her eyes, took a couple of slow deep breaths. "But that's me. Maybe you...What do you need, Ray?"

"Do you know anything about Karl? Is he alive? Does he still have a group?"

"I left a few months after you. And aside from talking to Lorraine every once in a while, I've stayed away from everyone. I haven't heard a thing. Maybe because I don't want to."

"We were never supposed to talk about stuff."

She nodded.

"Do you still believe that?"

She gave him a long look, her gaze working its way down into him. She closed her eyes, and the silence pooled with a dark, viscous feeling. She opened her eyes, looked through him. Her voice was barely hers, just a thin reed leeched of all its charm. "What I believe...is that you came here for a reason. One you aren't aware of."

"What?"

"So that I could *tell*. I've never spoken to a soul about it. Not even to Ted. He wouldn't understand. But you were there."

Her gaze focused on him from that faraway place for an instant, and something boiled out and into him. "Karl made me…made me get an abortion."

"Oh shit. Whose…"

"His. He told me my…stuff wasn't pure enough to mix with his. His seed."

"But *you* were pure enough to mix with?"

"I guess so. As with electricity and aspirin, he didn't believe in birth control. He demanded that I go off the pill."

"How did it happen?"

"That doesn't just happen. People do it."

"Did he make you?"

"Have the abortion? Absolutely. It was that or leave the group."

"No, I meant did he make you…" Unspoken: Did he rape you?

"Fuck him?" She started sobbing, got it under control. "That's the question I've been asking myself ever since I left. You know how he was. Did he make us do anything? Or everything? There was certainly no saying no to him."

"No."

She wasn't crying, but worse, trembling, the grief pouring off her in waves. "That's not the worst of it. Something went wrong. I can never have kids."

Ray moved his mouth, tried to voice the sympathy aching in his chest. But there were no words for this. He leaned over and hugged her, and she hugged him back. She didn't let go even when the saw whined from her husband's workshop.

She finally released him. They looked at each other. He said, "I'm so sorry. And sorry I came here."

"No, don't be. But you should go." She walked him to the door. She gave him a last look, devastating because of the kernel of hope in it. "Well, you came out the other side of it."

"You will too."

He wasn't at all sure she would. He drove to the bridge, Crystal's anguish a weight that pressed him into the seat. It was like her grief was his too. And buried in there was an incandescent core of anger that had him squeezing the wheel, his eyes blazing.

He passed the middle of the bridge, glanced to the railing. Up to now, he'd seen Bassman as the only truly nonrefundable price for his adventure with Karl. But Crystal wasn't getting any refund on her ovaries. And Ray...

He pictured himself knocking on the Portal to The House, the brick in hand. The door squeaking open, and Karl with a most un-Karl-like look of surprise. Smashing that long nose, that high forehead.

Back in Hudson, he headed for Bodine's.

He knew the secret of his friend's odd museum. It was private in more than the obvious sense that it wasn't public. Bodine collected items that had exclusively belonged to strangers, the standard of admission that an item represented loss, from the trivial to the catastrophic. Some of the loss was general—like those machines that were out of fashion. But most of it had been poignantly personal to someone, though someone Bodine had never known.

At the same time, like anyone his age, he'd lost things, not to speak of people. Parents, their friend Bassman, countless girlfriends. Yet, he never spoke of any of them, displayed no pictures of anyone from his past.

He held his sorrow at arm's length, projecting it onto these forgotten possessions of anonymous souls. And, being Bodine, he'd meticulously ordered them, keeping the wolf in his heart at bay.

Ray had no need for such a device—he had the writing. And, if that failed, there were always Jo and Bodine to tell his sorrows to.

But Crystal had set something off in him that he didn't understand. It lay in him hot and heavy, and he didn't know what to do with it.

He parked in back of the theater.

Bodine came to the door with Mingus. He poked his head out and shivered theatrically. "I thought winter was over." He looked at Ray. "What now?"

Ray pointed up at the office. When they got there, Bodine sat while Ray paced.

"I have an idea for a new category in your museum. Lost Children. Baby's booties and hospital tags from infants that didn't make it, maybe some of those old nineteenth-century photos of dead kids."

"I'm sorry. I've put some sad shit in there, but that's just too freaking dark. Where's this coming from?"

He told Bodine about Crystal's admission.

Bodine scowled. "I can't say I'm shocked to hear it. It was tough enough being a guy there. Can't imagine what it was like for the women."

Bodine was trying for sympathy, but words couldn't touch this feeling. "It was good to see her, even so."

"I'll bet. She was a nice lady, for a sorceress."

"She's married."

"Aw, Ray. You never catch the breaks."

"And she didn't have any idea where Karl is."

"That's all right. I think I know how he found out you're writing."

"Yeah?"

"The publishers wrote you a nice check, which was an investment. Books don't sell themselves."

"Where are you going with this?"

"I was on the right track with Lou and the editor talking the project up. But the publisher has pros to do that. Publicists."

Bodine sat at the computer and typed. He said, "Let me read you Google search result number three for Karl Maxwell. It's from *Publisher's World*. 'Top agent Louis Goldman announced today that Random House is publishing a book by musician Ray Watts, which will answer the question still on many minds— "Whatever happened to Karl Maxwell?" This tell-all account should put those minds to rest.'"

Ray was stunned. Acid gurgled in his gut. He looked over Bodine's shoulder. There was his *name,* next to *Karl's,* where anyone could see it. "Goddamn. The whole world knows I'm writing about Karl." He walked away from the computer and went over and leaned against the organ.

"What d'you think would happen if they published your book? Publish means 'make public.' This is how Karl got to you."

"But how would he see that article?"

"He just had to Google himself. He was never short on vanity. Or if he was lazy, he could set up a Google alert. Any time his name came up online he'd get an email."

"Can you get rid of this *Publisher's World* thing?"

"Nobody can. It's there for eternity."

"Fuck."

Ray drove home. He parked in the alley. Went up to the couch and sat. Bodine hadn't gone for his Lost Children idea, and no wonder. It was downright morbid. But the feeling behind it, the one he got from Crystal, was still strong.

He wasn't smashing Karl in the face with a brick, not today. And he wasn't going down to the bodega and getting a bottle of booze, much as he was tempted. Because even if he did, this feeling would still be with him tomorrow.

Maybe writing would cure it. But a promise was a promise. And a dead cat was a dead cat. Except, what was to stop him from writing—who was to stop him—if he didn't send it to Lou? He could hide it away in this computer. Bodine said they were getting his writing from his email, and he'd installed that software so they couldn't get it off his hard drive. Jo's was closed. It was just as well. He'd only gone to Jo's to write because he felt safer there.

But where the story was headed was so private, so sensitive that he didn't want to tell it in public. Of course, once the book was published… He shoved the thought away.

Lou liked the acid trip? Wanted more dirt?

He gritted his teeth and continued Susan's story.

***

In the early days, before the rule about not talking, Susan and I spoke excitedly about the group when we got home to the farmhouse. We went on about Karl and his ideas with this buzzy kind of energy. I imagined we dished about other members—Susan wasn't entirely a saint. I felt that those conversations were strengthening the bond between us. The discussions often ended up with us in bed, so I figured they must be good.

In the first months, a page appeared next to the task list in the Front Hall with words written in Karl's elegant hand:

STOP ALL NEGATIVE EMOTIONS

One weekend morning when we'd been there about a year, a new rule joined the first:

NEVER SPEAK

The animated exchanges between Susan and I stopped. And our relationship took a strange turn. All the juice in our lives was in the group, so we were left with empty phrases, such as "Did you remember to get milk?" or "How was work?"

It was several months before a third rule appeared on the bulletin board:

NO CIGARETTES

That didn't affect Susan or me. She'd never smoked, and I had quit a few years before. Shortly after that came:

NO DRUGS

This one required a little explanation, but of course, none was forthcoming from Karl. Did he mean caffeine? Alcohol? Coffee had always been served after lunch. That day there was herbal tea. So, caffeine was out.

I had a massive headache for several days. And life seemed grimmer.

But beer? As a musician, I'd always drunk at bar gigs. In the early days of the group, I'd gotten in the habit of having a beer when I came home from Karl's.

But by the time NO DRUGS showed up, drinking had become a whole other thing. I'd get home from Karl's, every part of my body and soul in a huge knot. I'd race to the fridge and chug an entire beer, then open a second. I'd always liked my booze, but this was the only time in my life that it felt existential.

I was convinced that, without drinking, the tension from Karl's was going to cause me to contract a deadly disease. Susan wouldn't join me—she'd never touched alcohol—but she didn't hassle me about it. I think she understood why I did it.

The day NO DRUGS appeared, I got home and sat at the kitchen table and wrestled with it a long time. I finally stepped deliberately to the fridge and gingerly removed a beer. Sipped it. I was fully aware that I was breaking the rule. It was that or something worse.

Susan came in, saw me drinking, and went upstairs without looking at me. She didn't say anything about it to me. Or anyone else I'm sure, except maybe Karl. Because there was another new stricture.

NO GOSSIP

I figured that was it for the rules, because there were no more for over a year. And then came:

NO SEX

Like the other rules, we weren't to talk about it. But a lot of meaningful glances and nervous smiles passed between people. Karl didn't say anything at the next meeting, but some brave fool brought it up. "Uh, this NO SEX, do you mean just in The House?"

That elicited a rare laugh from Karl. A sound that had me cringing such that I'd rather he would have roared. He held his hand up, thumb and forefinger an inch apart. He didn't address the guy who'd spoken, but me.

"Ray. You remember this."

"The, uh, diamond of consciousness."

"You don't have to say it like it's an enema bag. This is the prize. Now, I think I've been clear about your chances of ever possessing it, even for a moment."

My chances, or all of ours?

"Slender as it is, would you give that chance up for a little screwing? To gratify your miserable prick? I've explained too many times how talking wastes the precious energy we accumulate here. What do you know about sex, Ray?"

"I, uh..."

"You know less about sex than a pig. Allow me to explain. The sex act is one of the most sacred. Just because pigs copulate doesn't mean they know what they're doing. Though at least they know how. You think you're ready for sex, when you don't even know how to properly tie your shoes?"

I looked down, but of course my shoes were upstairs in the Front Hall, neatly lined up. And what did I know about tying them? By that point, I'd come to doubt my ability to stand, to walk, to breathe properly.

After a couple of weeks, Susan and I cheated on the new rule. I was relieved, but I could tell how guilty it made her. We kept cheating. Not nearly often enough for my taste. Susan seemed into it when we did it. But afterwards, she'd just shut down, totally withdrawing from me. We, of course, weren't allowed to talk about that.

And soon Susan and I weren't talking at all.

***

From time to time, Karl mentioned a guru back in England. A man whom he only identified as My Teacher. "He's one of the five highest men on the planet." I assumed he must be a god walking the earth. But I never got to meet him.

That privilege was reserved for a select few who traveled to England each spring on a pilgrimage. The fact that I was never invited was one of the things that convinced me I would never make the grade with Karl.

People returned from those trips with an unmistakable glow. They exchanged little smiles with each other. They avoided eye contact with us poor souls who'd stayed home. We'd spent a dreary two weeks wandering around The House, half-heartedly doing chores.

Yet at the same time, in their absence I was relieved to be temporarily free of Karl's presence. But when they returned, the envy burned. Left out! It was a taste of that Outer Darkness. The only thing that made me feel better was that Susan hadn't been invited either.

Until she was.

It was the year Karl instigated NO SEX. I remember because Bodine had recently left the group.

When Susan returned from the pilgrimage, it was no surprise that our teacher's pet beamed brightest of the pilgrims. But was she avoiding my gaze?

I told myself it was just me, that I was even more envious now that she had gone on that trip. But after a few weeks, when the others had returned to normal, Susan still seemed almost supernaturally lit up. She looked at me now, but with a smile that kept me out rather than invited me in.

A few days after she got back, I turned to her in bed. She shook her head. There would be no more cheating.

Up to this time, it was only men that disappeared into The Backroom. Now, women started going in. When Susan went missing, I assumed it was her turn.

She'd been gone almost a day. I'd been to town on shopping duty. I was carrying bags into The Kitchen when I glanced toward The Backroom. I knew I shouldn't, but I snuck over to listen at the door. I was surprised to find it slightly ajar.

I stood still. Silence. Biting my lip, I inched the door open. The room was dark and empty.

Where was Susan?

When she returned the next day, the glow she'd carried back from England had taken on an almost feverish cast. Hah, old straight-edge Susan had finally dropped acid! But later, I caught a glimpse of her when she wasn't looking. She looked haunted. Maybe it was me. Because I was half-crazy by that point.

When I got to Karl's the next day, I was surprised to see Karl. By then, he was almost never around. But there he was. He didn't sneak up on me as usual, but just came out of a door. He saw me, and it was almost as if I'd surprised him. He gave me a look. Not of scorn, which I expected, but a little smile. It felt like he was sticking his tongue out at me.

That night I got drunk. I knew it in my gut. But I refused to think it. Now, I turned away from Susan in bed, in anger.

Karl had said, "No man touches me." He never said anything about the women.

It must have started on that trip to England. I started doing some serious drinking.

***

Ray looked up. His eyes bugged. Writing about Susan was feeding an incandescent core of righteous rage. It was growing to the size of a sun. He wasn't worried about the brick or a dead cat.

Let Karl bring an army.

And paired with the anger came a taste of something else. What?

He sat still, and the word came.

Freedom. He was almost to the end of the story. Is that what awaited him?

Even so, he had an urge to delay, to savor the terrible pleasure of telling. There were also commercial considerations. Crystal's admission had opened another dimension to the story. Ray had suffered, but so had others. And ripe as the tale of Susan's betrayal was for him, it was far from X-rated, not quite Lou's dirt.

He headed back to Bodine's. His friend had never said much about his experience at Karl's. It was clear from his reaction when the cat came that something had happened to him that he didn't want to talk about.

Ray hadn't wanted to pry. Now, it was time to.

16.

Ray walked to Bodine's. It was four, still cold, but sunny.

Bodine and Mingus appeared at the door. "You couldn't stay away."

"Are you busy?"

"I'm done coding for the day." He smiled at Mingus. "And this guy wants out. Springtime, and a dog's heart turns to chasing squirrels."

"Well how about we all go for a walk down to the river? You never get out."

Bodine poked his head out and frowned. "It's still cold. Bah. It won't kill me." He leashed up Mingus, and they headed up to Warren Street and down toward the Hudson.

It was going to be some job getting Bodine to talk about the group. So, Ray didn't hit him with it right away. "I know I promised I wouldn't, but I'm, uh, writing again."

"And I'm, uh, *shocked*. What's it going to take to stop you?"

"Nothing, apparently. But I haven't sent anything to Lou."

"You will."

Ray laughed. "Not today."

Bodine glanced over at him. "That's what you came to talk to me about?"

Ray hadn't fooled his friend. But did Bodine sound wary? He rarely betrayed feelings, but that didn't mean he didn't have fine instincts. Okay. "You've never talked much about the group."

"Neither did you, until recently."

"But you don't believe in the taboo about speaking."

"I do not. It's just dirty water under the bridge. Why wallow in it?"

"Well, I'm a little curious."

"A little? You're slipping."

Ray said, "I can see why most of us went with Karl. Zealous Susan, poor Bassman, and weird Fred. But why you?"

"Ah. Now, there's a question."

Mingus had been sniffing every lamppost and building corner, marking off every third, Bodine tugging at the leash to try to keep him on track. "This is why I never walk the damned dog."

"He isn't used to it. You need to get him out more."

"No, he's just a dog. That's what they do." They kept walking. "Why me? Karl was a powerful guy, on stage and off. Which, I'll admit, drew me."

"But that was in the beginning. What about later?"

"Right." He was silent for a moment, "You know how Karl was always going on about how it's too hard, you can't do it, nobody has a prayer in a million years of getting there?"

"How could I forget. And what exactly was *it?*"

"You know, spiritual awakening, enlightenment. I was a young guy. Tell me something was too hard, and that's precisely what I was hell-bent on doing. The impossible thing." He shook his head and made a rude sound. Self-deprecation? That wasn't like him.

They were a block from Promenade Park. Ray never saw tourists down here, maybe because of the housing projects nearby. Today, there was no one. "Why did you leave the group? Was it all the money you gave Karl?"

"Where'd you hear about that? Oh. Lorraine. Of course."

Ray nodded.

"That was a blessing."

"Really?"

"Indeed. I'll get to that. Why did I leave?" He addressed the dog. "Now here's a tale to curl your whiskers." Mingus ignored him. "And we're headed to the right place to tell it."

Ray raised his eyebrows, but Bodine was silent.

They came up a short flight of steps into the park and stood against the railing with the cliff below. The trees across the river were dusted with the light green of fresh leaves. Ray pointed, and Bodine and Mingus looked. Ray said, "Spring's coming along nicely."

Bodine said, "When I left the group it was early summer."

"A little more than a year before me."

"One beautiful day, seventy, not a cloud in the sky. Karl led several of us men up a hidden back stairway in The House, all the way to the roof."

"The roof? I had no idea you could get up there." What had Bodine said yesterday after the dead cat? That he hadn't been upstairs…much.

"Neither did I. The stairs came out on a flat spot between the chimneys. Karl sat us down in a circle. He said, 'Perhaps one of you is ready to join us.' In the inner circle. The implication being that it was highly unlikely."

Even now, to his shame, Ray felt the envy burn, that he had never been invited up to that roof. Mingus sat still, staring intently at Bodine.

"I knew this was some kind of test. Karl said, 'You need to be willing to die for me.'"

"I remember him saying that too."

"Yeah. I figured, the guy's being his usual dramatic self. I suppose I wasn't alone in my skepticism, because he gave each of us in turn that you're-gonna-burn-in-the-pit-of-hell stare. You remember."

"Oh, yes."

"He said, 'I'm not playing with words here. I mean, literally die for me.' Karl again stared at each of us, this time for whole seconds. I could feel the others shrink back. I was last. When he reached me, it was hard to hold his gaze—there was a fire in him. He glanced around the circle once more then returned to me and nodded once.

"I said, 'What do you want?' The kind of question which usually would have had him giving you both guns, but he let it pass. He pointed with his index finger, which had that monster ring on it. I looked at where he was pointing. The edge of the roof. The finger moved, tracing a foot-wide ledge that ran around the perimeter above the cornice with those fucked-up gargoyles.

"He said, 'Walk that.' I gave him a look—What, now? 'Not next week.'

"I crawled down the ridge of the roof, stood carefully, and stepped onto the ledge." Now, Bodine peered over the railing at the drop to the railroad tracks. "I was a little higher than we are now. I walked, one foot before the other, and finally reached the corner. Karl said, 'Now, turn and continue. Go the whole way around.' I made it all the way around."

"Jeez." Ray shuddered. As Bodine spoke, Ray was inching back from the rail.

"By the time I was done, my legs were shaking. I wasn't afraid—it was just the tension of keeping on track. At that point, I did expect a little bit of positive feedback. But Karl just looked at me. He said, 'This time with your eyes closed.'

"I knew Karl well enough by then to know the game—I was going to close my eyes, take a step, and he'd say, 'Stop.' And I'd climb back up, and it would be over.

"Except with the way he'd been getting lately, I wasn't sure. What if he'd just let me keep walking until I hit the corner? By now, my legs were visibly trembling. And it was fear.

"I said, 'No. I won't do it.' I climbed up the ridge from the edge, all the time with him looking at me with this triumphant grin. He said, 'You're not ready.' I swear, I almost picked him up and threw him off the roof. Instead, I headed downstairs, got in my car and drove away. And never came back."

Bodine stepped from the railing and sat on a bench. Ray sat next to him.

"I remember, you didn't say goodbye. Just one day you were gone."

"That day."

"Why'd you go on that ledge? You never bought into Karl's trip like some of us."

"No. It was that macho thing." He snorted. "Ray, what are you getting me into? I can't believe I just told you that. That I remembered it."

"Sorry. You know why he got you up on that roof?"

Bodine shook his head.

"You were another alpha male. A threat to his authority. It was push you into leaving or push you literally off that roof."

"If you say so."

"You mind if I write about that?"

"It's no skin off my ass."

Ray was one of the few people who knew that Bodine had come from old money. His father had disowned him when he dropped out of college and pursued rock 'n' roll. The money explained Bodine's generosity back then. How he was always buying the dope and getting food. How he had a running car when the rest of them had clunkers.

"How could losing that money be a blessing? And hadn't your father already cut you off by that time?"

"There was a trust fund he couldn't touch. No fortune, but nothing to sniff at either. That fund didn't fully kick in until I hit a certain age. Which I reached the second year with Karl. The next day, I signed every penny over to him. And I was free. Free of the old man and his plans for me to take my place in the white old boy's establishment."

"So Karl was in it for the money?"

"I've never really thought about it. But no. He'd been a rock star. He had plenty then. It was something else." He looked at Ray. "Why were you afraid of him? He never got *you* up on a roof."

"He was intimidating."

"True. But that's circular logic. 'He was intimidating because I was afraid of him.'" Bodine snorted. "Hey, how about this? It's right up your alley. Those spooky sculptures of yours with the bones."

Bodine pointed back up Warren Street. "All that horror shit you love. Karl was a fucking vampire."

Ray scoffed. "You don't believe in vampires."

"He wasn't drinking our blood. But he sure as shit was sucking our life energy. You remember how tired we got?"

"Yeah. But we were working hard, not sleeping much."

"That's no different than being on the road. But tell me, did that ever make you so exhausted?"

Ray tried to recall. As he did, he slumped on the bench. He felt weak, almost faint. Those last months of the group, trying to get out of bed, feeling if he stood up too fast his heart would give out. Struggling to keep his eyes open as he drove to The House. And when he arrived, the only thing keeping him on his feet was the constant fear.

"Damn. I'd forgotten. No question, I'd never been so beat in my life."

"What work did Karl ever do? Did you ever see him so much as lift a rake, let alone a heavy stone? All that browbeating, all those embarrassing questions, they were sucking the souls out of us. Feeding his." Bodine made a noise of disgust. "I need to get home."

They stood and headed out of the park and back up Warren Street.

Ray said, "Lorraine thinks he was a con man."

"That's the same damned thing as a vampire. Only what Karl wanted was power."

"I hope this hasn't bummed you."

Bodine waved his hand. "You're the one writing the freaking book."

"Mingus is sniffing at all the same places he did on the way down and marking them all off again."

"My dog has the memory of a gnat."

"Or an elephant, depending on how you look at it."

Neither of them laughed, and Bodine seemed subdued. They continued in silence.

When they got to Bodine's, Ray said, "We should walk more often."

"Sure. But you won't get a roof story next time."

Back home, Ray sat on the couch and wrote down Bodine's ordeal. He could see it attracting a few of those eyeballs. He suppressed the urge to email it to Lou.

That night he dreamed.

He's up on the roof of The House. Susan stands on the ledge, naked, her back to him, a blindfold tied behind her head. He wants to shout, "Don't do it! Don't turn the next corner!" But his lips are frozen.

She turns and walks toward him. She bursts into flames, but keeps walking, smoldering skin flaking from her arms and drifting to the ground like fall leaves. Her nose caves in, the skull appearing, yet she still approaches.

An enormous black cat slinks from behind one of the chimneys, flashes a set of Dracula incisors, races over to her, and pounces on her back.

***

He woke from the dream to a gray morning. He made coffee and headed down to the gallery, flipped the sign to Open.

He'd dreamed Bodine's nightmare. He gazed at the rusted leaves twining up the spiral steps and thought of Lorraine and her grapevine. She must have more dirt. And now, he had something to trade.

He called her, told her Bodine's story. He paced the gallery as he talked.

She said, "I never heard that one. But did I tell you about the robberies?"

"Huh?"

"Karl made some of the guys go out and knock over gas stations, a hardware store. I was afraid at the time of getting busted myself. I think the statute of limitations covers it now."

"Why were you afraid?"

"My job was to get rid of the stuff."

"Fence it?"

"No, it was worthless. Karl would ask for, say, a single tire, specific make. Or a couple of balls of twine, a certain chisel. I buried it all out in the woods. It made me feel guilty as hell."

"Huh."

"I figured it was one of his tests. Karl trying to see just how far he could get people to go."

An old couple out on Warren Street approached the display window. They looked nice. They looked in the window. The woman looked at the man. They shook their heads and scurried away.

Lorraine said, "Later he sent Beaky of all people to knock over a couple of pharmacies."

"No!"

"Oh, yes. And this time, Karl wanted something of value."

"But didn't Beaky have to get clean as a condition for joining?"

"He did. That's the thing—it might have been a test, but it was cruel."

"No kidding. Waving dope in front of an ex-addict. What was he getting?"

"I don't know."

Ray said, "Wait. Bodine told me Karl was a junkie back before the group. I didn't believe him."

"A junkie? Huh. That really doesn't fit my picture of Karl. Then again, that picture has evolved."

"Was Beaky using what he stole?"

"I think we would have noticed."

"You're right. He was very different straight. So, who were the drugs for?"

She said, "Well, he dosed us with that acid."

"Did he have people in the Backroom on Vicodin or whatever?"

"That doesn't make sense."

"Who knows? Do you mind if I use this for my book?"

"Not a bit, as long as you keep my name out of it."

"Done."

"Thanks for all this."

"Least I can do for someone I've been to hell with."

"Hell and back."

"Thank God."

***

When he was home, Ray ate exactly at noon. He was sitting down with a salami sandwich when Bodine called. "I've got something on the blackmail idea."

"Right."

"I spent the morning digging into your ex-wife's finances."

"And?"

"Starting that summer before she died, her cash withdrawals grew from an average of a thousand a month to almost two."

"After that manila envelope arrived."

"I don't know exactly when it came but could be."

"That's some serious blackmail." Ray bit into his sandwich and held the phone away so Bodine couldn't hear.

"Oh, there's more. She had an IRA. Something she inherited, just in her name. I'm not sure old hubby even knew about it. Later that fall, she started withdrawing from that. She siphoned off about twenty grand. The last withdrawal was a week before she died."

"She must have really loved her family to protect them like that."

"And really been afraid of this guy. Ray, I can hear you chewing."

"Then don't call me at noon."

Bodine hung up. Ray went to Jo's for dessert.

She came over. "I haven't seen you in days."

"I've been busy."

"Writing your book. You were doing it here."

"Yeah. Uh, I can't deal with the distractions."

She looked over at a table with a couple of young women. "They need a check. And you need…"

"Chocolate pie."

"One of those days, huh? Though you look good."

"Every day is a chocolate pie day, as long as it's yours."

She brought the pie. As she headed into the kitchen, he inhaled it. He pondered a second piece.

Jo returned a few minutes later. "I see you licked your plate. More?"

"Mind-reader. But I'll pass this time."

She sat, and her smile got strained.

He said, "What?"

"I spoke to Liz. She feels badly about how she's handled things."

"She called you?"

"Yeah. Said she's worried."

"So why doesn't she call me?"

"I don't know. She's just sniffing around."

"She won't call me, but it's okay for her to get you to talk to me and report back?"

"I'm sorry, Ray. I don't know what to do here."

"You're fine. I'm not mad at you."

Ray headed across the street to home holding his collar up against a light rain. Liz was back with a cruel vengeance. Liz and her banker, banging away, not in a hotel king-sized bed but *hers,* at her apartment, the same one.

He got inside, slammed the door, sat at his desk. He flashed on what he and Bodine had speculated about—Susan and a mysterious lover. Ray had never met the guy, and he might just be a figment of his imagination, but he still hated the slimy prick.

He climbed up to his couch and the laptop.

***

Denial is a powerful thing. And if you're truly between a rock and a hard place, it can be the thing that keeps you alive, stops you from grinding yourself to a bloody pulp between two implacable things.

The rock was the mounting evidence that my beloved teacher didn't have my best interests at heart. That this group, far from offering salvation, was destroying my body, ruining my marriage. And killing my spirit—whose sustenance was my very reason for being there.

The hard place was my fear of leaving. Despite everything, it only grew. I was like the gambler who's holding a pair of threes and keeps tossing in chips until he has too much on the table to admit he might have a losing hand. It would take more than what I had to overcome that fear. Bodine was lucky. His life had come on the line up on that roof, and that had given him the strength to go.

I wasn't on the edge of any roof. Just feeling the walls pressing against me, squeezing and squeezing.

I wasn't shocked when Bodine left the group. If anything, I was surprised he'd stuck it out as long as he did. But then Ethan was gone. Why him? My eyes were wider, ears keener, looking for some reason. But aside from Karl's increasing absence, everything was exactly the same. Unfortunately. I suppose in some dark corner of my mind, there was hope—that if others left, maybe someday I might too. But it wasn't a conscious thing.

A light comes on for a second, and you see where you really are. Then it's dark, and you can pretend again.

One day, there's a light so glaring that it burns itself into your retinas, and you just can't forget.

Beaky clean and sober was not his old shuck-and-jive self. Instead he was awkward and raunchy. Like Fred, but without the nastiness. Beaky was almost sweet in his oddness. Maybe the drugs had been his way of hiding it.

One night in the Meeting Hall, Karl was pontificating. He'd gone on so long that even with him there I was on the verge of nodding off. From the corner of my eye, I caught Beaky standing and came wide awake. He interrupted Karl mid-sentence. "Karl Maxwell!" He spoke in an uncanny parody of Karl's portentous whisper. "Tell us what you had for lunch."

Karl reacted instantly. He rose from his cushion and hissed, "Eat shit and die!" pointing to the door, like God expelling Adam and Eve from Paradise.

I'd stopped breathing. From the silence in the room, I figured everyone else had too. No one moved a muscle. The Meeting Hall vibrated with our collective shock such that I was afraid the ceiling would come down. Karl's mask had slipped again, revealing the predator.

And this time, it was in public.

Finally, Beaky moved, shambling out of the room. We never saw him again. Karl resumed speaking as if nothing had happened, but everything was different.

Questions raced through my mind. What about those Negative Emotions? I argued to myself: It's only Karl teaching, doing his crazy wisdom thing. Shocking us into consciousness.

Except I knew. Nobody, let alone a spiritual teacher, beats on someone like Beaky, who isn't all there. It's just wrong.

When it came to Beaky's last stand, I think he might have been the one playing the crazy wisdom card. Because in all those years there striving for enlightenment, nothing opened my eyes like the sound of that "Karl Maxwell!" In that instant, I knew that Karl's voice, his slinking walk, his whole act was just a bag of cheap tricks.

With Beaky gone, Karl went after Bassman. It was like he suddenly had a license to torment our weakest members.

One night, Karl began the meeting by addressing our bass player. "Bass-MAN. Are you really a man? Then why haven't you ever been with a woman? Maybe I should call you Bass-BOY. But you're not ready for a woman yet. Practice being sexual with a tree."

What? Was he telling Bassman to go fuck a tree? And never mind that we were all under the stricture of NO SEX. So, what was he telling Bassman to do?

Bassman just sat there and took it, like he'd taken everything in life. Karl knew he would never defend himself, never dare pull a Beaky.

After that meeting, I approached Bassman. His face looked gray. I couldn't say anything, of course, but I gazed at him, tried to show him I understood what he must feel. He just slunk away.

Without thinking, I'd begun keeping track of him. As long as he didn't disappear, it meant he wasn't in The Backroom tripping his brains out. I knew that would be the last straw for him.

His cough, which had started when we laid those bricks, had never really stopped. The day he disappeared, I actually hoped it had landed him in the hospital.

But no. I was pruning trees out near the cliff the next day when he drifted toward me from The House with a listless gait, like a specter, a set of garden shears flopping in his hand against his pants. And I knew he'd been to The Backroom.

We looked at each other for long seconds in silence. It was strange, because it was the first time he'd ever really made eye contact with me. I stared into the black pools of his eyes and could see that he was still in The Backroom, in the darkness with a million colors. I had to look away. I was afraid that I might fall in there with him, to a place from which there was no coming back. I sometimes imagine him still wandering the reaches of some obscure dimension, forever lost.

He spoke in a voice devoid of all affect, except for a little tremor that made me feel like my whole body might start shaking in sympathy with it.

"I can't do it. I just can't."

He was breaking the rule against speaking. Now, so did I. "What, you can't prune these trees? This is nothing. You made that floor."

"No, I can't do any of it."

He was going to leave. Go out into the Outer Darkness. I said, "You need to think about this. Give it a few days. You can't…"

But he was turning away.

Even at that very late date, I still believed in everything Karl had fed us. So, I believed the worst thing that could happen to Bassman, to any of us, was to leave the group. But Karl had taken Bassman's soul, stolen what little life he had. I couldn't see that there was really only one thing Bassman could do.

He could take his life back from Karl.

I found out about it at home the next morning. Though Susan and I weren't

*speaking, she handed me the local paper, and left the room without looking at me:
"Musician plunges to death in river."*

*He'd driven down Route 145 to the Rip Van Winkle Bridge. Parked halfway
across, gotten out, leaving the motor running, and climbed the rail to the walkway.
He'd mounted the second rail, then jumped in the river. Only it was shallow there,
not deep enough to drown. He'd shattered both legs and lay there for a long time.
I imagine him down there, in the dark and cold, moaning in agony, crying for
somebody to help, but no one heard. Like none of us had really heard all along.*

*Karl called a meeting. As he spoke, he didn't assume a posture of grief, and never
lost his guru cool. "Life is a river, and death is the great ocean. Just as the rain falls on
the roof of this house and eventually finds its way to the sea, we all are destined…"*

*And I might have bought it, except for his choice of metaphor. It was in the
worst of bad taste. My friend had jumped into a real river and died. He wasn't
headed to some great ocean. He was going into a box in the ground and never
coming out.*

Karl ended with, "So he was just a tiny drop…"

*Was he saying this was no big deal? Because, no, it was huge. For some reason,
Karl looked at me. My mask was off, that blank face I'd carried for years. I don't
know exactly what showed on my face, but it felt like naked rage. And as his eyes
locked onto mine for a moment, I saw the strangest thing. A little nervous smile
twitched across his lips. It was gone in an instant, but he didn't finish his sentence:
"a tiny drop…" In the bucket? Or in the great ocean?*

*That marked the beginning of Karl's facade slipping. I left that meeting feeling
as if I'd been slipped another drug, one stranger even than LSD. My body was
numb and sluggish yet filled with crazy energy.*

*Over the next weeks, it was like seeing an actual mask crumble away in slow
motion. The twitching in his lips spread to his eyes, which darted around the room.
The way he walked, hunched over, he seemed to have actually shrunk.*

*He was afraid. What was underneath the mask? It didn't seem to be a
dangerous animal anymore. More like the silly Wizard of Oz flailing at his knobs
with the curtain torn back.*

*During this time I ran into Lorraine out on the road on the way to my car. She
smiled at me, a wide knowing smile, the first real smile I'd seen on any of us in years.*

I was seeing the first crack in another façade—our collective face, that impassive mask we'd all worn.

The next day Lorraine flashed me another smile, and I returned it. That night she called me, explicitly breaking the taboo against speaking. And she kept calling me. She told me stories. It was clear that a lot of members had been worse than me at obeying Karl's command to NEVER SPEAK.

I said only, "Unh-huh" and "I see," clutching the receiver until my knuckles were bone white. At first, I held the phone like it was a handle to hold onto the group, frantically trying to come up with alternate explanations for her stories.

And then, I crossed some threshold, and the phone became a lifeline, pulling me away.

Lorraine told me about Bodine and the money. About cruelties I'd known of, but that by this point no longer shocked. The mundane stuff was almost as damning. All those weekend Sundays while we slaved away, Karl was apparently upstairs, "watching the game on TV."

Football? And where did the electricity come from for the TV? I found this somehow the hardest to swallow. To this day, I still don't quite believe it.

***

And yet, Karl was there in The House, now. With a computer. Or was he? It made no sense, but Ray needed it to. He needed to know where Karl was, what he was doing, and who he was doing it with…but how?

By going to The House. He'd knock on the door, and Karl would answer, shake his hand, invite him in, *Ray, how have you been?* with all the shadings of meaning he'd put in a seemingly superficial question.

Ray laughed darkly. He wasn't going there. He'd gone through twenty conniptions, had to dose himself half-crazy with acid just to get in that house with the writing. He dove back into it.

***

It was only later that I realized Lorraine only spoke of what happened to others. That she might have been hiding something from me. It wasn't hard to guess what that could be.

But outwardly she kept smiling, and it spread through the group like a contagion. As Karl stooped and shrank before us, we stood taller. Walked faster, our bodies looser as the chains of constriction fell away.

But not Susan. She clung to her slack face, her measured movements. We hadn't spoken in months. She'd moved into the spare bedroom. I avoided her, waiting for the sound of her door when we returned from The House before going down to the kitchen for my beer.

Yet deep as I was in grief at the disintegration of our marriage, there came moments when I tasted imminent freedom. My head still couldn't wrap around it. But somewhere in me I knew.

It was uncanny, how something we'd so believed in for so long could just fall apart so fast. Life with Karl, which was supposed to be so vivid, was simply fading like an old Polaroid in reverse, the events of only a week ago distant as ancient memories. The House, which we'd considered more solid than any on earth, seemed to shimmer, appearing translucent as if it was in the process of dissolving into the air.

I'd bought Karl's rap about the great lineage of teachers. I'd believed the group would last long past our individual lives, down the generations until the sun burned out. But in a matter of days, it was over.

I'd always dreaded Karl's unexpected appearances out of fear. Now, I dreaded them out of embarrassment. He was suddenly around a lot. He must have sensed the end was coming. But it was too late. After that initial slip, his mouth, which he'd always held in a firm line, now seemed to constantly struggle to suppress something: an apology, an explanation? What radiated off of him was not psychic power, but enormous sheepishness. It was as though he'd been caught out doing something far more embarrassing than the stuff he'd once made us stand and admit to.

By the very last meal, the group had shrunk so that there were only twelve of us. Karl said, "I've always thought twelve was the right number." We laughed, but the joke of comparing himself to Jesus was obviously terrible—as pathetic as his river metaphor after Bassman died. I understood why Beaky had so enraged Karl. In imitating him, he'd pointed out what was just the other side of all that pretension. Ridiculousness. I later thought of it as Karl's Last Supper.

Those final days had the unreality of a fairy tale, as though Bassman's hitting the river had broken a spell, waking us up. We blinked, rubbed our eyes and looked around in wonder. It's ironic, because Karl always said our goal was awakening to consciousness. But the group had actually been deep in slumber.

One of the very last days—though I couldn't know yet that it was –started normally. We sat meditating in the Meeting Hall. Karl assigned some exercise, then we milled around the bulletin board upstairs to see what our job was for the day.

At the bottom of the list:

Karl—Painting.

His name had never been on the list before. He'd never worked with us peons. After the morning meeting, he'd disappear until lunch, unless he popped out to surprise you with one of his takedowns.

But there he was, carrying a can of paint out back. I walked behind him on my way to prune trees. For once, he didn't see me. He stopped at the corner of The House and stooped over the can. I stood, frozen, not wanting to interrupt whatever he was doing, not intending to eavesdrop, but also afraid to move in case he noticed me.

The paint was white—of course, what other color? It took me some moments to figure out what he was doing, because he was so bad at it. He was trying to get the can open. Drips down the side indicated it had been opened before. And unless it had just been closed, the paint would have dried, sealing it. It was easy enough to open if you had a screwdriver and you knew how.

He had a set of keys. He worked at the thing, to my amazement, visibly becoming more and more frustrated. Karl, unknowledgeable about a simple practical matter, Karl incompetent, was hard to believe.

But frustrated? That was a Negative Emotion.

He picked the can up with a snarl and flung it at the side of The House. The lid finally came off and gobs of paint sprayed over the stones. Karl stalked off.

I still didn't move. I'd just witnessed my teacher being quite stupid and very pissed off.

***

Karl didn't show up for Bassman's funeral. But Bodine did. The service was held in that little church down the road from The House. Bodine played an out-of-tune upright, a simple hymn that segued into a long, sprawling blues. Bassman had loved the blues. There were many tears.

Afterward, Bodine came up to me outside. "Man, I should have brought you a guitar. But I have something else in my car."

He opened the trunk. There was a six-pack of beer. I'd been cheating on NO DRUGS at home with my own beer. But as I clinked bottles with Bodine and exchanged a look—for Bassman—I knew I was done.

Karl hadn't bothered to show up at the funeral. The next day, I just didn't show up at The House. There was no drama. I didn't say goodbye to him. How could I have? I may not have been able to speak, but I was finished with lying.

***

It was true, every word he'd written. As best as memory could serve, that's how it had gone down. So, why was he rubbing his fingers nervously on the couch?

He kept rubbing, stared from the window, and then it came. He'd missed a piece. He'd missed it in the writing because he hadn't been aware of it at the time.

Grief and rage had done what nothing else could and driven him from Karl's house. But even as he walked away, he'd carried something that remained buried in him for decades.

Doubt. What if Karl had been a true holy man, and Ray's leaving him had been the biggest mistake of his life? The doubt was what was behind that recurrent dream where he was back with Karl, and all was forgiven. It's what had him Googling Susan. It's what had him struggling to get into The House, through the writing.

At the same time, he wished he could erase it. Because if he didn't, he was never going to be free.

For all the terrible things he'd just evoked from the past, there was a new bad thing: malignant thoughts, infecting his brain. So, he was suddenly convinced that Karl had sent the brick and dead cat not as warnings but *teachings,* designed to wake Ray to that ever-elusive higher state. But it was a waste of Karl's oh-so-precious time, because Ray still wasn't learning.

But God save him, he wanted to.

He shook his head and reached to his throat. Just like that, the lump was back, so big that his breath was rasping. That was part of Karl's new teaching too. He'd told them not to speak for a good reason. It had something to do with energy, but Ray was so freaked out he couldn't for the life of him remember what.

He remembered Bassman at one of their last gigs, just standing there like he did, those fingers pumping out that hellacious bottom. It practically brought tears but pulled him away from the poisonous thoughts.

17.

It was almost five. Ray went down to the bodega, bought a six of Magic Hat, and carried it over to Bodine's. He heard no barking as he approached the door. He knocked, and a minute later Bodine opened it.

Ray said, "Is Mingus okay?"

"Fine. You've been over here so often lately he didn't bother to get up when you came. Good thing I was working here in the theater or I wouldn't have heard you."

"You need a new doorbell."

"I was about to call you." He looked at the beer. "What's that for?"

"For Bassman."

"Huh?"

"Remember his funeral?"

Bodine's face turned solemn. "I do. You mind sitting outside? It's not too cold."

They sat on lawn chairs by the back wall, and Ray told Bodine what he'd written.

Bodine said, "Oh, man, I never heard the gory details before."

"Because I couldn't speak."

"You know I'm not big on second-guessing. But I will confess that I still sometimes wonder if we couldn't have done better by him." He laughed ruefully. "One time I tried to help him out. There was this skinny little chick, I forget her name, she obviously had the hots for him. I told him she liked him. Set up for them to meet. She was sweet, gentle, shy herself, utterly unintimidating. But it was a disaster. I shouldn't have pushed it."

"How could you know? How could you understand someone like that, who doesn't believe he deserves anything good? I have plenty of my own guilt. What if we'd never driven him up to Karl's? Because he didn't have a license, never learned to drive."

"No. He's not on us. He's on Karl Maxwell. Karl wasn't there that night on the bridge, but he might as well have been. Might as well have pushed Bassman right in the river. I don't hold personal grudges. But this isn't about me. If I believed in an afterlife, I'd like to think Karl is going to spend eternity with his cold, shriveled heart getting munched on by giant cockroaches." He stood and walked over to the filthy remains of the snowbank and gave it a few kicks.

Ray followed him and leaned against Bodine's Mustang. "Why were you going to call me?"

"I got into Susan's cell phone records."

"How'd you—"

"Never mind. I tracked down every number to and from her in the year before she died. Ruled out calls with her husband, work, and commercial stuff. Came up with a handful of cell numbers. All of them belong to people in New Jersey, except for one. Starting that September, she made five calls to a prepaid phone with an upstate New York area code."

"Five-one-eight. That's ours."

"It is. But I dug deeper, into phone company records. Found the cell tower that phone was pinging off. It's smack in the middle of the Helderberg Mountains."

"Where The House is. Fuck. A while ago, you suggested she might have been on her way back from seeing Karl the day she crashed. I didn't buy it, because there are a lot of places she could have been coming from." Ray's body was filled with jangly energy. He paced in a tight circuit.

Bodine said, "I'm afraid Karl's *there*. In The House."

So it wasn't a new lover she was seeing. It was a very old one.

Bodine said, "The phone calls were right around the time she started spending that money."

"But Karl was rich, a rock star."

"Was. That was ages ago."

"Why would she pay him?"

"Blackmail, like I said with this lover we were imagining. Her husband didn't know about her sordid past in a cult, and Karl threatened to tell and ruin her family. Who knows, maybe he still had the old power over her." Bodine leaned against the car.

Ray continued to pace. "So she was on her way home from there when she crashed. Why did she see him? What happened when she did? Was she..." Back with him. "Back with the group?"

"If she was, it wasn't for long. I got into her E-Z Pass records. She only came up that way the one time."

"So Karl sent the emails and delivered the dead cat."

"Not necessarily. If Susan went up there, others might have too. Which suggests another possibility—that he's started up a new group. In which case, he has a minion to do his dirty work."

"Our postmodern teen geek." Ray looked at Bodine. "You've been busy."

"You know me. I start a job, I have to finish it."

That made two of them. "I have to go."

"You only had one beer."

"Don't worry, I'll be back for more."

When he got home, he headed straight for the laptop up on the couch.

***

When I got home from going to The House for the last time, I told Susan, "I'm leaving. Are you staying?" Not, Are you coming with me?

She said, "I don't know, Ray."

In that moment I realized that I, at least, was free of the stricture NO SEX. Maybe I was just horny, but I saw the possibility that leaving might make it right between us. I actually smiled. "If you're leaving, we don't need to obey the rules."

She was already unbuttoning her shirt, backing up to our couch. But not exactly looking at me.

***

Ray looked up. He couldn't write this part. He didn't want to remember it, and what he did remember was all confused with that last sorry time with Liz.

***

Afterwards, we got off the couch. I reached to hug her, but she was moving to the corner of the room, where she faced me. I didn't come closer. She was fixing her shirt, combing her hair back with her hand as she talked, finally breaking silence. Which I first thought meant she was leaving the group.

I imagine that, in some twisted sense, she believed she was giving me a gift: the gift of an explanation.

Now she looked at me. "I was with Karl."

"With him."

"You know."

I'd known it for months, but still it socked me in the gut. I stopped breathing. But she wasn't done.

"Ray, it was so beautiful."

How could she evoke my name in the same sentence as that execrable notion?

What could possess her to tell me this now, with what had just happened on that couch? "Susan, maybe you want to stop."

A volcanic process stirred in me. The next day, I'd see the bruises where my fingernails had cut into my palms. But she still wasn't done.

"Ray, you remember the sound of his voice. He spoke when he was inside of me. I could feel that sound in my whole body."

I saw it. The great cat looming over her, all its natural grace gone. Pounding into her. Her mouth coming open, making cries she never made with me.

My face was on fire. The pressure was building, building in me. If I didn't release it, I was going to explode. I needed to open my mouth. Except I couldn't trust what might come out. Couldn't be sure that once I got screaming my hands wouldn't get involved. My eyes flicked to the poker in the fireplace.

I raced upstairs and grabbed a few things—guitars, clothes. I was almost to the car when I heard her.

"Ray."

I turned to her.

"I'm sorry." Her face was heavy with sorrow, but she didn't look sorry. Like she'd had no hand in what had happened, no choice.

I drove away. That's the last time I saw her.

***

In the terrible weeks after leaving the group, leaving Susan, I had literally no idea what to do. Bodine kindly let me crash at his apartment in the city. Once he got a whiff of where I was at, he mostly hung out at his girlfriend's while I paced the two tiny rooms and drank endless cups of instant coffee. I felt like the needle of a broken compass that no longer pointed True North, to Karl, but skittered around from one impossible question to another.

Where was I going to live? What would I do for money? What would I do with the rest of my life? Music wasn't even an option. The idea of getting on a stage after being on the same stage Karl had performed on made me physically ill.

The rule about not talking survived in me, so I couldn't make myself say a word to Bodine. The one about negative emotions crumbled. My rage about Karl and Susan spilled into my mind in the form of terrible sarcasm.

So, if it was Cooking that happened in The Kitchen and Eating in The Dining Hall, what went on in The Bedroom with Karl was no ordinary adultery, no mere sex, but COSMIC FUCKING. Karl's supreme gift to my wife, for which I should thank him.

With a bullet in the head if I ever ran across him again.

***

The Bedroom? He'd never heard such a place mentioned, but of course Karl had to have one. Or did he call it the Love Den? Ray's fingers hovered trembling over the keyboard for some minutes, until he realized—the story was done. He eased the laptop closed. It was the coffer that now contained his fortune, spoils of mining the past.

He'd worked through five bells, and six too. It was almost seven. But daylight saving time had come, and it was still light.

The story was done, but the process wasn't. The last thing was to deliver it to Lou. Bodine had said Ray was going to write it. And he had. Fuck Karl.

Let him bring a shit-ton of bricks and a truckload of dead cats. Ray composed an email and punched Send.

Ray headed outside and down toward the river. He squinted against the glare of the last sun. It was too bright but without an ounce of warmth. A steady wind buffeted his face. The sidewalk sucked at his feet. He stumbled on the curb, almost stepped into a turning truck.

It was always like this finishing a big project. Liz called it his post-partum depression. And it *was* a little sad. But usually there was a feeling of satisfaction.

Not this time. He was just bone tired. He'd finished telling the story, but for some reason he didn't feel done.

But he was done for today. He turned back home, lumbering like an oil tanker changing course. He fumbled with the keys, creaked the door open. Picked up the laptop, almost too heavy to carry, and trudged upstairs one clank at a time. He climbed into bed, opened the computer, started looking at the news and was out. Though usually a light sleeper, tonight he slept the sleep of the dead.

***

He came wide awake, bolting up in the bed, heart pounding, listening for tinkling glass. There'd been a crash, and now silence. Dim light crept into the window. It felt like very early morning. Earlier than he usually woke, but he'd passed out last night at, what, eight?

He looked around for the computer. It was lying on the floor next to the bed. The crash hadn't been a brick, let alone a car accident, but the computer falling on the floor.

He picked it up and punched a key. The screen stayed black for a moment then lit up with the same news site he'd last visited. The screen refreshed with a story about road rage. A moment later, an ad popped up with a car and smiling woman and the sound came on and blared some fucked-up music. He slammed the computer shut and got up.

It was freezing in here. He'd left the window open. Dank air streamed in. He needed coffee. But first he had to get warm. He padded across the icy floor to the bathroom. Funny, he'd been dreaming he was sneaking around Karl's dark place. Something had fallen in the dream too. And then he was running. How did that work, hearing the sound before it happened? He shook his head. This is what you got with a brain and no caffeine.

He closed the bathroom door by habit—not that it mattered with no one else in the house. He stepped in the shower and cranked the knobs. A clanking of old pipes and then the stream burst from the showerhead. He stepped back, but it hit his chest. The cold always shocked, no matter how carefully you set the temperature. A moment later, the water warmed, and he melted into it. The water pressure was great here, like back when he lived in the city. A big improvement over the piddling trickle from those new green showerheads.

Growing up in the fifties, he had the notion drummed into him that history was a series of great leaps forward, science racing toward some unimaginably bright future. It hadn't turned out that way. He'd watched "progress" swallow the remaining farmlands of his native Long Island, spawning millions of crummy little houses like the one he'd grown up in. What ex-smoker didn't pine for the innocent days before the sixties, when you could suck down a pack a day without a worry about cancer? Pretty soon, a good shower would become just a memory too.

He thought about Art in the twentieth century. Who in their right mind could say Andy Warhol was a step up from Rembrandt? Stockhausen from Bach? Punk rock from the Beatles? History was not a great upward ramp, but a bumpy ride down a muddy track. It had the occasional up—and a lot of downs. He laughed. He'd been thinking the same exact thoughts for years in the shower. He turned the tap, water came out, and along with it his mind spewed the same cranky shit.

What the fuck? The pipes were clanking again. That was new. It was a miracle the shower was still working. It sounded like the whole business was collapsing inside the walls. That was all he needed, to hire a plumber. Those suckers didn't come cheap. At least he had that money now. Split the bill with Liz?

Goddamn Liz.

A louder sound interrupted the stream of thoughts. It wasn't pipes. He cranked the water off. Now came a bang. That was a door slamming, downstairs. He leapt from the shower, threw a towel around his waist, smashed the bathroom door open and tore through the kitchen and down the spiral staircase. Foul smoke streamed up from below. He ran into it, coughing. He reached the floor and stopped. The smoke was coming from the front of the gallery, obscuring the ceiling. But he could see his chair.

Someone was sitting in it, faced away from Ray. Looking out the window, which gleamed in the first morning sun. Wearing his leather jacket and wool watch cap that yesterday had been on hooks by the back door.

Smoke billowed from the figure. Ray raced toward it and skipped around to the front.

It was a man, his legs and lower stomach ablaze. Ray whipped the towel off and reached in to smother the flames, vaguely aware that he was naked to the street. He looked at the face and froze. Ray was looking at *himself*. A crummy version of Ray Watts. It reminded him of some Dada collage—his eyes, nose, mouth and ears were cutouts from a photo of him, pasted to a head of papier-mâché.

He tamped the flames out and carefully wrapped the towel around himself. If anyone saw him from the street, they'd probably call the police, or the men in white coats, but he couldn't stop looking.

On the papier-mâché he made out fragments of typing: "After that initial slip, his mouth…Bassman's funeral…no goodbye to Karl."

It was stuff he'd just written about Karl. The head was intact. From the neck down, the figure was blackened and smoldering. Stapled to the front of Ray's leather jacket, over the heart, was a charred fragment of a blurry black-and-white photo of a face. All that remained was an eye, a cheek, and a hank of hair.

Susan. But she didn't look right.

He raced upstairs and threw on clothes. Back downstairs, he became aware of the stench. Breathing through his mouth, he inspected the horror in his chair, poking with a pen at the still-smoking thing. It was not a corpse, thank God. But part of one. Foot bones protruded from the legs of the pants—tibia, metatarsals? His memory of anatomy class at art school was foggy. A ribcage was visible where the coat had come open. He didn't remember what they called these, aside from ribs, but they looked real. Human. The stink was not just of burning paper and leather, but bone.

He called Bodine. "You awake?"

"I am now. This is early for you."

"You need to come over here, right now."

Bodine must have heard the panic in Ray's voice, because five minutes later, he came running down the sidewalk and banged in through the front door. He stopped. He looked at Ray then at the thing in the chair. He didn't say anything but stepped over and studied it. He laughed. "Burning Man!"

"Huh?"

"That festival out in the desert, Woodstock for the Gen-Yers."

"Ha."

"Never mind." Bodine got serious. He poked around at the mannequin. He picked up a piece of cardboard from the floor. It was a sign, made of letters torn from newspaper headlines, echoing the collage that was Ray's face: ReliquaRAY.

"They're still copping my style." He pointed at the cardboard. "That's the title. I can't say much for their aesthetic sense. But it's another reliquary."

"The name is even a bad pun."

"Touché."

Bodine shook his head. "Karl hated ugly things, and this is nothing if not butt-ugly. But remember how down he was on 'Ego Arts'?"

"Oh yeah."

"No offense at all, but your sculptures would qualify in his book. This mess is him ridiculing your art."

"Which *is* like him."

"Exactly." Bodine pulled up one of the pant legs and studied the bone.

Ray said, "That's real, isn't it?"

"You tell me—you're the bone guy. But, yes. I believe it's a human skeleton. A reliquary for *you*."

"I'm not dead yet. But if I hadn't come down just then, I might be a smoking corpse now. Because once the rest of the room caught fire…" The sense of his house, his self, being attacked had him shrinking inside to a tight ball of loathing.

Bodine must have felt it, because he groaned and shook his head.

"They didn't only invade my shop, ruin my favorite jacket. It's like they've crawled in my head. I don't get it. Could they have copped my style so well just from my website? It's like they know me."

"Well Karl does, of course. At least this is more grown-up than that cat business."

Ray scoffed. "Yeah, he's gone from fifteen to sixteen." He frowned. "What if Karl sent someone here, posing as a customer, and they saw my stuff?"

"Who's been here recently?"

"A couple from the City who bought one of Maurice's sculptures. Some hipsters from Brooklyn."

Bodine shook his head. "They could have gotten all this from your website. What I don't understand is how they could have set this up with you right upstairs. Now, tell me exactly what happened."

"I woke up, really early."

"Tell me about it." Bodine yawned theatrically. "What woke you?"

"I knocked my computer on the floor... No, wait. That's what woke me. There was this crash a little earlier in my dream."

"So another sound woke you up."

"What else? We don't have earthquakes around here."

"It was the sound of whoever delivered this monstrosity."

"I guess. Anyway, I looked at the computer for a minute, got in the shower. I thought I was hearing the pipes complaining, but it was something else. I heard a door slam and raced downstairs."

"So they woke you up, heard the laptop fall and stopped what they were doing."

"Then they heard me get in the shower and finished it."

"Something's not right here. How'd they know you went in the shower?"

"I told you, they heard it."

"Maybe. This is an old house, with thick walls. Go upstairs and turn on the shower."

Ray went in the bathroom, closed the door the way it had been and cranked the taps. The pipes clanked, followed by the roar of water. He came out into the bedroom and Bodine appeared in the doorway.

"From downstairs, that sound could have been anything. Radiator pipes. If I wasn't listening for it, it might have been next door, anywhere."

"Where are you going with this?"

Bodine was silent. He looked around the room.

"Okay, Mister Mysterioso, gimme a clue."

"I'm looking for something little and round. A spy cam."

Ray looked. "What—they were watching me sleep? When did they install it? Karl with computers is weird enough. He's into spy stuff now?"

Bodine shook his head. He pointed to the laptop, which was open on the bed. "When they delivered that dead cat, they also sent emails."

"Which woke me up. I was sleeping then too. Let me check." Ray picked the computer up and looked. "There's a new email. But it's from five minutes ago, so it didn't... It's just spam. The same one came before."

LAZY **SUSAN**, VOTIVE **CANDLES**

Ray said, "Shit. The one before said 'Susans' plural. This is singular." He opened it. There was no text, just a photo. It looked like a copy of the one pinned to the mannequin, only whole and in color. It was Susan's face, all right, but not an expression he'd ever seen. A hand clutched a red cover to her throat. Ray set the computer so Bodine could see, and they both leaned over it.

Bodine said, "Susan?"

"Yes."

"A young Susan. Looks like she did last time I saw her."

"What's that look on her face?"

"Not exactly lazy."

"Scared?"

"Maybe."

Her long dark hair was a mess, splayed over a pillow. "She's in bed." Ray pointed to an ornate headboard at the top of the picture. "This is the same period as the furniture in The House."

"Victorian. I don't know. So's your couch upstairs, and this house."

"True. But that red cover…" Ray found the cat video in his downloads and hit play.

Bodine said, "The cover looks the same. Though Karl was so fussy. It's hard to imagine him having the same bedspread for thirty years."

Ray stared at Susan's face. It took him a moment to put it together. "Oh, God. I had nightmares, imagining this place. The Bedroom." Ray gave it Karl's funny intonation.

"The Bedroom?"

"Karl's. That's his bed. I never told you. Karl was…fucking Susan near the end. I guess I was kind of ashamed to tell you."

"Oh. I'm sorry, man."

"I assumed he was doing it in The Backroom, where he dosed people with acid."

"I knew things were getting funky, but, Jesus. He did that to you?"

"Yeah. In pitch dark. It was after you left. But there wasn't any bed there. It was the last time I tripped before you gave me that Owsley last week."

"I never would have done that if I'd known."

"It's water under the bridge. But Karl took her up to his bedroom. Look at that face again."

"She's tripping her brains out."

Ray said, "Exactly. He dosed her up there."

"Susan wasn't much into drugs, if I remember."

"She wasn't into drugs at all."

This concrete reminder of Susan and Karl's betrayal pitched him back to the day her trip must have happened. He'd spent it hoeing in the garden. If only he'd known. Then what? What difference would it have made? He pictured himself going inside with the hoe, upstairs, into The Bedroom. Ray shook the memory away and scrolled down the laptop screen. The caption was "She's burning again."

Ray flashed on Susan in the car, Susan on the roof in that dream. "The picture was on fire. Susan died in a fire." He looked at Bodine. "It was seeing Susan's obituary that started all this."

"So Karl must have seen it too."

"Not just that. She was coming from visiting him when she crashed. Which still doesn't make sense."

"Not yet. But I think we're getting there." Bodine scrolled the email up to the picture and studied it.

He had that odd look again. Ray said, "What is it?"

"I don't know. Maybe it'll come later. The question is, where is that damned spy cam?" He closed his eyes. Opened them and grabbed the laptop. "Where was this when you were sleeping?"

"Right here on the bed."

"Wait." Bodine clicked around on the keyboard.

Ray leapt back. "Oh fuck!"

He and Bodine were staring from the screen. Looking at themselves, like it was a mirror, in real time. Bodine pointed to a little dark circle above the screen. "There's the cam. This is a light that's supposed to come on, to warn that the computer is recording video, but on this model, it can be disabled remotely from another computer. Which can then see this." Bodine pointed at himself on the monitor, and the image pointed back.

"They're seeing us now!"

"No. Whoever set that fire is on their way back to Karl's. And I'm about to poke their eye out." Bodine popped the battery from the laptop. He pulled a little set of tools from his pocket, used a tiny screwdriver to tweeze the cam from above the screen and pocketed it. He tweezed a tiny microphone from the computer, too. "They're blind now. Deaf, too."

"So they were also listening?"

"I'm afraid so. Not to get too personal, but do you always sleep with the laptop?"

"Yeah. I like to read the news last thing at night."

"And in the morning?"

"First thing when I wake up."

"They've been doing this for a while."

"Watching me in bed?"

"Yep. Today as they carted that monstrosity in here, they kept an eye on their phone. Soon as you woke up, so would your computer. And they'd see. They heard it crash on the floor first."

"They heard the real crash, because they were downstairs setting that thing up."

"Yes. Then you woke the computer, and they saw the virtual you. And saw you go in the shower. And heard you in there. They deliberately slammed the door so you'd come down and see their work before it burned your house down. At least they weren't trying to kill you."

"I suppose."

"I must hand it to the asshole who's doing this. It's some serious hacking."

"How did this spy cam get in my computer?"

"I'll bet if I check that original Lazy Susan email that it has an attachment."

"How'd they get in the house?"

Bodine led the way down to the back door. He pulled a credit card from his wallet and a moment later they were inside again. "Like that. This lock is ancient."

Bodine helped Ray shovel the mess into a couple of garbage cans.

Ray's leather jacket was ruined. "This is the only winter coat I have."

"Why am I not surprised? I have something that should fit you. And let me get rid of this crap for you."

"Hey, you took care of the dead cat too."

Bodine waved his hand. "Maybe I can put it in the museum? No. It's too awful. And stinky. I'm going to get my car. You can come."

"I'll be all right."

Ray sat at the edge of his desk, waiting for Bodine to return. His chair was ruined. He'd have to buy a new one.

When did the camera hack become active? Had they been watching him write? His breath came in short gasps. His imagination let loose. He saw his oculus upstairs, his eye on the world, shrink down to the plastic eye on his computer. He recalled the dream when it rained marbles and he ran from the Eye of God. He'd had it right. They *were* watching him. Literally. And he should run.

He was about to. The energy which had coursed through his hands, which had him writing, no matter how badly Karl wanted him to stop, had over the last minutes spread into arms and legs.

He wasn't running from them. He was going to run *after* them. He couldn't stay here and just let them get him.

And if they saw him through the eye of his computer, he needed to see them. Not with his computer, or by writing. Those were new for him. He needed to see using his old, reliable tool—the naked eye he was born with.

He needed to see, because he needed to know. The questions swirled in his head again—*where's Karl, and what's he doing?* Does he have a group, and, if so, who's in it? He couldn't retreat to the writing anymore. It was done.

He'd known for a while what he had to do.

Bodine came in the back door carrying a coat and hat. "These are pretty warm." He glanced at Ray and said, "What?"

"I'm going to The House."

"And doing what?"

"I'm going to find out who's there."

Bodine slowly nodded. "Okay. But I'm coming too."

"No. This is my business. I'm just planning to look. Then I'll come right back, and we can figure out what to do."

"You're not confronting anybody."

"No!"

"How long are you going for?"

"Long as it takes."

"Well, you'll need some things."

18.

They loaded the garbage cans into Bodine's car and drove them to his house. Mingus came out and went crazy sniffing. Bodine said, "This shit is going to the dump first thing, or I'll have bones all over the place."

They sat in the office. Bodine said, "What's your plan?"

"I need a place to spy from where I can't be seen."

"Given the lay of land as I remember it, that's going to be tough."

"Yeah." Ray pointed to the closet. "You have maps in there?"

"Of course. But there's one right here." He pointed to his main computer. He sat at it and pulled up Google Maps as Ray looked over his shoulder. "First we have to find The House. It was close to that little town, what was it?"

"Piedmont."

"That makes sense. Piedmont means 'foot of the mountain.'" Bodine searched. "Here it is. All this map has is street and town names. I'm going to the US Geological Survey site."

Bodine opened another map in a new window and pointed. "These contour lines are every twenty vertical feet. Houses appear as little squares." As he scrolled around, he pointed. "Here's Piedmont on this map. It's in the valley, which is relatively flat, so the contour lines make these big lazy loops. To the south is the escarpment of the plateau—a steep slope a thousand feet high, where the lines bunch up, and on top hundred-foot cliffs, where the lines are so close, they're almost black. Further south up on the plateau, the lines relax again.

"Just north of the escarpment and running east west parallel to it is the road we took to Karl's. See this square icon with a flag on it? That's the church that was the landmark for our turn. And here's the dirt road that switchbacks up the escarpment. Just as it reaches the top it goes through that slot cut in the cliffs. And this little square is…The House."

The dinky icon didn't do Karl's place justice.

"This crossed-pick symbol next to The House is the old quarry, which it's set in. That's why it's surrounded by cliffs. They're a hundred feet high."

He remembered how oppressive it felt having those cliffs always frowning down. Ray said, "So, there's a new quarry."

Bodine pointed to another cross-pick symbol to the south of the other one. "Here."

"Right. I remember hearing trucks and blasting."

Bodine pointed. "Between the quarries, on the level of the plateau, is this saddle. The road past Karl's winds up more switchbacks to the same level. This turn off leads to the new quarry.

"How old is this map?"

Bodine scrolled. "From the seventies. Let's see how it looks now, with Google Earth."

He opened a third window. The screen was blank for a second, then filled in a square at a time with blurry green and brown blotches, which then snapped into clear focus. Fields and forest with actual trees visible.

Ray said, "The Earth."

"From outer space."

"The Eye of God." Ray wasn't sure if his tone of awe was ironic or the real thing. But it roused Mingus from his bed. He came over and looked up at the computer.

Bodine said, "Huh?"

"Just a dream I had. Never mind." His Googling Susan had been child's play. And his oculus? It was a quaint tool from another century. "Everything looks all squashed down."

"This may be the Eye of God, but the dude's got shitty depth perception. The wages of omnipotence. But check this out." Bodine zoomed in. "Here's The House. We're looking straight down on the roof. See the chimneys? This is the last place I saw that asshole Karl."

It was one thing seeing that dinky square on a map. It was another whole story to view the actual house. Ray's pulse ticked in his neck. "How am I supposed to hide with Google watching me? Won't they be able to see on their computer, just like whoever it was saw me at my house?"

Ray's eyes bugged as he stared at the gardens at the back of The House. He imagined

Karl standing, waving up at him, *Ray, it's been so long...*

Bodine laughed. "Don't worry. This isn't in real time."

"When was it recorded?"

Bodine shook his head. "That's probably some huge secret down at Google. But it wasn't this time of year. See—there's no snow. Up in those mountains, there will still be some now."

Mingus lay down on the floor but stayed awake. Ray pointed to the cliff across the road from The House, to the west. "Why can't I watch from here?"

Bodine zoomed out and traced his finger on the screen. "You'd have to hike miles across these open fields. Someone might see you."

"Right. And I need to be able to peek into the window of The Bedroom. Where do you think it is?"

"Remember those LOLcat photos? There were two reflections in the computer monitor in the picture. According to the clock on the screen, they were taken in the morning. So, we're talking about a corner room, with eastern exposure. Either the northeast or the southeast. It can't be the southeast. That was Karl's office."

"You were up there?"

"Yeah." Bodine looked uncomfortable. "So, The Bedroom's got to be at the northeast corner. Which puts you out of luck. To the east—" he scrolled the map, "—there isn't a road for miles, so you're going to have to bushwhack it. And to the north is that escarpment with the cliff on top.

Bodine zoomed in. "Here's another problem. See these dark lines? They're cracks in the limestone, some of them tens of feet deep. They're a feature of karst topography. I was up there one time. You go wandering in there, you're going to break a leg, or worse. The closest you'll get is that saddle." He pointed. "If you can find a way into the new quarry, you can reach it by following this fence line along the edge of the workings. Once you're there, you'll be able to look right down on The House and gardens, but not into the windows of The Bedroom. You'll still see a light at night."

"But I want to know who's in there."

"Then you're going to have to bushwhack."

"Even with this map, I'm having trouble picturing the lay of the land. How am I going to remember it?"

"I'm going to draw you a map." He did, then handed it to Ray.

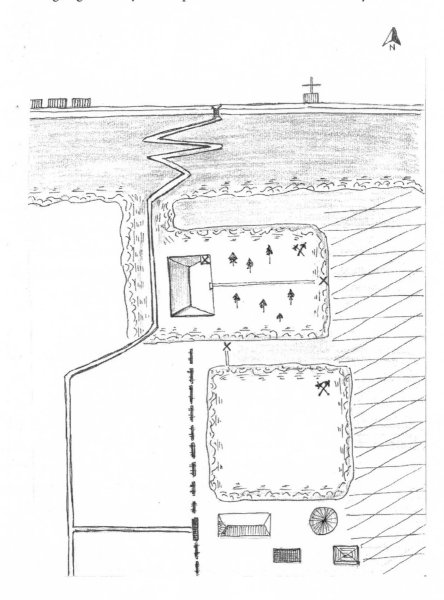

Ray looked at it. "Cartography. Another of your hidden talents."

He put it in his pocket. "You think the quarry is still open?"

"This is as far as we can zoom in. These buildings and vehicles look funky, but that's the nature of quarries. It would obviously be easier if it's closed."

"It was operating then. Working in the garden you'd hear the rumble of trucks and explosions. You ever go up there?"

Bodine laughed. "Remember that big-ass stone, Karl's fucking 'Threshold'?"

Ray said, "How could I forget? He said, 'A door is a *portal*. Be especially aware when you step through.'"

"The Portal to his realm. That's our Karl. Never passed up a chance to be pretentious. He never just walked through a door in his life. The front steps were crumbling, made of some soft stone. Not a fitting entrance for our great leader. So, Karl brought me out there one day, said, 'Find me a *threshold* for my house. Can you believe we bought into that shit?"

It *was* hard to believe. Especially of Bodine. But they had.

"We snuck into the quarry in the night. Climbed the fence. What a pain in the ass—it was fifteen feet high if it was an inch. We found the perfect stone—flat and a nice shape. But we could barely lift it. It was at least four hundred pounds. No way was it going over that fence. We wheeled it there on a cart."

"How'd you open the gate?"

"It had this big old padlock." Bodine grinned. "I'll be right back."

He disappeared into the closet and returned with a key and a can of Liquid Wrench.

Ray shook his head. "You still have it. Where'd you get it?"

"I made it."

"Same as you make programs to hack into other people's computers."

He nodded with a little smile. "Some say."

He handed Ray the key, then the Liquid Wrench. "You'll probably need this."

"What do I do if the quarry's still in business?"

"You'll figure something out."

Ray was having doubts. "This is going to be harder than I thought."

"Most things are once you get into the details."

Bodine returned to the closet and emerged with a sleeping bag and a fistful of Power Bars. Provisions for camping solo in the Adirondacks when he did his yearly acid trip. Ray followed him into the theater, and Bodine headed for one of the museum cases. It was labeled *Dead Eyes* and contained antique viewing devices. Bodine cranked the lid open.

A monocle, spyglass, and Victorian microscope. Bodine handed Ray a cracked leather case. "These binoculars were the best."

"In 1803. Thanks."

Ray glanced to the door. He wanted to get there while it was still light. But Bodine was staring at the museum case, an odd expression on his face.

Ray said, "What?"

"I need to look at those emails again."

They climbed upstairs, and Bodine got into Ray's account. He found the picture of Susan. "I knew there was something about this. You see how crappy the quality is? These lines?" He pointed.

"A bad scan?"

"No. This isn't a photo. And it's not from a cell phone. It's a still. From a video."

"How do you know? Graphics are more my thing than yours, and I can't tell."

"You never told me about Susan and Karl. Well here's something I never told you, that I'm not proud of." He led Ray into the theater and back to the open case. He picked up an old, but not ancient device.

Ray asked, "Is that a video camera?"

"One of the first commercial ones, from the seventies."

"And?"

"Karl had me install one just like it in the wall of his office."

"That's how he taped Susan. Flying on acid."

Bodine nodded. "His office had all these books on religion, and a nice chair. I figured maybe he'd tape himself giving one of his spiels for posterity."

"That doesn't make sense. If you remember, Susan was a bit of a photographer. Early on she told me how she brought a camera to The House.

She tried to take Karl's picture, but Karl said, 'No graven images!' Susan explained that meant no images of God."

"I didn't know that. Maybe he thought it was different if he was doing the taping himself."

"So he got you to do one part of the dirty work, then made someone else move the bed in. The left hand didn't know what the right hand was doing."

"Yep. But this puts you back in luck. You'll be able to see right down into The Bedroom, if he's there."

And avoid bushwhacking with those lethal cracks.

Bodine said, "That's if he's still using it. There are a lot of rooms in that house."

They stood looking at each other. Bodine looked away. He wasn't big on guilt, but even though it was a different camera, it was a glaring exception to his rule about no personal items in his museum. Had he put it there to remind himself? Ray let it go.

He picked up the sleeping bag and headed for the door. "If you don't mind, I'm bringing the laptop you gave me."

"Why?"

"In case I want to write."

"*Writers.* Just don't get it wet. And charge it up. You keep the screen dim it should have three, maybe four hours of life. Uh, I've got one more thing in my closet." He headed up to the office. He returned with a sheepish look and a handgun.

Ray blanched. "What the hell are you doing with that? You're a pacifist!"

"It's a long, long story. I would never use it. I keep meaning to get rid of it."

"Not by pawning it off on me. I'm not taking it."

Bodine followed Ray to the door and grabbed a nylon parka from its hook on the wall. "Well take this, in case it rains. Stay in touch with your cell—but make it short. You need to conserve your batteries. Then again, they may not even have service up there."

"But Susan spoke to Karl."

"He always called her. He could have gone somewhere to call."

Ray opened the door.

Bodine said, "Promise me one thing. You won't go in that house."

Ray looked away. "My promises aren't too good. I seem to remember promising not to write."

"Well, then, don't do anything stupid. You hear me?"

"Yeah." Except the whole time he'd been at Bodine's, that volcano had been simmering in him. Karl had thrown Susan right in his face, a naked, tripping Susan. On that Victorian bed, the same one where he fucked her and taped it for posterity.

Bodine was staring at him. "You're not listening to a word I say. You need to get your shit on the ball. I don't know what you're headed for, but it's no picnic in the mountains this time of year. It's going to be cold at night. You'll have to sleep in your car."

But Ray was barely listening. Karl hadn't just had Susan in that bed. He'd had Crystal.

Which made the flames burn hotter. "I always thought Bassman was the only thing Karl took that couldn't be gotten back. I was wrong. He stole Crystal's chance of having babies. And mine, too."

"How?"

"I was a mess after Susan. It was years before I had a decent relationship. And then it was too late. My girlfriends were too old. Susan and I were going to have kids, before we met Karl."

"I'm sorry. That is some poisonous regret. But right now, you need to focus."

"I hear you."

Mingus trotted over, and Ray gave him some serious petting. He headed home. It was almost balmy out.

Up in the kitchen, he threw food in a backpack, along with the Power Bars and bottles of water. He was a little miffed that Bodine hadn't told him before about installing that video camera. But he'd admitted he was ashamed of it. Which must have been hard. Who knew what damage even macho Bodine had sustained in his time with Karl? Ray thought of the roof and shuddered.

But Bodine's gun? Bodine was as strictly committed to nonviolence as anyone Ray had ever known. He could barely get himself to kill mosquitos when he went camping. Ray shook his head and smiled. Who wanted predictable friends? They were boring.

He remembered something from back then. Ray had been even more weirded out when he found out about Karl's gun.

It was time to go, but he needed to write this while the laptop had power.

***

I was allowed upstairs in The House one time, early on. Ethan ushered me up. With each step, my excitement grew. I was entering the realm of the inner circle! I sniffed the air like it was fresher, looked for signs.

I followed Ethan down a long hall, with closed doors on either side. They were polished to a fine luster. The walls were freshly plastered and painted Karl's signature white. We reached the end of the hall, and Ethan opened a closet and handed me a mop and bucket.

I was disappointed. I got mopping, afraid that at any moment Karl might pop out of one of those doors and give me a withering look. Is that how you mop a floor?

But he didn't show. When I'd mopped the whole floor twice and couldn't get it any cleaner, I opened the closet to return the tools. With one eye out for Karl, I took a guilty look inside.

A broom and dustpan. Rags. A suitcase.

And a rifle. I didn't know anything about guns. This had two barrels. Was it a shotgun? No, the barrels were too slender. The gun looked old, perhaps antique, but the stock was freshly oiled, and the hardware gleamed. The only things in that place that saw such care belonged to Karl. That meant the weapon was his. But what was Karl Maxwell, spiritual master, doing with a gun? Coming out of the sixties, I'd naturally assumed my guru would be a man of peace.

Now I wasn't so sure. Later, when Karl's anger showed, the gun haunted me.

***

Ray emailed this last bit to Lou. They might intercept it. It didn't matter, anyway, because if they came back to his place, he'd be gone. He called his artist friend Maurice, who, once Ray offered him cash, was eager to man the store.

It was getting dark. Too late to leave today.

He had a big breakfast at Jo's early the next morning. He didn't know when he'd eat another decent meal.

As he left, he told her, "I'm leaving for a couple of days."

"Where are you going? You never—"

"Go anywhere. I know. I just need to get away."

She gave him a skeptical look. "So you need food?"

"Now that you mention it, how about one of those little chocolate cakes?"

Back home down in the gallery, he checked his email a last time. Just opening the account made him jumpy—would there be another threat?

A message from Lou: "Call me!"

Ray stood, rocking from foot to foot as he called.

Lou was pumped. "This new stuff is the balls! I cleaned it up, sent it over to that editor and he loves it. Bodine on the roof? That's hardcore. But…sorry about your wife."

"It was a long time ago."

"Your friend, Bassman. That abortion. I knew Karl was a wicked harmonica player. I had no idea he was plain wicked."

"It feels good to be done."

There was a pause. "Done? What about the last thirty years? What's he doing now? Is he even alive? Does he still have that group?"

"Uh, I haven't been able to find any trace of him after that."

"Well, you need to. This is a good beginning. But it doesn't make a book." Lou paused. "Hey—what's this new email from you?"

"I just sent it."

"I'm reading it…a gun! Now we're really talking. How do you know he didn't use it?"

"Maybe he did."

"Well, keep sending me this good stuff. And there's got to be something on Karl on Google. Do I need to do your job for you?"

"No. I'm on it."

Lou hung up. Ray winced. He was never writing about what was happening now with Karl. So, how was the book getting published? He wasn't sure he cared anymore.

***

Ray drove north on I-87. He exited off the highway south of Albany and headed west, past weary houses with scrubby lawns. The neighborhood was unfamiliar. Had he taken the wrong exit?

No. This had been farmland last time he'd been here. Now, it was a crummy suburb of the state capitol. In the years since he'd come this way, these sad houses had been built and had already worn out. As the road started climbing onto the limestone plateau, the falling-down barns and blown-out trailers became familiar. This area was still dirt poor.

As he gained altitude, spring slipped back into winter. Dirty snow smudged the north edges of lifeless brown fields.

Ray rode the rolling hills for a good twenty minutes without crossing a bridge and remembered the reason. Bodine had told him that these Helderberg Mountains concealed a secret: a vast network of caves. A natural sewer system carved in the limestone that swallowed all the streams entering its domain. The rock lay just inches below the skin of soil and in the higher places protruded in layers of dark blue. Pastures dipped down into depressions that funneled rain underground via deep pits. They hid behind clumps of trees left to grow by farmers to keep cows from falling in. The trees now appeared like heaps of cigarette ash. Even in his car Ray felt precarious riding over this hollow earth, as if it might at any moment open and swallow him. Like that cave Bodine had taken him in that time.

He shuddered.

Bodine had said something about rain, but the sky was mostly clear. Even if it poured, every drop would disappear underground. Ray licked his lips, grateful for the bottles of water in the back of the car.

The ruined farms and dreary landscape sucked at his mood. For all the trouble the writing had created over the last weeks, it had given him purpose, pulling him from the worst of his depression. But with each mile, he could feel that purpose leaking away into this dry plateau at the ass-end of winter.

A moment's paranoia made Ray glance in the rearview mirror. No one was following him. There was no one on the road at all. Then he remembered: Karl and the mirror.

Karl had come up once, gotten in Ray's face and stared wordlessly. Ray felt stripped naked, certain Karl was seeing his every thought and feeling. Karl whispered, "I'm a mirror," and was gone. What could he have meant? Ray spent years trying to figure it out.

Now he knew. He'd been looking for some profound explanation. It was so simple, so obvious that he'd missed it. Karl mirrored whatever you presented to him. If you looked scared, he would draw his face back and widen his eyes. He mimicked surprise by raising his eyebrows. If you felt unsure, his lips would quiver. Betray an ounce of anger and Karl would lock demon eyes with yours.

Terror, self-doubt, rage: Karl's famous Negative Emotions. Ray had assumed Karl's role was to reflect their higher selves. What if he hadn't offered the limpid surface of wisdom, but a funhouse mirror, distorting, bringing out the worst in them?

Ray turned off the plateau and descended into a deep hollow. With a shock he saw the first landmark on the way to The House: that church. Up to now, he'd somehow doubted any of this could be real. Though every flake of paint was gone, and the windows were all broken, Ray recognized the church like he'd last driven by yesterday. At its sight, his body began a series of reactions precisely as it had back then whenever he approached Karl's domain.

They were his own somatic Stations of the Cross. The church triggered a hard ticking in his temples. As he swung onto the dirt road, the car lurched into a rut and butterflies swarmed in his gut. Coming up the switchbacks and the butterflies became frenzied, hating the altitude. As he entered the darkness of the slot in the cliff, scrambling to turn on the headlights, he held his breath.

As the reactions accelerated, he slipped into the future, anticipating the coming reactions. In just seconds, with the first glimpse of the blue walls of The House, his palms would turn slippery on the wheel. By the time he parked—and not in the ditch, but not in the road either, *or else!*—he'd be practically hyperventilating. Walking down the hill from his car, his whole body would thrum with his pulse. And then pausing before the door, he'd hit the top of the crescendo of anxiety, every muscle coiling in upon itself. Inside, and suddenly he'd be numb with resignation.

As he reached the exit of the slot, he slammed on the brakes. He wasn't going in that door, or even driving past The House. He'd come to snoop on whoever was there, but what was to stop them from seeing him? What if they were waiting for him, had lookouts, in the windows, atop the cliffs? Whoever had placed a dead cat in this car would recognize it. How many old blue Volvos were there out in this poor part of the state? The few vehicles he'd seen were ancient pickup trucks, rusted out jalopies.

He slowly backed up, out of the slot and down the switchbacks. With nowhere to turn around, death was just a slip of the wheel away. He white-knuckled it down, his neck straining from staring into the rearview.

He reached the bottom, pulled out onto the main road and headed back the way he'd come. He felt a huge letting down, as he had every time leaving The House. And the sudden urge for a beer. Not today.

He had a rough idea how to reach the quarry. He climbed again onto the plateau. He drove maybe twenty minutes, but they seemed interminable. Stained teeth of limestone loomed high above the trees, and he slowed.

The road ahead on the right must be the one. Ray's skin again prickled with paranoia. His eyes darted around. There was no one behind him. No one in that field. No one in the woods. He slowed, turned, and gunned the car into the turn.

It was barely a track, with no signs of recent use. Which suggested that the quarry was closed. The road crossed an area of broken rock spotted with anemic bushes. There was no snow here to show his tracks.

He entered a line of trees and slammed into a foot of snow. He slid across, hit mud. It slurped at the tires, and he gunned the engine, slipping to one side, just missing a tree. What the hell was he going to do if he got stuck? It was not an option. He found himself driving with a skill he didn't have.

He was relieved to reach the tall iron fence. It was rusted, but still appeared solid. Ray climbed out. It had the biggest padlock he'd ever seen. He squirted Liquid Wrench into the hole and waited. A gust of cold wind slapped his face. All he could see over the enclosure were those limestone teeth, which up close seemed not only discolored but suffering serious decay.

The lock succumbed to Bodine's key with a rude creak. He hung the lock on the hasp and pushed the gate open with a shriek that chewed at his nerves. He relaxed. The mountain between him and The House had muffled dynamite before. He put the key in his pants pocket.

He drove through and closed the gate. Should he lock it? Nobody had been in here in years. But he'd feel safer if he did.

It was tricky fumbling blindly around the gate post to close the lock, but the shackle finally snapped home.

He got in the car and followed a faint track past a dilapidated warehouse. He turned a corner and the limestone workings revealed themselves. He stopped the car. There was no doubt about its being abandoned. No one had been here in years. Though Ray considered himself ecologically minded, he'd thought talk of the "rape of mother earth" was over the top. No longer.

It wasn't just that quarry men had torn half of the mountain away. They'd left the place an obscene mess. A crumpled network of rusted conveyor belts and sluiceways fed shattered concrete silos. A gantry had collapsed on itself, soot-black, like a monster grasshopper caught in a brush fire.

Ray followed the road around the side of the silos, He squeezed the Volvo between a shed and one of the larger buildings, satisfied that it was well hidden. Not that anyone was coming here.

He got out of the car and stood surveying the scene. A series of wide ramps cut into the stone descended from where he stood to a pond filled with some black substance. Across it, he faced a sheer hundred-foot cliff. The right side of it was half buried in a chaos of rotted timbers and bent corrugated sheets. To the left side was the fence, this side hugged by a narrow path leading up to the saddle, just inches from a sheer wall of the quarry.

The wind picked up, whistling in the structures, a moment later startling him as it angrily slapped tarpaper against the remains of a caved in roof.

His dark mood from the plateau returned and deepened. During the last year, before the writing, Ray had imagined himself at the bottom of something. Even in the bitter weeks after Liz's departure, even at his most vilely hung-over, he'd never gotten this low. He tumbled into an abyss of black thoughts.

His true love, the past, was doomed. All his attempts to remember, all the attempts anyone had made to remember, all the history books, photo albums, memoirs added up to nothing against the landslide of forgetting. From the dreams of these quarrymen long dead to all the lost ancestors of the human race, it was all gone. Trillions of sea creatures had died to make this limestone, and no one gave a thought to them. All the memories of everyone alive were merely feeble wisps crushed under mountains of forgetting.

He'd set his history with Karl in words, thinking it would set him free. That was delusion. All along the writing had just been a final embrace from his true love.

There was a word for this feeling. Despair. It was substantial, black and viscous, like that poison in the quarry pit. It seeped into his veins, weighing his limbs down. The muscles in the back of his neck strained to keep his head from rolling down onto his chest. He felt a terrible urge to lie down on the dirty rock, shut his eyes, and just give up.

But he kept standing for long minutes, as the place worked its malignant spell on him. Finally, he shook it off like a wet dog and dragged himself back to the car.

19.

He strapped the sleeping bag to the pack, put it on and hiked along the fence, the quarry yawning just past it to his right. The fence ended at a tower of rock, all that remained of the original top of the mountain. He skirted it to the right and reached the saddle between the lips of the two quarries. They were fifteen feet apart. The ground was flat, bare limestone. It was midafternoon and sunny. The wind was steady, with a bite that quickly chilled his sweaty chest and promised a bitter night. He stood and drank in the sight of the Mohawk valley with hazy bumps of the Adirondacks in the distance. A fine view, but not the one he'd come for.

Now that he was here, he was reluctant to look. Some superstition told him that once he set eyes on the thing, he'd be committed. There was also the cliff before him. He didn't like heights, and it was a hundred feet to the bottom. In order to see, he'd need to get close to its edge.

But the desire to see rose in him and pushed him forward a single step, and then another. The torpor of a few minutes ago was gone. A new feeling arose: dread. In just a moment, he'd see, and then it would be too late. He took another step.

The top of a chimney. He froze. Seeing the roof on Google Earth at Bodine's had been a shock. This was hyperreal, as jolting as a sudden hallucination. He stared, and the bricks and concrete lost their solidity and shimmered against the sky.

Another step and half of the roof came into view. *They can see me!* No, not unless they were up on the roof, which was very unlikely. Ray inched forward a half step, and there was the edge of the roof, and he was in Bodine's shoes, eyes closed, walking that lethal perimeter. The cliff edge before Ray, the great expanse of air below tugged at his core, pulling him down, toward disaster.

He hopped back from the precipice, turned and ran several paces. He stopped short. The other cliff yawned right in front of him. He pivoted back toward The House. Got down on hands and knees and crawled toward it. With his head a foot from the edge, he fell to his belly and squirmed forward the last inches. His chin rested on the edge.

He could see the whole back of The House. He focused on the center of the first floor, on two bricked in windows.

The Backroom.

Karl knew everything about Ray. Certainly about his compulsion to watch. Karl had known Ray would eventually come here, which was why he'd sealed those openings, so Ray couldn't see in...

Craziness. He shook it off. It was just sealed windows in a big, ugly house. Not Google's picture of it, or Ray's recent words depicting it, or the fantastic place that had lived all these years in his imagination, but the actual house, as real and solid as this mountain of limestone.

And it was made of that same limestone. It was what gave these mountains their name, Helderberg. In Dutch, it meant "light stone." Which was how it looked in the quarry. But it was moody stuff. This time of day, the back of The House cast a massive shadow that swallowed most of the garden, and the stone appeared a dark blue-gray that seemed to bleed a chill out into the yard.

He sat cross-legged on the hard ground. He tried the cellphone. No bars. And he was high up. Karl must have gone someplace to call Susan. The wind had died down. He listened. He picked up a faint rushing sound—traffic up on the interstate? blood in his ears?—but not a peep from The House.

Ray looked down at the window of The Bedroom. All he saw inside were the vague shapes of blinds. Karl might be there. Or not. From what Bodine said, depending on how many people were there, they could be in any or all of the rooms of The House.

Whoever was there would presumably use the kitchen. It was on the first floor, in the northeast corner, its three windows extending toward him. He could, in theory, see into the nearest, but right now, it was dark.

Come night, whoever was in there would use a light. And he'd see who was there. See Karl, even if he just had a candle.

Ray studied the tower of rock that had been the top of the mountain. Its surface facing him was flat except for a dark opening at the bottom, two feet high and extending the width of the saddle from one cliff to the other. He crouched down and poked his head in. A little cave, going in about six feet. He flashed on that cave Bodine had taken him in. It had started with hundreds of feet of crawlway. He didn't like tight places. Didn't like caves.

This one had been truncated by the quarrying. That was probably the reason they'd stopped working the limestone up here. If it were riddled with holes, it would be useless. According to Bodine, all the caves in the area were connected, though in some cases "you'd have to be a flea to make the connection." By that token, this teeny one was connected to the huge one he'd gone in with Bodine as well as the grotto in the garden below.

While he didn't like caves, he hated camping and waking up with it raining. The sky was clear now, but the wind suggested that might change. If it stayed clear, it was going to be cold tonight. Bodine had said something about caves maintaining the temperature of the earth. So, he should be warmer sleeping it the cave. And drier if it rained.

He inched into the low opening, pulling his gear in with him, fighting the shrinking inside as he breached the tight space. He turned and crawled toward The House. He lay with his head at the edge of the cliff and looked. His loathing of the closed space was somewhat mollified by the sense that the ceiling would keep him from tumbling over. He was also invisible to anyone looking from The House, even if they were on the roof.

This was his new aerie, with hard rock to lie on instead of a comfy couch. There was no round window to keep out the elements. But it provided the essential of any aerie: a place to spy on prey unseen.

Now that he was safe, he could really look. The House was as ugly and ill-proportioned as he remembered. This angle did not flatter it. The roof was too tall, the cornice too wide, its edge laden with the ruins of concrete gargoyles. The effect was not only rude to the eye but caused a visceral sense that the whole top of the house might at any moment tumble down on anyone looking up from below.

In truth, the roof looked sound. Karl had said of it, "This will last a hundred years, longer than any of us," adding with a twinkle, "Probably."

Was he hinting he might live forever?

The gargoyles had suffered in the years since the group. Some were missing, leaving scars like yanked teeth. It was impossible to tell if the remaining lumps of concrete had been intended to be gods or demons, for the weather had eroded most of their features. In the center of the roof's edge a few segments of a serpent remained.

Birds periodically flew up and squawked. Had he taken their nesting place? Would Karl notice their fuss? He remembered how silent it had been in there with those thick stone walls. He'd never heard a thing from outside except once during a violent storm. Even then, the thunder was just distant thuds.

Ray studied the house for signs of occupation. The stones of its back wall gave no clue. They'd look the same in three hundred years whether someone was there or not. The windows were framed in stone, so there was no telltale peeling paint. The only difference he could see in the gardens from then and now was the trees. He remembered planting some of them. Now, they were thirty feet tall. They'd actually turned out okay once they'd grown high enough to get some sun.

There was no group in there. The place was just too silent. Someone had always been going out to the well to the right side of The House. He looked in that direction for a path in the snow but couldn't see it because the land dipped down there.

Then he remembered. It was this time of year, early spring, that Karl led the pilgrimage to his teacher in England. That guy, miraculous longevity aside, had to be dead by now. But maybe they still went anyway, out of habit. For all Ray knew, they were there at this moment, and he'd come to spy on a vacant house.

On pilgrimage, when Karl began fucking Susan.

Ray shook away the thought. What was important was that Karl always left some people behind when they went. Including the deliverer of Ray's smoking doppelganger, who Karl presumably directed via email. So, where were they? Ray was missing something. He stared a long time.

What was it about the chimneys? He stared at them.

There was no smoke. Unless someone was in there freezing their ass off, the place was empty.

Except some person had shot the video of the cat in that room right in front of him. Had they left? Just come to The House to do that? None of it made any sense.

He enjoyed sitting at home on a comfy couch with a drink and looking out his window. This was a whole other gig: surveillance. The boredom manifested as a sickness in his muscles. It must be lactic acid buildup or some such. What had happened to that volcano of rage? It was dormant, but not likely extinct.

Ray had a moment's clarity. His heart was like the karst landscape of this plateau, subject to subterranean forces he couldn't understand. And this was no mere intellectual theory. These mysterious influences were what had him up on this cliff, trying to see, and damn the consequences.

He returned from his reverie, scooted forward a few inches and looked down at the back yard.

The path. It was free of snow. He felt a fluttering inside. The first thing he'd written about Karl involved that path. He hadn't finished it. He fussed the computer out of his backpack. He could barely get it open in the cave. This was too awkward for writing. He brought it out onto the rock saddle. It was windy but not too cold. Bodine's binoculars were ready by his side in case he heard something.

The battery was already down by a half-hour, and he hadn't even used the laptop. He hadn't remembered to shut it down before bringing it here. He must be more careful.

He found the file and read: *It was chilly that morning working in the shadow of The House…*

He continued.

***

Karl brushed the dirt away from the stones. "You've found a path." I struggled frantically to understand his meaning. This physical path? The Secret Path he sometimes spoke about? Or both?

How could Karl not see the silver gash I'd made in the stone? Was he deliberately overlooking it, setting me up? As far as I knew, nothing escaped his gaze.

He drew a line in the air from the three stones, projecting it toward the foot of the cliff. "Dig it up. Bring it up from the earth, then clean it." I pictured the path when it was done. Every stone washed, gleaming in the sun, me stepping onto it barefoot, stepping into a perfect future. I'd have arrived on The Path. I was replaying my first time on acid, when I'd stepped barefoot into a perfect spring day. That time I had arrived somewhere.

Not now. As I labored to uncover the stones, I entered an all-too-familiar and mundane state: anxiety. I mustn't leave the hint of another shovel mark on what I uncovered. And I had to work fast, because that's how everything was done. Karl had me well trained by now. He didn't have to stalk up and glare at me. No dawdling! I could see him do it without him even being there.

A week and a half, and I was almost finished. The line of stones ended at a pile of junk at the base of the cliff with a black space behind it. Karl had been absent since I started the job. With his usual impeccable timing, he reappeared.

He pointed into the darkness. "What do you think that is?"

A cave? It couldn't be that easy. Like all his questions, this was a challenge, a teaching moment. If I could only make some leap of consciousness I'd come up with the right answer. Not just the right words, but I'd learn whatever it was he was trying to impart.

But all I had was a mumbled "I don't know."

He said, "Find out. You have until this afternoon."

Finding out involved cleaning up all the junk. I humped it. I hauled old tires, a rotting mattress, and broken shutters around the north side of the house and neatly stacked them by the trash cans.

When I was done, I saw the entrance of a small cave. I consulted Bodine, who'd somehow found the time to become quite the expert on the local caves. Talking to him was permitted because it involved my task.

He pointed to a dried-up pool surrounded by bad knock-offs of Greek statues. "This is a grotto," he said. "They were all the rage back in the Victorian times. Just the thing if you owned a mansion or castle with a formal garden and wanted to get over on your neighbors. Often, they were artificial, but it helped to have a real cave to work with. Which it looks like this is."

He pointed to stalactites wired to the ceiling, which appeared dusty and lifeless. He said, "Those look real, but Karl isn't going to like them."

He was right. When Karl came to see them, his face twisted into a pained expression. He looked at me deadpan. "This is appalling. Fix it." He stalked away.

I told Bodine. He said, "I don't know what you can do about it. But I do know some cavers around here."

I raised my eyebrows. How? We weren't to have contact with outsiders.

"Never mind." He wrote a phone number down on a piece of paper. "Call this guy."

I met the caver at the pizza joint down in Piedmont. He was grizzled, with a lopsided grin. About what you'd expect for a guy who got off on crawling around in the dark and mud.

He asked, "You new to the area?"

"Uh, I've been here a few years. I'm helping someone fix up their house."

"You're a carpenter? Contractor."

"No, actually it's their garden."

"You're a gardener."

"Right. There's this little cave at the back of the garden." I explained what I'd seen.

"A grotto." He curled his lip. "The reason those stalactites in there look like shit is because they're dead. They've been cut off from their blood supply—water."

"So if I found new ones and hung them in there, how long would they look alive? Maybe you know where I can get some?"

He groaned with disgust, closing his eyes. Opened them and looked at me as if I was asking him to join a ring of child molesters. He gave me the rap. It didn't sound like the first time. "Cave formations are irreplaceable. It can take a hundred years for them to grow a single centimeter. Besides, around here most of the good stuff was plundered long ago by assholes like whoever made that grotto."

"I'm sorry. I had no idea. Any way I can hook the existing stalactites up again? Or fake it?"

The guy shook his head mournfully. But then he got a gleam in his eye. "This house with a grotto—it must be big. Fancy. It wouldn't be that ugly place up that switchback road where the quarries are?" He pointed up the mountain toward Karl's.

I scrambled. I'm not a good liar. "No, no, it's up by Albany."

He cocked an eyebrow but let that go. "You ever seen the house here?"

"Never heard of it."

"There's an old rumor of a monster cave on that property. And the geology's just right. Some cavers went up there years ago, but the owner didn't seem too friendly, chased them away. The place was abandoned after that. But I hear there have been cars up there recently."

He was getting way too close. I said, "Well, I have to go. Have to get up, go to work. But thank you."

"Any time. And hey—you want to go caving sometime, give me a call. We have a nice beginner's cave. See how you like it."

No thanks.

"And if you hear anything about that big cave…I'd give my left nut to get in there."

I drove back to the farmhouse Susan and I were renting. What was I going to do with that cave? I bought some polyurethane and painted the dead formations. It made them gleam as if they were for sale at Wal-Mart. Karl would never buy it. The only solution was to clean everything out, speleothems and lame statues, make it pristine. I could hook up a pump and fill the pool. Find a tasteful statue— a Buddha? Something Hindu? It was too dangerous second-guessing Karl on that, so I left the statue out.

Karl came to inspect. He swept his hands over the walls where the dead speleothems had hung. "You've ruined it."

I felt like I'd done something terrible, but at the same time I was certain— what he'd demanded of me was impossible. He could ask you for a rainbow, and you'd bring him a real one, wrapped with a bow, and he'd say, "Ray, you got the wrong one."

***

Caves. He remembered another part of the story. It was just a little anecdote, but Lou might like it.

***

It turned out that caver guy was right about the big cave. Burt was one of Karl's old roadies, not too bright, but hulking and muscled from years of lugging around giant PA systems. Karl pulled a version of his mirror trick on Burt, letting the big guy see himself in the task Karl assigned.

The basement flooded in spring. Karl told Burt to dig a hundred-foot-long trench, six feet deep. It was a job for a bulldozer. All Burt had was a shovel and his machismo. Without dynamite, it turned out to be just about impossible. The soil lying on the old quarry floor was at most only a few feet thick. As Burt dug down, he kept hitting bedrock. As I hoed in the garden, I'd hear the regular pings of his shovel on stone, followed by anguished growls.

He was persistent. Did Burt ever get what Karl was trying to make him see? In any case, at some point he got smart. He gave up on digging outside and moved inside to the little room at the north end of the basement, opposite the foyer. He'd heard about that cave system in the area, that there'd once been an entrance in the bowels of The House.

It was filled with dirt, but in a few hours, he dug into open passage. Burt trenched the floor and the next spring the water in the basement drained away into the cave. He made a wall of loose bricks to cover the entrance.

***

Karl was away the Sunday Bodine took me into the cave. He sidled up to me where I was working, grinned, and placed a finger to his lips. This was definitely not part of our practice with Karl. He handed me a flashlight and led me to the basement.

Bodine pulled the bricks from the entrance and clicked his light on and pointed it in. It looked like a natural sewer pipe, about three feet around.

I asked, "We're going in there?"

"It'll be fun."

"It doesn't look like fun."

"Burt told me he reached the end and popped out on the side of the mountain.

Said it was a real trip, coming out from that cold, dark place into glorious sunshine, bright green leaves. A literal rite of passage."

"Burt called it that? That doesn't sound his style."

"No, actually he said it was like 'getting born from Mother Nature's muddy snatch.' You'll like it."

I was a sucker for mythic experiences.

"The moment you want to turn back, we'll leave."

Sure.

***

Ray shut the computer down and crawled back into his little cave. He ate a couple of granola bars then waited for dusk. What time was it? He fumbled for his cell phone. Six-thirty. He remembered Bodine warning him about the batteries and turned the phone off. Up here, it was just a glorified clock.

A brilliant flash of light. Ray recoiled and banged his head against the ceiling of his lair.

He scurried back into the gloom, his head throbbing.

Karl was on the roof, training a klieg light onto Ray. Karl had known he was there all afternoon, was just waiting to... No. It was only the last of the sun peeking into the narrow cave entrance.

He lay motionless. The sun crept into the lair, drenching him in light. In minutes, it was gone. It must only shine in here that brief time each day. *Like the light of awareness.* Something Karl would say.

The dark came fast, and with it the temperature plunged. The cold penetrated his legs first, borne by a breeze blowing into the cave. He struggled into the sleeping bag and watched.

The House gradually dissolved in the murk. Finally, its back was just a black mass, the roof peak lit by the moon, itself invisible from this narrow aperture. The dread had leaked away over the hours, leaving him bored and lethargic. He struggled to stay conscious.

A faint whirring sound and he looked up. The blinds in the two windows of The Bedroom glowed like great lamps, like demonic eyes. *He sees me.* Ray came wide awake, his heart thundering.

Karl couldn't see him—not with it light in there and dark out here—but he was there.

In The House, just a few hundred feet away. In The Bedroom. And that was no candlelight illuminating the window, spilling out onto the limestone walls. He had electricity. Which was why there was no smoke coming from the chimneys. He had electric heat. Karl was probably at the computer right now, checking his email. As Bodine said, people change.

Fuck. Karl couldn't see Ray, but Ray couldn't see him. He stared as if his eyes could burn through the shades. He didn't hear anything aside from the faint rustling of leaves. But if stuff outside was inaudible when you were in The House, the converse would be true.

That whirring was the sound of a generator staring up. What if the group was on pilgrimage and the light on a timer, and no one was there? Could a generator start by itself?

A momentary blur, and a silhouette appeared behind the shade. It electrified him, and his body sprung up, his back slamming into the ceiling.

Karl. Though his back screamed with pain, Ray lay frozen, transfixed, waiting for another shadowy appearance. There was nothing. Finally, the light winked out and the whirring sound stopped. It was around eleven.

It was time to leave. He'd gotten what he came for. Karl was there. But he wasn't hiking down next to that gaping quarry in the dark, even if there was a fence.

He'd get up tomorrow and go home. Bring a six-pack over to Bodine's, tell him all about it. Bodine would be amused. Ray would send Lou an email, saying he couldn't finish the book. Karl, in turn, would intercept it, which would deliver Ray's message to him: I'm done. Done with writing. He'd have to return the money to that publisher, find another place to live, get a job.

Right now, he needed to get some sleep. He huddled in the sleeping bag. The rock hurt to lie on no matter which way he turned. This morning's despair seeped back into him, as though it originated in the limestone itself, the grave of those long dead sea-things.

Finally, he dozed.

***

He woke to the sound of rustling. His body launched up and his head slammed on the rock ceiling. He let out a cry. As the agony subsided, he became acutely aware of his vulnerability, trapped in this rat-hole with only one exit. He pictured Karl, creeping up from the quarry with that gun. Coming to shoot Ray, or just shove him over the cliff. Was Karl here already, waiting for Ray to fall asleep again?

The rustling came again. It wasn't subtle, not the sound of someone creeping around. Ray pulled the Mag-Lite from the pack and lay still waiting for the sound. When it came, he clicked the light on. He flinched at the sight of movement from the corner of his eye.

A rat. A cave rat.

After they'd emerged from the cave, Bodine had carefully stacked the bricks to cover the entrance. Ray asked why. "We wouldn't want cave rats getting in The House. They're hungry bastards with nothing to eat down there. They get in The Kitchen, who knows what kind of fit Karl will throw."

Ray was relieved to know that Karl was not up here stalking him. Except when he opened his pack, he found that the little fuckers had pinched the last of his food. Now, he was going to have to go home tomorrow.

Ray tried to get back to sleep. The rock was hard, and he was cold, but that wasn't the problem. The fluttering feeling him from before was back with a vengeance. He was jazzed, like he'd sucked down a quart of coffee.

He'd seen Karl, and the old doubt was back. Was Karl a living god or an asshole? Had Ray escaped by the skin of his teeth or made the biggest mistake of his life?

There was also the issue of Susan. The question of just what had happened to her had been eating at him, but now it was urgent. She'd been married with kids, had a good job. She'd walked away from the group and, according to Lorraine, never looked back. No matter how he tried, he could not picture Susan coming up to this spooky house to see Karl.

Karl might have blackmailed her, and maybe she'd sent him money. But why in the world would she come here? And why then would she crash her car on the way home?

There might be no answers in that house, but there certainly weren't any back in Hudson.

He had to *know* about Karl, and about Susan. The questions assumed visceral life in a tight ball of energy at his core. It radiated out into coiled muscles. Despair, dread, and certainly boredom were gone. There was just this urgency.

To do what? His fingers were twitching. He got the laptop out. There were only seven minutes left on the battery. But he'd forgotten something. Something important.

He had to scoot back in the cave to make room for the computer. Typing was still awkward. He turned down the screen light in case Karl woke, looked out the window and caught a strange electronic glow up on the cliff.

***

One day in the last months of the group, I was taking the trash out when Karl appeared. Was I holding the bags wrong? Had I missed the enlightened way to carry garbage? These were the same kind of dreary thoughts his appearance had evoked for years, but with a new edge of sarcasm. I still didn't know consciously, but I was very close to leaving.

Karl deadpanned his face and drilled me with those eyes. In retrospect, it was his final shot at getting over on me. And it was a direct hit. "It's time."

My mind whirled. Time for what? Time to get your shit together. Time to get serious with the exercises—but how much more serious could anyone be in a day than five thousand attempts to follow a mantra that made no sense, a million instances of bearing down inside, pushing to reach Karl's level?

Now, "It's time" became my mantra. I was getting nowhere with it, grinding my mental gears until they slipped. All I could come up with was the argument: I'm not ready. I'm never going to be ready. But it no longer had me in a panic. It just made me tired.

Yet in no time, magically, it was time. Time to leave the group.

20.

It's time. Ray looked at the silent, dark house. He noticed that his head was nodding. His body had known for a while and his head had just caught up.

It was time to go in The House. Not with the writing, but for real. He needed to see just how Karl was living, see if he had a group. And maybe there were clues to Susan's last day.

Had he just made this decision, or was it made when that silhouette appeared in the window? Was it when he got in the car in Hudson, or when he first Googled Susan? Or even before? It didn't matter.

But he didn't want to see Karl face to face. He shuddered. What if he did?

In the months after leaving the group, he'd often been visited by a vivid fantasy, a recurring waking dream.

Ray hides in the garden in back of The House. Karl inspects the trees— they're growing too slowly! Ray sneaks up on Karl from behind, soundlessly, turning the tables. He slaps a hood soaked in chloroform over Karl's big head. Karl slumps down. Ray drags him over to the well. He yanks off the heavy concrete top and lowers Karl down on a rope. Gets a ladder and climbs down there and sets him lying face up. Drowning would be too easy. Ray climbs out, pulls up the ladder, and replaces the lid.

Karl wakes in pitch black. When his seductive whisper doesn't bring some minion to the rescue, he raises his voice and finally bellows. The sound is very undignified, very unlike Karl. He cowers in the dark, shivering in the cold and pondering his sins: wife-fucking and mind-fucking. Scamming money. Wasting years of his disciples' precious youth in fruitless and self-destructive pursuit, all to feed his monstrous insatiable ego.

Every morning Ray throws him a sack of rotten meat and a bottle of water, to keep him alive for another day of torment.

The scenario had a fairy-tale cast to it, of kids fallen down wells, of monsters caught and punished. His face burned. Here was that volcano. It wasn't extinct. And it had been here ever since the end of the group.

If Ray had come here intending to face Karl, he would have marched up to the Front Door this afternoon and knocked. He wasn't going in the Front Door, period. Karl would definitely keep it locked, and unlike Bodine, Ray was no lock-picker.

He needed to sneak in, now, while Karl was asleep.

How? The cave in the basement had that other entrance. All he knew was that it was "out on the mountain." Even if he found it, he didn't know what the passage would entail. But what Ray had seen that time with Bodine was bad enough. They'd turned around because he'd chickened out.

He looked down on the gardens. At the junction of the north and east cliffs was a steep slope of quarry rubble—the one place you could descend without a rope. But getting there would mean bushwhacking in the dark with those lethal cracks lurking.

Even if he got past them and down the cliff, he'd have to walk across muddy ground or snow to get to The House, leaving obvious tracks.

He could just picture Karl strolling out back, rubbing his hands together like he did, smiling up at the sun, *time for the vernal equinox.* It would not do for him to look down and see footprints in the snow.

Ray's eyes moved down. Gleaming wetly in the light of a three-quarter moon, free of snow, were the dark stones of the path. The thing he'd just been writing about. If he walked across it in stocking feet, whatever traces he left would burn away in the morning sun. He remembered how the east cliff was overhung at the bottom. He looked. That overhang was hidden behind a ridge of snow that had fallen from the cliff top. Once he reached the bottom of the rubble slope, he could work his way behind the ridge of snow to the beginning of the path.

Was he really going to do this? His body, which had been agitating to go, was suddenly heavy and drained of energy, as if the agitation had abandoned it for his mind. He lay there as it fretted, raising objections, doing its job. Because what he was contemplating was crazy.

The wind stirred, its fingers shaking the new leaves in the woods. Now, it reached into the back of the cave. It was warmer than the previous breeze.

The moonlight faltered, then went out, and darkness fell, like an immense blanket. A moment later the moon came on again. If he was going, it had to be now, while there was still a chance of moonlight.

He crawled from the cave, stepped onto the saddle and headed east. Half the sky was filled with clouds, their edge playing with the moon. It lit his way across the saddle, but as he entered the trees it flickered out again. He fished the Mag-Lite from his pocket and clicked it on, then immediately off. It was too bright. If Karl happened to look out the window, he would see it.

Ray stopped. He needed to walk some distance into the woods, away from the house, then make a diagonal toward the rubble slope. With the cliff higher than the window the light should be no problem. But that wouldn't help with the noise. The wind in those leaves was intermittent and unpredictable.

Ray stepped forward, then stopped again. *Those cracks.* He was going to need to take his shoes off before crossing the path below if he wanted to avoid leaving muddy prints. He might as well do it now and have the sole and toes of his feet to sense with.

He crept forward, feeling with a foot, keeping his weight back in case it found a crack. His lower back started complaining right away. Not ten feet into the woods, his toes sensed a void and he jerked it back, staggering, crashing into a bush, almost falling on his ass. The noise was like thunder.

Had he woken Karl up? He could picture him lying there wondering. Listening for another sound. One that Ray couldn't make.

He cupped the Mag-Lite in a hand, switched it on—*did Karl hear that?*—and pointed it down. The crack was over a yard wide. He inched forward to the edge. The crack went down as far as the light could reach. He shuddered. He could maybe jump it, but Karl would surely hear, would know it was no animal up here.

What now? The wind died down. He reached to his left and brushed an arm against a bush. It didn't sound different than that breeze. If he moved very slowly, very carefully, he'd be covered.

He'd come east into the woods. The crack was perpendicular to him, which meant it was roughly parallel to the cliff. He moved north along the crack, staying a good foot away from it. Ray couldn't believe how dark it was. Even with the flashlight on, the darkness was like a sentient thing that chewed at the edges of the tiny circle of light he cast on the ground.

He felt pressure at his chest and jerked away, something slapping him in the face. He trained the light up. He'd walked into a tree. He carefully skirted it and got back to the crack. It would not do to get lost up here.

The trees became sparse and the undergrowth thick. He zigged and zagged to avoid the bigger bushes. Moving at this snail's pace, it was impossible to know how far he'd come. And it was far more taxing than running flat out. He was panting, out of shape, long-idle muscles complaining. The temperature was in the forties, but the exertion had him soaked.

He clicked the Mag-Lite off and stood in the dark. With an intense fanfare of wind, the moon reappeared. The wind settled down. He looked to his left and saw the top of the roof. He was just about even with the top of the rubble slope. The wind was picking up, rattling leaves and making branches creak. And he was done with this excruciating pace. He waded fast through the undergrowth to the slope.

It was steeper than it had looked from his aerie. He scrambled, then half-fell down it, clutching at bushes so he wouldn't fall on his face. He hunched over and inched along the recess in the cliff behind the snowbank. His back didn't like it, but he soon reached the grotto and the head of The Path.

How could he get to it without leaving footprints in the snow ridge? It was too high and wide to jump over. He rolled over it on his back, landing with a foot on the first stone. He'd left an indentation in the snow, but no footprints. He hopscotched toward The House. Once he got going, he couldn't stop. He didn't miss any stones. He crossed the snow ridge on the other side the same way, rolling on his back. He was learning all kinds of new tricks.

Because of the cut of the old quarry, the basement lay underground on the south and west sides of The House. It was a walk-out here. The Path led to a door, which had always been locked. He tried it. It still was.

The wide eaves of the roof made it easy to walk between the snowbank and the back wall. He headed south and around the corner. The snowbank continued. Inside of it six feet away was his goal—the casement window in its brick well. He lay down with his chin on the edge of the bricks and peered into the window. The glass was thick with dust, but a dim light flickered inside. Blood beat in his temples.

Karl's new group is meeting down there.

He knew this window because Ethan had once tasked him with cleaning it. When Ray had reached the top of the ten-foot ladder, he found that the latch was broken. He knew he should fix it, but it was a hundred years old, impossible to duplicate. So, he'd left it. Who would ever know? With luck, no one had fixed it since.

The window opened in, which was good, because otherwise there'd be no room to both get it open and squeeze inside. He pushed against the glass, and it moved an inch. The latch was still broken. But as he tried to move it further it gave a loud creak. He stopped. Karl was in the bedroom right overhead. *Unless he's in the basement already.* Though the wind was getting worked up, it sounded distant here with a cliff so close to The House. But how would it sound up there?

What the hell. He shoved the window all the way in, making a screech you could hear down the valley. The window was only a foot high, but almost as wide as the well. It was overbuilt, like everything from a hundred years ago, and heavy. Ray sat up and worked his bottom half in until he was sitting on the frame, facing The House, legs dangling into the basement, the sash resting on his thighs. He pushed himself further in. He needed to wrench himself around onto his stomach. It seemed impossible, but it was the only way to get in without ripping his face to shreds.

He did it, but not without making a great roar. He was on his stomach, panting, sweat streaming down his face. He was going to have a lot of bruises tomorrow.

He was halfway in, the window weighing on his butt, when he realized he was committed. The weight of the window had him pinned so that he could work his way in, but not out, like a finger in a Chinese puzzle.

As he wormed further in, the sill cut into his belly and the weight of the window pressed on his back. A few inches more, and gravity took over. He slid in and down, the front of his thighs scraping the wall, the back of his head skating down the glass, and the sash giving it a good bump. Now, he hung, his hands gripping the frame, the sash cutting into their backs. He was trying to figure out how to get them out without crushing his fingers when he fell.

Instinct whipped his arms down so his fingers wouldn't get caught. A searing pain in the middle one. Instinct bent his legs so as to not break them when he hit. His knees slammed into the wall and knocked him backward. He landed on his butt.

His finger screamed. The nail was half torn off, blood steadily dripping. He'd caught it in the window. But he could move it, so it wasn't broken. He squeezed it with his other hand to stop the bleeding. That worsened the pain and a wave of nausea convulsed his gut. He lay on the floor, on his back, and closed his eyes. The bricks were cold.

He flinched at a sound. Where? Upstairs in The House, or was that a car going by? He hadn't noticed any when he was up on the cliff, but he wasn't listening for them. Now he did. There was only silence.

He opened his eyes and looked for the source of the light. He stood, and his head swam. It cleared, and he approached the light.

It came from two tall candles on a wooden shelf in a niche in the wall. He remembered this—it was a shrine. The centerpiece had been a photo of Karl's teacher in England, a canny geezer with piercing eyes and a shaved head. Now, in its place stood a picture of Karl. So, the old guy had finally died. Between the candle on the left and the photo, a sheaf of dead flowers drooped in a slender oriental vase. He smelled something he hadn't in a long time, since the group. Incense.

The picture was a black-and-white headshot. It showed Karl at his most soulful, his lips set in deep seriousness, eyes staring out, through and beyond Ray, beyond this world. He seemed about the same age as when Ray knew him. Or perhaps a little older, because Ray didn't remember those smudges under his eyes. Was he tired? Karl never got tired. It must be the photo.

Ray realized he was *staring* at Karl, and his eyes flicked away from Karl's gaze, as he'd always done when he saw him in the flesh. And it all came back. He shrank down inside, suddenly that guy who didn't know anything, not how to walk across a room or brush his teeth in the proper way. A man whose every thought was suspect. *Unbecoming.* The word appeared in his mind in Karl's voice, as if the picture had spoken. Above all, he was a worthless piece of shit in the eyes of his teacher, his god.

To his shame, his chest swelled with a kind of love. He looked back at Karl, then away again, biting his lip.

What if a select few had stayed with Karl and ascended to some celestial realm? Ray remembered his recurrent dream of Karl and the others in the clearing, everyone smiling, Karl telling him all was forgiven. It had been no dream, but a premonition.

He'd thought he'd come here to spy, but he was the Prodigal Son. All he had to do was climb these stairs and, *Surprise!* His brothers and sisters would be there, beaming like angels, arms wide to embrace him.

Welcome home.

Leaving Karl had been a terrible mistake. His whole life since then had been a nightmare of illusion, Karl's world the only real one. Was it too late?

But what was the chance Karl would let him just waltz back after all these years? His mouth fell. He sobbed, and a tear ran down his cheek. All the time he'd missed when he could have been here.

He looked at Karl again, widened his focus from the photo to the dead flowers. He shuddered as the delusions flew away. The volcano roared to life and set his torso on fire. He was sorry, yes, but for all the years he'd wasted with the group.

And there was something wrong about this shrine. He couldn't put his finger on it, but he felt the wrongness as an icicle down his middle.

Would Karl, even with his monstrous ego, build a shrine to himself? No. That meant someone else was with him. That he still had followers. They must be living in the front rooms, whose lights he couldn't see. They were up there, now.

He needed to get out, right now. He looked up to the window he'd come through. There was no way to climb out without a ladder. Should he creep upstairs, slip out the Front Door? Or try for that cave?

He stood, frozen with uncertainty, and stared at the shrine. What was wrong?

The dead flowers. They were *sloppy*, something Karl would never tolerate in his house, let alone this shrine.

Ray gazed at the floor, at the bricks he and Bassman had laid. They still looked good. But his finger had left drops of blood, which someone might see. He kneeled, licked his sleeve and scrubbed at the stain. It wasn't coming out.

Down here on the floor there was an odor, beneath the incense and burning wax. A damp cellar smell, or the clayey exhalation of that cave? No, it was organic. Rotten. But it wasn't dead flowers...

The smell was wrong. More wrong than the flowers. It must be coming from upstairs. He pictured the first floor reverted to the state of decrepitude it had been in when they first started working up there. It had stunk of rotting carpets and moldy upholstery.

Except this was more like the dead mice in the walls of the old farmhouse Susan and he lived in back then, though there were plenty of live ones to skitter around at night keeping them awake. Dead cave rats?

He shrank down inside again, only this was different. It was the cowering of an animal trying to hide from its prey.

As he stood, he felt a faint breeze. He wet a finger and held it up. The air came from further into the basement, from The Meeting Hall, and flowed upstairs, not down from above. Which made sense, if it was unheated up there. This time of year, the air down here was warmer than above, and should rise. So, the odor wasn't coming from up there, but from further in The Basement.

He pulled out the Mag-Lite and headed through the door into the dark Meeting Hall. As he stepped through, the smell got stronger. His light sliced a narrow beam in the gloom, making the room seem bigger than he remembered. He directed the beam onto the brick floor, then to the far wall, where cushions were stacked halfway to the high ceiling.

Ah. Now, he relaxed. He'd forgotten about those. They'd been rotting for all these years. That was the smell.

The cushions…and he was back sitting in the last row, Karl intoning, *Ray, I hear you've been breaking the rule about sex, with your wife,* spitting out the last word with contempt. *NO SEX, Ray. Maybe she should come stay here in The House where I can keep an eye on her.*

Ray snapped back to the present. His face was on fire, despite the chill. He'd been standing here, looking everywhere in the room but up front, to Karl's cushion. As if Karl might still be there.

He slowly swept the light to the front. Karl's cushion was gone.

21.

In place of the cushion was a long wooden box sitting on two chairs. Ray's thoughts stopped. He was only aware of the pulse throbbing in his smashed finger, clammy air on his cheeks, and the sweat-damp shirt clinging to his chest.

Karl spoke in his head: *It's time.* Time to leave. But he crept up to the box, quietly as he could, though why bother to be quiet? He was alone here. He peered down. The box was open.

Karl lay still, eyes closed, his mouth shut tight. Ray suppressed the impulse to hold a hand under his nose, see if he was breathing. Because he was quite dead. Why was Ray thinking of Lenin in his tomb, of some saint in the crypt of an Italian church? Of the mummies at The Met?

Because Karl had been *mummified.* How did he know? Because Karl should have been in his sixties, and this guy was barely fifty. Though being younger wasn't doing much for his look.

This mummification job wasn't quite up to Egyptian standards. And there was the stink, so strong here that Ray was breathing through his mouth and forcing his stomach not to heave.

Karl's skin was too dark, too loose. His face had lost its symmetry, one side collapsed down, pulling his lips into an uncharacteristic sneer.

Ray's skin crawled. He'd been running the gamut of emotions. Add disgust. What had he been worried about those last weeks? Karl had been *dead* for years.

Though that shrine had warned him of something bad, he could never have imagined this. He was stunned, but as the numbness started to pass, he felt Karl, even in death, reaching out to fuck with his head.

All Ray's weird art—which started with the mummy in the museum—had led him here. What had Karl once said? We are what we think. We make our own reality. And Ray had been thinking macabre thoughts all these years, dreaming up faux reliquaries, and here was the real thing. A mummy in a coffin—not exactly a reliquary, but close enough.

Ray stared at those dusky eyelids, certain Karl was about to open them, nail him with that molten gaze, paralyzing him. He was terrified that Karl was about to part those shriveled lips and say, *Ray, It's time.*

Ray snapped back to the reality of Karl's badly embalmed body in its coffin and asked himself the obvious question. Who had preserved him? And who lit those candles in the shrine, sent the emails, killed a cat? Who the hell was living upstairs?

A sound, and Ray jumped. *Karl's eyes, rolling open!* No. It wasn't coming from the coffin, but somewhere *behind* him. Bright light spilled from that direction, pitching his shadow against the wall, like a giant's, and he flinched from it. The hand with the flashlight fell to his side.

Ray turned with excruciating slowness—or was it time that had slipped into slow-mo? Wordless screaming filled his head, but he could translate: *Don't turn. Don't Look. Run for your life from this hall of horrors!* But there was nowhere to run.

Even now, his curiosity ruled. He must see.

At first, he was blinded by the light. He threw a hand up to shield his eyes. They adjusted.

A man, standing in the door. Ray couldn't make out his face. But the height, the heft he knew. His stomach turned over. His skin prickled like it no longer fit his flesh.

Run! Hide! Fight! But no.

He. Had. To. See.

As if reading his mind, the figure lowered the light, and Ray was no longer blind. His lovely floor came into focus, every brick as solidly mortared as when he first laid it.

He raised his eyes.

It was Karl.

Ray's imagined vision of a minute ago had become real. Karl's gaze burned into him, paralyzing him. This Karl didn't look like he'd aged a month since Ray had last seen him. If anything, he looked younger. Which was impossible…but so was his double in the coffin behind Ray.

Karl was still as ever. Scary as ever. Scarier, because of this doppelgänger business. Had Bodine laced one of those granola bars with acid? Ray felt his world flip upside down, inside out, guts on the outside and skin in. Bile jetted up into his throat, and a thread spilled from his lips.

Karl took a step toward him and something glittered at the side of his head. He was wearing an earring. What in the living, breathing fuck? Karl would never in a thousand lifetimes wear an earring.

But as Bodine liked to say, people change. Except Karl was wearing a tee-shirt. That was wrong, too. Karl hated tee-shirts. And this couldn't be Karl of course, because Karl was dead in that coffin. But somehow it *was* him…

He walked just like Karl: light and graceful as a cat. He stepped toward Ray, and Ray couldn't move, couldn't flee, just felt this enormous pressure building in his head.

Karl stopped a step in front of him, close enough to touch. Ray suppressed the impulse to reach out and finger his face, to see if it was made of flesh, or rubber, or just incense smoke.

Ray's eyes fell to Karl's hands. They were large and wide, most definitely Karl's. To Ray's relief, they carried no weapons, only an old key in one and in the other one of those industrial lanterns with a fat six-volt battery. But he was one big guy. With Karl's face, though with the light he pointed illuminating his chin it was mostly in shadow. Ray resisted the urge to shine his puny light on it.

Ray's eyes adjusted further. That wasn't Karl's nose. Or his mouth, exactly, either. His smell hit Ray's nose, overpowering the stench from the coffin. It was the stink of a homeless person: filthy clothes and shit.

Karl never smelled like anything. He never broke a sweat.

This wasn't Karl. Then who?

Still, the man whispered, as only Karl could, "Why are you here?" Ray leaped back a step. It was Karl's precise intonation, only it issued from the wrong pipes. This voice was not soft and seductive like a breeze through willows. It was harsh and a little nasal. Maybe he had a cold?

Why are you here? They were Karl's words, some of the first he'd ever spoken to Ray. And now, as then, they were ambiguous. Why are you standing here, in this house? Or Why are you on this planet?

Ray tried to turn the tables, hit the man with a Karl question. "Who are you?"

"You've heard of the brother's keeper?" A pedantic tone has crept into his voice.

"Of course."

"I am my father's keeper. The keeper of the teachings. Some fathers are of the flesh. Some of the spirit. Mine was both."

It was the same face, almost. The same way of talking. But he was much younger than Karl should be. About…a generation. Ray said, "You're Karl's son." He should be glad to have an explanation for the inexplicable, but all he felt was an icy calm.

The man's throat emitted a little, familiar sound, Karl's way of scoffing at something too obvious. "He said you would come."

Ray glanced over at the coffin and his calm disintegrated. What, Karl knew he was coming here, told his son? How could he know? He was dead long before Ray thought of writing.

"He said you would come, to speak of what should never be spoken, to spread lies about the teachings…"

Ray got it. Karl didn't prophesize that he would come personally, but that *someone* would come. Someone would come and finally speak.

"…And the teachers. The line stretches back to Leonardo and Johann Sebastian Bach, to Jesus, the Buddha and Mohammed. The secret masters. I am the sum of all their wisdom."

"What the hell does a dead cat with a dirty joke and that mannequin have to do with the teachings?"

"I needed you to stop writing. And my father taught me about mirrors."

Oh God. Ray's smoking form in the chair had been this kid's version of Karl's technique. He was trying to show Ray who he was, but with none of Karl's subtlety. Ray had been right that someone was attempting to teach him, just wrong about who.

Ray asked again. "Who are you?"

"Seth. You are done writing, Ray."

How did he know who Ray was, what he looked like? Seth must have recognized him from his website. The man's body tensed—to run? To fight? But he turned and stalked out into the anteroom. Ray heard the thunder of big feet pounding upstairs. He pictured that gun in the closet on the second floor. Even closer was one of those knives in The Kitchen. Karl had insisted on only the best.

And Ray had…this baby flashlight.

He needed to get up there, out the Front Door before Seth returned. He raced into the foyer and hit the steps. A slam and he stopped. At the creaking of a key, hope drained from him. He'd never noticed a door at the top of those stairs, because it was always open. Now, it was locked.

Ray stood frozen on the steps. He was locked in the basement with Karl's corpse. Maybe Seth wasn't about to return with a knife or a gun, but was going to just leave him here, take off and never come back. Leave him here to join Seth's father in this mausoleum of the damned.

The door was locked, and like the others in The House probably solid oak. There were other ways out. Ray raced down into the foyer. He looked up at the window he'd crawled in. There used to be a ladder in the far room. He ran there. No ladder, but the stack of bricks was there.

He picked one up. A weapon. But what did they say? You don't bring a knife to a gunfight. And you certainly don't bring a brick to a knife fight or a gunfight. Seth had one or the other. Ray dropped the brick.

He ran to the back door. It was locked with one of those old jobs that needed a key for both sides. He crashed a shoulder into the door. It didn't budge.

He raced back to the pile of bricks. If he carried them into the foyer and stacked them up, could he reach the window? There were only about a hundred. Not nearly enough.

He'd known there was only one way out. He'd been avoiding it. It was right here, behind the stack of bricks.

The cave.

Did Seth know about it? Had he ever been in there? Ray frantically tossed the bricks from the entrance. He should cover it back up once he was inside, but there was no time to do it. Seth would figure out he came in here, anyway. Where else could Ray be?

He needed to move. He crawled in on hands and knees. He paused to listen. Not a sound, in here or out there.

The first part would be easy, just a little painful on his knees, if not for that throbbing finger. He made that hand into a fist and proceeded on the knuckles though that was more than a little painful. The other hand held that blessed flashlight. He must be careful not to damage it. A narrow crack ran along the bottom of the passage. It gradually widened until he had to jam his elbows against the wall to keep from slipping in. The ceiling stayed at the same level, but the crack got deeper and deeper. The way forward started undulating like a snake. It narrowed, forcing him to move sideways.

He paused for a moment to rest. A scraping sound echoed down the passage. Shit. Seth was coming. He turned off the Mag-Lite and froze, stopped breathing. It was pitch dark. Where was Seth's lantern? The sound got louder and resolved into two. Cloth rubbing on stone, which was his clothes, and a periodic clink. Was it the lantern? A knife? A *gun*? Ray waited. A flicker of light reflected on the rock walls. Seth had a light but was still around a corner or two.

If he had the lantern he had before, it was a plus and a minus. It was ten candlepower stronger than Ray's Mag-Lite, which was a major asset in this place of eternal night. But it didn't fit in the palm of a hand. And you needed both hands down here.

Seth was getting closer and Ray had to move. But he needed to know just what his pursuer carried. He listened. There were *three* sounds: clothes on stone, that original clink, and a clank, duller and lower in pitch. Was the clink a knife and the clank the lantern? Or was the clink the lantern and the clank…a gun?

Ray inched on, past a dark opening in the wall.

When he'd seen that with Bodine, he asked, "How the hell are we going to keep from getting lost?"

Bodine said, "That's a side passage. See, it's smaller. If we stick to this main one, we'll be fine."

Now, Ray stopped again to listen: clink, clank, and a grunt. Seth was still coming, gaining on him.

Ray humped it. The crack in the floor widened. Though he'd come in here with Bodine decades ago, the memory was as clear as if it happened yesterday. Which was good. He needed to remember in order to get through this.

***

Bodine explained how the crack went down thirty or forty feet. He laughed and said, "You don't want to fall down here and get stuck. Though, I suppose we could fish you out. I heard about this fat guy who got stuck in a cave near here. They somehow got his clothes off, greased him up with Crisco, tied a rope around him and popped him out like a champagne cork."

Bodine taught Ray how to "chimney," to get his knees against one wall and back on the other and sidle along, using the pressure to keep from falling.

***

Maybe Seth didn't know how to do it. It must be hard toting the gun and lantern, which was maybe why his sounds were getting fainter. Hopefully, it'd get to be too much, and he'd just go back.

Ray stopped. Ten feet in front of him the crack closed up and the passageway abruptly turned into a crawlway. He flashed back to the trip with Bodine.

***

Bodine pointed ahead. "That, my friend, is the notorious 'lemon-squeezer.'"

It had made the crawlway that started the cave look like Grand Central Station. A body couldn't fit in there.

Yet Bodine's did. He crawled in on his belly until all Ray could see were the soles of his boots. Bodine grunted with the effort. Ray followed. The only way to move forward was a combination of kicking against the walls and slithering. He was hyperventilating but refused to stop and rest until he was through. *If* he got through. There was a little space above his back, which was good, but his arms were pinned to his sides.

The passage widened a hair. He said with relief. "That was tough. But we're through."

"Uh, we aren't quite there yet. This coming up is the lemon-squeezer. Here's what you need to do. Breathe out so your chest is smaller, then slide through fast as you can. It's only a few feet. Then you'll have room to breathe again."

Bodine's boots receded… Ray swallowed his panic and squirmed through.

It was when he was on the other side, lying on the cold floor, able to breathe again, that it hit him. It had been like being in a coffin, in your grave, unable to breath. Buried alive, as in that old Poe story.

***

A deafening sound and stinging in his shoulder rocketed Ray back to the present. His knees let go and he fell. How far? It took enough time to think to splay all four limbs against the walls, to stop his descent. He scraped the shit out of his hands and knees and heard his pants tearing, but it slowed him enough so that when his feet hit the floor, he didn't break an ankle. He crumbled in a heap.

A second explosion rang out. The fall had saved his life. There was no third shot. He had his answer—Seth had a lantern and gun. It must be Karl's, from the closet upstairs. It had had two barrels. Seth needed to reload before shooting again. If Ray was silent, maybe Seth would think he was dead.

Bodine had said there was a passage below, parallel to the one we were in. That was where Ray must be now. He'd dropped his light in the fall. Seth's flickered above.

There were no sounds of reloading but scraping again. There was less clink and clank. Seth was learning. With the echoes, the sounds could be coming from anywhere, but not the light. It was getting brighter. He was overhead. Ray stopped breathing. Could the kid see down here? If so, Ray was dead.

But he'd fallen some distance. The way the passage was shaped, the upper route was the obvious way to go. The light above moved past him, but illuminated the way ahead here below, which must pass under the nasty crawlway that culminated in the lemon squeezer. And there was Ray's flashlight on the floor, where he'd dropped it. A rush of hope. With luck, it wasn't broken.

Seth's light dimmed, then was gone. He was in the crawlway. The question was—had he been in this cave before? If not, would he know how to exhale, get past the lemon-squeezer? He was bigger than Ray, like his father. Maybe he couldn't fit at all. Another thing– it was hard enough squeezing a body through there. Getting through there with that light and gun would be grueling, perhaps impossible. When Ray had gone through, his hands had been pinned to his sides. Maybe Seth would quit and leave, though good luck to him backing out of that thing.

There was silence. Seth had either suffocated or was heading on.

Ray groped his way to the Mag-Lite, grabbed it and jiggled it. After a few horrible seconds, it came on. He didn't have to worry about Seth seeing it. Ray's shoulder was bleeding, but he hadn't been shot. He'd just gotten nailed by a splinter of stone from the bullet hitting the rock.

Ray was at the bottom of a canyon. Unlike the rest of the cave so far, it was a place where you could stand.

Bodine had said that his chimneying technique worked for going up and down too. If Ray could chimney up where he fell, he could go back out of the cave and escape! He clamped the light in his teeth and tried to climb. But the narrow slot that had broken his fall widened in the last few feet. And the walls were smooth, with no footholds or handholds, no way to get purchase on the rock and propel himself up.

He ran back toward the entrance of the cave, but the crack narrowed, and finally pinched in. He couldn't squeeze through.

He raced the other way, past where he'd fallen, a couple of hundred feet. He must be past the lemon squeezer above. Seth couldn't have made it through by now, not with all that baggage. So, Ray was ahead of him.

He trained the Mag-Lite up. Here the passage gradually widened the higher it went. He should be able to chimney up. He got his back against one wall, feet against the other, and inched his way up. He finally made it to the top. He stopped—ignoring the fact that he was straddling a forty-foot drop—and listened. There were sounds, very faint. It wasn't cave rats.

He chimneyed forward. The canyon narrowed, then petered out and for the first time he was *walking*. But the easy passage only lasted thirty feet. It ended at a place he'd never forget. Again memory froze him.

***

The floor had been flat, and for the first time in the cave, they could walk. Ray said, "This is more like it."

Bodine said, "Yeah. The calm before the storm."

"What storm?"

"We're almost there." His last words echoed.

Ray moved up to him and Bodine grabbed his arm. "Watch it."

They stood on the lip of a chamber that belled out from their perch. It was roughly cylindrical, thirty feet across with sheer walls. Bodine said, "This is called a dome-pit. Here's the dome." He shined his flashlight up. Ray couldn't see a ceiling, only water drops falling, oddly lazy in the light. "And the pit." Bodine pointed the light down. Ray peered down into blackness. He couldn't see the bottom, either.

"How deep is this thing?"

"I haven't been down to measure. There's an easy way to find out." Bodine stepped back into the passage and returned with a small rock. He dropped it down the hole.

"One Mississippi, two Mississi—" Boom. "A little less than two seconds. Sixty, seventy feet. You don't want to fall."

Funny how that information made the dark below suddenly crawl with malevolence. Ray shrunk back from the edge, almost crashing into Bodine.

He said, "Whoa."

The walls were vertical. "There's no way across that."

"There is." He trained his flashlight along the left side of the pit, to a ledge about four feet down. "That goes to the other side. It's solid and flat. The passage continues on past there, and we can easily climb up into it."

But Ray was pointing his flashlight down past their feet, to a gap in the ledge before it began. "What about that?"

"That's a little tricky." He demonstrated. "You can't see it, but there's a slot below me where I'm putting my foot. Now, I grab this nub of rock on this side and—" He swung a leg over the gap, shifted his weight, let go of the handhold and was on the ledge.

Ray imitated him. It wasn't so bad. He followed him out onto the ledge. It was solid and flat. But it was ten inches wide at best, so he had to face the wall and sidle. It was also muddy. As he shuffled his foot, it slipped. He stopped. His body revolted. "I can't do this."

Ray had to hand it to Bodine. He'd heard his voice and knew he was done. Bodine didn't try to cajole him into continuing. "Go back the way you came. And be careful." As if Ray needed him to tell him that.

Ray inched back. He was almost there when he saw the problem. "I'm stuck."

"Yeah, that last bit is harder on the return. Reach your leg across and into the slot. Now you have to kind of lunge for that handhold."

There was no reason, in theory, he shouldn't be able to get his foot in that slot, except from this angle he could *see* the chasm he was about to step over. Before he could second-guess, he rammed his foot across and lunged for the handhold.

He crumpled in a heap on the floor, his body quivering with relief. Until He remembered the lemon-squeezer.

***

The sounds behind Ray got louder, yanking him back to the present. It had taken him a long time, but Seth had made it through the lemon squeezer. He was coming. And, like it or not, Ray was going.

He set the light in his teeth again. There was that nub of rock. His foot found the invisible slot and before he could think, he was past the gap with his other foot on the ledge. He faced the wall and sidled across. He moved fast, faster than the fearful thoughts. But not too fast. He'd gotten further than he did last time. That's why he didn't know how to negotiate this next spot. The wall bulged. He needed to get his right hand on the bulge and crouch down.

He was past it, over halfway across when the shot rang out. It echoed discordantly in the dome-pit. His body spasmed, and he almost lost his footing. He heard little splashes below. The bullet must have knocked mud off the wall. He didn't remember there being water down there before. But it had been summer. The water must be up now from all the melting snow.

A few steps later came a second shot. Why hadn't Seth hit him? Ray turned his head back. Seth hadn't made it to the edge of the pit yet. He'd missed Ray because the pit belled out and he didn't know it. That suggested he'd never gotten this far in the cave before. He was going to see the pit any second.

Ray heard a metallic snap. Seth was reloading. Ray was less than ten feet from the other side of the dome. The ledge ended at an upward slope—there was no gap on this side—with blackness at the top. It looked like the continuation of the passage before. The slope looked easy.

Except any moment Seth going to reach the edge of the pit and see Ray. And shoot him like a drunken duck, especially if he saw his light. Ray memorized the contours of the slope then turned it off.

He made it to the top, scurried a few feet further from the edge of the pit then lay with his head at the top of the slope. Seth appeared on the other side, his face lit ghostly by the lantern. He waved the light around the dome-pit. He pointed it right at the passage Ray was in but moved it away. Seth couldn't see him. Maybe he didn't know where he was. Seth stared down at his feet, at the gap. If he hadn't been this far in the cave before, he didn't know about that handhold and invisible foothold. He couldn't get across.

22.

Ray was hopeful for the first time in what seemed like hours. He needed to see how the passage continued. He inched back from the pit, turned, and clicked his light on.

The gun boomed, and he dropped to the floor. He wasn't hit. He scrambled forward, leaving the light on—he didn't want to be falling into some other pit. With the second boom, he was free. Seth needed to reload, and by that time Ray would be far out of range. There was no pit ahead, just a sewer passage similar to the start of the cave. Which, by the standards of the rest of this hellhole, was an easy crawlway. He scurried on hands and knees for a couple of hundred feet. It occurred to him that he was headed toward that exit.

The floor sloped down, then got gradually steeper. Now, it was so steep that he had to creep down on his butt. The rock was muddy, soaking through the back of his pants and making his ass cold.

The incline became even steeper, and he was sliding, out of control. He landed with a big splash on his feet in water above his knees. He was standing in a pool at the bottom of a dome-pit like the previous one. Aside from the slot he'd shot down, this was almost perfectly cylindrical. Water rained down from the ceiling, clattering on the pool.

He splashed around looking for the way on. The only passage was a low crawlway. He leaned down and pointed the flashlight in. It was less than two feet high and half submerged. He crawled in, the flashlight in his mouth. The water struck his chest, so cold that it burned. As he crept forward, the icy liquid hit his diaphragm, and it seized up. He couldn't breathe! His body squirmed backward involuntarily. A moment later, he was breathing again, though in shallow gasps.

He forced himself forward again. The walls closed in, pressing his arms against his sides. The roof lowered. His mouth was an inch from the surface of the water. His body rebelled and backed out again. He willed it to stop.

He wasn't going back. Seth was there.

He crawled in once more, and this time got further in. He came around a corner to the left. The crawlway widened into a pool. His movements had roiled the water so that it slapped against the rock with a sickening rhythm. A few feet further in, it was up to the ceiling.

Bodine had told him of cavers "free diving" in spots like this: holding their breath, plunging in, swimming underwater and counting the seconds to half the time they knew they could hold their breath before either popping out into air-filled passage, or returning. It had seemed suicidal. It still did, except it was the only way out.

Was this Mag-Lite waterproof? Ray was about to find out. He sucked in as much air as his lungs would hold and ducked his head under. He shoved forward a couple of feet. He wasn't swimming but *crawling* underwater.

He backed out. There was a limit to the craziness his body would take, and he'd reached it.

He was almost certain the exit was flooded. He'd never know, because he wasn't going in there again.

He stood in the dome, water raining on his head. Was Seth still at the pit? Was he getting reinforcements? Locking Ray in the basement again, for good this time?

Like that, Ray was violently shivering. If he didn't get out of this waterfall and start moving, it was all going to be moot. He needed to return to the pit and see.

He stared up at the slope he'd come down. It was muddy, and he was wet. He began climbing. A few feet up, and he slipped back into the water. The second time was harder, because his wet clothes had greased the mud incline.

Sheer physical effort wasn't going to get him up there. He studied the slope. There were no handholds, but the rock sides were solid and close together. He leaned his body in, kicked up a few feet and jammed his elbows against the rock, punching the toes of his boots into the mud. Rinse and repeat. It was exhausting, but there was no resting, or he'd slip back down.

Halfway up, his foot got stuck. He wiggled it until it plopped out with a sucking sound and threw him off balance, but he hung on. Finally, he was past the steepest part. He slithered up to the level passage and collapsed in a heap, panting, like a fish out of water. At least he wasn't shivering any more.

He crawled on and approached the pit. He clicked his light off and saw faint reflections of Seth's. Why was he still there? Did he know the exit was flooded? Was he aware that there was an exit at all? It didn't matter. He was waiting for Ray.

Ray crept up to the edge on his belly, quietly as he could. But the dome-pit must have amplified his sounds, because they were answered by the boom of the gun. Ray scurried back. A second shot came, then the clatter of Seth reloading. They'd done this before. Only last time Ray thought he had an exit. How was he going to get by him?

Ray needed to think about who Seth was. Based on a short conversation, but that's all he had. Karl, it seems, had subjected him to a rare form of homeschooling, grooming him as the next in the lineage of teachers. He taught Seth that no one should speak of the teachings, which is why Seth was compelled to stop Ray's writing.

Despite all the evidence, that doubting part of Ray still wondered whether Karl was a con man or a holy man. And what had Karl believed? It was unknowable. But those were the wrong questions. What Ray needed to know was what Seth believed. He wasn't slick like his father. He didn't seem like someone who hid things well. In their brief conversation Ray had gotten two vibes.

Seth seemed crazy, which Ray already knew from his attacks on him at home. But Seth was also a True Believer. Like Susan. Where the crazy came in was that the person Seth truly believed in was himself. He was on a unique mission on the planet to save the chosen few. Ray hoped he was right. He didn't know the end point, but he knew the first step of his plan. It sounded like Seth was done reloading, and he hadn't taken another shot. Ray crept up to the edge again on his belly, close enough that he could see Seth, and Seth could see him. Seth was standing there.

Ray started talking before he knew what he was saying. "Seth, please put the gun down and listen." The echo distorted his words. There was silence, but at least Seth didn't answer with a shot. Ray spoke more slowly to accommodate the acoustics.

"I was wrong. Wrong to write. And wrong to leave your father." Silence. "I want to come back. Finish with you what I should have with your father."

"Why did you come back now? There's no way out, is there?" The sound of him speaking was even stranger here than it had been in the Meeting Room. Ray was struck by the sureality of the two of them here in the bowels of the earth.

Ray want to laugh. *No way out.* Seth probably meant the cave. But like his father, everything seemed to have at least two meanings. And it came to Ray with a jolt, along with a flicker of hope—two could play at that.

Ray said, "There *is* a way out. Which I'll get to. But the only way out...out of my situation, my suffering, is with you. Traveling the hidden path."

There was a long, long pause. In order to stay alive, Ray needed to stay here, now, in this moment. Stay alert and away from his thoughts, the well of fears. He listened to the drops falling from the ceiling and counted, like breaths in meditation. One, two, three...he was at twelve when Seth finally answered.

"If you want to come back, you need to come to me. Here, now."

"I'm not coming there if you have that gun. Throw it in the pit." That was dumb. If Seth got rid of the gun, Ray would have to come to him. As he was climbing up that last bit Seth could push him. But Seth didn't answer.

Ray said "That lemon-squeezer must have been hard. You're a big man." Big man could have a second meaning. "And with that gun and light."

"The lemon-squeezer. *That's* what it's called."

Did Ray hear a shudder in his voice? He was pretty sure the reason Seth was still there was not because he was waiting for Ray, but because he didn't want to go back through that awful crawlway again. That made them both stuck in both directions. Seth didn't want to go back and didn't know how to cross the pit. Ray couldn't get past him and wasn't trying that exit again.

The first step in Ray's plan had been getting Seth to talk spiritual turkey with him. That accomplished, the next step revealed itself: getting Seth to come to him. Ray said, "You don't have to go through that crawlway again. There's another way out of here, past me. It's much easier than the way in."

"Then why didn't you take it?"

"Because, as you of all people should know, there is no easier way. There's only The Way. Your way." This multiple-meaning trip was seductive. Ray was starting to almost believe his own bullshit. Maybe that was what had happened to Karl. He started believing his own bullshit.

Seth pointed the lantern down at the ledge like he had before. "How do I do it?"

Had Ray made the sale? Maybe. But Seth still had the gun. Except Ray didn't need to worry about it. That first move required a hand for that nub of rock. Both of Seth's were occupied. So, he had to lose the weapon or the lantern. Advantage Ray.

And he didn't need to worry about whether Seth bought Ray's scam or not. Whether he thought Ray was going to follow him as a teacher or not, he wanted to get across this pit and avoid that lemon-squeezer.

Even as Ray was thinking this hopeful thought, Seth slung the gun over his right shoulder, leaving the lantern in his right hand and the left free. The gun had a strap. Fuck. But the next part of the plan came to Ray, and it didn't matter.

"Okay. You can't see the foothold, but it's there." *Trust me.* "Step down and put your weight on…" *On your right foot. Where there's no slot. And fall into the void.*

But Ray couldn't say it. He couldn't just send Seth to his death. "Your left foot. Now, grab that nub of rock and swing over the hole, shifting your weight." Betrayed by his weenie tongue. What the living fuck was he going to do now?

Seth was over the gap in no time and moving carefully toward Ray. He'd inherited some of his father's feline agility. That gun was heavy. So was the lantern. Heavy enough that having them must make balancing hard. But he seemed to be managing fine.

When they'd been talking, Seth could see Ray and hadn't taken another shot. Why? Because he needed him to get across the pit.

Ray spoke softly so as to not startle him. "Seth. You need my help to get out of here. There's a second climb, like that one."

Seth stopped, glanced up at Ray, then kept moving.

If he thought he needed Ray's help, he wouldn't shoot him when he got up here. Then Ray would tell him, "Your light's brighter than mine, you should go first," but when they reached the next pit and Seth was busy climbing, Ray would turn around. And hightail it out.

Ray was shivering again. The cold had worked its way into his core. If he didn't get moving, the shaking was going to become uncontrollable.

Seth was halfway across the ledge when he stopped. Why? He'd reached that bulge that Ray had put his hand on to balance as he crouched under it. Seth's hand was busy holding the lantern. And he was taller than Ray, so he needed to crouch lower.

Seth asked, "What do I do here?"

It was a good damned question. "I told you that you needed my help. You need your hand. Put the light down."

"Where?"

"On the ledge in front of you. Reach for that bulge in the rock, step over the light, crouch down and get past the bulge. Then you can turn and pick up the light again."

Seth was agile. He put the light down, got to the bulge, was crouching, moving forward...

A wild arc of light. Silence and then a splash. And they were in the dark, because Ray's light was still off, and Seth had just knocked his lantern into the pit.

"Help me!" It was no whisper, no voice of Karl's, but that of a terrified kid.

Ray noticed his own ragged breathing, out of sync with the steady drip, drip of groundwater from far above. Seth couldn't make it back across that ledge in the dark. If he came this way, Ray would just have to wait until he was at the top of the slope then give him a push.

What if he shot Ray? He couldn't. That slope was impossible without both hands.

"Please. You have to help me." What had it been like growing up with the great junkie Karl Maxwell? Whatever Seth had done, he did not deserve to die.

Ray clutched a second time. He snapped the light on and trained it on Seth, who was frozen on the ledge. Ray said, "Okay. No funny business. Come here. Carefully."

Seth looked right at him, huge animal eyes gleaming. He inched forward.

Seth reached the slope, hesitated for a moment, then bolted up like a rocket. He lunged for Ray's head, which jerked up and smashed into the roof. Ray's arms thrust forward and shoved Seth's shoulders. His hands sensed resistance for a moment, then nothing.

An instant of yawning silence, then a grunt and the scraping of cloth on mud. A longer silence, almost two whole seconds. Then a big splash, echoing up the walls of the pit. Only it wasn't a pure splash, but had this *crunch* element to it.

Seth had fallen into water, which was better than hitting rock. But it wasn't deep enough. That crunch heard Ray wasn't the gun hitting the floor. It was Seth's bones breaking. Ray listened for signs of life below. But there was just that drip, drip, and now his breath as it started up again.

Seth had joined his father.

Ray lay there for minutes, violently shivering, but he didn't care. His body flooded with animal relief, and his mind was wiped clean.

He was sure he must have lost the Mag-Lite pushing Seth. But here it was in his palm, gripped so tightly that he wondered if he'd ever play guitar again. His arms had known to push Seth. His hand had known he needed light. He clicked it on,

Ray inched to the edge of the pit and peered down into the blackness. He couldn't see it, but down there in the water was the broken body of Seth. Nobody survived a seventy-foot fall.

And Ray had killed him. A torrent of feeling rose up, but there was no time for it now. Not if he wanted to live.

Had Seth been alone in The House? Ray imagined someone up there, wondering where Seth went, eventually coming down here.

He had to cross the pit. He'd been dry on the way in. Now, he was wet and muddy. He'd have to be extra careful. He started across. He restrained the shaking in his arms and legs but couldn't keep his teeth from chattering. And they held the Mag-Lite.

He was almost there! He relaxed. Just a little, but enough so that the flashlight slipped from his mouth and clattered down into the pit. A splash, and he was in the black of deepest midnight. Absolute darkness, Bodine had called it.

Ray's body went numb as he shrank down inside to a tight ball of terror. And in the absence of light he was not sure where or who he was anymore. Whether he was a man in a cave or a black hole at the end of the universe.

A breath, and Ray knew he was here, on this ledge. And he remembered: that last bit was tricky. He latched every ounce of consciousness onto the tips of fingers touching rock and the soles of feet on the ledge. There was no pit, no cave, only inching forward. Skin of fingers and feet, breath and movement.

He felt for the gap in the ledge with his foot. This must be it.

He was panting, thoughts spinning out to the abyss yawning in front of him. He slowed his breath and reeled in his mind. He reached a foot over the gap. He told himself: it's easier if you can't see it.

He tentatively shifted his weight. But that wasn't it. If he hesitated, he'd overthink it. He lunged for the handhold. The next part happened so fast that he didn't know how he did it. But he was lying on the flat floor, gasping, quivering.

The lemon-squeezer was nothing now. He was through in a minute.

He was chimneying now, careful not to slip into the crack in the floor. It *was* better if you couldn't see it. Past the worst of it, he restrained the desire to rush, to get the hell out of there. He was crawling now. He stopped. Where was the crack in the floor? It had started near the entrance and continued until it widened into the canyon he'd just passed. Now the passage was growing smaller and smaller. Then too small. He panicked, pounding hands on the rock. He hit that bum finger and let out a yell.

He was *lost*. Lost in pitch black in this fucking huge cave. As hope leaked from him, his body became listless until the whole of him was paralyzed, the only activity the thought loop, *I'm lost, I'm lost, lost, lost...*

An abrupt spasm, and he was shivering again. This was the sub-arctic big-time version, completely out of control, arms and legs convulsing, whapping against the rock.

He couldn't stop it, but he could get his mind working. He remembered coming in here with Bodine. He must be in that side passage, at the end of it. Or was this another one he hadn't noticed then? There was only one way to go, out, and only one way to do it, backward. It was cumbersome but warmed him up so that the shivers were only periodic.

How would he know when he got to the main passage? If he turned the wrong way, he'd be headed into the cave again. He groped the floor, feeling for that crack. When it was there, he'd be back in the main passage.

But which side of the cave did this passage come off of? His memory of passing it coming in an hour ago was confused with when he came *out* with Bodine. Left or right? Fuck if he knew.

Relief flooded him as icy fingers sensed the crack. But should he go right or left? He hugged the rock. Breathed and let his mind go blank.

He was cold, yes, but his face was especially so. There was air blowing on it. It should be headed out into the basement then upstairs into The House, where it was colder. What direction was it going?

He licked a finger and held it up.

He crawled into the wind. Minutes later his hand crashed onto the pile of bricks. It hurt, but he wanted to kiss every one of them. Marry them.

He stood and felt his way toward the door. As he entered the Meeting Room, he became aware of the dim light of the candles in the foyer, and his light-starved eyes actually narrowed. He passed the midpoint of the room with Karl's coffin in the gloom to his right.

It occurred to him that the cave was a crime scene. He lifted one of the candles from the shrine and returned to the mouth of the cavern. He stacked bricks up to hide it.

He was passing the coffin again when he stopped. He needed to see Karl one last time. He stood over the body, dripping wax on the floor. Karl didn't care anymore. Neither did Seth.

Karl had never had any fat on him, but he looked even thinner. As usual, he wore a long-sleeved shirt, quietly elegant, fine cloth in a pleasing shade of dark blue. This one was buttoned at the wrists, the way they'd always been, even in the August heat. It was typical of his fastidiousness.

Or maybe it was something else. Crystal had said Karl was a junkie, and Ray hadn't believed it. Still couldn't.

He closed his eyes. A second later, he was dizzy and intensely nauseated. He opened them again and looked out into the room. Did he really want to see? To know?

He reached down—even at the risk of touching dead flesh—and undid a sleeve button. There was a bad moment, thinking the skin might adhere, slough off as his hand tugged on the cloth.

He teased the sleeve up the arm, and the skin didn't slide off. But the inner forearm was a mess. And it wasn't rot. Scabby circles extended from the pit of the elbow down a vein toward the hand.

Ray had never seen the tracks of a heroin addict, but he knew that's what he was seeing. Bodine said Karl had been into smack in the sixties. Lorraine spoke about Karl getting Beaky to rob drugstores. Ray hadn't believed them. But Karl had been a user. A heavy user.

And Ray didn't know why, but he was pretty sure his teacher had OD'd.

Had he been using at the end of the group? Is that why he'd gotten so weird, why the mask slipped? Ray would never know. Karl might have had a "Way" at some point, but he'd surely lost it. Forsaken it for the way of the needle.

One thing was clear. Whatever the truth of Karl's great spiritual lineage, stretching back to Jesus Christ, it had just ended with Seth. According to Karl, that should mean the end of all hope for mankind. Though it seems that line had fizzled out a bit earlier, around the time Karl started poking a spike in his arm.

23.

Ray gave Karl's face a last look and headed to the foyer. *It's Time.* Time to get the car and go home. He felt a great letting down inside, and his body checked in with its complaints: a stabbing pain at the end of his finger and a jaw aching from biting on the flashlight. Oh, and he was desperately thirsty.

He reached the bottom of the stairs and stopped. He knew now who'd been doing the computer stuff, the hacking, and anonymous remailers. Seth was from a generation that knew technology. Ray also knew that he was crazy, but crazy enough to mummify his own father? Had he really been living alone in this place, all by himself? It didn't make sense. Unless Seth hadn't been alone.

Ray listened. Not a sound.

But...they must be setting him up. Suddenly he was six years old, alone in a basement in a dark house, the shadows outside the dim circle of candlelight crawling with menace. They were upstairs in the original Meeting Room, sitting waiting for him, along with an empty cushion.

Waiting, not to embrace him, not even to punish him, but to begin it all again. The endless days of boring physical work and the browbeating and the terrible, awkward meals.

A tremor arose in his chest and, a moment later, his whole body convulsed with violent shivers. He needed to get warm, right now, people upstairs be damned. He sprang for the steps, but his feet had turned sluggish and he missed. He crashed into the wall, knocking the candle out.

He prized the other one from the niche, hands shaking, and trudged up the steps. What if Seth had locked the door? He tried to be quiet, but the shivers had his arms thumping into the wood-paneled walls of the stairwell.

The door was open. He stopped to listen. The shaking got worse. He crept into the great room with the stairs to the second floor. He felt The House around him, its enormous weight. It felt empty. And it was definitely unheated.

He should leave. But it was probably colder outside. He had to get warm before doing anything else. He was no expert on hypothermia, but he was surely well into it. Seth had been living here. There must be a coat.

Back in the group they'd hung theirs up by the Front Door. He stumbled through the room he'd first worked on all those years ago. He slowed down so the candle didn't go out. The same furniture was here, but the wood has lost the gleam they'd labored so to give it. Dust covered everything. It smelled like a museum unvisited in decades. No group had been here in a long time.

Coat hooks still lined the wall of the foyer, but there were no coats. He headed back then turned to the hall with the grand stairway.

Light streamed from The Bedroom upstairs. He bounded up, and the candle went out.

As he entered the room, he caught a strong whiff of that homeless person stench, mingled with another incongruous smell: tuna fish. The faint thrumming of the generator came from down the hall.

His eyes jumped to the bed. Where Karl had videotaped Susan. Where Seth slept. He saw the red cover at the bottom edge, looking its age, threadbare and faded. Otherwise the bed was piled high with a tangle of blankets and coats. Seth's smell was strongest here. Ray wrestled one of the coats on. It reeked, but it was wool.

He rushed to a space heater by the window, turned it on, and huddled over it, toasting his hands. It would take more than this to dry his clothes, but he finally got the shaking to stop. Thirst returned with a vengeance. He looked around frantically and saw a half-filled water bottle. Seth had drunk from it, but Ray chugged the contents.

As his body climbed out of survival mode, questions rushed in. When did Karl die? How did Seth live?

A bookcase next to the bed was crammed with religious texts, from the

Bhagavad-Gita to The Bible. There were odder things. *The Mysteries of Chartres Cathedral.* Something about Atlantis, and *Secrets of the Pharaohs.* Was that where Seth got his embalming technique?

The bottom shelf contained bound notebooks. Ray opened one and recognized Karl's ornate hand. Here was his philosophy, laid out in quotes, some lifted from the books above, many of which he remembered Karl saying.

Without the charm of his intonation it all seemed a bit fussy. Here was a nugget Ray had heard from him once. "If a man doesn't find his way by age fifty, he might as well blow his brains out." Ray had obsessed about that one at the time, but when the big five-oh rolled around he had mercifully forgotten it. Now, it seemed overheated, portentous.

Wait. How old had Karl been when he died? According to Wikipedia, he'd been born about 1950. Even figuring in the ravages of heroin, his corpse hadn't look sixty. So, maybe Seth's embalming hadn't been so bad. Karl could have been as young as fifty when he died.

Across the room from the bed stood a pyramid more than three feet high made of cat food cans, source of the tuna smell. Next to it were empty food and water bowls. Ray remembered the cat in the video, poor thing. On a table sat an open can, half eaten, a fork beside it. He'd heard of old poor people doing this. Seth had been living on cat food, along with his cat. Until he killed it. And it must have been his only companion.

These were not the digs of a great teacher. Seth couldn't have had a group.

So what had Susan been doing here? She hadn't come to resume her affair with Karl. And there was no group. And she was giving Seth money. Why?

Next to the unfinished meal sat a Nintendo video game console, a monitor, and games. But where was Seth's computer? The console was plugged into a power strip hooked to a heavy orange extension cord that snaked out the door and down the right side of the hall. Ray found matches and lit the candle again. He traced the cord to the last room. The windows were empty of glass. Here was the generator, and a satellite dish, which explained Seth's internet access. It was a clever place to install them, out of the rain, but where the generator fumes vented to the outside. He might have been a loon, but Seth was not impractical.

A second orange extension cord also led out of the room, hugging the other side of the hall. Ray followed it downstairs and down another hall. It disappeared into a hole outside The Backroom.

What the hell? The door was locked.

He returned to The Bedroom and searched for keys. Seth had locked him in the basement. And unlocked the door when he came back down to go in the cave. He'd had the keys with him when he fell. Shit.

His computer must be in The Backroom. And why had he locked that door?

Maybe he'd left the keys in the door to the basement. Ray went downstairs, and there they were hanging from the lock. He tried keys at the Backroom door, holding the candle in the other hand. Karl had been wrong about electricity. Living without it was a pain in the ass.

The door finally swished open. He hesitated on the threshold. Last time he'd been in here was during that nightmare trip. The room had been empty. Now, there was a trestle table covered with electronic devices. He walked up to it.

The laptop had black smears on the keyboard. The cat's blood. The mantelpiece of the baroque fireplace was lined with VHS tapes. A VCR sat on the table. He hadn't seen one in years. It was on.

The tapes were labeled in Karl's elegant hand: Crystal, Lorraine, a half-dozen other women.

And Susan. Ray flashed on the emailed picture of her, the one that was burning on the chest of the mannequin. Bodine had said it was a still from a video. Ray's hands clenched.

He knew he should stop. But he needed to see. He grabbed the box. It was empty. He hit "play" on the VCR and it ratcheted and whined. The TV monitor above it came to life. But nothing was on the screen. He fussed with the controls. It was near the end of the tape.

He rewound to the top. This was the same scene as in the still Seth had emailed him. Susan lay on the bed, her hand gripping the red cover. Her eyes were wide, staring off at some distant planet. A minute later they flitted from side to side, blinking in a mechanical rhythm. She was terrified, tripping her brains out. She clutched at the cover as something below the frame tugged at it. She lost the battle, and it slipped down, exposing a breast.

Big fingers appeared from the bottom of the frame and plucked at the nipple of the breast like snatching change from a store counter. Another hand appeared and yanked the cover from her hand, exposing the other breast, then pounced on it. The hands kneaded in the same rhythm as her blinking eyes. Had there been music? The video didn't have sound. Tufts of dark hair bobbed in and out of the bottom of the picture on the upbeats of the hands.

It was Karl, going down on Ray's wife. The Susan he'd known had sexual tastes that ranged from vanilla to Presbyterian. She hadn't liked oral sex. But there was no telling what Susan had emerged under a thousand mics of acid and in bed with her beloved teacher.

Up to now, only Susan's eyes had moved, but now her mouth got into it, her lower lip trembling, her tongue darting out. She was making sounds. Ray was grateful there was no audio, just the faint squeak of the tape crawling past the heads of the old machine.

Karl was definitely getting an intense reaction from her, but it didn't look like pleasure. She looked like she was being devoured by a ravenous predator. Talk about oral transmission.

He stopped the video, his own eyes wide. His hands trembled, but he wasn't cold anymore. He felt like he was spiking a fever. He fumbled for the switch on the machine and punched it off.

He'd come to this house intent on seeing Karl. Even after the sight of his corpse, even after his son was dead, he'd still wanted to see. No more. It was good to know his desire to see had a limit.

He couldn't say the same for Karl, who'd made this tape. Or, for that matter, for Seth. He was no expert, but the tape seemed well-worn. Seth had somehow loaded a still from it into the computer. From what Bodine had said about that camera he'd installed in The Bedroom, Susan and the others hadn't been aware they were being taped.

Karl and his "no graven images." So, what had the top of his head been doing in that video? Was it hypocrisy, or did it not matter if only God was acting and looking?

Hold on. How old had Seth been? Ray had only seen him for less than a minute, most of which he'd spent believing he was seeing some reincarnation of Karl, and then across that pit in bad light.

But he'd looked about the same age as Karl last time Ray saw him, in 1978. Which was partially why Ray had freaked so badly, thinking Seth was Karl. Karl had been around thirty when Ray left the group. He couldn't have been hiding a kid when they were all here. So, Seth must have been born shortly after Ray left.

Who was his mother? It had to be one of the group members. Ray's eyes flitted up to the shelf of videos. It wasn't Crystal. She'd been sterile after that abortion. Or Lorraine, for that matter. She'd left when Ray did.

After Seth had come into the Meeting Room, in that moment when Ray knew he wasn't looking at Karl, he'd been relieved that he wasn't going crazy. But as he stared at Seth's face, he'd gotten a bad feeling. Because, though there was a lot of Karl in his face, there was someone else there as well. He'd been pretty sure who but wasn't admitting it until he absolutely had to.

He ejected the tape and was placing it back on the shelf when he noticed something at the end of the set of tapes: a CD, without a label.

He slotted it in the computer and the screen came awake. There were no videos on the CD, just a couple handfuls of photos. Karl's dirty picture collection, to go with the videos.

But no. They were baby pictures. A large, chubby fellow, looking goofy, then a little older, smiling. He was alone in a few, but in most he was held by one of three women. They'd still been with the group when he left. Crystal and Lorraine weren't among them.

Neither was Susan, which brought a huge sigh of relief. But which one was the mom? He stared at the pictures. The women beamed down at the baby, no one more than the others.

He tried to get into the email on the computer. As he suspected, it required a password. But why did he need it? He knew what was in it: the dead cat video and the threats.

The computer desktop was littered with folders, so it took me a minute to find the folder labeled "Susan." Inside was a file with a .mov suffix. The bad feeling was back.

He wasn't done watching after all. He clicked on the file. A window opened, and it started playing. This had much better quality than the earlier Susan video. It was crisper. Recent, technology marching forward. To his relief, she was fully dressed in this one, in a blouse and skirt, sitting where? He looked around the room. She'd been on the old couch across from the table. If the computer had sat where it did now, she could have been recorded on its webcam.

Seth was not in the picture. As Ray watched, he had the sense that she again didn't know she was being taped. Ray hadn't known when Seth spied on him in his house using Ray's computer. Seth must have used the same trick on her.

She looked about the age of her last picture online, at that corporate thing. The hint of a shadow on her face in that photo had deepened. She looked tortured. Damned. For the first time since the terrible day when Ray had last seen her, his heart flooded with all the love he'd been hiding away somewhere all those years. The feeling was excruciating.

This video had sound. It was deeper, older, sadder, but it was her voice. He'd seen those pictures of her online. He hadn't heard her voice since that last day. As she spoke, the tumult in his chest got even worse.

She said, "I have your money, dear. Do you need anything else?"

"What else could you give me? You've had nothing, been nothing since you left."

"I didn't leave, Seth. He *sent me away.*"

No! Ray flinched hearing those old words of doom. He'd assumed Susan had finally seen the truth and left of her own accord, like the rest of them. If Karl had sent Susan away, she'd never get over it. Karl's approval had been like the air she breathed.

But the tape continued.

Seth said, "He sent you away because you defied his will, giving into your lower nature."

"Did he tell you that? Oh, Seth, I'm so sorry." She was starting to cry. "No, all I did was nurse you, one time. All I did was try to be your mother. Karl was everything to me before you came. And then…you were everything.

And he was jealous. First, he wouldn't let me touch you. Then he wouldn't let me see you. He passed you around to those other women. One of them caught me sneaking in to feed you and told him. He sent me away."

Karl had sent her into the Outer Darkness. Sent her to hell.

"And he threatened me, told me if I ever came back, ever tried to see you, he'd hurt you."

"You think you can lie to me? He would never harm a hair on this head. He knew who I was."

Susan had been incapable of such a lie. She might have been after The Truth, but she also believed in truth with a small t. It's why she'd been so brutally honest about Karl the last time Ray saw her.

But she was still talking. "The last thing he said to me was he'd take care of you. He didn't take care of you. He..." She sobbed uncontrollably.

"Enough! I have no mother. I never needed a mother. You were just a vessel of weak flesh. Now, get out. Don't come here again."

She lost it completely, howling with grief, but the clip ended. It started playing again. Ray punched the window on the computer shut and slammed the lid.

Susan had been sent away again. By her delusional son, whom she'd abandoned to a monster. And she'd seen how that had turned out. The son was as bad as the father, only cruder. And he was crazy.

How had it gone for him as a kid? Ray had read about cults, how children can be made communal property so as to keep the love and attention on the leader. On that vampire who needs every ounce of it for his craven self.

Those baby pictures had a professional look. He could imagine Karl forcing Susan to take them, as a kind of punishment, recording her son in the arms of other women, while she was forbidden to touch him. And he didn't think Seth considered them ordinary baby pictures. He'd been keeping them, had scanned them and burned them on a CD. Pictures of the enlightened one, the Great Teacher, just arrived on the planet. Good News!

Ray looked at the creation date on the video. He couldn't remember the date of the crash.

But he was sure it was that day.

Why did Susan return to The House? Seth had sent the photo in the manila envelope that she shredded. What was in it—the still from the acid trip video or a baby picture? It didn't matter. Either one would have been enough to get her to start sending him money. Not because he was blackmailing her, but out of guilt. Out of love.

Seth had told her Karl was dead, and he needed money. With Karl gone, she no longer had to stay away from him. She wanted a relationship with him, and, being Susan, would have given Seth anything he desired.

She came to see him because she wanted to see her son. But why did he want to see her? In order to make the tape. And now that he had it, he was going to blackmail her. He figured pest-control hubby might be able to handle an old lover, even a kid. But Ray had talked to the guy. He would never understand his wife being in a wacko cult. If Seth revealed it, her world would blow up.

Then Seth had gotten greedy. He could have hit her up on a permanent basis. Instead he had sent the golden goose to her death. When he saw her, he couldn't help himself. He couldn't help lashing out and saying things a mother should never have to hear.

All this came to Ray in a flurry. He wasn't sure of the details but believed he had it pretty much right.

And now, he was finally done with Karl. The doubt was over. He'd lost the last shred of belief.

There was no relief, just terrible fatigue, and an empty place in him, like what he imagined it felt like when they cut out an organ. A diseased organ.

But what about Seth? The kid had watched tapes of his father getting it on with disciples. Was he studying the perks of his future life as the Great World Teacher? But he hadn't just watched his father. He'd seen his parents. Maybe he was searching, looking for the time when he was conceived. Which, for all Ray knew, is what he'd seen a few minutes ago.

He clutched the reeking overcoat around him, but the shivering returned. There was no heater in this room.

The emails in Seth's laptop were the only thing tying him to Ray. He grabbed it. He locked the door of The Backroom and pocketed the keys and stalked to the Front Door.

The bulletin board was still in the foyer. The Rules were there on a curled page. Ray flattened it out. The ink had faded, but was still legible, in Karl's inimitable fancy public school hand.

NEVER SPEAK ABOUT WHAT WE DO

NO CIGARETTES

NO DRUGS

NO GOSSIP

NO SEX

STOP ALL NEGATIVE EMOTIONS

He tore the paper off the board and stuffed it in a pocket. He passed through Karl's Portal for the last time.

He glanced up at the façade of The House. It was ugly as ever. He was half-running around the side toward the back, headed to his lair, when he stopped. He'd locked the quarry gate. It had been difficult enough closing that padlock from inside through the gate. It would be harder to get the key in from that direction, and his hands were frozen and sluggish. He reached in his pocket. At least he still had the key.

He turned and hightailed it up the road toward the quarry. It wouldn't do for someone to see him, though it was unlikely at this hour, which must to be past midnight. Seth must be known in town. Once he stopped showing up, they'd wonder, and they might remember seeing Ray.

At the quarry gate he carefully plucked the key from his pocket and grabbed the icy padlock with his other hand. He trained the key at the keyhole, but his hands were shaking from the cold. It wouldn't go in. In frustration, he pushed, and the key flew away someplace, dinging against metal.

He set Seth's laptop on a tree stump and crawled around in slush looking for the key. His pants were getting soaked again and the snowmelt burned. He couldn't get any colder. And there was no key. It must be on the other side of the fence.

He eyed the fence, then climbed. There was a bad moment at the top as he launched a leg over, but then he was down. In just a minute he'd gone from freezing to drenched in sweat. His body heat had roused even more stink from the coat. He tore it off and ran it to the black pool and threw it in. He'd have the car heat soon enough.

He hiked up to the saddle and fumbled in the little cave for his stuff. His car keys were still in the backpack.

He drove his ancient Volvo toward the gate. When he was twenty feet away, he gunned it. If the gate fell forward, he'd drive over it. If it fell toward him, it would smash the windshield. Most likely it wouldn't budge. In which case he'd be doing some very cold hitchhiking in the middle of nowhere. What if he was picked up by a local who'd remember when Seth went missing? If he could hike to a place with cell service, he could call a locksmith. And tell him what?

He rammed the gate twice. This third shot should do it. That's what Karl would say. It took five attempts before the rusted steel collapsed outward. The front of his car was battered but had been was on its way to being an old wreck to begin with. He remembered Seth's laptop and retrieved it from the stump. He drove away.

24.

Ray looked up from his laptop and blinked. He'd been so ensconced in typing into it that for a moment he didn't know where he was. He was sitting at a narrow Formica counter, gleaming blue under harsh fluorescents. Outside stood gas pumps.

He was at an all-night rest stop, the parking lot empty aside from his Volvo and a car that must belong to the girl behind the register. He glanced over. She seemed uninterested in the fact that he'd been sitting here all this time, writing. How long? Long enough for the coffee in the Styrofoam cup to be stone cold. It was undrinkable anyway.

He'd stopped here to pee and realized he was starving. All they had was junk food. That was just the ticket. He bought a large coffee, a couple of crumb cakes, a Ring Ding, and some candy. He was sitting here gobbling the junk food, waiting for the coffee to cool, when he noticed a laptop on the table. He'd picked it up from the car without thinking. His eyes darted to the girl behind the counter in a moment of panic—was this Seth's? She didn't seem like someone who did curious, at least this time of night. And Seth's laptop was in the backseat under his pack. This was his.

He'd poked the power button, but it was dead. He plugged it into an outlet under the counter and after a long minute it stirred. And he was furiously typing.

Now he closed the computer. The whole scene from the moment he'd seen Karl embalmed in the coffin had been so intense that he just had to write it, as if by getting it out on the page he could purge himself of it. Maybe it had worked. Because all he felt was bone-tired, and drained, which must be why he was famished.

He hadn't finished his coffee, but must have demolished the sweet stuff, though he had no memory of it. He bought another Ring Ding. The girl gave him his change and said, "Have a good one."

"You too." He suppressed a laugh. Whatever he was having tonight, it did not qualify as a *good one*. She didn't seem all that thrilled to be here either.

Ray drove south on I-87. He ate the Ring Ding, and the sugar went right to his brain and stirred up a flurry of questions. Did Seth even officially exist? Did he have a birth certificate? When had the last of the group members left, including his surrogate mothers? How long had it been just him and Karl, and how much of that time had Karl been using? There were no answers and wouldn't be any.

He was twenty minutes from home, almost to the Rip Van Winkle Bridge when he found himself looking for the overpass. The place where Susan died. He'd assumed it was south of the exit for Hudson, but that was back when he thought she was visiting him that night. What had the report said? "North of Saugerties." So, this could be it coming up.

As he got close, he slowed and looked at the concrete for signs of a fire. There was nothing, just a flash of gray as he passed under the road above. But even if it had shown evidence of the accident, it wouldn't give a clue to how it had happened.

How did a car just crash into an overpass abutment? It was November. She could have hit a patch of ice. But what were the odds she'd slip right at that moment, jump the curb and hit the concrete?

Susan had loved life, yes, by she'd also never been big on accepting human frailty, and least of all her own. It was the downside to her burning spiritual aspiration. If you're looking way up to some god, it's a long way down.

Seeing Seth, she knew she'd fucked up. Abandoning Ray for Karl, perhaps she'd forgive herself. But abandoning her son, and then finding out she'd left him in the hands of a junkie? A son who turned into a malignant parody of the spiritual teacher she was always seeking?

But Seth wasn't her only child. How could she abandon the other two?

It was terrible, likely to obsess him for the rest of his life, but he was never going to know if it had been bad luck on a slippery road or if she'd killed herself.

If she had, Ray could see her steering into the concrete, even welcoming the flames—a hell she believed she richly deserved.

But what did *he* deserve? Susan would never have died if Ray hadn't introduced her to Karl. And he hadn't done it with her welfare in mind, but only in the hope of getting points with both of them.

Without Ray introducing them, there would have been no Seth. And if Ray hadn't gone into The House, hadn't started writing, Seth would still be alive.

What about the police? Ray must have left fingerprints all over, in The Bedroom, The Backroom, in the caves, on Karl's shirtsleeve. And what about DNA? But the only evidence of connection between him and Seth was on the computers in this car and in the emails Seth sent.

He supposed they were on some server, too, but without the laptops, how could anyone know they existed? Even if the police came looking for Seth and found evidence, they still wouldn't know to link it to Ray. Plus, without Seth's body, they wouldn't even know there was a murder.

It was almost inconceivable the law would ever punish him. But he was going to punish himself. His writing at the rest stop hadn't purged him of anything. The residue of those terrible hours was still in him, and it was welling up like a poison tide.

He was coming up to the Rip Van Winkle Bridge. He hit the toll. The guy was half-asleep. As Ray started across the bridge, he opened the passenger window. The river roared below, in spring flood. Blackness welled in his chest. He slowed the car.

Bassman had died right here. And he got it—his friend had died just like *Seth*, falling a long way into cold water. Bassman had lived for hours, his bones shattered. They'd theorized that he'd survived as long as he did because the water had partially broken his fall. But not enough so it didn't break half his bones.

Which meant Seth might still be alive.

Should he call the police? By the time they got up there he'd be dead. Eventually the spring waters would carry what was left of him down to the Mohawk River, then into the Hudson, and under this very bridge.

Ray had given Karl his blessing back when Bassman was at that crucial juncture, trying to decide whether to join the group. Ray's thoughts had been spiraling down into the shadows. Now, they entered the darkest place.

With Ray's last shred of belief in Karl as some higher being gone, there was no one to hide behind anymore. He knew who Karl was, but who was Ray? He imagined Karl in his final minutes, as the final dose clutched him and dragged him under. Karl might have been smacked to the gills, but he'd never go out without the drama of last words, even if his crazed son was the only one to hear them: *It's time.*

It was time. Time to pay.

Ray stopped the car halfway across the bridge, where Bassman had parked. He left the motor running, just like Bassman had. He turned to the backseat and pulled Seth's computer from under the pack. He glanced at his own on the passenger seat, glinting silver in the yellow bridge lights. He carried both out of the car and awkwardly hustled them and himself over the first railing onto the walkway. That toll guy had been half asleep, but Ray was really pushing his luck. And he could sense dawn coming. He set the computers down, leaned over the second railing and looked down at the Hudson River. The roiling waters shattered the reflections of lights on the bridge into senseless patterns.

Just a few feet away, fastened to a strut, was a call box with the sign:

WHEN IT SEEMS LIKE THERE IS NO HOPE – THERE IS HELP – OPEN THE
DOOR, PICK UP THE RECEIVER.
LIFE IS WORTH LIVING.
- NATIONAL SUICIDE PREVENTION HOTLINE

This was apparently a popular spot to kill yourself. He gripped the icy railing, leaned over, and stared down at the black, roiling water. This sensation in the palms had been Bassman's last before the agony below. The roar of the river was deafening, a vibration that hummed in the rail under his hands, shaking his bones. It was like the mighty sound of rock 'n' roll, of the Nightcrawlers in their prime, with Bassman laying down that bottom as no one else could.

Ray looked over at the suicide prevention sign. Had it been there back then? It didn't matter. It wasn't convincing if you were determined to do it.

Long before his gallery, before finding a soulmate in Edgar Allan Poe, even before that mummy, he'd been Ray of Darkness. *It's time.* Time to stop resisting, to embrace his true nature. Ashes to ashes, and dust to dust. Darkness to darkness. Just one leg over the rail, and then a second—as Bassman must have done—and down into the dark night and into the black waters.

Jo's voice appeared in his head, clear as though she was standing beside him, speaking as she had sometime last year. "I read about this fucking idiot who jumped off the Golden Gate Bridge—and lived to tell about it. He said that in the moment after he leaped, before he hit the water, he realized that it was all fixable. All of it. Except for what he'd just done. Fucking idiot." As she'd told him this, her eyes had teared, and so had his. He'd wanted to hug her. Now, he wished he had.

He felt the vibrations in his hands before he heard the chugging sound above the rushing water. A train was coming.

Bassman hadn't had Jo, hadn't had anybody, really. Susan, and Karl, and Seth were ghosts. Jo wasn't. Ray could go over and hug her anytime, though she might call him a fucking idiot. Bodine wasn't a ghost.

Neither was Ray. And he didn't want to become one.

He leaned back from the rail and removed his hands. He feet felt solid on the walkway. Cold air kissed his cheeks as his breath came in and went out. He counted three breaths then smiled. The number three might be Karl's, but Ray's breath was his.

He lifted Seth's computer and slung it out over the river. He didn't see or hear it land.

The train rounded the bend and its headlight pierced the night. Ray threw his computer over. Just before it hit the water, the light caught it, and it gleamed like a big fish coming up for air.

He had a last piece of baggage: Karl's rules. Ray tweezed them from his pocket, tore the page into scraps and tossed them to the wind. He got back in the car, jammed it in gear, and headed home.

As he drove, he was keenly aware of palms gripping the wheel, of air rushing past the windows, of the spring dawn stealing into winter woods at the corners of his vision. He sensed his body moving through space. Inside he was empty as a bass drum.

He parked in the alley behind his house. His hyper-physical awareness continued as he hauled himself from the car, shut the door, stepped onto the back stoop and twisted the key in the lock. But it was already open.

Someone was sitting in his chair, staring out the window. Karl. Seth. His doppelganger, Ray Watts.

The chair swiveled around, and Bodine said, "Good morning."

"Jesus! I thought you were—"

"Just me. I've been a little worried about you. Jo has been too."

"She called you?"

"I called her."

He must have been *really* worried.

Bodine said, "I told myself if you weren't here by noon today, I was coming up there. You saved me the trip."

Ray walked over and stood with his butt on the edge of the desk. "How did you get in?"

"The same way as Karl."

"Not Karl. *Seth.*"

"Who?" Bodine took a good look at Ray. He stared at Ray's finger, which was now purple and swollen twice its size, and his eyes widened. "What the hell did you do to that? I imagine you have a tale to tell."

Ray nodded. "One that requires at least a six pack, and it's too early to drink."

Bodine yawned. "I suppose it is, even for you. But I'll confess, though you're the cat with the curiosity, I'd like to hear it. How about a couple of Liz's famous lattes?"

Ray laughed. "Christ, I didn't bring any coffee up there. Can you believe? I forgot all about it."

"You *have* been busy. And now, I'm insisting you tell me with what."

Up in the kitchen, Bodine sat while Ray worked the espresso machine. He told Bodine the short version of Karl, Seth, and The House.

Bodine said, "I told you Karl was a freaking junkie. And his kid—*Susan's* kid—sounds totally bonkers."

Ray sighed. "Man, his dying is on my head. Coming back here, I got into this whole dark riff, how if I had acted differently Susan and Bassman never would have been with Karl, Seth wouldn't be born, and they'd all still be alive." He didn't tell Bodine about almost jumping.

"Anyone can play that game. It's bullshit. Tell me exactly what happened in that cave."

Ray told. It already seemed like it had happened to someone else, years ago.

Bodine said, "You had the chance to let him fall twice. You could have told him the wrong foot to put down. You could have left him on that ledge in the dark. And you didn't."

"Yeah, but the third time—"

"Look at me. I would have done the same thing. He lunged for you, and you instinctively pushed him away. If you hadn't, he would have pulled you right down in the hole with him."

"Thanks." Ray felt immense gratitude. Bodine was a confirmed pacifist, and for him to admit that he would have done the same thing was right now the ultimate in kindness. Even if he was lying. Ray wanted to hug him. But that wasn't what they did. And Bodine wouldn't like it.

He handed Bodine his coffee. He sat and sipped his own.

Ray said, "I couldn't drink that stuff I had out on the interstate if my life depended on it. Which it practically did."

Bodine shook his head at the espresso machine. "You've gotten hooked on that damned thing. You can't stomach real coffee anymore."

Ray laughed, then looked away. "I, uh, don't have your computer."

"You lose it in that cave?"

"No. I threw it in the Hudson River."

Bodine burst out laughing. "What about the book?"

"It's over. That's what I was throwing in."

"That seems a tad dramatic. But haven't you been emailing it to Lou as you write?"

"Damn. What was I thinking? He has the whole book." Except for what he wrote on the cliff. And that last bit.

Bodine got still, which meant serious. "Are you done with Karl?"

Ray didn't hesitate. "I am. Finally. And there's one upside to that whole sorry trip with the group. I'm incapable of doing something like that again. I'm never following any man down any old path again. If Jesus Christ waltzed in here and asked me to join up with him, I'd say, 'Very pleased to meet you, sir, and thanks, but no thanks. I'm done. I believe I'm going to sit right here in my house.'"

"Which you can stay in now. With Karl and Seth out of the picture, you have nothing to worry about in publishing your book. And who knows? Maybe somebody will read it and think twice about going down that road."

"I can't publish the last part without incriminating myself, and Lou. But that's a decision for another day."

Bodine nodded his head sagely. "You *are* done."

Ray raised his coffee cup. "After three days without, this is practically a psychedelic experience. The good kind. But I'm starved. Come over to Jo's with me, we can have breakfast."

Bodine actually seemed to think about it. "Naw. I must skedaddle. The dog needs fed."

Right.

***

Ray stepped into Jo's. The smells of fresh pastries, more coffee had his mouth watering, his tongue practically hanging down. She saw him and rushed out from behind the counter. He gave her an enormous hug. She reciprocated. She said, "Am I ever glad to see you."

She was smiling, of course, but it was the astonished, incredulous version.

She beamed it at him for a long uncomfortable moment, then said, "Have you found religion?"

He exploded in laughter.

She said, "Hey, I'm not kidding. You've got the glow." She frowned. "Are you on drugs?"

"No."

She noticed his hand. "What the living fuck did you do to that finger?"

"Just had a little adventure."

Her smile turned to plain skeptical.

He said, "Camping."

"Oh. You're crazy. It's practically winter! Camping. I hate that shit, even in the summer. Bears, mosquitos, poison ivy. Got my fill of mother nature out in Minnesota, thank you very much."

"That makes two of us. I'm never going camping again."

Breakfast was fine, and so was Jo's coffee. He'd like to stay here all morning, but bed was calling.

***

Back home, he was on his way upstairs when he thought to check his email. He fired up the old clunker computer. It still worked.

Liz: "Just wanted to let you know. That relationship I was in is over. Now, don't get your hopes up…"

Then, why the hell did she tell him? She had a sixth sense, but then, so did he. He was done with Karl.

But he wasn't done with Liz.

Keep reading for an excerpt from the next book in the Ray of Darkness series, *If I Fell.*

1.

"Bob?" At first, I thought it was a wrong number. Nobody had called me Bob in a long time. I was Bodine.

"Bob Hutchinson?"

"Yeah. Who's this?" The voice sounded familiar. The dying AC in my office in the theater's old projection booth cycled on with a roar. "Hold on." I could turn it off, but with this August humidity, the computers wouldn't like it. I stood and headed to the theater. Opened the door and hot, musty air blasted me in the face. Mingus lifted his furry head, raised a bleary eye, and glanced mournfully down into the dark hall. I squatted to give his ears a squeeze, but he'd already given up and collapsed onto his bed. They didn't call them dog days for nothing.

I closed the door, stepped downstairs into the dark, and sat on the bottom step. "Sorry."

"It's Buzzy."

"Well, I'll be dipped in shit. Knew I recognized your voice. It's been a while."

"Forty years, actually."

"Not exactly. Thirty-eight years, three months, and—"

Buzzy laughed. "You're still Mr. Precise."

A comfortable silence. We'd picked up right where we left off.

"Waldo's dead."

"Damn." The news kicked me out of my head, into sensations. The T-shirt, already damp against my chest in the minute I'd been down here. Light from the office streaming down through the old projection slots, glinting on the brass and gleaming on the glass of neatly lined museum cases housing my private collection.

I pulled myself back to the call. "Waldo. Oh man, that's terrible. How did you find out?"

"His wife, Jeannie, called me. It happened a few days ago."

"What happened?"

"He fell."

I gripped the phone tighter. "Fell? In the bathtub or something?"

"Off a cliff."

"No."

"Into the ocean, not..."

Into a snowbank, at the height of a blizzard? No, it was August. And it wasn't 1969. It was 2007. My lungs seized up. My mind squeezed down to a single word. The same one Buzzy had to be thinking.

Angela.

I glanced at the wall, still graced by Art Deco arabesques and sconces from when this was a working theater.

I closed my eyes and tumbled into the past. To the night Angela had gone missing, with its endless, swirling snow. A million flakes, every one a different color and size to a mind chemically blasted past the edges of the known universe.

I leapt forward a few months to that spring, the day they found Angela's body. Buzzy was in the kitchen, telling me, "We need to talk," but I was already out of there, out of that house and out of that life. I got in my car and drove away. That was the last time I saw him.

I opened my eyes, stood, and started pacing the aisle between the first two rows of display cases in my odd museum.

Buzzy asked, "You OK?" It was as if he'd heard my thoughts.

Lighten up the conversation. "How've you been all this time?"

"I've been a lot of things. Right now, I'm happy to be alive. And very sad."

"Yeah." Sorrow was the right feeling, but all I had was this knot in my chest. I stared into the nearest case, at a yellowed wedding dress still in desiccated cellophane, never worn. Now *there* was sad.

"And you? How have you been?"

"Fine. Just fine. It's good to hear your voice."

"And yours."

I laughed.

"What?"

"Your voice *sounds* like mine—kind of cooled out." Except it was the other way around. I sounded like him because I'd looked up to him from the moment we met and wanted to be like him.

"Hey, we all kind of got cooled out that year."

It wasn't just his voice I'd been carrying all these years. I'd been looking up to him all this time. Still was. "Where you living?"

"I'm still in sleepy old Middleburg. Never managed to leave the nest. But Waldo was living his dream. San Francisco. Remember how he was always talking about it?" Buzzy paused. "There's a service out there tomorrow. I know it's short notice, but I had trouble finding you. Maybe I'll see you there?"

"Maybe. I have to see what I've got going on—"

"Sure."

"But this has been good." Really good.

"It has." And Buzzy didn't lie about stuff like that.

"Have you talked to Rick?"

"Email. I got his from the alumni office. They didn't have a thing on you."

"Figures. I was only there the one year. So, how'd you find me?"

"I didn't think of it until this morning. Google, of course." He clicked off. What the hell. Google? No "of course" about it.

I scrambled upstairs into the relative cool of the office. Mingus got up and stared at me—*what's wrong?* I raced to the computer, Googled "Bodine Hutchinson."

I'm not one of those people who obsessively search for themselves online. In fact, I'd only done it once, a couple years ago. And come up with the same single hit as now. My name was buried in a blog post about bands of the early

'70s. A crummy posed photo of The Nightcrawlers, listing Ray on guitar, Frank on drums, Bassman on bass, and "keyboardist and lead singer Bodine Hutchinson." There was a scanned article about us from some long-defunct rock mag, hardly *Rolling Stone*, the writing somehow breathless and bored silly at the same time. Ancient history.

Buzzy hadn't gotten my phone number from that. I tapped my forehead. He didn't know me as Bodine. I tried "Bob Hutchinson." There were a mess of them. "Robert Hutchinson." Robert the attorney. Robert the woodworker. Some LinkedIn Robert. And fourth down the results, me.

What the fucking hell.

It was a website, a cheap-shit thing with cheesy retro '50s fonts. Stock cartoon figures of a grinning guy and gal from the same era, their thumbs up. Happy customers.

Pesky computer problems? Just call Bodine.

A list of my clients. The legal ones and a few of the others. Neither of which anyone in the world should know about.

Robert "Bodine" Hutchinson. Hudson, NY. Computer expert.

How did they know I was Robert? Or Bodine, for that matter? How did they get my phone number? How did they have any of it?

I'd been living for years under the radar. No phone listing. No Facebook. No nothing. My mailing address was a PO box. The only souls that even knew I was in Hudson were my buddy Ray and a few ex-girlfriends. Maintaining a low profile wasn't really about the fact that I'm not always quite on the right side of the law. It's just my nature. Probably some dark psychological explanation. I never bothered with such stuff.

But this website had me freaked. As if I were suddenly parading down the middle of Warren Street—Hudson's Main—without a stitch of clothing. Worse. On the inconceivable occasion that I found myself naked in public, I'd survive it.

No guarantee I'd survive this.

I stood and went over to the theater's old pump organ, sat, and silently fingered the keys, as I do when I'm thinking hard.

It couldn't have come from one of my corporate clients. They knew me only as "Bodine." They didn't have my phone number, just a deeply secure email address. They came to me via word of mouth as their last option, with security issues so embarrassing that they were as interested as I was in keeping things quiet.

But that was just the legit side of my business. Between paying gigs I played digital Robin Hood. I went after asshole companies that willfully spewed poison into the atmosphere, and people's bodies and minds. I slipped into their financial accounts and silently bled them, so little they wouldn't notice on a daily basis. Diverted the proceeds into anonymous donations to the good guys. Green energy, prison reform. I wasn't fooling myself. It was just a drop in the bucket. But it was my drop.

I was well aware of the dangers of do-gooding. So, I abided strictly by two rules: Never take a dime for myself, and never brag about it.

I didn't worry about getting caught. None of my targets had the technical IQ to ever know anyone had been pilfering, let alone that it was me.

But it was too easy, and I got bored. I started going after black-hat hackers. Somebody had to. Neither the cops nor even the FBI had the chops to stop them. Messing with cyber crooks was dangerous. These guys knew their stuff. Piss some of them off and they might steal my identity, a mega hassle. Piss off others, and I could end up floating in the Hudson River, an arm in Poughkeepsie and my head under the Tappan Zee Bridge. But I wasn't worried. I was very good. And very careful.

Until Brickman.

This had to be him. My eyes darted around, like he was looking in the window, lurking in the corner.

No time for him now. If I was going to this funeral, I had to get moving. I went online and booked the only affordable flight that would get me there on time. It left at six a.m.

Mingus raised an eyelid a crack and went back to sleep. It was hard to know what made dogs so tired when they slept all day. The vet calls him a "large tan hound." He eats, poops, lumbers around for a few minutes, then crashes. But he should never be mistaken for dumb. He knew I was just headed to Ray's.

I walked through the theater to the only currently usable door to the place, the old emergency exit. Headed to Warren Street, where the only reminder there'd ever been a working theater here was a scar where the marquee had hung above the now-chained public doors.

I walked up Warren, away from the river, past a dozen dusty antiques shops and newer art galleries. It was almost seven in the evening, but the sun was still fully cranked, beating buzz rolls on my head. It had been a brutal summer. With Hudson so close to the river, the air was positively gummy, as if the hot, thirsty sky had sucked up half the river. At the bodega I bought a six-pack of Ray's new favorite beer, Magic Hat, and carried it to his place.

His house was a tall, thin Victorian. The name of his art gallery, Ray of Darkness, was painted in gothic script on the picture window. I averted my eyes from whatever monstrosity was displayed there that week. I opened the door, jangling the discordant bells. Ray was seated behind his desk at his laptop.

He was tall and skinny, like his house. Scuffed leather jacket, ragged salt-and-pepper hair, leaning toward the salt. Between his messy looks and his mess of a life, he didn't make much sense until you saw him pick up a guitar. Like a magic wand, it transformed him into a confident master, a rock star whose incandescent solos had him owning whatever room he was in—whether a concert hall or this weird gallery.

But these days he wrote, working on some vague book project—but mostly he blogged. Before that it was art. I couldn't help thinking, what a waste of those hands.

Ray looked at me and raised his eyebrows. "What's up?"

I rarely visited him. He often came to the theater with his latest life conundrum, or when I got lucky, with his guitar.

"How's the writing going?"

He scowled and slammed his laptop shut. Smiled. "Already better. Actually, I was reading right-wing blogs. Useless fuckwits."

As I'd feared, *fuckwits* was Ray's new word of the month. Though I supposed it was a little easier on the ear than last month's *shitwad*.

"Torturing yourself, as usual," I said.

"Not as bad as writing. Hey, this is an essential part of my work."

Was it? I supposed if you blogged it might be. You'd think with the thirty-eight years I'd known him I'd be used to how loud he was. Not shouting loud but wearing his heart on his sleeve loud. And on his pant cuffs, and on a lanyard around his neck.

He smiled at the beer. "What's that for? Aside from drinking."

"Down payment on a favor."

He grabbed the six-pack and headed toward the stairs. I took the laptop from his desk and followed at my measured pace, threading my way through the thicket of sculptures, doing my best to ignore them. I have boring taste in art—bright colors and pleasing shapes. Though I know Ray is talented, his "sculptures" seem closer to horror movie props than museum pieces.

Ray clanked up the Art Nouveau spiral staircase. Ten years ago—when he and his ex, Liz, had moved in—*it* had been pleasing, a thicket of metal greenery. Now it was a mass of rust.

When I reached him in the kitchen, he'd already opened one of the beers, probably not his first of the evening. He handed me one. We stood leaning against countertops.

He said, "What's this favor?"

"Can you come feed Mingus for a few days?"

"Of course. I like your dog. Where you going?"

"Funeral."

"A musician?"

I shook my head.

"Oh no, not one of your exes?"

"No. One of the Four Brothers."

"Four Brothers? Remind me."

"At Middleburg College, back the year you and I met, I was living with three friends—Buzzy, Waldo, and Rick—in this decommissioned frat house. Theta Epsilon Phi Foe Fum. Gamma Lamma ding-dong or whatever."

"I remember. Big ugly old thing."

I nodded. "You were there a couple of times. When we moved in, the place was abandoned. It was totally trashed. Street people crashing there, using the furniture for firewood, pissing in the fireplaces. We kicked them out, cleaned the place up, more or less, and called it home."

Ray said, "*I* was a street person. Didn't go to no fancy-pants college."

"You were a *musician.*"

"Hey, at least I played the guitar, not some wussy keyboard."

"Touché. The Four Brothers was our joke. We weren't related by blood. We were way too hip to ever dream of joining a fraternity. But we *were* brothers in The Movement."

I paused, and Ray must have sensed something because he stopped pacing. "Waldo just died."

"Oh, man. Sorry to hear that."

"Thanks. You remember that blizzard in February of '69, the year we met?"

"I don't know. All I remember is freezing my ass off in the place I was crashing that winter."

"It snowed for a hundred hours straight. Major disaster, power lines down, roads a mess. So, we decided to do our part to help out."

Ray raised a hand. "What, you went out shoveling?"

"No, we all dropped a megadose of acid."

Ray laughed. "On the theory that you'd make the snow just go away, same as those freaks trying to levitate the Pentagon that time."

Now I laughed. "No. Our theory was that we just wouldn't care." I turned serious. "The acid was only the beginning. Even though it was coming down like a bastard, and we hadn't even heard a plow come by in hours, the cops somehow got up to campus and busted the four of us. Hauled us to the station. I suppose it was a blessing that we were past peaking. Except we were still whacked. Jail isn't what old Tim Leary would call an ideal 'set and setting.'"

"Middleburg cops. Useless fuckwits, in the vernacular." His vernacular. "How come I never heard about that bust? It's not like Middleburg was some teeming metropolis. And the grapevine was always humming with shit like that."

"That's the thing. There were never any charges. They simply let us walk. And Rick was a dope dealer."

"That doesn't make sense."

"No. We figured they'd screwed up the search warrant or something. Even so, the whole thing was weird, even for a majorly weird time. Which is why it took us a few days to realize the most important thing: that someone had gone missing that weekend." Her name had gone unspoken in the conversation with Buzzy. It stuck in my throat now. "Angela."

"I don't remember her."

"Waldo had a thing with her, but she…dumped him for another guy, around Thanksgiving. We hadn't seen her much until that night. She was there at some point during the trip—" I winced.

My tale was winding Ray up, had him pacing from one end of the kitchen to the other. I leaned back against the marble counter.

"Anyway, a week or so later it became clear that she was *gone*. There was a rumor that after the blizzard she'd had it with winter and split for California. It made sense. Folks were dropping out of school right and left. But it soured the atmosphere in the house. After that weekend we all stopped tripping. Months passed and we'd almost forgotten about Angela." Some of us, that is. "You remember Garnet Hill?"

"I heard about it."

"On the edge of campus, the steep side with a cliff facing west. It was a thing that year, getting high there, rooting around for garnets in the rocks, waiting for the sunset. By late spring the snow had melted, except for a deep pile at the foot of the cliff. With the warm days it had been steadily shrinking. First really fine day some poor kid went up there, got baked, and happened to look down. There was Angela's face, sticking out of the snow."

"Oh, man. She fell?"

"Yeah. They didn't think she suffered too long. Still."

"I can't believe you never told me about this."

"It's not something I like to remember."

"Hmm. What was she doing up there in the middle of a blizzard?"

"That hill was sacred to us pagan acid-gobblers. We could see someone getting high and going there to enhance their trip. What's spooky is that Waldo died…the same way," I explained.

Ray stopped pacing and looked at me. "If you consider water the same as snow. And if you ignore that it happened three thousand miles away, and forty years later. What it is, is a nasty coincidence."

"Yeah."

"You never told me about the Four Brothers, either."

I sighed and sat at the kitchen table. Ray slid into a chair across from me. "That Angela business was like our Altamont. The end of the dream. The one where we dropped acid and saw God and vowed to change the world."

"I had the same dream. Woke up on the road in a rock-and-roll band. Come to think of it, one of those guys looked a lot like you. Only a lot younger."

We laughed. He was always ragging on me for looking younger than my age.

"That was a different dream. A good one too, while it lasted."

"Sounds like you brothers were just an earlier incarnation of our band. Four guys out for a good time, deluded into thinking they were after something greater."

"I've never thought of it that way, but yeah. Except for Buzzy. He was a year older. Colonizing the old frat house was his idea. He lured us out of the dorms with the promise that 'Everything will be possible, man!' What was probable, of course, was a lot of drugs and, with luck, a few women. Except Buzzy was a truly spiritual cat. Already looking past psychedelics to Eastern religion. He had this crack in his smile, like he was in on some cosmic joke, and a gleam in his eyes, like he was looking out beyond the farthest horizon to the wonders of another world."

"What about the guy who died?"

Waldo. I tried to picture him, but the fact of my looking away every time I saw him in those last months before I split had somehow erased his features, leaving only vague dark hair and a scowl. "Science was his thing. Biology? *Micro*biology. Old Waldo really *cared* about those germs, or whatever they were. He certainly spent enough time at the lab. Might have won the Nobel Prize by now."

"Not that you'd ever know." Ray frowned. I didn't follow the news, politics, or sports.

"Once Waldo sunk his teeth into something, he just couldn't let it go. After Angela left him, we all knew she was never coming back. But he kept working it like it was one of his experiments, and if he just kept at it, it would finally come out right. And maybe it would have, but he never had the chance."

"The fourth brother?"

"Fucking Rick. A 'legend in his own time.' The most amazing hair on campus. Light brown afro, bigger than a basketball, exploding from his head, defying gravity. It hid his face, except for the squinty eyes and monster grin."

"Yeah, man, hair was a path to fame in those days."

I laughed. "He was peaking on mescaline one night and got down on all fours and ate with the dog. Barked at the poor thing, which hid behind the couch for the next week. Rick had crazy ideas about health. He read somewhere that it was essential to cook and eat outside, like our ancestors. That winter he crouched out in the snow cooking kielbasas on a hibachi when it was ten degrees below. Scarfed 'em down half-cooked and got an epic case of the runs. Which he thought was hilarious."

Ray cocked an eye. "He doesn't sound exactly your style."

"He was our dope dealer."

"Ah." He nodded his head, as if that explained everything. Which maybe it did. "How did Buzzy find you?"

I opened Ray's computer, showed him the website.

His mouth fell open and he slammed a hand against his head. "What happened to Bodine, Man of Mystery, with no known address? Who sneaks in the shadows? You that hard up for work?"

"No."

"And speaking of not your style, pardon me, but these graphics are butt ugly."

"I didn't design it."

"I hope not." Ray was scrolling down, looking at my client list. "These are big names! I had no idea."

I put a hand over the screen to block his view. He raised his hands in surrender. "Sorry. But what the hell is going on?"

I stood, looked away from him. "I've got some ideas." One, actually. "But I've got to get home, pack—"

"Pack what?" He got up and faced me. "Bodine, you need to tell me what's going on."

Part of never bragging about my Robin Hood business was never telling anyone. Because once a guy started blabbing, who wasn't going to take a little pride in his work? But damned if I didn't owe him some kind of explanation. This was a fucked-up scene to have me violating one of my rules.

"OK. You've heard of ransomware?"

"Maybe."

"Certain asshole coders use it to 'brick' people's computers, encrypting them remotely over the net such that without the password key they're useless. In theory, you pay the ransom and get a key, but more often than not they make off with the money and the computer's still a brick."

"That sounds like a major piss off. What's that got to do with your fake website?"

"I, uh, came across one of these gentlemen. I call him 'Brickman.' I found him *bragging* about it on an online forum. He said, 'I haven't had so much fun since I was boinking my little cousin. I'd do it for free, but a dude's got to make his nut.'"

Ray blinked. "That's some evil shit. So?"

"So I did something about it."

"Really. What?"

What to tell him? But he was getting there by himself.

"You hacked him!"

"You know I don't like that term. But yeah." Ray might not know about my sideline, but I'd dropped hints. You couldn't not brag about everything.

"I carved down through the layers of Brickman's bogus accounts. He's got more handles than the devil himself. But I discovered his real identity. And the crucial thing—what he wants. He's in the market for a young Asian wife. I set a honey trap, impersonating a Korean girl. Downloaded a picture from the net and Photoshopped it to unrecognizable. Sent him a sweet love letter.

Brickman got back to me in three minutes, dying to meet. Which revealed his IP address and location: Cambridge, Mass."

"Harvard?"

"MIT."

"Of course. So, what did you do?"

"I wasn't schlepping up to Cambridge to stalk him."

Ray smiled. "No, that's not you."

"A little research revealed that, like any profitable online scam, the Russian Mafia was on this bricking business like white on Anglo-Saxons. If they caught wind of some wimpy American geek—an ex-MIT geek—poaching on their turf, he'd soon be a very unhappy geek.

"Except there was no way I could in good conscience sic those boys on Brickman and live with it." I didn't have to tell Ray why. I might not believe in God, but I believed no one should play him. I'd long ago vowed to never do violence to another person. I'd stuck to pacifism all these years, though it was sometimes inconvenient.

"What to do? I wasn't getting him killed—or worse. But I had to stop him. I looked up notorious Russian mobsters. Vasily Chernoskylachenko, aka Vasily Chernobyl. Terrifying-looking guy—hold on." I got on Ray's computer again and found the photo of him. Pasty vodka-pickled cheeks, capital offense stare, and bull's neck with prison tats crawling up it.

Ray said, "Yow!"

"I attached this picture in an email to Brickman, saying, 'We know your ransom business. Know who you are, and where you live. Here is deal. You retire from bricking business in next five minutes, or Mr. Chernobyl will come visiting.'"

"And it worked."

"I thought it did. Like that he disappeared from his favorite forums."

"So he put up this fake website? Why?"

"It's his revenge."

"What are you going to do now?"

"I don't know. Right now, I'm going to a funeral."

We stood. Ray looked at my cowboy boots, jeans, the black embroidered shirt, straight, straight blond hair in its neat ponytail, with an amused grin. "You going like that?"

"How else?" I didn't own a suit.

"Where is this funeral?"

"San Francisco."

"If you have to go to a funeral, there are worse places."

Back home, I heated up some leftover chicken and rice for dinner. I felt bad leaving Mingus, so I gave him an extra dollop of wet food. He looked at it, then me, evoking a sharp pang of guilt. He knew I was leaving and was milking it for all it was worth. I gave him some of my chicken and a big hug.

It was ten, and I had to get up at four-thirty, but I headed into the office. I couldn't sleep until I got at least a start on Brickman. As I typed and thought and sat at the organ and played silently and thought some more, I realized I could be up all night and miss my flight and not get anywhere.

Brickman had turned invisible. I had his computer's IP address, only it was offline. Without that, or him on the forums, I had nothing aside from a physical address. I wasn't going to Cambridge, and definitely not hiring a private eye.

It was ironic. For years I'd been using the Internet to sneak into various company computers, disguised as their IT guy, or as a piece of boring maintenance software. And I was always secure in my anonymity. And here I was chasing a ghost.

I'd been so pumped when I finally outed Brickman. The sin of pride. But my worst mistake had been acting from anger. His bragging about his crimes had outraged me, convincing me to take him on as the latest conquest in my digital Robin Hood act. I lost my cool. Emotions should never rule in business. My anger had blinded me to the truth: he was very good.

Too good. As I'd been playing him, he was playing me.

It had been a long, strange day, and I was plain out of juice. Brickman was the kind of problem that required reinventing wheels and seeing things from a new perspective. Which required fresh energy. A night's sleep—or at least part of one.

The last thing I did was to unplug the router, killing the Internet on all my computers. However he'd found me, he wasn't sneaking back in that way while I was gone. And now, I was invisible to him. But as I lay in bed hoping for ten or twenty winks, I couldn't help the irrational thought: he sees me.

If I Fell is available now.

Visit www.johnkmanchester.com/free/ to sign up for my newsletter and receive an exclusive FREE Prequel Novella to the *Ray of Darkness* Series.

A Word from John

Thank you for reading *Never Speak!* And I want to thank everyone who's contributed to its coming into the world: my wife and sons, and all the friends who read the manuscript in various stages of development. Oh, and my dogs.

I'd love it if you could take a moment to write a short review and post it on **Amazon** and/or Goodreads. Reviews help others to discover my series.

John Manchester was born in Baltimore, which perhaps explains his early fascination with the works of Edgar Allan Poe. His passion for music led him to a performing career starting at age thirteen in a Beatles imitation band, where he posed as John Lennon in a wig. He later played guitar in a group that toured opening for Linda Ronstadt and Fleetwood Mac. He taught himself to compose and soon made a living at it. His compositions are heard worldwide on TV, radio, and the internet. They were popular for the happy, hopeful feelings they evoked. Wishing to indulge his darker impulses, he taught himself to write. His pieces about the arts, life, and growing up with his late father, the historian William Manchester have been published at Salon.com, Medium.com and on his blog. He's haunted by memories of strange, terrible, and even miraculous things. And so, he transforms them into fiction in the Ray of Darkness series of Deep Psychological Thrillers. After decades in New England, he moved to California with his family. He misses the seasons but not digging his car out of the snow. Sign up for his newsletter or visit his website at www.johnkmanchester.com.